JOURNEY
TO THE
HEART
OF THE
ABYSS

Also by London Shah

The Light the Abyss Series

The Light at the Bottom of the World
Journey to the Heart of the Abyss

JOURNEY
TO THE
HEART
OF THE
ABYSS

LIGHT THE ABYSS

LONDON SHAH

Little, Brown and Company
New York Boston

Little, Brown and Company
Hachette Book Group
1290 Avenue of the Americas, New York, NY 10104
Visit us at LBYR.com

First Edition: October 2021

Little, Brown and Company is a division of Hachette Book Group, Inc. The Little, Brown name and logo are trademarks of Hachette Book Group, Inc.

The publisher is not responsible for websites (or their content) that are not owned by the publisher.

Library of Congress Cataloging-in-Publication Data
Names: Shah, London, author.
Title: Journey to the heart of the abyss / London Shah.
Description: First edition. | New York : Little, Brown and Company, 2021. | Series: Light the abyss | Sequel to: The light at the bottom of the world. | Audience: Ages 12 & up. | Summary: In a post-apocalyptic future, teenaged Leyla feels compelled to search for Ari, while seeking to uncover the mystery behind her past.
Identifiers: LCCN 2020048434 | ISBN 9780759555075 (hardcover) | ISBN 9780759555068 (ebook) | ISBN 9780316103688 (ebook other)
Subjects: CYAC: Science fiction.
Classification: LCC PZ7.1.S4748 Jou 2021 | DDC [Fic]—dc23
LC record available at https://lccn.loc.gov/2020048434

ISBNs: 978-0-7595-5507-5 (hardcover), 978-0-7595-5506-8 (ebook)

Printed in the United States of America

LSC-C

Printing 1, 2021

For Aswila, Mariam, and Ibrahim.
Lights of my life.

A Note from the Author

Dear Reader,

Welcome back to the submerged world of the future.

Just a quick note from me before you dive right in.

Humanity living deep underwater has been a fantasy I've indulged in since childhood. I'm absolutely fascinated by the thought of our contemporary world completely submerged. A landscape where our current way of life is still very much visible, except it now exists deep below the waves. I've always found the surreality of such a setting utterly exciting.

It means everything to me that you would choose to read the Light the Abyss duology (*The Light at the Bottom of the World* and *Journey to the Heart of the Abyss*). The series is the first to feature a British Muslim main character in a sci-fi and also the first western science fiction or fantasy novel to feature a lead of Pashtun ethnicity. I myself am a British Muslim of Pashtun ethnicity, and so its representation is another reason the story is incredibly dear to me.

The Light the Abyss series is about surviving and embracing change. It's about valuing our differences and not being afraid of them. It's about reflecting on the past with a clear mind and looking around us now with clear hearts. It's about the unwavering pursuit of truth, no matter how painful. It is about never giving up hope. And above all, it's the realization of a long-held dream—of finally bringing to life the inescapable vision of humanity residing in the deep.

It's very touching to know that you wish to revisit my beloved Leyla in her underwater world and join her as her journey for answers deepens in every way. Thank you from the bottom of my heart. May you always find the light in everything you do.

London Shah

Where were we going now,
and what was reserved for the future?

Jules Verne

THE PRIME MINISTER   September 21, 2035

The Official Secrets Act binds the inviolability of this message. It is purposed solely for the attention of the Prime Minister of the United Kingdom.

Dear Rt. Hon. Prime Minister,

I congratulate you in advance now on your appointment as leader of this great nation of ours. I know you will agree with me when I say that to guide the United Kingdom is the highest honor. One that comes with untold responsibilities. I pen this letter to you because I must bring to your attention a matter of utmost gravity and sensitivity, and deepest regret. I urge you, as you read on, to please find it in your good self to remain magnanimous toward all involved. These are uncertain and testing times.

With the impending asteroid 2030 FM31 resolved on colliding with Earth and driving us into subaqueous existence, we are on the cusp of a catastrophe unlike any humanity has faced. It has at times forced us to consider solutions previously deemed unconscionable.

Project Amphibios was an initiative conceived by certain parties involved in Operation Ark and seated on the Resurrection Council. The scheme would see two hundred artificially designed humans, Homo amphibius, *created solely for the purposes of a workforce. Entirely unaffected by the environment themselves, they would aid the survivors after the disaster. Technically the scheme is a success. Amphis can safely breathe underwater and remain immune to its pressures.*

A marginal increase in body strength further ensures they would be up to any task assigned to them. In hindsight, however, the project was a profound error in moral judgment.

Those who knew of the scheme have arrived at a unanimous conclusion: We cannot in good faith proceed with this project. These are human beings. The only difference between us is their ability to remain extant underwater. They must be allowed to freely live out their lives, and not exist as a labor force for ours. I have proposed a thorough sterilization program, after which they will enter into society where they will live among us as equals. Which brings us to the crux of this note, my Rt. Hon. friend.

For their sakes, and the stability of our nation, it is of great consequence nobody else be made aware of the true identities and abilities of the amphis.

I implore you to help right our wrong by ensuring this note is passed on to all subsequent prime ministers until such a time when amphis no longer exist.

Yours sincerely,

Stephen John
Prime Minister of the
United Kingdom

JANUARY 20, 2087

PM GLADSTONE   [*clears throat*] Good evening, my fellow Britons. [*pause*] I swore when campaigning that I would always be forthright with you, the people of a once great nation. The safety of Britons is my top priority; it always has been. And after much deliberation, it's with a heavy heart that I must now share with you a very serious matter. In doing so, I'm breaking a sworn oath of office, but I feel confident you'll understand why I must. Secrets and lies were never my vision for leading this nation. Questions will be taken at the end. Thank you. [*deep sigh*] There's no easy way of saying this. The fact of the matter is: We are not alone. There lives among us an—an unnatural species. Artificially created humans. [*inaudible murmurings*] This species is the result of a *disastrous* endeavor by Old World scientists. It's been down here for as long as we have and—

REPORTER   Sir! Prime Minister Gladstone, when you say "artificially created humans" can you—

PM GLADSTONE   If I might finish, please. But yes, artificially designed humans, fashioned in some ill-founded hope they would help us once humanity was relegated to this darkness. It was a reckless venture—one of the more alarming of the countless errors the scientists made. Physically, these beings look just like us, but do not be fooled. They're *nothing* like us. They—

[*inaudible murmurings*]

REPORTER   Prime Minister, are you saying there are rogue humans out there and—

PM GLADSTONE   Please, I must insist on silence in the room until I've finished speaking. All of your questions will be answered at the end. And I'm saying this species is *here*, walking among us. These—these aberrations are our friends, neighbors, colleagues. They are around our children. [*inaudible murmurings*] They have abnormal traits—

REPORTER   Such as? What traits, Prime Minister?

PM GLADSTONE   Inhuman capabilities. And, crucially, they exhibit no telltale signs of such. We must—

REPORTERS   —Sir! How can they be identified?

—How could this have been allowed to happen?

—Are we in any immediate danger?

—What about your plans for the surface?

—Why the cover-up? Why are we only hearing of this now?

—Could we see some proof of these—

PM GLADSTONE   Order! That's better. Right, I'm afraid any further interruptions will result in the responsible party escorted out of the room. I understand how distressing and confusing the information I'm presenting you with is, but I really need you to employ patience and hold off questions until the end. [*sigh*] Now, if these creatures carry any ill intent toward us, and there's no proof they do not, then we're looking at a foe as formidable as the abyss. All is not lost, though. If I might remind everyone, I was elected on my surfacer policies. You placed your faith in me and I *will* deliver. Getting us out of this darkness and living up on the surface of the waters instead is what we as a nation want. It's what we need. And it's our *right*. This is not who we are, and we won't bow so readily to this life as the Old Worlders did. As for identification, we're currently in the process of developing a fail-safe test that would recognize these creatures, these Anthropoids if you will, so that we can eliminate the threat. As we speak, my cabinet is working hard on establishing, in almost every major settlement, a branch of the AWC—the Anthropoid Watch Council. Following today's broadcast, you should all find a specific AWC information booklet waiting for you. It's paramount you absorb every word in it. Your lives, and the lives of your loved ones, may depend on it. I want to say nobody is in any immediate danger, but that would be highly irresponsible of me. Stay alert, stay safe. They are cunning and we don't yet fully know what they're capable of. It's very likely they took control of the laboratories they were held at and slaughtered every scientist and technician present that day. But they underestimate our will. We are Britons. And we don't cower in anyone's presence. We once *ruled* these waves. We can do so again. Together we can fight both foes—the environment and these Anthropoids. We will overcome this madness and resume our rightful place at the top of the world, once more a great nation—the *greatest*. Right, yes, I will take your questions now.

Tous les changements, même les plus souhaités
ont leur mélancolie, car ce que nous quittons,
c'est une partie de nous-mêmes; il faut mourir
à une vie pour entrer dans une autre.

∞

All changes, even the most longed for,
have their melancholy; for what we leave behind
us is a part of ourselves; we must die to one
life before we can enter another.

Anatole France

CHAPTER ONE

EYSTUROY, THE FAROE ISLANDS,
NORTH ATLANTIC OCEAN, FEBRUARY 2100

The early morning waves of the North Atlantic Ocean roll wild around us, murky gray swells crashing into the submerged mountains and obscuring everything in sight with their churning. The submersible sways in the turbulent current and my heart races as I peer into the water. From our undercover spot among several huge boulders, all we can see is an unforgiving gloom.

Papa is sitting still beside me, his gaze fixed on the blurry forms outside. At last he takes a breath and speaks. "This is not what I wanted for you, Leyla."

He narrows his eyes when we sense a change. We twist and turn in the double-seated sub to peer into the cloaked surroundings from every angle.

As dark as it is with our craft shut down, there's no mistaking the telltale shadow of the vessel passing way overhead now, even when they're using minimum light. Only those wishing to stay concealed would risk these waters without full illumination. We should be safe on this ridge. I shut down the craft the moment it settled on the ledge so that nothing would give us away. Our fate now depends on how long they're prepared to spend in the area, and whether they decide to max out their vessel's lighting. There's no missing us if they do that.

It was Oscar who alerted us to the patrolling security sub. I always leave the *Kabul* in stealth mode on these trips so they didn't trace her, and

I've instructed the Navigator to move her a little. As long as nobody gets a visual on the submarine, she'll be safe where she's hiding now, hovering away between several imposing cliff faces far above us.

"They'll be gone soon, Papa." I keep my eyes on the shadowy presence that doesn't seem to be in any hurry.

This is not what I wanted for you. I twist my hair around my fingers. I'm letting him down, or at least causing him to worry.

"It's not what I wanted for myself either, Papa. But what choice do we have?"

The craft rocks again and I pray the boulders aren't suddenly lodged. The mountain ranges around here make for great hideouts I've found these past few weeks, but they're not without their risks. If only these depths were clearer, but they're murkier than even the deep gray-blue of the altitude we keep the *Kabul* at.

"I'm still not convinced these excursions are the best way to search for his community, Pickle." Papa sighs heavily as he strokes Jojo's white fur. The lazy Maltese puppy curled up in his lap and fell asleep soon after the submersible set off.

"It isn't ideal, but how else are we meant to find Ari's people? And you insist on coming along when you really don't need to. You and Jojo should be sitting comfortably back on the *Kabul*. We can stay in touch throughout. I never take more than a couple of hours." I'd worry a lot less about him if he remained on board the submarine instead of joining me on my searches.

Sometimes I have nightmares where I'm back in our flat in London and Papa's left for work. Jeeves delivers a message: *The Blackwatch has taken your father again.* Other times Papa's out there in a submersible and a net falls over the craft. The worst of the past few weeks seem to have merged, and every nightmare is so bloody real I'm shaking with relief when I open my eyes. They cannot get their hands on him a second time.

"We're not doing this again, Pickle. If you must make these trips, then I come along with you."

Something materializes from the thick gloom to my side and I startle.

The enormous round shape, as tall as the vessel, draws closer. It heads straight for us, slowly circling the sub. I hold my breath as it returns to the front. It looks strange, like a mammoth fish missing the latter half of its body.

"A giant mola," Papa marvels.

The hardened-looking creature is at least three meters tall and yet almost flat, its small mouth open in an O shape. I wave it away frantically as if it can understand me. It mustn't draw the security sub's attention to this spot. At last, the fish meanders on.

I face Papa just as he turns to gaze out to his side, and I slip my hand in his; he squeezes it tight.

He hasn't voiced it, but ever since his return he's been uneasy when left on his own. I can hear the low music he has playing all night, and he never used to sleep with a Lumi-Orb glowing. I hate the authorities so much. What they put him through at Broadmoor…He was in that hellhole of a prison for over three months. After weeks of them trying and failing to get him to reveal the names of everyone sympathetic toward amphis, they left him to rot in a freezing-cold, bare cell. When he caught an infection and the extended fever severely limited his movements, his condition escalated. We found him almost lifeless. He had several viral and bacterial infections, a raging temperature that had him delirious for days, and most heartbreaking of all, he was critically malnourished. Though he already looks like a completely different person to the one we'd broken out of Broadmoor, thank God, all I see when I look at him is a mind and body that's been through hell. He runs his hand now over very short dark-brown hair that still hasn't grown back long enough to curl. I had to shave his head because it was full of lice. But he's here, and sometimes I still can't believe it.

It's been just over a month since his rescue. A month since the prime minister's right-hand man, Captain Sebastian, placed a hefty bounty on our heads and labeled us terrorists—Britain's number one enemy, to be exact.

A month since Ari was dragged away from us.

A creature slinks into view as it becomes interested in the dome of the cockpit, gliding its body all over it. The Faroe Islands seem to draw the eeriest critters. The seconds stretch into minutes, and still the security sub circles the area. All I see, though, no matter where I look, is Ari's face.

It's hard to picture this part of the world as his home, impossible to imagine him once swimming out here. It's actually terrifying placing him in such an environment. He's too bright, too intense for such a grim setting. His dazzling gaze, so beautiful and tender. He'll randomly pop into my head and then it's a struggle to focus on anything else. Often his face taunts me at mealtimes, and I'll see him as he was, when we'd sit to eat together in the viewport. The way he smiled his small, secretive smile. Then I have to quickly steady myself because I really, really miss him.

And the mere thought that somebody might've hurt him shreds my insides.

I replay that moment over and over, how his then warm, affectionate expression turned so fierce when the net dropped around him and he found himself confined. The way they hauled him up through the waves as if he were an animal. How his features twisted in disbelief at first, and then in wild rage and resentment.

My heart sinks now as it always does every time I allow myself to think about him. It starts with wonder and ends in such emptiness.

Papa sighs as he shifts around in the seat. "This is their reality every day, Pickle. A life in hiding. It's no way to live."

Ari and his people aren't even Anthropoids. That's the name the current government gave them, Papa explained to me, in order to label them as something animal. But they're human beings—*Homo amphibius* to be exact. The scientists who created amphis knew their makeup, their DNA, was entirely human, and that the only difference between them and us is they can breathe underwater. I wish I'd known earlier; all those years I'd used the term Anthropoid for them.... I'm filled with shame anytime I remember. It was too dangerous to ever let me know the truth about the so-called threat of the Anthropoids, so Papa kept it from me to protect me and fully intended to tell me everything soon. But then he was arrested.

The minutes tick by as we sit, tense, my stomach hard. It's the third time we've found ourselves in this particular situation, and it doesn't get any less unnerving. But we hardly have any alternative. "I don't enjoy these daily trips either, Papa," I say gently. "But I can't stop now. Someone from Ari's community will spot us—they *have* to."

"It's too risky...."

Papa's biggest worry is the authorities capturing me on one of these searches. And it always reminds me of *his* arrest. More specifically, that I still don't know exactly why he was apprehended and imprisoned. Unfortunately he isn't yet ready to talk about it. But he's been through enough, and I know he'll share that with me, too, as soon as he's ready.

"If they spot us, I'll aim for a dense group of peaks like the ones behind us now. Our craft's tiny compared to theirs, and the clusters of rock will give me the upper hand, Papa. I'll play cat and mouse in the mountains until they run out of power."

"Out of the question." He gazes away into the water, deep in thought, before shaking his head softly. "You are so much like your mama." His voice always turns wistful whenever he mentions her. He releases a long sigh. "I must keep you safe—"

"Papa—"

"Hear me out, Pickle. No matter what you say, it's my job to ensure your safety. You're my child. It doesn't mean I don't think you can't look after yourself. It only means I need to look after you, too. Look at me, Leyla."

I meet his gaze and he breaks into a small, tender smile. Oh how I'd missed this lopsided grin of his all those months he was gone.

"I know I say it often, but you need to believe it. I'm so proud of you. And your mama...Soraya would have been the proudest. Even an adult would have struggled with what you've had to bear these past months. Leaving London in a submarine...I feel as if I hear about somebody else's journey, not yours. You used to feel uneasy if I even *spoke* of life beyond London's borders. And then...then you had to suffer all that. What did I put my Pickle through?" His voice fades and he swallows.

"*You* put me through nothing, Papa. You didn't cause it—they did. It was my decision to go looking for you. And I know I was rash with some of my choices, I see that now. But you're back, and that's the main thing, yes?" I rub his arm. "And now we must find Ari."

Papa pats my hand as he looks away, nodding. "Knowing you didn't go through all that alone is a balm whenever I think too much on everything that happened to you."

"We wouldn't be here without him," I whisper.

At last, it's been a full ten minutes since we caught a glimpse of the security sub. I cup my Bracelet with my other hand to shield its light, just in case, and bring up my wrist.

"Oscar? Verbal communication only."

Even dimmed, the immediate glow about my wrist puts me on edge, and I let my hair fall around my hands.

"My lady?" The Navigator's whimsical voice is always instantly comforting.

"Oscar, we can't see any sign of them anymore. Please check the area?"

It takes only seconds. "My dear, the rogue vessel is in motion some two leagues to the west of your location now, traversing in the opposite direction to ourselves. Any instructions?"

Papa utters a prayer in thanks.

I blow out my cheeks with relief. "All right, you can show yourself now, Oscar," I say, swiping his projection toward the cockpit so we can see him as I power up the craft.

I turn to Papa. "We carry on, yes?"

He nods and focuses on Oscar. "What is the status of the *Kabul*?"

The Navigator's affectionate gaze takes us in, and he dips his head with a warm smile. "All is quite satisfactory on this end, sir." He brings a crimson tulip to his nose and inhales it.

"Still, remain in stealth mode," I instruct him as I check the dashboard. "And don't take your eyes off the tracking system." The last time I stopped worrying and relaxed, a net fell out of nowhere, closed around Ari, and took him away.

A school of vividly striped mackerel immediately scatters from view when the sub lights up the water.

"Understood, my lady." Oscar tilts his head. "I do trust entirely in the *Kabul*'s flair for secrecy. The submarine is in her element when she must remain discreet. As ladies often are!"

We can't help grinning. The craft rises above the boulders and I take in the phantom silhouettes that surround us, all the endless, jagged peaks of Eysturoy.

The Navigator clears his throat. "Next time, my lady, perhaps I might suggest a smidgeon of firepower?" His doleful eyes shine. "I dare say it worked wonders the last time."

"Steady on, Oscar. We had no choice the other evening. But I've told you, we only fire in defense. Not to mention we don't want to waste our resources—you never know when we'll suddenly need the sub's full might."

"Of course." He straightens his silk cravat and nods. "Most prudent, my lady."

I dismiss the Navigator and we move on, the sudden lights and movement causing Jojo to stir awake. The puppy stretches in Papa's lap. She's been amazing for his recovery.

Negotiating the surrounding landscape as carefully as I can, I keep a lookout for any sign of a community. Papa, too, has his eyes pceled on the depths.

I steer by mountains now that look like towering water wraiths. All the churning here is maddening as the water breaks against the rock. As I round a pitch-black ridge, movement ahead catches my eye and I slow down. *Wow.*

Papa leans in. "Why have we— Oh…mashallah." His face lights up when he spots the mesmerizing sight.

It's several colossal chains of salps all merged together, and they're breathtaking. The gossamer form drifts directly in front of us now, glowing away. We watch as the lengthy, translucent creatures sway on the current. I can't believe such delicate animals can survive this tempestuous environment. Vivid orange lights dot their insides. They float away from sight.

And my breath hitches at what they reveal.

In the creatures' wake, suspended in the water mere feet from the sub, is a whole group of amphis. People breathing underwater.

Jojo jumps up in Papa's lap, her ears pricked.

"Alhamdulillah!" Papa says, thanking God. "Remember, there's nothing to fear, Pickle." He greets them with a wave.

They hover side by side, each carrying a laser gun, though the weapons aren't pointed at us. Hair fans around their faces, floating on the current, and the water flows freely in and out of their mouths as they stare back at us. My stomach quivers despite myself. But there's also relief—an entire wave of it washing over me. *At last.*

Papa communicates with them in sign language. It's how they interact with anyone not in the water. "I'm Hashem McQueen," he says. "I'm Gideon Abraham's son, and this is my daughter, Leyla. Gideon may have contacted you about us? It's been unsafe for us to keep in touch with him, with anyone at all. We're looking for Ari Sterling's family. He was with us when they took him." He also lets them know about the security sub in the area earlier, and they nod as if already aware of the fact.

They talk among themselves, their mouths moving exactly as if they were chatting inside and not actually hovering in a world of water. I can't look away. . . . It's unbelievable. They can hear one another out there.

One of them moves closer and signs right back. "Follow us," they say, before turning around and swimming away.

Despite my slight unease, I straighten in my seat. This is what I wanted. I've spent weeks searching for these people.

Ari. I slip my hand into the pocket of my sweater and wrap it around the smooth rock in there. *I have faith in you, Leyla,* he'd said, when he gave me the ancient flint tool. At last, we might be a little closer to finding him.

I reach for the throttle to my left, push it forward, and follow in their trail.

CHAPTER TWO

*W*e are fast, Ari once told me, but it's gripping to watch them in
action. One moment there's nobody there, and then someone
will suddenly appear, spearing back to the vessel to ensure we're still following. Though they're using a slightly different variant of sign language
to the version I'd learned from Jeeves, it's easy enough to grasp. As they
reach a wide clearing between several craggy peaks, they dive. I grab the
joystick to my right and, pushing it forward, do the same.

Ridge after ridge looms around us as we descend. It's a startling sight, all
spectral and gloomy. How can even a single person survive at these depths,
never mind an entire community? The water turns impossibly denser.

What would Theo and Tabby think if they could see us now? If they
knew we were heading for an entire amphi community? I haven't seen or
heard from the twins since we chatted at Cambridge about six weeks ago.
What I wouldn't give to hear from my friends again, to see their faces.
And Grandpa's. I know what Gramps would say if he saw us now; he worries so much. There's a familiar tugging at my heart.

The group we're following stop diving. They signal to us and disappear
around several cliff faces. As we catch up with them up, we find ourselves
between two great ridges. They beckon us on. I spotlight every beam we
have, but nothing.

"If they were easy to locate, there wouldn't be any of them left alive,"
Papa says quietly.

Sure enough, as they continue on, it becomes challenging for us to keep on their trail, and I find myself relying on every exterior lamp. I shake my head; not in a million years would I have found this place on one of my daily searches. The seabed comes into view. Though there's nowhere near as much debris here as we have in London, there's still too much. Cars, crates, the tail of a plane, huge container drums, and even furniture lie beneath us. Endless random shapes covered in rust, breadcrumb sponge, and coral.

"Almost there now," they say.

As we draw closer, it becomes apparent that unlike cities around the country, there are no streetlights here. I can't believe it; they somehow survive without either streetlights or solar spheres. At last as we glide through a broad cave-like passage and enter an open stretch of water, they pause and turn to us, indicating we've arrived.

Papa and I lean in and peer at the sight before us. We turn to stare at each other, before focusing again on the view all around us. It's as if we're inside a mountain. Colossal walls of rock surround us with no gaps in between. Then we notice the lights.

Expansive ridges jut out from the surrounding cliff faces, and oh goodness, on each one illumination glimmers from homes.

It's an entire community.

We haven't seen or spoken with anyone in over a month and the sudden sight of all this humanity has me light-headed. Papa and I turn to each other and grin. Even though it's only the homes that are lit up, it's such a welcome sight after the gloomy journey to reach the place. I sense a sudden yearning inside, an ache that brings Ari's face crashing into my head. I know he isn't here, but still—it's the closest I've felt to him since his absence.

The sub sways. Even tempered by looming rock faces, the current remains choppy here and the waves crash against the towering stone and ledges.

"Where there are no mountains to shield them, they build their communities in layers," Papa explains. "That way if they're attacked, they can hope to hide as the outer layer is obliterated. With any luck, security forces assume they've destroyed the place and everyone in it, and move on. It's easier than starting again from scratch. Many also construct an entire facade to hide the real settlement. Despite a lifetime of developing skills for hiding, though," he says, his voice growing tense, "too many communities are still discovered and..."

He can't finish, but he doesn't need to. Ari told me how the authorities slaughter them indiscriminately. Innocent people, including children. Because they're different.

A woman waves to catch my attention, and on her instruction I head toward a shaft of light indicating a moon pool. The silhouettes of inquisitive fish scatter as we move into the illumination.

"But I don't understand how they're still found, Papa. I mean this is the most hostile environment I've ever been in. Their existence is barely visible to anyone. How do security forces know exactly where to search? They can't send subs into every pocket of Great Britain. Do you think it's possible they have surveillance tech nobody knows about?" The sub rises.

He shakes his head. "I doubt it, Pickle. The Cambridge lot take care of that side of things, and they're good. No, it's just who the Blackwatch are; they're ready and waiting all the time. As soon as someone in the communities slips up security-wise and gives the location away, the authorities move in."

The craft bobs to the surface of the pool. The brightly lit room is in stark contrast to the darkness outside. I log the journey—it took us weeks to find this location, and I'm not losing it—and then I bury the info in case someone unsavory gets their hands on the sub.

Those who were guiding us surge through the water beside us and I jump in my seat. They climb out of the pool and disappear into a small row of cubicles lined up against the far wall.

Our sub moves to the very end, where Papa and I exit the vessel and enter the airlock to depressurize. As soon as we're in the clear, the sealed door before us opens and we step into the rest of the space. Those who were dripping wet only moments earlier are already waiting for us, dry and changed.

"A lifetime of practice," Papa says, grinning as he catches me staring.

They didn't even need to acclimatize, and it'll never be short of astonishing to me. I hold out my arms for Jojo, and as Papa hands her over to me, his gaze moves past me. His grin abruptly disappears. I whirl around to see several people pointing weapons at us.

"It's okay," Papa says to the nearest woman. "We're friends, I assure you. Please, contact Gideon Abraham." He turns to me. "It's fine, Pickle. They have good reason not to trust us."

"Hands where I can see them," the woman insists, her voice firm and her gaze wary.

Jojo whines and I comfort her.

They search us. A small guy then moves to a corner and speaks hurriedly into his Bracelet.

"That way," says the woman, and thrusts her weapon in the direction of the door.

Two others join us, and soon we're flanked by three armed people and walking toward who knows where. I will my heart to stop racing as we move through the pool room's hatch.

"They're wise to be cautious," Papa says, his voice low as he leans into me. "They'll see we mean them no harm. Your grandpa works with the communities this far north, so one of them will have to have heard of him."

Weirdly I don't think my pulse is racing only from fear. In fact, I feel we'll be all right. I think my heart's *thump-thumping* because *Ari, Ari, Ari.* We found his community; we're with his people.

The huge hatch leads into a corridor. The woman escorting us through pauses when her Bracelet bleeps, and she moves away for a whispered exchange. A moment later she rejoins us, nodding briefly to the others. They lower their weapons and walk away, taking with them any tension I was feeling about being here.

"Please follow me," she says. "Ben will be with you shortly."

Papa gives me a reassuring nod and we follow her.

Once we're through a second watertight door at the end, we find ourselves in a brightly lit interior. The place is sprawling. The air is filled with the aroma of baking—bread, I think. The space is surprisingly warm, both temperature-wise and also in its rugged, hearty decor. It's snug, all woods, mellow colors, and cozy textiles, and portraits and bookcases everywhere you look. Never in a million years could I have guessed this place existed in the surrounding darkness, at the heart of such a baleful landscape. Or that these people might live like this.

Back in London, I hadn't even imagined their homes. I can't believe how little I knew or understood about a whole people, how I was aware only of the few differences between us instead of the many ways in which we're exactly the same. And how oblivious I was to our treatment of them. Color floods my cheeks as I recall Ari's words to me:

You people . . . Always content with your own lives no matter what's going on with somebody else, somewhere else—as long as you're fine. Always believing everything you're told.

The delicious smell grows stronger as we pass a large room, its door open. An enormous oven burns at the center of the kitchen, and it's a bit like the model the twins have, its induction plates glowing red hot. Various pots simmer away over them. Its sides radiate warmth throughout the entire space. We move on until finally we enter a large room filled with at least a dozen people, and it instantly falls silent.

"Please wait here," the woman says, gesturing to a couple of chunky armchairs.

I look around the warm, bright space, taking in the faces turned toward us now. What are they doing here? Do they all live here? A few nod in greeting, while others throw cautious glances our way before whispering among themselves.

It wasn't too long ago that the sighting of a single amphi on the news would leave me frozen to the spot. And now I'm surrounded by them—people of every color, race, size, and age. And even the odd child. It's hard to imagine them in the water, hard to picture them attacking us. These people show no hint of being less than us in any way. All the lies and warped news footage swirl around inside my head as my eyes flit across the room. Years of being told amphis are the most violent species ever, when in reality they're a people who've been brutally victimized, their families and communities ripped apart by the very people meant to protect us all.

Since his recovery, anything new Papa tells me about Ari and others

21

with the same abilities, and where the government is failing us, continues to leave me stunned. Like how Papa and many others all around the country always worked hard to uncover and spread the truth about amphis, and did whatever they could to protect them. And that they'd always been friends with them and even visited them in secret.

Ari had told me how the original two hundred were marked for sterilization, but the disaster struck earlier than anticipated. They escaped confinement and chose to live quietly on the fringes of society, and nobody was the wiser. But then the current government needed to rationalize their single-minded goal of returning to the surface at all cost, and suddenly we lived among the most evil things to have ever been created and our lives were infinitely more in peril down here. The word "Anthropoid" swept in like a rogue wave.

Ari's words come back to me, how he pleaded with me to understand when I went into shock on discovering he was one: *We are* human, *Leyla. We are you. We lack nothing—we only possess more.* Hardly anything he said at the time registered with me. I was stunned to realize I'd been traveling with what I'd always been led to believe was our greatest enemy.

A man and woman around Papa's age enter the room and hurry forward to greet us.

"Ben Sterling," says the man. He's tall and pale with curly blond hair, and wears a haunted expression as he fixes warm brown eyes on us. "Ari's father. Welcome to our home."

I catch my breath. I'm actually in Ari's house. I battle a surge of emotions as I try to quickly focus.

Ari's mother, Ruby, is also pale and blond. I realize now Ari might possibly be an adoptee.

Ruby insists we have something to eat, but we settle on warm drinks.

Most of the room empties and Ben waves us over to a set of sprawling sofas in the corner. Ruby sits beside her husband, and a few others join us.

"Please," says Ben, clasping his wife's hand and leaning forward. His gaze flits frantically between Papa and me. "Tell us what happened. Where is our son?"

CHAPTER THREE

Ben and Ruby sit stunned as I tell them everything that happened when Ari was taken. His horrified face flashes before me again and again as I recall the events.

When I'm done, Ben stands, his face grim but determined, and starts pacing the room. Ruby's expression is somber, her eyes clouded as she processes everything. My heart goes out to them both. I wish there was something I could do.

"Okay," Ari's mother finally says, her face tight and jaw set. "So what are we going to do?"

"He's a fighter, our lad," Ben says, clearing his throat as he turns to Papa. "He'll be hanging on, wherever they've taken him. And if I know him, he'll be giving them hell." A brief glimmer of pride crosses his face, and Ruby nods absently in agreement.

"Papa told me," I say to her, "about how frequently your community go missing."

She swallows before speaking. "Very rarely do we ever see them again. But Ari will return to us, love. I know he will."

"Now that we finally know more about my son's fate, we can adjust our searches for him," says Ben, rolling back his sleeves. "We can't waste any time."

The minutes stretch as Ari's family and neighbors discuss the best way to organize an extensive search for him. Ben includes us in the discussion even though I don't have much to offer and end up mostly just listening to them as I feed Jojo a snack. Papa has plenty of experience to share, though, and for the first time in my life I see this side of him in action as he displays extensive knowledge of the security forces and their sly tactics.

"I wish we were coming together under very different circumstances, Hashem," Ben says after a while. "I've heard plenty about everything you've done for our people down south. I was honored when Gideon asked if Ari could accompany your lass." His face falls every time he says Ari's name. "And sorry about the 'welcome' you received," he adds. "It's difficult to relax around others until we know for sure they can be trusted. We were on the lookout for you, too—ever since we stopped hearing from Ari. He'd updated us on the breakout, but then you all fell off everyone's radar soon after."

"That's when we knew something was wrong," says Ruby with an empty stare. "Ari would never go that long without checking in with us, without assuring me he was okay."

Ben rubs his face. I notice the deep shadows under his eyes. "But we had to balance searching for you with ensuring the community wasn't made vulnerable as a result," he says. "It's been very slow going." He takes a deep breath and lets it out slowly before narrowing his eyes and turning to Papa. "Talking of protection...We were in the middle of a meeting. Hashem, you heard about the small settlement in Tórshavn?" Papa shakes his head. "Two days ago," Ari's dad continues. "Half a dozen dead and the rest were lucky to escape with their lives. No sign of the firepower they used this time either. The attack came as they slept."

It goes quiet.

How was I so completely oblivious to all this back in London? What is bloody wrong with us? I can't get rid of the images forming now, the possibilities of whatever took place in Tórshavn. First those people were here, living and breathing among us, and now they simply no longer exist. I don't know where to look. I can't help the overwhelming sense of resentment and frustration and anger flooding me now. The shame and the horror at what's been unfolding in our name. Without taking action to fix things, though, my feelings mean nothing.

"As for those they take alive, we don't know what they do with them." Ben rakes his fingers through his curls.

Not knowing where Papa was or why they'd taken him, and having to endure that endless silence from officials, was unbearably difficult. My heart goes out to Ben and Ruby and everyone else waiting on news of loved ones.

"I have a lot to catch up on," Papa says, his expression grave. "And as soon as we have secure communication on board, I'll reach out to my contacts down south, find out what they've heard about this latest attack."

Ben waves a hand as he remembers. "Ah yes, of course, you haven't been in touch with anyone. Feel free to contact Gideon and anybody else while you're here. Our systems are secure."

Papa and I stand immediately.

"Oh yes, please," I say to Ben, before turning to Papa. "I really need to speak to Grandpa and Theo and Tabby."

"This way." Ben leads us out of the room.

We make our way down a small passageway lined with more framed pictures. My breath hitches when I spot Ari in one. I pause and stare at it; it looks like some kind of celebration here at home. The little girl in the photograph must be Freya, his sister. The entire family looks relaxed and happy. Ari's bright eyes are lit up and as intense as ever, his black, shoulder-length hair falling in waves, and oh dear, I absolutely must touch the picture.

"Pickle?" Papa's paused ahead, watching me with his eyebrows squished together. I swiftly drop my hand and hurry along, my cheeks heating.

Despite its compact size, the communications room is impressive. All manner of technical equipment and anti-tracking systems are up and running, and I know Theo would happily spend an entire day inspecting it all. Ben shows us what to do before leaving the room.

First, we get in touch with Grandpa. He answers immediately and my heart lurches when I see him on-screen.

His pale-green eyes light up as he catches sight of Papa and me. "Ah, shalom, Queenie! Hashem…At long last."

"Salaam, Gramps!" Oh how I've missed him. Papa is almost tearful at the sight of him.

Grandpa is sitting in his study, blinking repeatedly as if he, too, can't quite believe it. He smooths down the jumble of white hair on his head as we quickly catch up. I've not spoken with him since we said our goodbyes back at the Mayfair Hangars on New Year's Eve, just before I set off in my submarine to search for Papa. We bring him up to speed on all the immediate stuff.

His eyes shine with tears as Papa briefly answers his questions about his time at Broadmoor.

"Isolation?" Grandpa asks, his eyes wide with disbelief. "It's bad enough they're imprisoning people without a trial. All those people kept from interacting with another soul. It's inhumane."

I quickly cover what we've been doing since Papa's rescue.

Grandpa keeps shaking his head in disbelief. He tells Papa everything going on in London. Then he explains how the authorities have shut down their labs.

Papa and Grandpa are astronomers. They worked together at the laboratories in Bloomsbury until the day of Papa's arrest. They live and breathe for researching our universe. Gramps goes on to update Papa with everything going on with Bia and the Cambridge lot.

"I'm checking in with them next," says Papa. "You look tired, Gideon. You must rest and we'll be in touch again very soon."

After we wrap things up with Grandpa, Papa inspects all the equipment while I contact the twins. Seconds later, Theo's face fills the screen.

His eyes widen. "Bloody hell, am I glad to see you!"

Warmth radiates through me at the sight of him. Jojo barks joyfully.

Theo peers closer. "How are you? *Where* are you? What's going on?"

We keep interrupting each other until finally we're over the shock of speaking again, and catch up.

"And then Bia updated your granddad after you broke your dad out of prison—Neptune, I still can't believe you did that!" Theo says. "Gideon brought us up to speed with everything that went down. We're helping him wherever we can. Your granddad's bloody brilliant with all his covert stuff." His eyes shine. "I've been in touch with the Cambridge lot through him, and do a fair bit of work with Charlie. He's amazing—works really hard to keep amphi communities safe. Loves his gaming, too!" Theo can't help beaming now; he's the most advanced gamer I know.

"That's fantastic about helping Gramps! Yeah, Charlie's great. Up until Papa's arrest, they used to work together looking out for the southern communities, and Charlie's saved so many lives."

Theo blows his cheeks out. "Mum's in shock about everything we've learned. And she's been really worried for you after what that treacherous little git Sebastian pulled off, slapping a price on your heads like that. Can't get over what you've been through. And your dad being held in Broadmoor after all that—Hey, Mr. McQueen!" Theo's mouth falls open as he spots Papa. "Oh wow, you're all right, you're safe. How—"

"Leyla!" Tabby squeezes into sight next to her brother. "Oh, Mr. McQueen, I'm so happy to see you! Holy Neptune, you don't look so good." Theo's twin sister frowns. "What happened to your hair? What's going on with you guys? You've got to stay in touch! I'm so sorry about Ari, hope he's okay. I still can't believe he's an Anthro— I mean amphi, sorry. We went into shock! He was on board your sub when we were saying goodbye. I was this close to one of *them*. And—"

"Tabs!" Theo says, scowling as he turns to face his sister. She rolls her eyes in response.

I shake my head. "Tabby, they're not what we've—"

"I know! But it's still all a bit shocking!" Her face darkens. "And we found out what caused the underground to collapse the day Dad died. His death could've been prevented if the government had done their jobs properly, but instead they held back on funds and killed all those people. I hate the lot of them. They need to answer for their crimes. As for that sly shit, Sebastian, calling you Britain's number one enemy…wish I could wipe that friggin' sneer off his face."

Theo shakes his head, his expression hardening. "He seriously wants locking up. It should be *him* in Broadmoor."

I hate our government for so many things, and their incompetence leading to the death of the twins' dad is one of them.

We talk more, eager to cover as much as we can in the short time we have. I can't believe I'm actually chatting again with my best friends. My face warms. It's been too long since I last heard their voices. I wish I could touch them, hug them.

"How did you cross into foreign territory?" Theo folds his arms. "You have papers?"

I bite my lip. "I couldn't risk applying for permission. I didn't want to do anything that left a trail. And it was too risky getting in touch with you to ask about it, so I checked the map for the least patrolled entry points, rose high, and sped through."

Theo's eyes widen. "What if you run into a security check? Okay, I have a mate who sorts out travel papers. Like, impossible to tell them from the real thing, believe me."

I can't nod fast enough. Being here without the necessary legal permissions is always on my mind anytime I go out there.

"Faroe Islands..." He taps his chin. "You're in Danish waters, I think. I'll get onto it right after and send them over soon as they're done. And let me know should you need papers for anywhere else, okay? You don't want to be without them."

"Wow, thanks, such a relief."

Papa joins me. "Theo, Tabby, it's so good to see you. And how is Vivian? You must tell me everything."

The twins update him on their mother and everything else going on back in the capital. They explain how some people are starting to question everything that's happened to me.

"They all watched you in the marathon, Leyla," Tabby says. "They saw the interviews and witnessed what went down during the prize-giving ceremony. People aren't happy about the PM not granting you your Ultimate Prize request to set your dad free. And they were livid when the committee asked for your sub back, you know. They really disagree with the bounty on your heads. Folk know you'd never even hurt krill." She flicks her short, platinum-blond bob. "Unlike me."

"Oh, speaking of the sub, we can keep in touch now!" Theo says, smiling. "You still using the same Bracelet I gave you?" He nods away when

I confirm. "You don't have to worry about them tracing you anymore. I came up with a program that safeguards all contact from the *Kabul* and blocks things our end, too. I didn't have any way of getting it to you safely before now. Forwarding it on to Ben's number. Transfer it to your Bracelet right away, and then pass it on to Oscar to upload it to the submarine's communications systems. We couldn't let you know until I'd found a way to remotely shield the *Kabul*'s network. But this way you can message anyone as long as you're certain nobody's monitoring things on their end. I already ensured your grandpa secured all his equipment. So get in touch with us whenever you want!"

"What? Oh wow! You're certain?" I can't believe it. At last we can chat regularly with Grandpa and the twins. We're no longer alone. We found Ari's people *and* we can keep in touch with everyone!

"Absolutely," says Theo, beaming. "Speaking of Oscar, is he operating okay? And what about the tracker I sent you at Cambridge, did it work?"

"Oh, Oscar's been a dream, thanks so much for him. As for the tracker…" I grimace. "We got the info, but it left the trace you warned it might, and Bia found out."

"What!" Tabby leans in. "Your granddad didn't tell us about that! How did she respond?"

Bia and her brilliant covert group in Cambridge push back against everything the authorities do, from inside their state-of-the-art hideout known as the Den. Ari and I stopped by there in our search for Papa. It became clear Bia's lot knew more about his situation than they were letting on; they even had their own rescue plans underway. But they wouldn't trust anyone else with the info. With Theo's help, I managed to uncover details that would eventually lead me to Broadmoor, and Papa. I was rumbled, though, and Ari and I found ourselves surrounded, with a very angry Bia demanding I return the stolen info. At that exact moment, Blackwatch chose to hit the place and we managed to escape. Thankfully with the information intact.

"I'm sending you what I discovered," I say to the twins now. "But basically the government has been outright lying about the surface, about us returning to it any day. Living up there's impossible. Scientists have tested and proven it. It's too hostile and won't be habitable for several decades at the soonest. It's all there in the Explorer reports. They've been tampering with them and releasing contradictory accounts."

The twins' eyes widen. "What the actual hell," says Tabby.

I was stunned when I saw the proof. Those meant to be looking after us are ignoring all the science and warnings and instead continue to pour vital funds into pointless projects for living up on the surface. And at such a heavy cost to our lives right now.

Theo and Tabby bring me up to speed with everyone back in London.

"And Malik has the seasickness," Tabby suddenly adds quietly, her voice flat now.

"Oh no…" My chest tightens. Poor Malik… It's hard to imagine him anything less than his spirited self. He was always my main competition during our weekly sub sprints around Tower Bridge.

A flicker of hope surfaces in Theo's eyes as he leans in. "Your granddad told us how Bia's lot discovered major info on it early last year." His gaze shifts to Papa, and he raises his eyebrows. "Did you know they treat the condition very differently abroad, Mr. McQueen?"

Papa presses his lips together in a slight grimace. Mention of the seasickness always triggers painful memories for him; the government used the illness to frame him and have him sent to Broadmoor. They had accused him of exploiting those suffering by encouraging their dying by suicide. A revolting lie that didn't even make sense. He'd actually been doing the opposite—trying to think of whatever he could to help them fight the terrible, deadly inertia.

I nod at Theo. "Papa knows; he told me about it."

We were wrong about the seasickness. A report I saw on one of the files I'd swiped while inside the prison had Bia declaring the government solely responsible for it. But Papa recently explained how that report was several years old, and he filled me in on what they've learned about the condition since.

Around a year ago, Bia's group managed to access classified files belonging to Westminster that revealed international scientific data. We now have a much clearer understanding of the seasickness. Though the government does make it so much worse with all its pervasive nostalgia for the Old World, and especially the unrelenting fearmongering of this world, they didn't actually create the seasickness. Its roots lie in how we've always struggled with living down here in the deep. Our minds still haven't adapted to the environment. It's a debilitating sense of claustrophobia, a malaise that requires proper remedy. Instead—and despite having access to medical findings that disclose real, proven treatments—the government insists it's uncontrollable, that it's just another of this world's deadly aspects. And our only solution is to ensure sufferers somehow increase their exposure to the Old World.... It's infuriating.

We talk some more before I have to cut short so Papa can catch up with Bia and everyone at Cambridge, but we promise to speak again soon.

I forward Oscar the file Theo just sent, so the communications system on board the *Kabul* can be secured. I notice Papa's smile as he stares away into space. The difference in him after chatting with Grandpa is immediate. It's the first time since that godforsaken prison that a smile's lingered on his face.

I'm thinking about rejoining the others so Papa can have some privacy for his call when there's a knock on the door, and a girl I recognize as Ari's sister pops her head around. She wanders in, around ten years old and a perfect blend of Ben and Ruby. I'm now certain Ari was adopted. Stopping beside me, she crosses her arms and tilts her head. "Where's Ari?" she asks, narrowing her round brown eyes.

"You're Freya, right?"

Her curls bounce as she nods. Her expression is torn. "When's Ari coming home?" she asks. "We haven't seen him since he left for London before Christmas."

"I'm so sorry but I don't know where he is. I wish I did.... But your dad and everyone are doing all they can to find him. Hopefully he'll be back very soon."

"In time for Aunt Linde's wedding? It's coming up. He has to be here for it, he promised me he would be." She unfolds her arms and puts her hands on her hips. "If he isn't here by then, I'll just have to go looking for him myself." She stops to smile at Jojo, who wags her tail in response. "Neptune, I can't believe you have a real dog! Want to see my rock collection?"

I turn to Papa and he nods. "I'll be along as soon as I've caught up with everyone at Cambridge, Pickle. Being able to contact Bia is such welcome news." His expression turns pensive. "Charlie will be waiting for information from me. He's done so much to help, but I was his primary source down south. Without my input his hands will mostly have been tied."

I leave Papa to catch up with everyone at the Den, and follow Freya out of the room, making sure to touch Ari's face when I pass his picture. Freya chats nonstop, taking it upon herself to show me around.

I try to imagine her brother here. How is Ari around his own people? What is he like with his family? How does he move around in this space he calls home? *Please, God, let him be all right, wherever he is.*

As we pass a couple of hatches, Freya points out the corridor that leads to their pool room.

"Does *everyone* have a moon pool?" I ask. "Back in London, only the houses of the rich or those considered important have one."

I realize now maybe *all* the homes here have access pools. I'd never given it any thought before. Imagine, a pool instead of a front door hatch. It's fascinating and still a little terrifying to think a part of the floor in your home opens onto the abyss. We have one on the *Kabul*, but that's a vessel. This place is stationary and it feels surreal.

Freya looks confused for a moment before her eyes widen. "Oh, that's because you can't swim, right? Every time you want to go out, you have to use the subs. Even for five minutes! They do it all the time on-screen and it takes forever."

I grin. "Compared with just diving into and climbing out of a pool, it's definitely more bothersome. And we can swim, just not..."

Freya continues the tour. Their home is hearty and spacious. There are hydroponic gardens of every size dotted around, random structures filled with fruit and vegetables all growing in the artificial light. Back in London, only the rich can afford their own gardens and the rest of us make do with what passes for fruit and veg from the London Markets. The *Kabul* has her very own garden, though, and maintaining it is an absolute joy. I continue to picture Ari living here as we walk on. "You'd never think it was this big inside!"

"Most community meetings are held in our house," Freya explains. "And there are extra rooms in case anyone needs somewhere to stay after an attack."

She says it so casually, so matter-of-fact, and I realize she's probably never known a time when the threat of an attack didn't exist. It's the saddest thought.

"We have even bigger buildings, like the hospital on the ledge above. And *this*"—Freya beams as a door slides open—"is my bedroom!"

It's a bit like Tabby's room back in London, all sleek spaces and soft lighting. Holographic posters of the latest music bands hover around the space, and she seems to be in the middle of a game of Whack-a-Seahorse. I haven't seen the vintage game for years. The old-fashioned neon hoops from a decade ago glimmer around the room, and every time a seahorse materializes over one, you have only two seconds to reach it and whack it back inside the ring. Tabby loved the game when we were younger, her reflexes impressively fast even back then. A sure sign she'd grow up to be a martial arts champ.

Jojo makes herself at home on Freya's bed, while I rush toward the large spherical window that's curved outward. It's as if I'm inside a bubble as I peer through the clear acrylic.

I gaze out, looking down, and as soon as my eyes adjust to the current I see a large portion of the community on a ledge opposite to this one. Plateaus of every size jut out from the surrounding jagged cliffs, and on each flattened space sits a maze of homes all lit up. Specks of yellow light glimmer like floating lanterns blinking on the current. My heart soars at the sight.

I whip my head around to Freya, who's busy dragging a sparkly poster of a trio of dancing girls across the room to reposition it beside a blue wardrobe. "I can't believe this place," I say. "It's like you live in a hollowed-out mountain. Do you feel safe when you're out there?"

Freya nods, joining me in the bubble. "If we ever suspect anything, we lock the pools and switch off all lights. Crafts can only reach us from either the secret long way around, like you did, or from up top." She jabs a finger upward. "But we have all kinds of security at work up there now. We'd know if a vessel were headed our way long before they got here. It doesn't happen often, but when it does, we send out distractions. So yep, we're safe since our security was updated after what happened at Christmas...." A haunted look breaks out on her expression. "They think they killed us all because they destroyed the decoy homes on a more visible ledge higher up." She ends far quieter than she'd started.

"I'm so sorry, Freya. I know Lance died in that attack."

Ari's face flashes before me, his expression dark as grief pooled into his eyes when he told me about his friend's death.

Freya stares into the space. "Lance was racing over to our house when he got caught up in the attack. Ari left to save him even though Mum and Dad begged him not to go outside. Just when my brother found him, Lance was hit. His sub exploded right in front of Ari, did you know?" She gazes up at me now, her eyes wide. "They never discovered the rest of the community. Dad says we would've lost so many more lives if they had." She blinks, her gaze so helpless it tears my insides.

"Don't forget to show me your rocks," I say, suddenly desperate to see her smile again.

Freya darts away from the window to grab a rusted tin box from under her bed. "Check it out!" she says proudly.

I join her to inspect her rock collection. Beautiful stones in every shape and texture.

"Mine's the best hoard of anyone's." She flashes a smug smile. "I don't just put anything in my pockets, you know. Sometimes I spend ages finding the best rock."

Freya holds up a hand when she remembers something, and hurries to a shelf to grab a Medi-bot. She pulls up her dress and tends to her left leg where there's a dressing on her thigh. The instrument removes the old dressing and starts cleaning the cut. Her right leg is a prosthetic limb, one of those translucent models with the lights and wires pulsing away inside.

Ari's words come back to me the night he had the nightmare on board the *Kabul*. He told me how security forces had attacked a group of them one day as they traveled to a wedding. The community lost many, including children. Freya lost her right leg and was lucky to have survived.

"Are you all right?" I ask when she winces as the Medi-bot does its job. "Do you need any help?"

She whips her head up, slight panic in her brown eyes, and swiftly commands the door shut. "Yes, I'm fine," she says hurriedly, lowering her voice. "And I can take care of it myself. It's only a tiny cut; you mustn't tell Dad. He worries too much and if he spots this scratch, I'll never be allowed out again." She blows her curls out of her eyes.

"How did you get it?"

"Out looking for rocks by the rift. The lights there are so cool, especially after a sandstorm." She pauses when she sees me frowning.

"The rift is lit up?" I ask.

She laughs. "Bioluminescence! When I wouldn't stop swimming out there to collect the rocks, Ari insisted on going with me. But he's not here and Dad doesn't like me being out there alone, even though it's dead close and I can look after myself. So I sometimes sneak out when they're still asleep in the mornings, poke around for the best rocks. You have to watch out for the eels, though, so slippery." She pauses to check the Medi-bot's work before returning her focus to me and tilting her head. "Nessie's not real, you know? If she existed, I'd have seen her by now. All that stuff about her swimming around these parts is bonkers. And that footage from last year was fake." She rolls her eyes. "I did a better tech job when I told my mates I was at a concert in Seoul."

I grin, and then ponder her words. The rift sounds scary as hell.

Back in London, before my world turned upside down, I'd have loved hearing how spirited Freya was. Despite being terrified of almost everything myself back then, others' adventures fascinated me to no end. So I hate that right now my only thought is concern for Ari's sister. I'm thrilled she has something she enjoys—she should be able to do anything and everything. And I'm also terrified for her. It feels like I'm suddenly getting a glimpse of Papa and myself, and I shift on my feet.

"There'll be good reason why Ari insisted on going with you. It must be dangerous. You have to be careful, Freya."

She sighs. "Not you too. I can take care of myself, you know."

My Bracelet flashes: It's Charlie. "Freya, I won't be a moment."

"Oh, you can take that in here," she says, and leaves the room.

Charlie's thin, pale face pops up, and his eyes brighten when they spot me. "Leyla—and Jojo's with you!"

His grin is contagious and I instantly feel lighter. Jojo jumps around at the sight of him. She took to him right away at Cambridge and wags her tail nonstop now.

"Just finished chatting with yer dad," Charlie says. "He's speaking with Bia now. Right, I wanna know everything that's happened since the breakout!" Charlie, along with many others Bia sent from Cambridge, helped us fight the prison's extensive security patrols.

The Den looks as busy as ever behind him. He glances over his shoulder now and pauses as someone approaches. I recognize Jas as he comes into view. The Blackwatch attack on the Den was frightening and I panicked when Jas chased me. I used the immobilizing spray in my brolly to stop him in his tracks. Jas doesn't take his eyes off us now as he walks by. Charlie turns back to me as soon as it's clear again, a thin line appearing between his eyebrows. He shrugs it away and we continue.

When I'm done summarizing what happened after we rescued Papa, he brings me up to speed with the Den, taking care to also pay Jojo the attention she's seeking. Bia's hard at work as usual, identifying communities at risk of being discovered, ensuring they receive help in time, and working with her contacts to keep tabs on the government's many questionable actions.

"Not possible to save everyone, though." His face falls. "You guys don't know any more about what went down at Tórshavn, do you? That one's got me well and truly stumped. No news of how they attacked, and half a dozen dead…"

I shake my head. "Ben's as mystified as you lot. They can't find a trace of any firepower at all. Papa told me security forces sometimes get to the communities right before you guys intend to. That's odd, right? Like, these people were undiscovered for that long and then as soon as the Den finds out, they're attacked. You don't think they could be listening in?"

Charlie presses his lips into a thin line and his expression turns heavy. "The sights we've met when we get there too late sometimes…" He shakes his head. "But if they were tracing us, they'd be onto every community we're protecting; they'd have all been wiped out ages ago. Our security's off the wall. Even when Blackwatch attacked the Trading Post that time you were here, they never discovered the Den beneath. If there's a weak spot, it ain't us, Leyla." He cocks his head. "Wait, hold yer horses. Are you serious thinking they might be tapping in?"

I shrug. "I'm not really sure, but it just doesn't make sense, you know?"

He bites his lip, worry clouding his gaze. "All I know is we're the best at what we do; everyone's skills in the Den are sound. But I'll see what I can find out. Might pick Theo's brains about this—there's nothing tech-related he doesn't know!" His eyes shine. "In the meantime, you mustn't fret over it. Send us footage of Jojo playing around?" He brightens when I nod. "You ever plan on visiting us again?"

We finish chatting and I open the door to find Freya waiting. She looks past me and, eyes wide, darts back in to thwack a seahorse that's materialized in the air over one of the glimmering hoops. Her Bracelet flashes yellow to indicate a hit and she beams triumphantly. We leave her room.

As we walk on, I can't help wondering… "Freya, do you think I could please see Ari's room?"

"But why? Boys' rooms stink."

"I don't mind."

"Well, only if I can hold Jojo." She waggles her eyebrows and holds out her arms.

The puppy buries her nose in Freya's sweater.

"Wow, thanks." Freya holds Jojo close and points to the second door along. "Ari's room. I'll just be in my own showing off Jojo to friends," she says over her shoulder as she walks back to her room. "Not going to let on she's real, see how long they fall for it!"

"That's great," I say, her words barely registering as, pulse racing, I step into Ari's room.

CHAPTER FOUR

Ari's room has a warm fragrance, woody and aromatic. Just beneath that is Ari's own smell—a wild and earthy musk scent, stirring and soothing and instantly transporting me into his arms. I snap out of it and take in the space. Like Freya's room, it's spacious with a single spherical window. It's all greens and blues, dark woods, and the glimmer of technology. I move farther inside.

I run my hand over the frame of Ari's bed. The quality of the wood is amazing; it looks and feels far more real than what we manufacture in London. Posters hover around: breathtaking underwater landscapes, sleek submersibles, the odd musician, a blue whale, fantasy gaming characters, and several extinct Old World creatures. A lion roars on the far wall beside a target board and an eagle bristles atop a bare branch on the back of the door. An entire wall is set up for gaming; I'd never realized he was such a keen gamer. He'd get on well with Theo and Charlie. There's a set of spears standing in one corner and a guitar in another. I recall the deep melodic notes of the music resounding around the sub whenever he played his sax. I still hear it every night as I lie in bed.

On a shelf sits a basket full of things I think Ari's collected when out and about. I rummage through the hoard and pick up an enormous pointed tooth, bigger than my hand and stained yellow-brown. There's a glittering rock and a large polished stone. I turn the stone over and realize it's a fossil. My finger gently traces the swirly imprint of God knows what creature, and from how long ago. A couple of shawls hang from a hook, like the black one he always wore draped around his shoulders. I remember its smell. I remember the feeling of my face pressed against Ari's chest whenever we hugged, the beauty of the weight of his arms around me. The striking angles and mysterious hollows of his face.

The look in his eyes when he realized he was trapped.

I glance around the room, and like a tidal wave, sadness suddenly and inexplicably engulfs me. I move to sit on the end of his bed.

I should be happy. We found Ari's family, and we can stay in touch with everyone once we're back on the submarine. It's so much more than I could've hoped for. And I'm truly grateful for today.

But he's still missing. And he's not the only one.

The unfairness of it all has me by the throat. It's as if one of the rocks out there has lodged itself inside it and I can't swallow it away. It's obscene that this is a part of life for these people. Their loved ones go missing and rarely return home. Searches are conducted and then...Imagine never knowing whether someone you love is alive or dead. And God only knows what they do to those they take.

There's a sour taste rising in my throat; I take several deep breaths and lie back on Ari's bed. I roll on my side and imagine him next to me, his face so close to mine I can see the golden specks in his eyes. Where is he? What is he doing at exactly this moment? He's alive, I know he is. He *has* to be. For weeks I've been so focused on trying to find Ari's family, and didn't dare dwell on what comes after. I never imagined I'd be in his room, feeling his presence everywhere.

I startle when the door slides open and almost roll off the bed, my face flushing. Freya is bouncing on her toes, beckoning me. "Mum said come and have something to eat."

The kitchen is a hearty space, the oven spreading delicious aromas and warmth throughout the home. From what I've gathered, people drop in on Ben's place all the time due to him being one of the main leaders of the community. And now with news of our presence and Ari's situation already spreading through the neighborhood, quite a few people have shown up to determine exactly what's going on and offer their assistance. Several of the neighbors' children run in and out of the kitchen. Papa's sitting around a large oak table with a few others and is done eating.

"Sit, Pickle," he says, taking a sip of his tea. "You haven't eaten since breakfast."

Ruby, standing and chatting with Papa, tucks a curl behind her ears. "Help yourself, love."

As I take a seat, Papa points out someone sitting opposite to me. It's a white guy and he must be around seventeen, same age as Theo and Tabby, possibly a little older. He has a buzz cut and wears a white T-shirt, his muscular arms covered in tattoos. There's a mischievous look about him.

"Leyla, this is Lewis McGregor," says Papa. "His mother, Maud, helped us inside Broadmoor." He introduces me to Lewis.

I can't believe it—McGregor, the prison officer who helped cause a riot the morning we went to rescue Papa so that we could get him out unnoticed! Maud actually works for Bia, and was placed inside that godforsaken place so they could find out more about it. I couldn't ask anyone about her up until now due to the communication restrictions, but I'd wondered so many times if she got out of that hellhole.

"Hi," I say to Lewis as I scoop creamy chicken tagliatelle onto my plate and add some vibrant salad on the side. "Your mum, did she make it out of there?"

"Hey there." Lewis winks in greeting, his pale-green eyes sparkling. He shakes his head. "Me mam's still inside."

"Oh no. I'm so sorry. I'm not sure we'd have ever made it out of there without her help."

"Aye, Mam's something," he says, grinning. He has a strong Scottish accent like his mother and a permanent glint in his eyes like Tabby. "And she's not too bad; they haven't rumbled her. She just doesn't wanna blow her cover by asking to leave before her time. And at least you got yer dad out." He tilts his head and waggles his eyebrows. "You were *something* in the marathon, by the way." He reaches for the coffee pot and Ari's face again flashes before me.

I don't like tea, he'd said, when I offered him a drink that first day we met on the sub. *I only drink coffee.* At the time it only made me even more suspicious of him—who'd ever choose coffee over tea? I drag my mind away from the memory of him working away around the engine room with a veiled expression and a spark in his gaze, and force it back to the present.

The food is delicious and I tuck in, marveling at the succulence of the chicken—what do they do differently with the protein in the Faroe Islands? I clear my plate in no time and pour myself a cup of tea. Papa's chatting with Ruby and another woman. One of the kids mentions horses to the others and I call her over and request a piece of paper.

"How long have you known Ari?" I ask Lewis as I bend and fold the sheet of paper.

"Always, we grew up together. I've known his family and many of his friends and relatives me whole life. Ari, Lance, and me, we would get up to all sorts, used to drive me mam mad. Them two in the water and me in me sub."

"Why you in the sub?" I ask, and then it dawns on me. "Oh, sorry, I just assumed you could go into the water, too."

He shakes his head. "If only. Though...I wouldn't wish their lives on anyone." Lewis stares into his coffee. "Lance died. It was hard for all of us, but Neptune, I'd never seen Ari so cut up." He falls silent for a moment, before gesturing to me. "And then his dad sent him round your way a week later, hoping it'd keep him from lashing out. So...what do you think of our Ari then?"

"How do you mean? Did somebody say something?" My cheeks warm, curse them.

Lewis grins, the glint returning to his eyes, and then his gaze moves past me and he waves at someone. I crane my neck and spot Jack Taylor's bright red hair across the room. I still can't believe he's alive.

Jack's from London. We've known the Taylors our whole lives. Two years ago Jack's sub malfunctioned during the London Marathon and he sank out of sight; they never found his body. All that time everyone thought he'd died. And then out of the blue he showed up at the prison to help me when I went in to break Papa out.

"I never knew the Taylors were amphis until I saw Jack at the prison," I say to Lewis. "His little sister, Becca, and his mum, all this time—"

"Eh, no," says Lewis, reaching for a slice of fruitcake. "Not Becca and Mrs. Taylor. Only Jack."

"Wait, how can Jack be one, but not his sister or mother?"

I finish fashioning the paper horse and hand it to the little girl, who grins widely and makes growling sounds as she waves it around to show her brother. For some reason children associate roaring and growling with the magnificent Old World creatures, except there's plenty of footage to show horses didn't make those sounds.

"Er, the IMAS gene?" says Lewis, eyebrow raised as if it's common knowledge. "It's rare, but some have the relevant gene only kick in after a trigger, usually a massive trauma."

"Wait, they're not all born—"

"Neptune, what do they put in the water around London? They really don't want you knowing anything, do they? IMAS is an undetectable dormant gene found in a wee number of folk who have amphi DNA in—"

"Lewis, you scoundrel," says a tall, athletic white girl entering the kitchen. She has the same blond curls as Ari's family. She spots me and offers a quick nod and smile.

Lewis grins. "Samantha, Leyla. Leyla, Samantha's a cousin of Ari's. And a mean shot with a Lastar."

"Congrats on winning the marathon," Samantha says, her smile widening. "That's no mean feat. Pity those dipshits refused you your prize." We chat a bit and I realize I haven't seen Ben since earlier.

I turn to Ari's mother. "Ruby, what's been decided?"

"Ben's gone, love. He left with several others. We tried to persuade him to wait until tomorrow, but he wouldn't hear of it. He doesn't want to waste any time. He has a point. They've taken our largest sub and want to go speak to friends of ours, about half a day's travel east. They have bigger vessels and that means more firepower for when they go searching wider." She rubs her arms, thinking.

"I'm so sorry, Ruby."

Ari's mother moves closer and pats my arm. "He's a shy boy," she says with a sad smile. "And a private soul. And of course most people assume he's aloof because of that. But he has the biggest heart of anybody I've ever known. I won't entertain the idea of never seeing my boy again. I don't accept that possibility."

"No," I say quietly, "that's unimaginable."

Her face softens as she watches me. Ruby's Bracelet flashes and she moves aside to take a message.

I feel like time's stood still, or at least slowed down considerably, and I can't stop tapping my feet. Draining my cup, I check on Jojo. The puppy's basking in all the attention Freya's lavishing on her. I leave them to it and walk around the home aimlessly, a million things swirling in my head.

Ever since I set off in the submarine from London I've felt uncomfortable, restless, inside any fixed building for too long. In a vessel you know you can move anytime you want or need to. This inability to be anything other than stationary feels so limiting. And with all the other stuff pressing against the insides of my skull, I feel like I can hardly breathe.

Sabr, Papa's always advising me: patience. I really wish it came easily to me. Taking several deep breaths, I return to the kitchen.

"Papa, I'm going for a quick spin just around here."

"No, Leyla."

"Please."

"No, Pickle, it's far too dangerous."

Argh. Now that we're here, I don't know exactly what we're doing, what we're going to do next.

"Actually, Hashem, it's probably the safest spot in the entire islands," says Ruby, and I hold my breath. "We have extensive security measures—I should know, I manage them. As long as Leyla remains inside our boundaries, she'll have help right away should she need it."

Papa presses his lips flat. "I don't know, Ruby…"

"I promise she'll be all right out there as long as she doesn't stray from the area. We have eyes and ears on every wave around here. Overhauled the system myself after what happened last Christmas."

"Aye," chimes in Lewis. "And if it makes you feel any better, Mr. McQueen, I can jump in me sub and keep a watch out."

"I don't—" I begin.

"Okay, son." Papa nods, and for once I quit while I'm ahead.

The submersible sways as it lowers into the choppy current. I message Oscar for another update. Everything's fine with the submarine.

I hover there, taking in the homes on the ledges as I adjust to the rocking sensation. Illumination glimmers from the windows, wavy forms of light defying the harsh environment, and the odd sub moves around the space. They would never believe this back in London. An entire community residing in the mountains.

I stifle a yawn as I wait for Lewis to join me. I had another bad night last night. The same old nightmare has returned with fervor.

I used to have it regularly as a child, and then it revisited the night before I had to leave London to search for Papa. It must be linked to my stress levels because ever since Ari was taken from us, the dark dreams have visited me several times a week. Always the same. Always heart-stoppingly terrifying.

I'm around four or five years old, and I'm staring out of a window. I can barely breathe for the fear crawling through me. The depths outside are an inky, palpable dark, and I just know there's something horrific lingering in the cloaked current. Watching, waiting. I always want to turn away, but even that seems like too much, as if it'll attract the attention of whatever's lurking in the dense gloom. So I stay rooted to the spot in front of the window. Sometimes, when I wake up, it's with the overwhelming sense I saw a person in the water. Except I never actually do. So why do I always feel as if I did?

Flashing lights bring me out of my thoughts as Lewis indicates we're good to go. We've swapped Bracelet info so we can keep in touch. I move to the center of the enclosed space and pull the joystick all the way back until the sub's nose points upward. The propeller whirls at full speed as I push forward on the throttle, and the craft rockets. The lights fall away as I climb, and only the hazy shapes of empty ledges pass me by as the vessel continues to ascend. Higher and higher until finally we exit the inhabited mountains and I pause, waiting for Lewis. When he joins me, we cruise away a little before descending until several cliff faces come into view. Speeding around obstacles ensures a more satisfying run.

I take in the shadowy ridges and peaks; the choppy, wildering waves; and the dense darkness around me, and straighten. Even if solar spheres had existed on the surface around these parts, I doubt they'd have made much difference. The North Atlantic Ocean is tempestuous here as it tussles with the Norwegian Sea, and with the added ominous landscape, I don't think any amount of lighting could illuminate these waters enough. This environment is a far cry from the milder waters of London.

I pick my music, and as the Purple Floyd track plays, its epic guitar riff bouncing off the sub's insides, I thrust forward and don't look back.

I'm moving with the current, the craft twisting and turning through wave after wave, rounding the cliff faces and swerving past endless ledges. *Escape.* I dip into the rift valleys in between before climbing and rising above jagged peaks. It's exhilarating and my heartbeat matches the speed. Lewis mostly prefers to watch, flashing his lights anytime I pass by him.

The weekly sprints I reveled in back in London seem like a lifetime ago now, and oh how I've missed the rush from charging carefree through the water. Racing is freedom; it's escaping from everything confusing and painful, and hurtling toward some unidentifiable hope.

At last, with a flushed face and warmth radiating throughout my body, I right the vessel and sit still, my breathing fast. *Wow.* Speeding away from security subs isn't quite the same thing! Lewis's vessel comes into view as my Bracelet flashes, and I turn down the music a little.

"Mad skills!" he says. "I love it. Follow me!"

He takes the lead and dives low. We continue descending until the water is the most dense I've ever experienced.

"We're still within the community's safety boundaries, right?" I ask him. Letting me race out here was quite big for Papa and I don't want him to regret it.

"Och yeah!" he says. "Quit yer worrying, yer safe with me!"

Gradually the seabed comes into view with its dark, cindery sand. The altitude warning light blinks away, and I level and rise a few feet until I'm in the clear. I follow Lewis as we cruise along, taking in the eerie gloom around us.

Several eco-bots that clearly malfunctioned years ago drift aimlessly past the sub. I switch my focus to the sights below as we pass over endless debris. A shoal of bright purple fish flicker seemingly in and out of existence as they swim among rusted cranes and human bone. The corroded body of an ancient fire truck lies on the seabed covered in giant clams and attracting an array of vibrant creatures. A frilly disc-like animal spins away over what remains of a ladder, keeping its distance from the clams.

Farther on, the decaying body of a whale is stuck in the side of half an antiquated cruise ship. Old Worlders would sail on the seas for days, writing epic poems and stories about them and filling them with waste—especially all their deadly, devastating plastic. The cursed stuff gets everywhere, causing us infinite problems. The countless sheets and containers dislodged with every sandstorm and earthquake float around creating endless damage, and prove especially perilous for drivers. And the smaller pieces just about get into everything, cramming our water filters, blocking power farms, and filling the throats and bellies of so many creatures.

One of the post-flood religions believes all the waters are the tears of the planet, after centuries of abuse at the hands of humans. They don't have as many followers as Neptune worshippers, but still.

As I continue to scan the ground beneath me, I spot something that makes me pause. The seafloor looks like it's moving. I stare, frowning. Could it be the start of a sandstorm? A quake? I'll need to move fast if it is. Once again the ground seems to shake, and then it ripples.

"Lewis, are you seeing this?"

My pulse races. I rise a little, not taking my eyes off the sight. It looks like…a limb. A huge, never-ending limb wriggling just beneath the top layer of sand and grit. There's no response from Lewis. I glance up and realize I can't see him anymore.

"Lewis!"

Silence. I spin around in the craft, flashing my lights to let him know where I am, but still there's no sign of him. *Oh hell.* And then a cloud of dust and sand engulfs me and I can't see a thing. I switch my sandstorm beam on, but it's no good. There's a *thud* against the sub and I freeze. And then another. A third hit is so strong it sends me whirling away and I cry out. I lose control of the vessel.

An alarm rings out in the sub. Around and around the craft spins, moving forward at unmanageable speed. I grab the sides, my hair covering my face as some kind of force carries us along. My heart pounds away and my lungs feel as if they can no longer contain it. All I can see outside is a million bubbles, and a thunderous roar echoes around me. The sub lurches and there's a *boom* when something knocks into it again, sending it careening in another direction. The current is smoother and slower here. I tighten my grip on the throttle and joystick, and concentrate on maneuvering the wings to counter the force. It works, thank God. The vessel stops spinning and the alarm is silenced. My pulse hammers away in my ears as I wipe my sweaty palms on my thighs and peer out. The waves are a lot clearer and the noise is gone.

"Lewis!" I try again as I check all systems. Everything seems to be in order.

"Leyla, can you hear me? Are you okay?"

My shoulders sag with relief on hearing his voice. "I don't know what happened! I thought I saw something on the seabed, and before I knew it I was hit. And then I was caught up in some weird current and dragged along. I've never experienced anything like it.…Are you all right? You didn't respond and I couldn't see you."

"Och sorry, I'm good. But yeah, I've taken a hit, too. Kept trying to contact you but no luck. Who the fuck hit us? Where are you? Are yer systems working?"

I get my bearings and Lewis whistles when I share my location.

"Okay, yer far out. I reckon you were swept up in the drift, for sure. Stay there and I'll come fetch you. Might be a while cos me tail's taken some damage. Security doesn't stretch that end, so watch yer back until I get there."

"No," I say. "If you're closer from where you are, then maybe we should each just make our own way back? Especially if you've been hit. I don't think either of us should be hanging around. I have the coordinates logged from my trip earlier."

"Yer sure about this? That does make more sense, especially with me tail playing up, but as long as yer confident you can make it. I can send someone for you?"

"No, don't call for anyone. I'm all right and I can make it. You forget I've been out here nearly every day for over a month. Let me know if you stall with that tail?"

Lewis agrees we shouldn't waste time meeting up, and he sets off after I promise we'll stay in touch until we're both back. I initiate the journey to Ari's community. Taking a deep breath and blowing out my cheeks, I follow the onboard computer. Who or what hit us?

It's not long before Lewis lets me know he's got back safely. I continue on, determined to do the same.

After a while, I could swear there's a faint light pulsing on the edge of my vision. When I turn to look, though, there's only patchy darkness, and I return my focus to what's ahead. A little farther and once more I suspect there's someone in the water with me—this time on my tail. I throw a glance over my shoulders.

During sprints back in London, no matter how hard the person trailing me would try to hide their presence, there was always a telltale glimmer on the current. Even the subtlest light dances on the waves. And I see that glimmer now—a tiny flicker glowing in the gloom. I take in the source of the light, its murky shape moving at seahorse speed.

There's a security sub following me.

I throw a swift glance all around me for signs of anyone else. It seems to be the only craft. Don't they *ever* take a day off from sniffing around these islands, dammit? I swiftly pause the coordinates—I was leading them right to their target. The community's defense systems won't have picked up the security sub yet; Lewis said I was too far out of their boundaries and I doubt we're close enough even now. I very gradually lean right.

I message Papa to alert everyone to security forces in the area. Their systems will trace the sub as it draws closer, but there's no harm in a heads-up.

Papa's immediately beside himself with worry. "I don't want you doing anything rash, do you hear me, Pickle? Lewis just told us what happened. Thank God you're both okay, but it's clearly an unpredictable environment."

"I'll be careful, Papa, promise."

Ruby speaks next. "Leyla, let me know if you have any difficulty losing them, love. We have subs ready in the water. We never attack, only defend, so let's hope they tire and move on." She lets out a heavy sigh. "You were both within our boundaries when you were hit, so I don't understand how our systems missed the culprits. Stay in touch."

I continue pretending to cruise along, oblivious, all the while looking out for a suitable landscape to speed up and lose them in.

"Oscar?"

The Navigator materializes in the craft and I transfer him to the dashboard. "Oscar, is the *Kabul* all right? And she's still in stealth mode, yes?"

He flashes one of his timid smiles. "My lady, the *Kabul* remains wholly unscathed and is currently lying low. There is nothing of concern in her immediate vicinity. Dare I say, unlike the highly unsavory rumpus that was going on in the waters around the submersible earlier. My sensors were rather off the charts!"

"Something hit me and I lost control. Then I ended up in some wild current and couldn't stop spinning!"

The Navigator waves his hand lazily in the air. "My dear, why burden yourself with such indelicate capers? I implore you to relax," he says with a puzzled look. "Hard work is simply the refuge of people who have nothing whatever to do." He gives a slight shake of his head. "You must understand, my lady, you are in a different class to that."

"Right, then…Oscar, if those dicks come anywhere near the *Kabul*, stay hidden and let me know right away, please. There's a security sub in the area, keep an eye on it. You probably already know; it's on my tail."

"Of course, my dear. A most cumbersome matter, being followed. This one night in Dublin I was terribly ruffled when I sensed someone trailing me back to Trinity. I wish I'd possessed the fortitude to turn around and interrogate the perpetrator, but alas! My lady, experience is simply…"

I check where I am, and where I intend on leading the shadowing sub. "Oscar, sorry, I must stay focused. That'll be all, thanks."

He disappears with a flourish and I subtly check behind me; they're still there.

And then the Navigator's words register, and I chew on my lip, wondering if it's worth mentioning.

"Papa?" I say as soon as he answers my call. "Please get Ruby."

"Sit tight, love," says Ruby almost immediately. "I'm sending someone."

"No, I was thinking what if I *do* lead them to you, and they're captured? Maybe they might be intimidated into telling you where Ari is?"

"That wouldn't work, Pickle," Papa says. "The moment they realize they've discovered the community, its exact location would be reported to Westminster before we restrained them."

"Unfortunately that's right," says Ruby. "We'd be surrounded before we got a single word out of them. However…if we could disable their onboard systems first, then that wouldn't be a problem."

During the marathon, the organizers used flares to immobilize our subs. Nothing on board worked until their effect wore off. And the prison did the same; when we closed in on Broadmoor's location, they released bots that started messing with the *Kabul*'s systems.

"Bringing them here, Ruby…has that ever happened before?" Papa asks, tension in his voice.

"It hasn't. And, Hashem, I want my son back, but this isn't just about Ari," she says. "Too many are dead in Tórshavn. If there's any way of discovering where they plan on hitting next, or yes, where our loved ones are, and if it can be done without putting our people at risk, then I want to consider it. Impairing their vessel would mean word can't get out about us. We have blockers powerful enough to shut down everything technological on board, including their Bracelets."

"Aye, and then we could drag it back here," Lewis adds in the background.

"We have the capability," Ruby continues. "We just need to go about it the right way. Leyla, sit tight, love, and keep the line open."

It's over in another forty-five minutes. I lead the security sub into a small range of peaks and hide, only coming out once I've guided the others to it. Not one but three vessels confront it, impairing all its systems before they know what hit them. The waters crinkle around the craft, holding it inside what looks like a shimmery bubble. And then a huge claw drops from the bulky sub above to clamp the immobilized vessel and carry it away. My heart races from watching it all. The sub that was following me is long—I'm guessing a four-seater at least. Hopefully there aren't four of them on board. . . . I make my way back.

Unlike the others who'll be heading straight for the top of the mountain because a clamped sub would never fit through the cave-like passage, I have to take the longer but safer route. An extra precaution Ruby insisted upon, in light of security showing up here. At last the glowing lights from the homes on the ledges greet me, and the relief is instant. I shoot up through the pool of Ari's house and exit the airlock to find Papa waiting for me.

He wraps his arms around me. "Alhamdulillah," he says. "I've been so worried hoping nothing else goes wrong out there, Pickle."

"Salaam, Papa. I'm all right. Are the others back yet?"

"Yes. They just restrained the officer in a back room. And the blockers worked; he wasn't able to sound the alarm. Ben has been updated. He wanted to return home immediately, but Ruby insisted he rest and set off in the morning." He takes a deep breath and exhales slowly as he thinks. "So now we must pray they reveal what happened at Tórshavn—and where they plan on attacking next."

"Yes. And what they've done with Ari."

Papa yawns and I step back to look at him. His color has paled and his eyes are bloodshot. Today's been the busiest day for him since his rescue, and he looks worryingly exhausted. He's still nowhere near as healthy as he used to be.

"Papa? It's late, and the day's been never-ending. We can catch up with everything going on here in the morning. Let's get back to the *Kabul*."

CHAPTER FIVE

The mountains once more loom around us, baleful and defiant. *Bismillah.* I select the house icon and follow the route back to the submarine. The submersible is connected to the *Kabul* and she will guide us to her.

"Your grandpa..." Sadness creeps into Papa's voice. He strokes Jojo as he speaks. "He looked so much weaker than when I last saw him, Pickle."

"Gramps was a shadow of what you saw today," I say, keeping my gaze fixed on the temperamental landscape. "He was so frail....The attack on the laboratories, your arrest, the silence from the authorities afterward. It was all too much and that's when he had his heart attack. But he pulled through. And don't forget you can now call him anytime you miss him, Papa."

I feel infinitely lighter knowing we're now in touch with everyone. The last month was all the more difficult for being cut off from the ones we loved and trusted.

The waves are wild and inscrutable as I weave our way back. At last I round a cliff and keep my eyes peeled; she should be coming up any second. "Oscar, if the waters are clear, then please lift stealth mode. I can barely see what I'm doing and could do with some help."

The *Kabul* materializes out of the gloom in the distance, her lights glowing on the current. A wave of warmth spreads through me. She feels more home to me than any other place ever and I'd be completely lost

JOURNEY TO THE HEART OF THE ABYSS

without her. She looks so powerful hovering there between cliff faces as we approach. The submarine is thirty-five meters of high-strength alloyed steel, her surface a gunmetal gray. Across her middle is a single row of circular viewports, and her bow is mostly made up of transparent acrylic.

The Marathon Committee asked for her back. They rescind my prize, they said, in light of my now being a terrorist. They can dream on of her return.

We close in and I'm up through the moon pool in no time. Oscar secures the opening and dims the sub's exterior lights once more. I instruct him to keep us here for the night.

Jojo's almost asleep in Papa's arms, and he heads upstairs to put her to bed while I make a quick trip to the control room. Despite Oscar being far more adept than myself at tracking all systems, it's always reassuring to quickly take in the status of the major systems on board. All looks satisfactory. It feels too long every time I leave the sub, but today has been an especially mammoth day, and the vessel's familiar *thrum* now is the best sound in the world.

I yawn as I climb the winding iron-and-maple-wood staircase to the upper floor and make my way to the galley. Almost two months on board and I'm still not used to the quiet thrill I get from walking through the *Kabul*'s passageway. The space has an industrial look about it. All manner of pipes and thick, grouped wires run its length, and yet the blend of metals and earthy hues of reds, browns, and mustard yellow make the passageway such a snug space.

In the galley, I instruct the Tea-lady to make us warm drinks, and while the machine does her thing, I make up a plate of biscuits. The space is lined with copper-handled alder cabinets, and bronze pipework stretches along every wall. Old World styling hides an array of the latest gadgets. Though I hate technology—only because it hates me—I'm very grateful for it when preparing meals. I grab the tray and head for the saloon at the tip of the sub. The doors slide open and I see Papa's already inside. I join him on the sofas.

"Your milk, Papa."

The seats are plush and a violet color, adding to the soft crimson, yellow, coral, and green of the upholstery in the rest of the room. An Old World globe stands at the end of the run of seating, and on the opposite side a bronze cat sits curled up on the floor.

We sip our warm drinks in the soft, golden light of a Lumi-Orb. I still can't get used to it: Papa, here with me. It's like a dream. Back at the prison, I'd feared the worst when I glanced down at his emaciated state. He's of medium height and slim build, but when I first set eyes on him lying there on that cold slab, he'd deteriorated so much I'd missed him completely until he moved. But alhamdulillah, he made it, and I mustn't ever lose sight of that. I glance around as I nibble on a ginger biscuit.

The floors and fixed furniture are a warm cherry wood. Built-in wooden cabinets make up the entire wall on the right. It's probably the wall we use the most as it houses all communications and multimedia systems. The opposite wall has several bookcases, and it's the best feeling ever when you sit on the chunky lavender chair beside them and lose yourself in another world. As Papa's health gradually improved enough for him to venture into the saloon, he found a welcome escape in those books. He needed it.

"We must talk, my child," he says now, rubbing his eyes. "There's something—"

Oscar materializes before us, head to toe in midnight blue and busy securing the satin ropelike belt of his dressing gown. "My lady, we are all set for the night."

"Thanks, Oscar. What about Theo's file—has the program been installed?"

"Indeed. It is already up and running, my dear."

"Ah, that's great."

Papa gestures to the Navigator. "Oscar, you will join us for a cup of chai?"

Papa's still not fully used to the Navigator. Our regular Jeeves back in London wasn't personified. Oscar's such an advanced program, thanks to Theo, that if he didn't flicker in and out of existence in front of our eyes, you'd never guess he was a hologram. Papa can't help but feel it rude not to offer him salaams and hospitality, even though he knows he isn't real.

"Oh I say, it would be an honor, sir." Oscar smiles, taking a seat on the opposite sofa. "Though I make it a point to always bring my own." A dainty—and very realistic—teapot, cup and saucer, and delicious-looking cake stand all appear before the Navigator. He discerningly rotates the stand around and around, until finally settling on a scone.

I glance at Papa. "What were you saying, Papa?"

He stifles a yawn and pats my hand. "Nothing that can't wait, Pickle. Tomorrow is a new day, inshallah." We finish our warm drinks and he retires for Isha prayer and bed.

My own bedroom is, as ever, immediately soothing from the moment I step into it and I dig my feet into the plush floor—the first carpeted room I've ever had. The space is decorated in a Far Eastern style. It's all dark woods, plum velvets, and olive brocades. The walls are actually papered, with delicate pale blossoms reaching out across their coppery sheen.

Jojo's fast asleep inside her Bliss-Pod by the single large porthole, and I move the pebble-like shape next to my bed where she's closer to me. I've barely looked at the puppy today, bless her. What a day. After a quick shower and prayer, I sink into the comfort of my bed.

Maybe because it's bedtime and that's when I usually let my guard down and allow his absence to creep in, or maybe it's because today I met his family and was in his bedroom—whatever the reason, I've never missed Ari more.

I select a low, rosy glow to the lighting, turn on my side, and hope to God the security officer talks.

CHAPTER SIX

"**A**ll right, that's enough, Oscar," I say, and the *Kabul* stops rising. I stand in the viewport at the tip of the vessel, peering out through the expansive floor-to-ceiling windows and into the morning current. The landscape lower down was way too dark for my liking and the familiar deep blue waves rolling before us now lift my spirits. They lap against the sub's nose, and a shimmering school of large coalfish plays leisurely in the distance. Huge, decorative arches—bronze and intricately detailed—edge the windows, framing every view we look out on.

"Hashem."

I turn around to see Ruby on-screen. She's on her Bracelet, in their kitchen, and I can hear multiple voices in the background.

Papa's paused to chat with her in front of the communications wall. "The officer talked?"

She nods. "We have something."

I suck in my breath and rush over to join them. "Ari?"

Ruby shakes her head slowly, her lips pressed tight. "But it's something. There's some kind of 'lab'.…A classified place." She hesitates, her voice strained. "He didn't reveal what goes on there, but it's clear something does. And that it concerns us. With a little more *persuading* from Lewis and our neighbors, the officer has also guided us to blueprints—and coordinates."

A lab. So many unthinkable possibilities swirl around in my head. My stomach rolls and I try to relax, but it's impossible. Why have a secret lab?

"And he did allude to the attack on Tórshavn, as we'd hoped." Ruby bites on her lip. "Something about that assault has him hinting at a 'surprise' we're not aware of. A weapon none of us can evade. According to him, it'll see the end of all of us, every community still existing." She grimaces. "He gloated about how it was already too late because something is going down *tomorrow*. And again, it's linked to this lab. He seems regretful of what he's let slip out, and refuses to say any more."

Voices rise in the background behind Ruby, everyone talking over one another, some even shouting.

"Do you want me to come down?" Papa asks.

"Don't trouble yourself, Hashem," she insists. "But if you have a moment, it'd help if you joined in with immediate discussions? Ben should also be coming through any second. We need to find this lab and discover what goes on there. And we need to do it pronto."

Ben's face fills the adjacent screen on our wall. Ruby has gathered others, all folk who work together to keep the community safe. Some focus only on Eysturoy while others venture wider to try and keep an eye on what the security forces are up to elsewhere. Papa takes a seat on the sofas as they discuss the best way to deal with the new information. My thoughts are a whirlpool and I can't stop fidgeting as I listen to everyone.

Papa turns to Ben. "How many submersibles can you get ahold of, and how soon can we expect your return?"

"That's just it," says Ben, throwing his hands in the air. "The mother of all storms has broken out here. Could take a couple of days to clear, and we can't head back to Eysturoy until it does."

"We need those submersibles now more than ever," says Ruby.

"Aye," says Max, a close friend of Ben's who now seems to be in charge of matters alongside Ruby. I remember seeing him back at Ben's, his bushy red hair and beard hard to miss. "We need to do something right away before that filth attack us with this new weapon."

"We have no choice," says Ari's cousin Samantha. "We'll have to go investigate the lab without backup."

"If we do this, then there's no going back," says a girl standing beside

Samantha. She's around my age, Black, petite, and breaks into a warm grin when our gazes meet. Ruby introduces her as Kiara, Ari's neighbor.

"Going anywhere near a classified location is dangerous enough," says Papa. "But doing it without adequate assistance will ensure nobody returns."

"What are our options?" Ruby's expression grows tense once more. "Those who perished in Tórshavn will not be forgotten. We need answers. And I want to know what's happened to my boy."

"Ruby, what's at those coordinates the officer revealed?" I ask.

She picks up a scrap of paper and reads from it. "The coordinates 70°59'N 8°32'W indicate Jan Mayen. It's an island in the Arctic Ocean, love. But despite our advanced systems, we can't dig up anything on the place."

Leaving them to chat, I move into the viewport and summon the Navigator.

"Oscar," I whisper. "What do you know about the coordinates 70°59'N 8°32'W? We already know the location is Jan Mayen in the Arctic Ocean, but are you able to see what lies there?" It's worth a try.

The Navigator tilts his head as he scans the info. "Alas, I appear unable to discern any details for the disclosed bearings, my dear. Oh I say!" He tugs on his brown silk waistcoat. "Are we headed for even colder climates? I once voyaged—"

"No, not us...But, erm, please look into any necessary travel permissions if we were. I think those are Norwegian waters?"

His eyes shine. "My lady." He bows his head and disappears.

I pace the viewport; I've no idea why I'm asking. *Yes you do.*

They're still discussing everything and I head for the galley to make breakfast, my mind racing. By the time I enter the saloon with the tray, Papa's done chatting.

"Breakfast, Papa. What's going on? What have they decided?"

He shakes his head. "It's simply too dangerous to venture out without sufficient backup. They'll need to wait for the storm to die down so Ben can bring home the larger subs. The moment he arrives, they're setting off in search of this lab."

I pour out our tea, processing his words. It might be too late if they wait until Ben's back. Something's going to happen tomorrow, Ruby said.

We eat our breakfast in silence, buttery parathas, scrambled eggs, and tea. Words burn in my throat, but every time I open my mouth to let them out, I end up dousing them with tea. I really don't want to add to his worries.

In the end, though, I can hardly breathe for not saying something. "We could help them, Papa. The *Kabul* could join them in finding this lab. It might tell us what's happened to Ari."

His gaze is conflicted; he's definitely thought about it. We eat in silence for a bit until finally he pauses. "It's too dangerous. We don't know what the place holds. The *Kabul*—"

"Is one of the most secure subs. She has every kind of firepower and saw us through a prison breakout. This vessel survived *that*." I nod eagerly. "We can do it, Papa. I know we can."

What else are we going to do? I want to ask. We found Ari's home. Ari's missing, and his people are being treated horrifically. And something's about to go down. How can we look away?

"We could be facing the might of the entire Blackwatch." Papa rubs his face and sighs.

"God knows how long Ben is going to be stranded before he can return with the vessels. Who knows what might happen between now and then? And submersibles alone might not even be enough. How do Ari's friends and family stand a chance of surviving a trip to this lab if they don't have powerful enough transport and defense? Bia's lot tried several times to break you out, but they never got past the prison's first line of defense. No submersible can match the firepower of Blackwatch. Only a submarine can. You know I'm right, Papa."

He chews quietly, a small line appearing between his eyebrows as he absorbs my words.

I press on. "I've been managing the sub for almost two months, remember." *Please have more faith in me.* "I've guided her over the London borders, taken her through ambushes, Blackwatch raids, a prison breakout that threw a zillion hostile bots our way. Her defense systems are the best

60

of any civic submarine and she's proven herself worthy. Nobody knows what they're going to find at this lab, or even on the way to that island." I take a breath and touch his arm. "She's my sub and I've had to get to know her inside out. I can do this, Papa. You stay at Ben's until I get back."

He shakes his head and breaks into a small reluctant smile. "Ya Allah, what am I going to do with you...? Do you really think I would stay behind and watch you leave without me?" He sighs, and resignation breaks across his expression as he nods. "We're in a position to help them."

Yes. We discuss it some more and then message Ruby. Everyone's still sitting around the kitchen table, their postures tense. Papa tells them we can accompany them to the lab.

Lewis claps his hands. "There you go," he says, crossing his arms behind his head and leaning back in his chair. "Escorted by the champ. We're doing this."

There's a cacophony of voices. Max, Ben's friend, is relieved and on board with the idea. Ruby is torn between not wanting to involve us and knowing they stand a much greater chance of survival if the *Kabul* is there to defend everyone should they need it. The others express immediate relief and enthusiasm.

Now more than ever, I need to know the plan thoroughly. My stomach churns as I listen and participate. Though it brings home the severity of what we're attempting to do, I feel stronger for knowing exactly what's going on.

Within the hour we're already decided on several things. The security sub they captured, a four-seater, will also be going, and it'll lead the way in when we get there. A neighbor of Ben's, the closest in resemblance to the officer, will assume his identity, and three others will occupy the remaining seats. The Bracelet and access codes they obtained should prove enough. Ruby and the others will pore over the blueprints further before we leave. On our end, Papa and I must ensure the submarine is ready for the trip. All her systems and supplies will need checking and updating where necessary. We aim to leave as soon as possible. Several submersibles will join us, and some of the people coming along will be on board so that if need be, they can get into the water and help in ways those traveling in vessels can't.

"I want to go." We watch as Freya comes into view on-screen, arms folded as she joins her mother's side and stares at Papa and me. "I've never been inside a submarine, and I promise to stay out of everyone's way."

Ruby pinches the bridge of her nose. "Freya, this is urgent business."

I wave at Freya. "If your parents are all right with it, then you can come check out the *Kabul* before Papa and I leave the Faroe Islands."

Ruby nods in agreement and Freya beams, satisfied.

When we're all done discussing matters, Papa ends the call. Once we're at the location and discover the lab's purpose, we'll alert Ruby and the others and take things from there. Ruby's staying behind. As head of security for their community, she's in charge of ensuring everyone stays protected. I confirm with Oscar, then message Theo and let him know we'll need travel papers for Norwegian waters.

Papa looks deep in thought. "We must be prepared for anything at that lab, my child. Understood?" He says it quietly and my stomach knots as I nod in reply. "Right," he says, clapping his hands. "I'll check on the engine room and then get a rundown on our firepower status."

He leaves with purpose in his stride. Though I never knew it at the time, this is something he used to do down south—watch out for amphi communities and help them wherever he could. He'd pass on info to Charlie at Cambridge, and then Bia's lot would get to work trying to protect those most vulnerable.

We spend the day preparing the sub. I let Ruby know anyone going is more than welcome to stay on board. Though the amount of submersibles we're able to store is limited, we can take on any number of the individuals headed there. It's late afternoon when Lewis is the first to join us.

As I run my gaze over his sub, I realize he downplayed the damage it suffered when he offered to come meet me after we were hit. The tail took a real blow. He assures me now it's seaworthy again.

"Ayeeee!" He marvels at the submarine and whistles when we enter the saloon.

"I know," I say, unable to wipe the smile off my face. "Oh, one moment. You'll be needing access so the Navigator can keep on top of everything. Oscar?"

Oscar materializes and nods. "My lady?" He catches sight of Lewis and his gaze flickers. "I say, and who is the young gentleman gracing us with their fine company?"

"Oscar, this is Lewis. He'll be needing visitor clearance."

Lewis winks at the Navigator. "All right, Oscar?" He turns to me, impressed. "I've been all over but seen very few Housekeepers with this level of clarity. Nice one!"

"I know," I say again, sounding increasingly smug. "My friend Theo did it. Same friend who adapted the brolly I told you about, and modified the sub's systems."

I could never thank Theo enough for everything he's done for me. And continues to do. Oh how I wish he and Tabby were here.

Oscar turns to Lewis and offers a small bow. "Might I welcome the gentleman Lewis on board the *Kabul*? Your visitor access has been taken care of, sir. It's a pleasure to have you with us." A flush enters the Navigator's cheeks. "And what does Lewis like to do?"

"Pretty much everything, Oscar," Lewis replies, his smile wide as he takes in the multimedia wall.

The Navigator nods to indicate approval. "Ah yes, enjoying oneself is a sage decision. To live is the rarest thing in the world. Most people exist, that is all. I do hope you're fond of a little game of chess? Perhaps some reading aloud?"

Lewis whistles as he strides into the viewport. "Aye, whatever you say, Oscar!"

"Champion, sir," says the Navigator, his soft eyes lighting up.

I motion the Navigator. "Oscar, as soon as everyone's here, we're heading in the direction of those coordinates I passed on to you—the ones for Jan Mayen. Any word on the travel papers?"

"We have acquired suitable documentation for crossing into Norwegian territory, my lady."

Brilliant. The chances of being stopped by border patrol are always very low, especially at the altitude I choose, but still I'd rather be prepared.

I get to work completing a thorough rundown of the control room before heading for the galley to check all supplies. When I return to the saloon, Lewis has taken all the cushions piled to one side of the viewport, scattered them in front of the window, and placed Jojo at the center. He's busy setting up a small easel, and links it to his Bracelet. I watch as he swishes a paint palette into existence and begins choosing his colors from the hovering selection.

"I saw an Old World easel once, you know," I say as I join him. "Well, three-quarters of one—it had suffered a lot of wear and tear. It was at one of those Days Past events the Royal Preservation Society holds."

"Eh." He shakes his head. "London's a fucking cult." He flings colors at the easel.

"Oi, it's the best city on the planet." I can't help grinning as I take a peek at his work. My little Jojo looks like some leviathan from the deep.

The sight of Lewis painting brings Mama crashing into my head. Papa's always told me how she was endlessly creative and took so much joy in painting and crafts. We lost her creations when Blackwatch ransacked our flat while I was racing the marathon; they destroyed everything. My gaze wanders to the picture hanging above the sofa and I move closer to take it in.

I'm sitting on Mama's lap and we're at Kensington Gardens, her favorite place in London. It's winter in the indoor gardens and Mama's face is practically glowing as we experience the light snowfall. I can't get over how much I resemble her. Pictures of Mama and me are almost identical, at any age. We're both petite, have the same golden-sandy skin color, long black hair, and green eyes. Mama's gaze is fixed on me, her smile so bright and beautiful. Every time I look on the picture, I feel the same tug inside. I wonder if it'll ever fade. I sigh and look away.

It's evening by the time everyone is gathered and we're ready to set off.

There are around half a dozen large submersibles, including the security vessel, and they'll be traveling under the belly of the *Kabul*. It's the safest place for them—out of sight and close to the pool if we encounter trouble. They'll take it in turns to board the submarine when they need to. Several people are staying with us, including Samantha and Kiara, and have chosen to crash in the saloon. We'll be traveling through the night, with Lewis insisting he take the first shift when the rest of us retire later. Jan Mayen lies almost two hundred leagues north of here so we're looking at a twenty hours' journey minimum.

Papa leaves to pray. Oscar and I stand in the viewport and gaze out into the evening current.

Everyone's armed individually, and the larger submersibles all have built-in weaponry. We've no idea what we might encounter. The fact that Oscar can't trace anything at the location means nothing—Broadmoor doesn't show up anywhere either. Nobody advertises their evil.

Oscar bows his head as the *Kabul* thrums with power and ascends the waters around the Faroe Islands. The sub turns and speeds up. Lewis joins us, clapping his hands at the sight of the Navigator.

"Oscar! Psyched for the trip?"

"Indeed, old boy. One shall endeavor to keep you entertained."

"Hope yer all set for me to pick yer brains?"

"My dear young man, one is quite primed for all manner of picking, I assure you. Though, as no doubt you're already aware, nothing that is worth knowing can be taught." Oscar has a gleam in his eye, and I'm left slightly in awe of his realistic programming.

Theo told me he'd gone full Type 3—the most thorough character and personality programming you can assign to your chosen Housekeeper persona, and it's fascinating watching it in action. Every time it's Tabby's turn to choose their Housekeeper back home, she ensures they're in love with her and the results are always hilarious.

"Nice one, Oscar, that's exactly what I'm talking about," says Lewis. "That quotable stuff right there. The lasses are mad for all that Old World crap. Sorry, no offense."

"Oh, none taken, old chap—I quite understand. After all, illusion is the first of all pleasures...."

My Bracelet flashes; it's a message from Theo. News of the attack in Tórshavn is spreading down south and tensions are rising. People are demanding their leaders do something.

I look out into the shifting waves as the *Kabul*'s bow slices through the North Atlantic Ocean. I take in a deep breath and blow out my cheeks.

We're aware the authorities have a secret weapon that took the lives of many in Tórshavn. And that something significant is scheduled to take place tomorrow. We're chasing a classified location we know nothing of, in the hope the place will provide some answers.

I clasp my hands and think of everyone traveling with us now, and I fear for all our safety. There are endless dangers I still don't know about. But doing nothing achieves exactly nothing. We're as prepared as we can be, and now we're going to have to hope for the best.

There's just no way this lab doesn't hold some answers.

CHAPTER SEVEN

"What in the Lord's name..."

"What is it, Kiara?" I look up in the direction of the viewport where she stands drinking tea and staring into the early morning waters of the Arctic Region. "What can you see?"

I top up my own cup, grab another slice of toast, and join her.

The *Kabul* is momentarily stationary so that those in submersibles can take turns boarding her to wash and eat. Lewis has been ordered to get some sleep. He was meant to wake me up for my shift but pulled an all-nighter instead. We're over halfway now and he needs to be fully alert for when we get there.

There are several of us gathered in the viewport, curious.

"Yikes." I stop chewing and stare at the sight.

"They look like those viperfish," says Samantha. "You can catch sight of them in the rifts sometimes—always give me the creeps. But what the hell is wrong with *these* guys?" She takes a step back.

The silver-brown creatures are too slow. As for their appearance... their pointed teeth are terrifyingly long, so long they can't even close their mouths, and their hinged jaws send a shudder through me. But the worst thing about them is the group of fish looks almost lifeless as it drifts past the window at a barely perceptible speed. The sight of the listless creatures is only one in several strange and frightening encounters this morning. I guess wild waters really do attract some horrors.

"Whoa," says Kiara. "Look at the sides of their bodies."

I peer closer and spot it, biting my lip. They're all bearing man-made scars—clear signs of human interference. Some have holes cut into their sides while others still carry hooks embedded into their flesh. One of the fish swims as close to the windows as possible. Its eyes are empty gray bubbles.

"Actually, I think they're anglerfish," says Samantha. "Wait, look, the fishing rod thingy on its head—it's fake. Oh shit, these guys have *really* been tampered with."

I swiftly summon the Navigator and have him on guard in case the creatures are here to attack, even though they look barely alive.

On our way to the prison, Ari and I encountered a truly pitiful animal, its insides all carved out and replaced with technology. *There are many more like it*, he'd said.

I move away from the viewport. "Ari told me how the government experiments on the creatures, use them for their own gains."

Kiara rubs at her temples. "You wouldn't believe what we stumble across out there. But I've never seen anything like what we've witnessed this morning. Too much weird behavior in these waters for my liking." She grimaces and moves to sit on the sofa, tapping her Bracelet until there's a glimmering piano in front of her. A soothing tune plays throughout the saloon as she masterfully commands the floating keys. Jojo sits transfixed beside her.

I top up the warm drinks and plates of food as the last of the folk in submersibles come on board to have their breakfast. Papa's showered and they all sit to eat together.

"Oscar?" I beckon the Navigator. "Wow, you look fab."

He's seriously dressed up; an emerald-green velvet cape drapes his shoulders over a silk shirt with billowing sleeves. He runs a hand over his hair as he eyes the room. "The gentleman Lewis does not harbor a desire for some morning nourishment, my lady?" He raises an eyebrow.

"What? Oh. No, Lewis is asleep. Oscar, please prepare for us to move on as soon as I give word. Once everyone's eaten and back in the water, we resume our journey. Everything all right out there?"

His eyes dim but he nods to confirm. "Understood, my dear. An

Explorer sub is in the vicinity, though it currently bears no perceivable threat to us. It remains engrossed in its work some five hundred feet above. There are no other vessels in our midst to trouble yourself with, my lady."

As everyone returns to the water, I refill my teacup and stand in the viewport. The sub hums, ready to move once more. Something drifts into the edge of my vision. When I turn, my breath hitches with joy at the sight, and I stare, unblinking.

A single colossal jellyfish hovers beside the vessel, swaying on the current. It's the most beautiful creature. It's imposing and magnificent and still so utterly delicate, all translucent and golden yellow. An abyssal sun. I can't believe its size; its bell alone is as large as my submersible. And oh, how it pulses! It's like the skirt of a ball gown that keeps flaring and gathering again. Lengthy tentacles, speckled and frill-edged, sway beneath the bell. I remember when Ari commanded the sub to rise high enough to catch a little sunlight and, oh, what must this ethereal creature look like in natural light. I can't take my eyes off it.

I kind of wish I had, though.

The enormous, diaphanous jellyfish rips apart in front of me, convulsing and twitching as something attacks it. I yelp and Papa abandons his breakfast and rushes over.

Whatever's tearing into the creature moves incredibly fast, over and through it, shredding the bell and slicing its tentacles until piece after piece falls through the frothy waves. I flinch when the animals attacking the jellyfish become clearer.

It's a mass of the longest and thinnest silver snipe eels. They look like lengthy snakes, no more than an inch wide. My hands go all clammy. The creatures are fast, slipping in and around what's left of the poor jellyfish. They dart out of sight. My pulse races as I rush across the viewport to peer out in the other direction. When I swing my gaze back, everything's a blur of frenzied movement again. This time one of our subs is spinning out of control. What's going on?! Oscar appears beside me just as Ari's cousin and several others swim into view and try to help the submersible. It's the snipe eels again. Samantha and the others wrestle frantically with the slippery animals.

"My lady, our companions appear to be in distress. I propose blasting the—"

"No, wait, Oscar," I say, gulping at the air to stem the sense of rising nausea. "You risk hurting our friends!"

Papa nods in agreement.

The eels suddenly move back from those hovering between them and the vessel. Their eyes change color, flashing now like the telltale blips on the Eyeballs—the remote security cameras always hovering around the water—and my heart sinks. These creatures have been interfered with. Who knows what they've been trained to do. . . . My hand flies to my throat as I stare at them. They link themselves to one another by wrapping their thin tails around each other as if a single, wriggly creature. And then the tangled mass charges right past everyone.

Straight into the sub's propeller.

I stumble back a step. Beside me Papa utters a prayer. Blood clouds the water as the creatures are pulverized. The current churns in all the action and visibility is immediately reduced. I wait, holding my breath. "Oscar, stand by!"

The waves clear and I spot everyone as they help stabilize the spinning sub. At last they communicate that all are unharmed and the submersible isn't damaged. I nearly slump with relief. The vessels take their place once more beneath the *Kabul*'s belly, and those who'd jumped into the depths to help out swiftly return aboard and head for the showers.

Papa turns to me, despair in his eyes. "What madness is this, implanting technology inside innocent creatures? And they trained them to do that. They taught the animals to attack at all costs." He's visibly shaking.

Oh, how sheltered we are back in London. . . . I thought I'd seen everything. A sour taste fills my mouth and I feel so utterly hollow. What are we doing to the creatures of the oceans?

Old Worlders caused the extinction of so many animals. I've seen footage of the creatures: panda bears, rhinoceroses, gorillas, polar bears, leopards, orangutans, tigers—and more. All stunning and fearsome. And they all died, starved to death after their natural environment was destroyed.

We practically worship the Old Worlders and think of the pre-floods world as beyond perfect. Yet they wiped out so much life. And now we're doing the same down here.

My stomach twists into knots for the animals the snipe eels had once been, swimming wild and free in their own home. Until we trapped them and tried to manipulate their nature.

"Oscar," I say quietly, wrapping my arms around myself, "it's time to get back on the waves. I want her at full speed, please."

We race on and I try to stay focused on the task ahead. Lewis awakens and joins Papa for breakfast.

Soon we enter the Arctic Circle. The water, even deep down here, turns noticeably purer as the sub's nose pierces the cleaner waves.

We spend the hours communicating with Ben and everyone, and Papa also chats with Bia in Cambridge, updating her and gauging her advice. They don't have anything on Jan Mayen; the location has never come up. But a lab would answer a lot of questions, Bia says. She urges us to proceed with caution and to update them every step. Charlie looks concerned for Papa, despite receiving assurances, and demands to know everything, pressing us to ensure we're not rushing in. I leave to pray and end it with a special invocation for times of uncertainty. Back in the saloon, Samantha teaches me how to use a small but effective Lastar03. I really hope I never need more than my modified brolly.

The hours tick by and the nerves kick in as we draw ever closer. Papa switches on the news for any possible sign of what the authorities have planned for today, but instead it's filled with somber coverage of Prime Minister Gladstone. The PM is laying a wreath by the Memorial Fountain in Kensington Gardens. The camera zooms in to focus on the inscription on the plaque of the fountain: *In memory of Eva and Winston Gladstone, beloved sister and darling nephew, sleep peacefully, Edmund Gladstone 2087.*

The exact details of the attack were held from the media out of respect for the newly elected PM. It's one of those times in the year when we all come together in collective mourning, and it always leaves you feeling so sad. Not just for the PM's sister and nephew, but also for him. You can see him visibly withdraw around the anniversary of their deaths.

A group of enraged amphis ambushed and murdered Eva and her little boy, Winston Gladstone. They were aboard a submersible, almost home, when the unprovoked attack took place. Their murders shocked the entire nation. It's horrific and unthinkable and so, so wrong. And so is what Captain Sebastian does to amphis. Gazing at his calm and gentle demeanor, I wonder how much the PM knows about what Sebastian does.

When we're ten leagues from our destination, I instruct the Navigator to rise until the vessel is just inside the general no-go zone for submersibles. They might not be wasting any surveillance measures where they least expect any trouble to come from. The *Kabul* hums as she ascends the waters.

It's early evening when Oscar materializes to announce we're here. "Instructions, my lady?"

As the sub slows to a stop, we crowd the viewport and peer out, taking in the surrounding seascape. At this altitude, all around us is a vast and vivid blue. The Norwegian Sea clashes here with the Greenland Sea, the waves coursing over the *Kabul*'s bow. Who knows what secrets are concealed in their depths.... The vessel sways slightly in the choppier current, all the churning lapping against the windows.

"Oscar, any security crafts nearby?"

"We appear to be alone at this altitude, my lady."

"Still, we have to assume they have eyes everywhere—technology beyond our system's knowledge. It's the only way to stay safe. Remain on high alert, Oscar, and tell me if you pick up anything at all."

Soon everyone's going over the details with Ruby and the others back in Eysturoy. I pay close attention so I know exactly what's going on. The plan is more detailed now and has slightly changed since they've had adequate time to consult the lab's blueprints.

Those posing as security officers will head in first. Once their sub is through, their immediate goal is to take over the lab's command center. If they have control of the place's security systems, it'll ease the way for the rest of the submersibles to board the lab and search it. Kiara, Samantha, and the others without vessels will only go near the lab after it's been secured. The *Kabul* will stay here, hovering safely high above in stealth mode. She's ready to attack at the first sign of trouble.

Papa rolls his tasbih, muttering prayers as he passes the beads through his fingers.

I look around. "Where's Lewis?"

Ruby frowns on-screen. "He wouldn't..."

"He's just sped right past me, foolish lad!" says Max. "Wouldn't answer when I asked where he's going."

"Where are you off to?!" Samantha demands into her Bracelet.

"Och, come on!" Lewis says. "Why risk everything? You know it makes more sense for only one of us to head down first. No big deal. I just wanna see if I can spot anything!"

"Lewis McGregor, get back up here right now!" says Ruby.

He doesn't respond.

Ruby pinches her mouth. "Let's get back to the plan, we don't have time to waste." She goes through everything one more time, ensuring all possible scenarios have been covered, and everyone knows what to do.

I turn when Samantha whispers something urgently into her Bracelet, her brow wrinkled.

"What is it?" Ruby asks.

Samantha places her Bracelet on speaker once more, and Lewis's voice echoes back, tinged with frustration.

"I'm stuck," he says. And then a stream of swears fills the air.

"Are you exposed?" Papa asks.

"I don't think so—no sign of anyone. Tail just started burning up and then the engine slowed down. I parked her so I could check her out, but now she's not budging."

"Tell me you didn't climb back into her before all repairs to your tail had been carried out?" Ruby demands, her voice rising.

"There was no time!" he says.

She puts her head into her hands. "Anyone free to give Lewis a hand in getting back to the submarine? Should they spot him..."

If it were any one of the others, the situation wouldn't be as critical. Even if they were discovered and hit, then as long as they weren't injured, they could survive the craft flooding. But Lewis wouldn't stand a chance.

"Papa, I'm going to help him."

"Pickle," he says, his eyes clouding. "I'll go."

Others also volunteer but I press on. "We don't have time for this." I take Papa's hands in mine. "Everyone else is part of the plan, and we shouldn't delay anyone. I'm free to do this. I'll be in touch and will be back before you know it." I turn to Ruby. "Please, stick to the schedule—we don't want to run out of time."

Max and the others agree and begin heading out for the lab.

I rush out of the saloon and grab the umbrella from my room. I won't be exiting the submersible, but I always feel a lot better knowing it's there. It's saved me so many times. As I stand in the airlock waiting for the pressure to blow down to ambient, I inspect the brolly. The canister's still topped up and the tase function is at maximum power. Before long I'm in the water. Running the thruster at full speed, I follow Lewis's instructions and race the submersible in his direction. I squint into the current as I descend, and it isn't until I'm just above the seabed that I finally spot his craft. The tail looks a mess. He offers an apologetic shrug, his expression super frustrated.

"I've found him, Papa; looks like he just needs a nudge. There's nobody else around. I'm going to help him and we'll be back in no time. Any news on the others?"

I try pushing the vessel from the front, my own sub groaning with the effort. Lewis's craft refuses to move. It's going to take longer than I'd anticipated. I cast another swift glance around to ensure we're still in the clear. Papa keeps me up to date with what's going on with the others as I work to find a way to dislodge the trapped vessel.

"They've located the lab," he says, as I'm busy tilting my nose and aiming for the lower body of Lewis's craft. "And Max is through. Watch your back, Pickle."

Yes. At least something's going right! I keep one eye on the water as I work away, my heartbeat steadily rising the longer it takes.

"The place is light on security," Papa says with an edge to his voice. I circle Lewis's sub trying to work out the best place to apply pressure. "Something's going on. Max is inside the control room now and says all exterior security and half the guards were ordered someplace else."

"Papa, is Ari's community secure? They said something was going down today, remember."

"Ruby's taken action at home, and sent word to everyone else up north to remain on high alert."

My chest tightens as I imagine an army of security vessels headed for who knows where, and with what kind of new weapon. It must be top priority if they needed to divert so much of the lab's security to it. Lewis and I need to get out of the water right away.

At last, as I grit my teeth and ram the side of Lewis's sub in my desperation to shift it, the craft comes free. And just as it does, there's movement in the far distance. I take in the shape and jolt. A security sub.

"They're onto us!" I shout into my Bracelet. "Everyone watch out!"

I gesture frantically to Lewis. "Quick, we need to get out of here!"

And then the sub fires in our direction.

"What the fuck!" Lewis's yelling echoes inside my craft. "Where did they come from? Get yerself to the submarine, Leyla! Don't wait for me!"

"After you!" I shout. "Your tail looks seriously dodgy!"

A figure swims toward us through the waves, and for a split second I imagine it's Ari, and my heart lurches. But it's Kiara.

"Go!" she shouts. "You two need to get out of here! I'll try and distract them!" She darts away, and Lewis and I move ahead while dodging persistent sharp-green lasers.

I pull back on the joystick and ram the throttle forward, rocketing just as a bright ray passes beneath the vessel. My whole body tenses. Another sub has joined the first. Lewis continues to tell me to get away as we scramble directionless. I focus on shaking off their attacks. We can't go back to the *Kabul*, not like this. It'd lead them right to her. I spot Kiara as she disappears beneath a sprawling pale ridge and I realize it must be the lab. It's chaos as Lewis and I dodge the onslaught around the structure. I circle it to get a better look. The place is massive, and there are hatches on its side where several Blackwatch vessels sit docked. And then I watch as smoke trails from Lewis's tail.

"Quick, get inside the place, Lewis!" I shout. "You'll never make it back to the submarine now!"

My heart in my mouth, I wipe my palms on my thighs and draw the hostile subs away from Lewis. I rise and dip and spin away as I evade their attacks, until I finally see his craft crawl beneath the lab. And then I make a dash for the spot myself.

On my own now, I could probably find my way back to the *Kabul* without being sighted. But something's going on at this lab and I want to see what. And I might be able to aid the others in some way.

Kiara's helping Lewis up into the shaft of illumination beneath the lab. Her eyes widen when she spots me, before beckoning me to hurry.

As I draw closer, a body exits the lab, falling into the light and sinking below. And then another. They both wear clinical white coats. Finally Samantha appears as she dives into the glowing waves.

"Quick!" she says.

As soon as Lewis's sub is out of the way, I follow him up into the lab until I'm bobbing on the moon pool's surface and the surrounding water is replaced with an expansive interior. I quickly scan the space and update Papa. He pleads with me to return at once to the submarine, but I can't.

The lab's pool room is huge. Lewis and I rush to the airlock to depressurize. There's frenzied movement when we exit into the adjoining chamber, and my gaze locks with that of an armed technician's. They raise their gun. Before I've had a chance to react, they stagger back when Lewis aims his weapon and brings them down.

"One sec, lassie," he says, reaching into his backpack. "Here, yer gonna need this."

I take the Lastar03 I practiced on earlier and hold on tight. My brolly suddenly feels inadequate.

Samantha stops and stares at me. "I want it on record that I urged you to leave," she says, before getting busy. She removes the woman's ID, drags her across the floor, through the hatch, and throws her into the pool. Her eyebrows rise when she takes in my expression. "Trust me, they deserve it." She gestures to a door, her face tightening.

My chest feels rock hard as I scan the room. All manner of heavy-duty containers, crates, and stretchers are piled high in the corners.

Lewis strides to the front. Kiara tosses him an access card she took off those they threw into the water. In seconds we're all through the door, down several corridors, and then abruptly find ourselves standing in a vast space.

It's white and clinical, and alarms ring throughout. Lifts and staircases feature like columns, and bridges link them to the walls. Walkways wrap around the whole interior, marking out different levels. There are at least three more floors above us and each one is filled with screens and technological equipment. The place is dotted with projections, all playing slick marketing-type footage. *Marketing what, though?* But I can't stop to find out as the *ping* of a weapon is far too close for comfort. The others rush forward, attacking and defending, with Lewis joining them. I duck just in time to spot Kiara and Samantha heading determinedly in the opposite direction and disappearing around a corner.

"What's going on? What have you found so far?" I ask Samantha, shouting into my Bracelet through the din of the alarms. "How can I help?"

"Look at the walls! Ask Lewis for a bag of shells and fix them to any tank you see. We've covered this floor now, so you two need to head higher up. Call for cover if you need it!"

"Have any missing people been found?"

"Not yet, but we're clearing one floor at a time! Max had to join the others in protecting the control room because they're keeping all the files there. The rest of us are searching the place. Make sure you're always with—" She's cut off by the crackling of crossfire.

There's a reason this place is off everyone's radar—and the security officer said it concerned amphis. As soon as Lewis has dealt with two hostile individuals, I beckon him over.

"There are enough people in the control room and we have to join the others in searching the place. And you have to give me some shells!"

He nods and we run toward the central column. Lewis takes out a couple of armed technicians as we rush up a stairway. We race across the first bridge. And I falter when I suddenly see them.

I see why the place is lined with walkways, why all the bridges from the center lead to its walls. I breathe hard and fast now. Lewis stills beside me. We gaze at the endless columns and rows of tanks before us. At the living creatures trapped and writhing in agony inside them.

CHAPTER EIGHT

"They're not getting away with this," Lewis says through gritted teeth.

Everywhere you look, what had at first appeared as screens are actually tanks. Inside each one are the most pitiful sea creatures I've ever seen. Some drift around the limited space, listless and drowning in wires. Some appear dead, just lying there at the bottom of their tanks. And others... They actually dart to the back of their containers, cowering away when we approach. But the vast majority toss and turn; they jerk their bodies and twitch uncontrollably as various wires and pipes and robotic arms do who knows what to them. Rods, mechanical probes, and giant steel claws rest at the bottom of each tank.

My hand flies to my mouth as I try to process what I'm seeing. Shouts and sirens and the odd *ping* and *whoosh* of firepower all echo around me, but I can't take my eyes off the tanks.

By the edge of each container, files glimmer away with every manner of charted information. A sharp-blue one displays a price and list of the creature's hostile capabilities. My stomach rolls. Weapons. They're imprisoning and torturing these animals—living beings—to create weapons so we can hurt one another. My chest aches as I try to see as many of the creatures as I can.

In one row all the animals are abyssal and they glow in the darkened water. Strange substances pour into their tanks through tiny pipes. The row above has creatures you'd find in higher, warmer streams. On yet another level each animal is unique and compelling to look at. Some seem invisible; you only notice their form if you concentrate your gaze slightly off center. In a large tank in front of us, several creatures appear as if you're looking through a kaleidoscope, a perfect arrangement of multicolored pulsing light. And every one of the animals we've seen is behaving erratically and even aggressively.

"Look what those bastards are doing. . . ." Lewis pauses in front of one of the tanks.

I join him and peer into the container. A milky-white tentacled creature shrinks as far back as possible. But then something jolts it forward and it writhes in agony, its small mouth opening and closing. And then it's repeated. It's the sorriest space I've ever stood in. I turn away, my head spinning, and gulp past the lump in my throat.

"We need to get to task," I say. "And if we're to work fast and not be distracted, then we're going to need cover."

Lewis messages Max for an update, and tells the others where we are. He whips off his backpack and delves inside.

"Here," he says, opening a box and passing me one of many pouches filled with tiny resin discs. "Good job we came prepared for anything."

I learned how the shells work back on the sub, but still he quickly shows me again.

"Remember, stick them on the tanks, removing their cover like this. One each is enough. These guys deserve a fighting chance when we're done with this place."

There's no time to waste. At each tank, we first free any creatures held in place. The controls for all the equipment inside are straightforward enough. And then we peel the backs off the tiny devices and place them against the center of the containers.

"Watch out!" Lewis shouts as we catch the attention of several people in blue coats. They scramble across the bridge toward us.

"Keep going, we've got this!" cries Kiara as she and two others charge at them from the opposite direction. "We've checked all rooms on the south side, no sign of anyone!"

"We're almost done!" I say.

Nausea surfaces and I try not to make eye contact with the animals as I finish up. But my heart is racing now, pounding away in my ears as I attach the disc to a tank in which a peach-colored blob with lights pulsing in its mouth drifts aimlessly around and around.

These are living things. They don't belong here. Confined and reduced to such a horrifying state, made to endure who knows what.

Fighting goes on around us as the others clash with the place's security, and further alarms join the increasing chaos. We hurry, climbing the levels and working away on the tanks. Thankfully it's the columns where most of the clashes are focused, as staff battle for access to the lifts and stairs. The screen directly in front of me now catches my eye as a recording plays.

A man in gray speaks earnestly to a crowded room of business types. "Once they're gone, they're gone. We're talking powerful jewels of the abyss here. State-of-the-art defense systems. Biotechnology you can't even imagine. We are talking capabilities that would blow your mind. Literally!" He chuckles and everyone laughs. "Security for the next generation, my friends. For a safer world. For your children." The people in the room nod away.

I can't stand any more of it.

As if he's read my mind, Lewis pauses, his fists balled. "Enough. Let's be done with this place now."

"One more floor to go. We check every corner," I say. "And then we can get the hell out of here."

We rush up to the topmost level. Footsteps sound behind us as soon as we're on the walkway, and we whirl around, lifting our weapons.

"Only me!" says Samantha, waving her hands wildly. "You'll be needing these if you want to search up here, but I can't see any tanks." She throws several security passes at us and gestures around.

I stop to take the level in and see it's different from the others. Only technical equipment lines the walls, no tanks. Every ten or so meters along there are small passages that lead to doors.

"I must get back down, and you guys need to hurry!" Samantha continues. "We've almost got control of the second floor, only the last pocket of guards to get rid of!"

"Nice one," says Lewis. He suddenly swings his hand around and aims right behind me. I pivot to see a technician drop several meters away.

I turn back to Ari's cousin. "Samantha, did you...did you find anyone?"

She shakes her head, her face falling. They desperately want to locate their missing loved ones. But I wonder if it might be a mixed blessing not to have discovered them here.

"We've cleared the west side for you," she says. "The plan remains the same?"

Lewis nods. "Just heard from Max. They aren't having much luck accessing more than they already have. Soon as the place has been checked and the tanks are sorted, we take it apart."

Samantha glances around. "Just make it quick!"

"But we have to check *every* room," I say. "You never know what we might find!"

"We only have so long, Leyla!" She races back the way she came.

"Samantha's right," says Lewis. "There's no way we can search every room. And I can't see any tanks up here, reckon this floor is admin or whatever. Possibly domestic quarters. Come on, let's move along until we spot more tanks. Go, go, go!"

I take in the small passageways leading off to doors and shake my head. "No. I'm not ignoring all those doors. We need to know we did everything we could!"

"We can't do everything—nobody can!" Lewis shouts, running ahead.

"We went through all this so we can learn more about what they do, and now we're not going to search every corner of this place? You go on ahead, look for tanks, I'm checking out where those doors lead to!"

He places his hands on his head, his expression pleading. "You don't understand! We don't have time!"

"We're here now and we're searching the place!"

And then my Bracelet flashes and it's Papa. "Pickle, where are you? You

82

must return immediately! Ya Allah, I'm going out of my mind! Please—for my sake, get inside your sub and come back!"

Lewis catches my eye, gesturing frantically for me to join him.

I leave him swearing and rush along the first passageway.

As I use one of the passes on the door before me, he joins me.

"Yer off yer head!" he says, holding up his weapon in the direction of the door. "We don't have the time! They've called for more backup!"

Once we're through, we face another door. We scan everything we have but with no success. I move back and fire at the security panel until it hangs off the wall and the doors slide open.

We step inside a small space to find laser beams targeting us, causing us to blink.

Everything spins around me and I force myself to focus. Beside me, Lewis curses. There are two security officers, and they're guarding a pair of reinforced doors at the end of the compact room. What are they protecting? The walls are lined with all manner of surveillance and technical equipment.

"Stop! And drop your weapons," says one of them, pointing her gun at us. Her eyes fill with contempt.

Lewis and I lower our weapons.

"I said *drop* them."

There's a thud as our guns hit the floor. I can practically *feel* the tension rising from Lewis now.

"Turn around, and move!" the second officer barks at us.

And then I remember. As we're turning, I meet Lewis's gaze and drop mine to my arm. He follows my eyes, and his own flicker when he understands.

I whip around, my brolly aimed at the guard opposite me and my finger pressed down on the button along its handle. The small space fills with the dull zapping sounds of the tase function and the officer twitches away. Lewis launches himself at the guy in front of him, knocking him out before he can blink. He grabs our weapons and whistles as the woman drops.

"Not bad, lassie."

He looks around and nods, voicing my thoughts. "What are they guarding...?"

I snatch one of the officer's Bracelets and look to Lewis to ensure he's prepared. Taking a breath and holding my weapon up at the ready, I scan the panel by the heavy doors. They slide open. My gaze flits across the huge space. It's twice as high as the ground floor. And there are more tanks. Except these ones are much bigger, scattered around randomly. I step forward.

And I think my heart stops in my chest.

"Oh fuck..." says Lewis.

We stare into the nearest tank.

My gaze locks with that of a little girl's, her hair swaying around her face and endless wires connected to her temples. She blinks at us, and as we peer back, her face crumples and she begins sobbing. I freeze, unable to process what I'm seeing.

They're holding people captive in tanks.

CHAPTER NINE

I quickly glance at the nearest tanks, and oh God yes, there are others. All trapped.

My mind races ahead. So many thoughts. Too many. But there's no time for them. "We free everyone, ensure the place is a hundred percent clear before doing anything else," I say to Lewis. I recall Papa's horrific state back at the prison and my eyes scan the walls. "There. A lift. Anyone we find, we group them over there. They'll most likely be unable to make the walkways and stairs."

Lewis nods, his mouth twisted as he clenches and unclenches his fists. We scan the space around us for any sign of a technician, but it appears to be empty. "They could be hiding," he says, lowering his voice.

"I'll see if we can get some cover." I bring up my Bracelet as Lewis rushes to the little girl's tank. "Samantha, Kiara, we've found people. Top level—exactly where you left us, through that first set of doors. Someone needs to get them to the *Kabul* at once. I'm updating Papa right now!"

I sprint from tank to tank while alerting Papa to our discovery. "And, Papa, tell Oscar to expect quite a few people. And to bring her out of stealth mode. You need to descend about three hundred feet so they can find and board her faster, but no lower. Oh, and have the Medi-bot ready!"

Lewis was right, and the odd technician darts out of hiding. Luckily for us, it's only to sprint across the space, and they escape the room as we work away. It takes several moments before I can wrap my head around the different hovering files and work out which ones control entry and exit to the containers, and the horrific equipment used to hold each person inside them. The ones used for the creatures' tanks were much simpler. God, I hate technology. At last, I free my first person and help the elderly man across the room. As he rests by the lift, he coughs nonstop, before vomiting. Everyone we're managing to free is disorientated, dizzy even. Kiara and Samantha burst into the room.

"Sorry!" says Kiara. "Met with trouble on the stairs. We're set to go, planted what we needed to. We— Oh my Lord…" She stops talking as she stares at the tanks; tears fill her eyes. Samantha's already spinning around taking it all in, her posture tense. They rush around the room, checking the containers.

A little boy's eyes widen when he realizes he's about to be freed and he can't swim to the top fast enough. When I see him restrained again in another tank, I do a double take until I realize they're identical twins. It's a challenge to stay focused; I want to scream.

The boys rush toward a group of tanks by the opposite wall, crying as they spot those inside. Their parents. Kiara joins me in freeing them, and the family is soon huddled by the lift, all of them overcome.

Samantha abandons the tanks and rushes to the doorway, defending us against several employees who've returned with weapons.

In no time there's a considerable group of people by the lift, and Lewis and Kiara come back empty from another row of tanks. "We're done."

Those old enough are handed weapons the officers were carrying.

We usher everyone inside the lift and Samantha jumps in with them, her gaze still concentrated on the room's doorway.

Kiara frowns. "Quick, get in, Leyla!" She holds the door open.

I shake my head. "No, we haven't checked every corner yet."

"But we found them and now we have to get out of here!" says Lewis.

"No. I just…I can't go yet. We have to be dead certain there's nobody else here."

He rubs his face. "Then I'll stay with you."

Kiara shakes her head, fear surfacing in her dark-brown eyes. Samantha points her index finger at us. "No, you both have to come with us right now. Neither of you can swim!"

"Listen to me, please," I urge her. "Get these people out of here and on board the sub. Oscar's expecting them. I'll be right behind, promise. And we have Max and everyone else still inside, we're not alone. Only a very quick last check!"

Lewis refuses to leave with them, no matter what I say. I press the doors shut, and with a *ping* the lift starts moving. *Please, God, let them get off this nightmare safely.*

I start with the farthest row of tanks. Nothing. Soon I'm done with every tank in the room and still no sign of anyone else. I hear Lewis exchange fire with someone across the room. Maybe I should've gone with the others. We'd have been out of here by now. My head spins with what to do. This room had people in it. And there are other rooms up here. I can't help imagining myself as one of the people in the tanks, in some other room, still trapped. And oh how much I'd want someone to find and help me.

I beckon Lewis and we exit the room, keeping a look out as we sneak along the walkway. While we can no longer see anyone up here, the lower level is chaos, with the *whoosh* and *ping* of their weapons echoing around the expansive place. We edge along and turn into another of the small passageways. One by one we enter and search the rooms. Each one seems to have a different purpose, and though two others also contained tanks, there were only a few and all were empty. We continue on until we're standing in the last room and there's nobody in sight.

"I'll have a quick glance in there," says Lewis, pointing to an interior door. "And then we head straight down, lassie."

"I'll be over on that side." I gesture to a busy wall to our right. "I want to check it before we go."

He disappears through the door, and I make my way to the wall, casting my glance over large workstations and benches. I'm halfway done when a voice, low and urgent, reaches my ears from between two workstations near the wall. The whispering drifts from behind a thick strip curtain. I turn around but Lewis isn't back yet. I move toward the hushed tones, my weapon aimed. When I'm close enough, it becomes clear it's one of the employees and he's alerting someone to our presence. And then it goes quiet. I take a deep breath and slowly part the thick strips.

Someone reaches through, grabs me by the hair before I can even register what's going on, and pulls me inside. They clamp a hand over my mouth and drag me backward until we enter a larger space, where they push me down to the floor. I shudder, my body trembling all over and my pulse racing.

It's a young technician, brawny and raging. He twists his hand in my hair again and pulls even harder. Nerves explode everywhere. The pain is unbearable. I remember these sensations. The agony takes me right back to the engine room, to when the first amphi I'd ever encountered in person boarded the submarine and attacked us. Beat me. But I survived.

His hand moves very close to my face now. I grab a finger, pull it toward me, and bite down hard. Cursing, he pushes me back and I roll across the floor. He turns to the bench behind him, and grabs a short metal rod.

I scan the floor for the gun. I've lost it. I feel along my arm. *Please.* I could cry when my hand finds the smooth handle of the brolly. Wrapping my fingers around it, I bring it up and press down on the tase function, willing my hand to stop shaking. He drops the rod and twitches, shock and fury contorting his face. His eyes bulge as the dull droning sound echoes around. He reaches again for the bench behind him for something to throw at me.

And that's when I see it.

My finger slacks on the tase button. My hands won't stop trembling. I try to steady my breathing as I gaze on the bench. There's a doll, several Bracelets, knives, and a necklace.

Everything stands still.

I stare at the necklace. My legs quivering, and my brolly still aimed at the guy, I slowly walk around him and pick it up, turning the beads over in my palm. My heart misses a beat. *Focus.* The others are waiting for me;

I must hurry. We need to get to safety immediately and end this place. So why can't I just go?

Because I would know these beads anywhere.

"Where is he?" I say, holding the necklace up.

"Fuck you."

I take a step back and press down on the tase button again. The second the sound hits the air, he throws his hands up and nods away. I release the button and he staggers back.

"I said, where is he?"

He steadies himself before pointing to the side.

I swing my gaze to the right and only now notice the long, wide space. There's sudden movement. I lift my arm automatically and tase the technician. The steel rod he'd grabbed slips from his hands. I keep my finger on the button until at last he slumps to the floor. I return my gaze to the lengthy space before me now. And I drop the necklace.

Please, God...Please.

It's like a corridor. And at the very end stand three more tanks. I walk toward them. They become gradually clearer.

The tank on the left is empty. There's nothing in the middle tank. I focus on the tank on the right, nodding away as I draw closer to it. I'm nodding because I know.

I know *him*. The boy suspended there in the water.

I place my hand on the glass. There are robotic arms keeping him in place. A clawlike contraption ensures he can't turn his head.

And still, oh God, despite all that, his eyes light up when they meet mine, as bright and fiery and gentle as I ever remember them, and I shiver as a rush spreads inside and leaves me breathless.

Ari.

CHAPTER TEN

*T*hank you, God.

I blink, trying to focus, but I can't stop staring at Ari. As I press my face against the glass, he closes his eyes for a second. When he reopens them, a whole chasm of emotions play across his face.

Distant shouting reaches my ears and I force myself into action.

I tear my gaze away and, reaching for the files and controls beside the tank, fiddle around frantically. It takes longer than it did for the others, but step by step—each one feeling excruciatingly long—I tackle the security measures and equipment. Finally Ari is free, and he immediately rises to the top of the tank.

"Just a sec..." I jab at a red file. "Okay, it's open."

Ari plunges through the surface as soon as the top slides back, and begins spluttering and coughing. He inhales sharply as oxygen rushes into his lungs.

I point to the side. "There's a ladder, Ari. Grab that and—"

He grips the edge of the tank, hauls himself out, and leaps down. When he staggers back several steps, I quickly reach out to grab hold of him, but he indicates he'll be okay. He shakes his body and stamps his feet before straightening tentatively to tower before me, water dripping everywhere.

I hold my breath as I take in his face. It's full of shadows. They linger in the dips below his high cheekbones, in the dark stubble covering his jaw, and even in his burning gaze. His usually warm color is pallid, his eyes red. *What did they do to you?*

He flicks his dark hair back, the water spraying the air as he locks eyes with mine, searching my face. His expression is dazed and I can't look away.

I move toward him just as his arms reach out for me.

"Leyla!" Lewis's voice carries over before we touch, and we turn, waiting for him to appear. "Where'd you go? You okay? I found yer weapon. Wait, did this little shit bother you?" His footsteps pick up pace as he turns into the corridor. "You weren't answering yer Brace—" He stops short and gasps.

Then he moves closer, staring at Ari, at the tank, and back at Ari. "Neptune, Ari…" Lewis slowly shakes his head as he joins us. He lets out his breath in a huff, his knuckles turning white as he clenches his fists. "I'll kill them all." He throws his arms around Ari, visibly trembling when he moves back to take him in. "Thank Neptune. Here, you'll be needing one of these." His hands shake as he passes Ari one of the guards' guns. He holds mine out for me, waving vaguely behind him as I take it. "Everything's clear back there," he says, his eyes glistening.

"This—" Ari clenches his jaw and stops to cough again before he continues. "This place," he says hoarsely. "We don't leave until—"

"We've checked every room, Ari." I force my voice out. "We found them. They should already be out of here. And we're definitely not leaving this place standing after us. But now we really need to go."

He stares at me, wrestling with what I've said, when shouting breaks out around us—loud voices, angry and tense. And they're drawing closer.

"Let's go!" I say.

We can't run because Ari doesn't have the energy, but supporting him as much as he'll allow, we move as fast as we can through the space. He pauses only to pick up his necklace and knife. The voices draw too close for comfort now, their footsteps pounding on the bridges outside. We wait, only stepping out after they enter the room next door. My pulse hammers away in my ears as we edge along the walkway as fast as we can.

I quickly bring up the blueprints on my Bracelet and then point toward the corner. "There's another lift just around there. It'll mean crossing the lower level to get to the pool room, but we'd never make it via any of the staircases now."

We head for the lift. "Drop!" I shout as we step inside. A laser beam slips in to scan the space erratically, missing us by a second. I break out into a sweat.

Footsteps and voices suddenly sound. I reach up for the control panel from my crouched position and jab the button repeatedly. Just as security come into sight, the lift door slides shut and we descend. My legs won't stop quivering.

"They'll be waiting for us." Lewis checks his gun's status, and scans the info on mine, too. "Yer all right."

Max's voice fills the lift. "We can't hold them off any longer—we're out of here! Their defense is returning. Get out. Anyone still inside, leave now!"

I message Papa for an update. All those we rescued are now safely on board. I could cry with relief. The *Kabul* is ready to race away, he assures me. And the others are waiting in the water.

I glance at the faces in the lift with me. Lewis looks wound up, as if ready to launch himself out of the lift, all guns blazing as he charges them. And Ari...He looks stunned, and he looks exhausted.

I return my focus to Lewis's concern about us walking out of the lift to a blitz. "We need a distraction," I say, and raise my Bracelet. "Oscar?"

The Navigator materializes beside us. "My lady?"

I explain the situation and tell him he must do his best to distract those out there for as long as possible. "Do you understand, Oscar? We're talking a grade-one emergency here. Please help us!"

He clutches his chest. "Oh I say, more drama on the high seas. How vexing! Allow me to offer my assistance, my dear."

The doors to the lift slide open, and it's hell. It's all we can do to crouch back into the space without being hit. Oscar steps out. It takes a few seconds for them to notice him, but when they do, the firing eases. We slowly edge to the opening and peek out. The guards all have their eyes firmly on the Navigator, their expressions confused as he confidently crosses the space.

"A marvelous day for me to ruin this fine establishment, don't you think? Why, you look offended, distinguished personages. Rejoice, for I choose my enemies for their intellects!"

Oscar hurries away in the opposite direction.

"All right, now," I say, and we exit the lift just as they advance after Oscar and open fire on him. We rush through, battling the few remaining guards we encounter on our way to the pool room.

At last, as we turn a corner, the corridor to the pool room comes into sight just opposite us. Alarms still ring out and shouting sounds all around us, but thankfully there's nobody else present. We start crossing the floor. Almost instantly a door opens somewhere behind us. The sounds of voices and brisk footsteps fill the air, with boots pounding the first-level walkway. I tense and we keep going. *Please, please, please don't notice us.*

The sounds pause.

"Well, if it isn't our little champion," says a voice.

A shiver zigzags down my spine on hearing the menacing tones. I shake my head in disbelief. We stop moving and slowly turn around. I look up at the walkway in front of us and freeze. It's him. The cause of everything that's gone wrong for Papa and me.

Captain Sebastian, the prime minister's right-hand man, stares back down at us.

These last few months he's snaked his way into my life like some persistent sea serpent. He's behind all the horrific attacks on settlements, behind Papa's arrest—responsible for having him locked up in that hellhole for a prison and left to rot away, and God knows what else.

His eyes bore into me, calculating as always, but there's also an unmistakable hint of surprise. He's with more than half a dozen armed guards. I turn to Lewis and Ari, and they have lasers targeted at their chests and even dotting their faces. I look down and see the same on my body. Ari straightens, his gaze burning into Sebastian's.

"Sir," says the guard closest to Sebastian. "We must get you to safety until the building's secure again. Procedure—"

Sebastian glances at him and the guard falls silent. He fixes his stare on me once more, the contempt in his gaze scathing as he traces the scar running across his left cheek. He always wears such a shrouded, conniving look, and it's unbearable having it so clearly directed at you. My legs quiver.

"Slide your weapons across the floor," he says.

Before we've had time to think, he nods and there's a *ping* so close to us we jump and do as he says.

"McQueen." His mouth twists on my name. "You've caused me nothing but one giant fucking migraine."

I stare back at him, at once wanting to scream but also feeling completely numb. He stops tracing the scar as a small guy hurries along the walkway toward him. I use the chance to check on Ari, very slowly leaning into him.

"Leyla." I have to strain to hear it. Ari uncurls his fist to slip his hand in mine. I feel a squeeze and he might as well be gripping my heart.

"Reckon we could get away with messaging?" Lewis mutters under his breath.

My chest tightens on his words. Lewis is still inside this place because of me.

"Look at them," I whisper back. "They just *want* you to reach for your Bracelet." We watch Captain Sebastian. "What is he doing here? What's going on today that he had to visit?"

The door leading to the pool room behind us slides open as officers rush through the space.

"*What?*" Sebastian suddenly raises his voice at the messenger. "How can you morons lose something that size? I put this place at risk by giving you all the backup you could ever need and you *still* messed up?"

The guy shakes his head. "Sorry, sir, but we're on it."

Sebastian grabs hold of the metal frame of the walkway as if restraining himself. "I want it found, do you hear? No matter what it takes. Find it now before it leaves the area. Where's our exterior patrol? Get the rest of them back here, with instructions to take out every one of the unauthorized subs out there, got it? *Now!*"

"Yes, sir. Patrol is only half a league away now, they'll be here any moment, sir." The guy hurries away again.

"Captain?" the guard to Sebastian's left hesitantly asks, nodding in our direction.

Sebastian stares into the space. "Months of planning and now I come all the way out here, and for what? You lose the greatest thing we ever discovered. We tame that thing and we win the war against the savages. One by one, it'll rip them apart. So I don't care how you do it, but bring it back." He tilts his head to run his gaze over us. "And you let a bunch of freaks run this place amok." He pauses, rubbing his jaw before continuing. "It's the anniversary of Eva and Winston's deaths—Ed will do his usual and lock himself away for a couple of days. I need this to be sorted while he's distracted grieving for his sister and nephew, got it?" He twists his face as his gaze rests on Ari. "Take it back upstairs, return it to its tank, and keep at it. This place is depleting funds. I need results. We make a breakthrough with *him*, and we've got them all."

I shift on my feet and feel strange, as if a tremor just ran through the space. It's over before I can pinpoint it. A few of the guards seem to have also felt it, looking around before shrugging.

Sebastian's eyes flit over Lewis and me. "Bring the girl to me. She goes back to the capital with us. I ignored my instincts once and look where it got me. It's time the McQueens learned a lesson." He waves a dismissive hand in Lewis's direction. "Do away with him."

Boom. The place vibrates and the walkways rattle. We lose our step, and I'm holding on to Ari's hand tighter than ever. The guards look at one another and spin around trying to locate the source of the ominous sound.

Sebastian snarls. "They dare attack us? I'll—"

Boom. This time it's louder. The ground shakes beneath our feet and we stagger back. New alarms ring out, and then we jump as the walkway immediately above Sebastian and his men comes crashing down, trapping some of them. They shout and get busy lifting heavy sheets of steel mesh off themselves.

We move at once, turning and sprinting toward the door.

We're through in no time and race on as I use the blueprints to guide us back to the pool room.

Max messages us. "We're out of time!" he shouts. "Their security's returning. And whatever that was, it wasn't us. Get out of there!"

"Who's attacking the place if it isn't us?" Lewis shouts at me as we turn into another corridor.

"I don't have a *clue* what's going on!" I say as we rush into the pool room. Apart from a technician hastening to escape the place and completely ignoring us, it's mercifully empty.

I quickly message Papa. "Oscar needs to strike their patrol! It'll be here any second, a pack of security vessels with orders to take us all out. We'll never make it back if we don't take care of them!" He assures me he's onto it.

As soon as we're through the airlock, Lewis runs to his sub, calling out to Ari as he does. "You need to get in with Leyla, mine's not at its best. Not sure it'll manage two!"

I rush to check on his tail. "What the hell, Lewis, you can't go out there in this!" I hurry around to the cockpit and lean in to check the dashboard. "And your oxygen regulator's playing up, the sensor's off the charts. Why didn't you say?"

"Lewis, sit with Leyla," says Ari. "I can hold on to one of the others."

I wring my hands at the thought of him exposed out there when he's not feeling too strong, but we don't have any other option. Lewis would never make it back in a vessel this damaged. We jump into my sub and I gesture to Ari to leave.

He stands still, his expression conflicted and eyes blazing.

"Ari," Lewis pleads with him. "They're not getting away with anything, I swear it. You have to trust us. But they're gonna be here any second!"

Ari clamps his jaw and nods. "Okay, but after you."

I seal the craft and push forward on the joystick. We descend just as I see guards burst into the pool room.

"We're out!" I shout into my Bracelet. "Dropping away as I speak. Lewis is with me, and Ari's in the water—look out for him! Where's everyone?"

"We're ready when you are!" says Max.

We exit the shaft of light beneath the lab just in time to see a Black-watch vessel speed away in the distance. I slam the throttle the second I spot Ari hanging on to our sub. When we join the others, one of Ben's neighbors beckons to Ari. He swims toward her and holds on to the fin of her craft. It bolts away, taking him back to the *Kabul*. The sense of relief from watching them go is overwhelming. We give them half a minute, and then spring into action.

"All right, everyone in the clear!" Max shouts. "No closer than what we'd agreed on!"

We speed away from the structure.

"This should be enough," says Lewis, and we group together.

My heart hammers away in my chest.

"Okay!" says Max.

There's a pause, and then a pulse of current jolts our vessels and a powerful wave spreads in all directions from the target. The water swells as it rolls toward us.

"Yikes, hold on," I say to Lewis, hoping those in the water will be all right.

The surge hits us, and despite my best efforts, the sub is sent spinning away. There's only endless churning and rocking as I battle to stabilize the craft. Wave after wave crashes over us. And then something flashes from deep within their fold. The sub tosses, and then there it is again. It's... Oh God, I think it's an eye. It blinks.

"Lewis! What's *that*?"

"Where? I can't see anything!" he shouts, holding on to whatever he can grab.

I didn't imagine it, though. My pulse races now. I don't know what the hell is going on anymore. At last, the turbulence ebbs a little.

"Everyone check in!" comes Ruby's voice.

We're all okay, thank God. I can't believe those in the water survived that. As soon as our vessels are steady enough, we navigate back to the spot of the lab. Our subs sway in the choppy current, but we press on, moving near the wreckage to see the result. The closer we get, the cloudier it becomes, and for a while all we can see is sea foam and floating debris. I switch on the sandstorm beam to help combat the grainy haze surrounding us now. The others dart through the water and get even closer. The light aids visibility and my pulse hammers away as I take in the sight before us.

With its supporting columns blasted, the lab has slumped to the seabed and is falling apart before our eyes. As we watch, a chunk of its shell breaks away to roll slowly across the ocean floor. A creature drifts out of the remains. And another. And then there's a trickle of animals as they find themselves suddenly free.

Whoosh. Something whips right past my side of the submersible and I jump in my seat. Something longer than anything I've seen before.

"Did you see that!" I say to Lewis. "What *was* it?"

He peers into the water and shrugs. "Debris. Or one of the poor creatures."

I shudder. We need to get the hell out of here. . . . Relief floods my body as we turn around to leave. It's all too much.

"Message," says Lewis, pointing to my flashing Bracelet, and I shake myself alert.

It's Papa, his voice low and urgent, and far too heavy for comfort. "Leyla, Charlie called. As we speak, a dozen Blackwatch vessels are headed for the lab. We need to go!"

CHAPTER ELEVEN

I t's almost midnight. The *Kabul* hums away as she speeds through the freezing blue of the Greenland Sea. I'm in the galley, waiting on the Tea-lady to produce warm milk for the twin boys we rescued.

Ari lies asleep in the room he stayed in before they captured him. He swallowed a Prognosis Pill; the Medi-bot just isn't equipped for deeper analysis. The nanobot's stream of data didn't reveal anything serious, but advised various remedies for whatever they'd done to him in the lab. There are all kinds of drips on him, and he has to remain sedated throughout the treatment. A very tearful Ben and Ruby keep checking in on their Bracelets, and even watch him sleep for a bit. Freya was beside herself with joy on-screen. She *knew* he'd be back for their aunt Linde's wedding, she said.

Almost the entire Blackwatch fleet showed up, but with the *Kabul* running at full speed, we got away just before they arrived. The people we rescued were split between the submersibles and are being dropped off at their own communities. Lewis has borrowed my craft to take the little girl from the lab home. Ben identified her from the missing persons files all their communities keep updated. She was taken from a small settlement on the other side of Greenland. Though she was understandably keen on immediately getting home to her family, she had to wait until the Medi-bot had treated several urgent wounds she'd received from the equipment inside the tank. Lewis will meet us back in Eysturoy. And everyone else left hours ago, not wishing to prolong the journey by staying with us. Because instead of returning to the Faroe Islands, we're headed farther north. To Svalbard.

The family with the twin boys is from there. Only one of the larger submersibles would be able to take them, and that prolongs how long Ari's community remains vulnerable without their defense vessels. Plus, the submarine's much faster. Even with the *Kabul*'s speed, Svalbard is well over twenty-four hours away. We don't need to worry about new travel papers as it's within Norwegian territory.

We've given the family the space and privacy of the saloon, though they've requested Papa's presence for most of the evening. He's great with helping people.

The twins' drinks are ready and I head for the saloon. Voices drift out into the passageway as the boys quietly sing their nursery rhymes:

London Bridge is sinking fast
Sinking fast, sinking fast
London Bridge is sinking fast
My fair lady!

When I enter the saloon, Papa's seated in the corner, chatting with the twins' parents as they talk about the lab. Jojo makes a tired sound from the viewport to acknowledge me. She should've been asleep hours ago but instead played nonstop with the twins. The boys are now obsessed with her Bliss-Pod as the puppy finally curls up inside, and they take turns playing with its settings. By the time I place down their drinks, the interior of Jojo's pod twinkles with soft lighting, plays soothing music for her, and gently rocks the puppy. The twins' faces glow as they sip their milk and watch her fall asleep.

I look around the saloon. Even though there's a whole extra family with us, it's much quieter with everyone else gone. Papa yawns.

"It's late, Papa, you should get some sleep."

He nods. "I want to make sure Ari's comfortable for the night, and then I'm calling it a day, Pickle." He keeps checking in on him, and earlier recited prayers over him as he slept.

He mentions Ari so casually while I still can't believe he's even here. "I can do it, Papa."

After collecting blankets and pillows for the family, who prefer to spend the night together in the spacious saloon, I drop in on Ari.

A Lumi-Orb casts a soft, golden flush over the room, and I quietly slip inside.

The drips are working away. One of the fluids will need topping up any minute now, but the others will last until morning. The stream of data from the Prognosis Pill hovers behind Ari. He's responding well to the treatment, thank goodness. And there's already a noticeable difference in his color.

I carefully sit on his bed and take in his sleeping face. A face I'd missed more than anything.

I'd barely breathed a sigh of relief after Papa's rescue when Ari's capture replaced that nightmare. I'd never imagined the trip to the lab would end like this. At long last they're both here. It's unbelievable. I feel lighter than I have in a long time. I take in the deepest breath and let it out slowly. Hot tears prickle my eyes until they spill over my cheeks. Papa's back, and now Ari, too, is safe. I gaze at his sleeping form.

I couldn't bear it if he was placed in danger ever again.

Once Ari recovers, he has to stay away from us. We're Britain's most wanted. He's enough of a target already without adding his connection to us. God only knows what they put him through in that place.... We're taking him home, and then we must limit contact with him.

I stare at his face. I want so badly to run my fingers over it, smooth his hair back, slip my hand in his. Curl up beside him until he regains consciousness. It's going to be unimaginably hard to keep my distance.

The drip makes a soft bleeping sound, and I tear my gaze away from him to replace the bag. Ensuring everything else is set for the night, I quietly exit his room.

I call Oscar as I make my way to my own.

"My lady?"

"Oscar, please alert me if there's any change in Ari's condition."

"My dear." He bows his head to acknowledge, before raising his eyebrows a fraction. "I say, the gentleman Lewis appears to have forsaken us?"

"Huh? Oh. Yes, Lewis had to drop the little girl off. We'll meet up with him in Eysturoy."

What a day. Back in my room, I'm exhausted beyond words and stumble half-asleep through my prayers. At last, I lie in bed. I want to fall asleep, except images flash before me from the lab—the little girl's face when she cowered away in terror on spotting us, the twins when they ran crying toward their parents' tanks, the animals. Ari.

As for Captain Sebastian... How will he have taken the news of what we did to the lab? I recall his expression and I shiver. It was so full of contempt for us. He was adamant I return to London with him. What did he have in mind for me? He's responsible for everything gone wrong, and he's put so many through hell. What else might he be capable of?

Max is on his way back to Eysturoy and will share whatever info they gleaned from the lab with Ruby, Ben, and the others. Together with Bia and the gang in Cambridge, they'll see if they can find out where the other missing people are. I scoured the news but there was nothing about the entire thing. And no word of Sebastian. I'll bet anything it was him that escaped in the Blackwatch vessel.

I squeeze my eyes shut to rid my mind of the draining thoughts.

We were lucky today, too. We found and saved so many creatures and innocent people from pain and torture. None of us who set off from Eysturoy were hurt or captured in the process. And Ari's safe; he's back. These are the things I should be focusing on for God's sake, and give all the worrying a rest.

Warmth spreads in my chest at the thought of Ari lying next door. For the first time in weeks I smile as I drift into sleep.

London's drowning, London's drowning
Fetch your wellies, fetch your wellies,

Higher, higher! Higher, higher!
Rising water, rising water.

Apparently little boys can be extremely hyper in the morning. Jojo's trying to catch her holographic juicy bone as it darts around the viewport and the twins are chasing her, singing more nursery rhymes at the top of their voices.

The children look carefree for the first time since leaving that horrific place. If all goes well, we should be at Svalbard by nightfall latest.

The boys' parents are having their breakfast. Papa's chatting with Bia on-screen. He's been exchanging messages with the Cambridge lot ever since he woke up. Charlie's a stickler for details. Ari's still out of it but should start to come around some time tonight or early tomorrow.

I rub my arms, trying to shake off the mood I woke up in. The nightmare revisited me last night and it's left me with the usual sense of unnerving this morning.

It was the same as always, except this time it merged with everything we saw back at the lab. I'm gazing out of a small window and can hear Papa's voice calling for me in the background. I want to reply, but I can't because I'm frozen, transfixed by the depths outside. There's something dreadful in the water and I don't dare look at it. Scenes from the lab slipped into the nightmare, and I saw Ari thrashing around in the tank. And then he was pressed against it, his face inches from mine, disbelief in his gaze that I'd come to rescue him. He placed his hand on the glass and I reached out to cover it with my own. As soon as I did, something unfathomable from behind Ari grabbed him and he was gone. There was only an empty tank, blood clouding the water.

I think as a child I witnessed a predatory creature in the midst of an attack and my brain never made sense of it, that I've still not processed what I saw. But how can I do that if I can't recall it clearly enough once I awaken? Each time my eyes open, it's with the overwhelming feeling a *person* was also out there, in the water. That's all I know. It's exhausting. I can never make sense of the nightmare and I hate the state it leaves me in the next day. I shake my head to try and rid myself of the thoughts, and force myself to push through the day.

We reach Svalbard in the evening.

The boys' parents insist they'll be safe traveling to their home on their own from here, but Papa remains worried. For his sake, they contact relatives and give our location. In no time at all the depths fill with several people as they swim frantically toward the *Kabul*, and oh goodness, we're not prepared for the reunion. The adults cry so hard as they greet and hug one another, and Papa and I have tears streaming down our faces, too.

They leave and I order the pool door shut. I blow out my cheeks as I slump onto the sofa. That's that, then. Everyone's safely returned to their families. In the morning we'll set off back to Eysturoy.

I summon the Navigator. "Oscar, keep her stationary for the night."

I desperately need at least one night of no worrying, and moving as we sleep never sits easy with me. The family assured us it's safe to stay overnight in the area. They were discovered and captured on a day out well away from here, the mother explained.

Although Ari's still out of it when I check in on him, he's moving his head and his eyelids flicker. He should come fully around sometime during the night. I leave him a note briefly explaining what's happened since he came on board and alerting him to food in the galley, just in case.

I say my prayers so I can finally get some sleep myself. Slipping into bed, I tug at the duvet and block out any worries.

There's only Papa, Ari, Jojo, and me on board the *Kabul* now. We're inside the Arctic Circle. By all accounts, we're safe here. What is it like in the daytime this far north?

I snuggle farther into the sheets, and despite my resolve to distance myself from Ari, for the first time in months I actually look forward to the morning. I find escape in reliving our kiss—my first ever—as sleep washes over me.

CHAPTER TWELVE

A Lumi-Orb casts its soft, apricot-colored light over the entire view-port. The early morning water outside is the cleanest I've ever set eyes on. I feel light-headed as I gaze into the jade-colored waves. The clash of the various currents around Svalbard—the Greenland, Norwegian, and Barents Seas, and the Arctic Ocean—has a strange, soothing effect. Even the buoyancy around here feels different. The depths are clear and there's this indiscernible magic to the water.

"Leyla…"

Warmth spreads through me, fuzzy and fluttery and like a wonderful memory that suddenly comes to you. There's also a little rage that I'm still in my plain black robe.

Ari joins me in the viewport, looking out into the water.

I turn his way and my breath hitches from the sight of him. He's really here. "How do you feel?"

Thank goodness he isn't looking too weak physically. Papa was in such horrific shape when we rescued him from Broadmoor. Ari's hair has grown even longer, and the dark waves, still slightly damp from his shower, tumble past his shoulders now. He's back in his own clothes, the usual T-shirt and trousers, always black. His skin gleams in the soft light. His chest expands and falls as he gazes out, his expression conflicted. He's all angles and strength and disquiet.

He turns to face me, warm amber eyes fixed on mine, and clears his throat. "I'm okay. I feel much better already." His voice softens. "What about you?"

I nod. "I'm all right."

He breaks into a small smile. Oh how I'd missed that smile.... How many times I'd conjured it into existence in my head. I want to throw my arms around him so bad, but for his sake, I resist.

"Yes, you're okay...." His lips part, his eyes widening a little. "You've been evading them for over a month. How has it been?"

"Bloody hard." I grin.

His smile falters. "I'm sorry," he mutters, pain edging his features. "I couldn't be there for you."

"What, no, you've nothing to apologize for. Hey, I went to your home and met your family and went through your things."

His face relaxes, his mouth twitching as he cocks an eyebrow in that way he does, and I can't tear my eyes away from him. Dammit, it's so hard not to embrace him. This isn't me; I don't know how to be this person.... My every instinct is to bury my face in his chest.

I clasp my hands, not trusting them. "Have you spoken with your family?"

"Yes, everyone, as soon as they awoke. Lewis too."

"Right. Well, you're probably starving. What would you like to eat?"

"Have you had your breakfast? And your father?"

"Papa's still asleep. It always takes him a while to fall back asleep after dawn prayers and so he sleeps in unless he's worried about something. And nope, I haven't even had my breakfast yet," I say, genuinely surprised.

He grins again, remembering how shocking this is, and points to the plush cushions piled in the viewport. "You must rest now. The waters around here are special—I used to swim up here. I've instructed Oscar to dive a little if that's okay? I'll bring breakfast."

"No, no. You rest and I'll—"

But he's already exiting the room, with Jojo launching herself at him when she spots him in the passageway. He scoops her up and they head for the galley.

I spread the cushions on the floor. The temperature of the sub remains constant, but still these are the coldest waters I've ever traveled through, and a visible fire would be perfect as we enjoy this landscape before heading back to Eysturoy.

"Oscar?"

"My lady." Like me, the Navigator's still dressed in his nightwear. But unlike my plain hooded robe, he's totally kitted out in satin burgundy pajamas and matching velvet gown.

"You once asked me if I wanted a fire. I'd love a cozy one right here, please." I gesture to the water. "Look at it. Isn't it just magical?"

"Of course, my dear. And yes, a most splendid view. Though I hesitate to clarify why. To define is to limit, I say."

"Oh. Well don't forget my cozy fire!"

A small campfire materializes in the viewport, in front of the windows. Bright saffron-colored flames flicker and dance away, their tips licking the spaces around them, and tiny logs sit crackling at the base. It looks astonishingly real and I feel instantly warmer.

The people we rescued will be with their families now, all having breakfast together in God knows how long. Such a heartwarming thought. I gaze into the waves lapping the sub's nose as we descend; so many wonders I still haven't seen. Ari said these waters were special and I don't want to miss a thing.

I bring up the simulated sea chart. Immediately the room turns into a deep-sea landscape. Blue water fills the space and waves ripple everywhere. Creatures and landmarks sway on the underwater vista. It's as if you're directly in the sea. Using my hands to zoom in and out, I locate several things I'd love to see around here and then wave my arms to dismiss the map.

Ari enters the saloon with our breakfast tray and Jojo's bowl. His face lights up at the sight of the fire. We sit on the cushions around the campfire, facing the windows, and eat from the mix of breakfast foods he's thrown together. This was always his approach to rustling up a meal—prepare a little of everything. Jojo curls up beside us and tucks into her own food.

Lewis told me those captured were fed only through tubes at the lab, and it's clear just how ravenous Ari is now. I can't bear the thought of what they might've gone through in those tanks. I pour us glasses of orange juice and start on pancakes. There isn't another meal in the whole day that can match breakfast. I'd happily have breakfast food for lunch and dinner, too. Ari plates himself a full English. The *Kabul*'s *thrum* tempers as she stops diving; the depths are a pure turquoise now.

Ari clears his throat and I look at him. The waves outside are reflected over the viewport and ripples dance on his face. "Leyla," he says, as he reaches for more sausages and eggs. "I don't know what your plans are, but there's a family wedding coming up—my favorite aunt's... Do you think maybe you could..."

A wedding! Exactly what we need after all the chaos of the last few days. Except... I need to stay away from Ari so he isn't on Sebastian's radar so much. There's a sinking feeling in my stomach.

"Are you up for it?" I ask.

He considers my question a moment. "It's in a few days. I'll be ready."

"Right. I'm not really sure, sorry. . . . I'll check with Papa."

He nods slowly as he watches me, his expression unreadable, before returning to his plate. It takes all my will not to say *I'd love to go anywhere with you*.

I butter a slice of toast and take a bite, disappointed in my wavering self-control. This is definitely not going to be easy. But if I care about him at all, then it has to be this way.

When we're done eating, I pour us warm drinks—tea for me, coffee for him—and we sit cradling our cups as we watch the captivating world go by. I catch my breath when I see it.

"Ari..."

An iceberg. It looms over us in the depths, glowing-white and spectral. Goodness, it eclipses everything, lighting up all the water around it. So this is what they look like... so defiant and otherworldly. I shake my head at the majestic sight.

"These ones melt in the summer but always form again in the winter," says Ari softly, taking a sip of his drink.

"In the Old World they had a few that stayed frozen all year round. And they were huge. I spotted something else on the map that I'd love to see." I instruct Oscar to descend another fifty feet and turn west a little. I move to sit up against the windows, peering through them until at last I spot it on our left. "Stop!"

A whirlpool. The swirling vortex is both terrifying and compulsive to look at. They'd sprung up all over after the disaster and still remain. "Look at that, Ari. I've watched so much footage of them and always wanted to see one for myself. Have you ever been up close to one?"

He makes his way over. "Yes, we have to watch out for them when we're swimming."

"Some of the vortices disappear into the seabed." I sigh. "Where do the things they suck inside end up?" I put down my cup and place my hands on the window so I can get a better view. They're such an ominous yet spectacular sight; the water looks alive. I turn my face to see Ari watching me, his gaze thoughtful, before he fixes it on the whirlpool.

He sits beside me and we stare at the sight. Around and around the vortex spins, the thunderous funnel at its heart devouring whatever it can. How moody the waters are in places! We watch in silence as we finish up our warm drinks. I instruct Oscar to move slowly through the area; I want to see as much as possible before we have to set off back to Eysturoy. When I turn to Ari, his expression is suddenly heavy as he looks into the current. I'm about to move closer to him when I remember and stop myself.

"What is it, Ari?"

He lowers his eyes, staring into his cup before tossing his head back to drain it. There's unease on his face, his muscles all tense. He swallows before speaking. "I don't know what I was forced to take in that place. But I started hallucinating. There was a woman in the water, and someone else, elsewhere...and blood...the water bleeding around me. It wouldn't go away, intense every time." His shoulders rise and fall and his gaze grows stormy. "I couldn't bear it."

I've never hated Captain Sebastian more.

Ari waves his hand absently. "I thrashed around so much I broke the restraints and they moved me to a separate tank away from the others."

"Have you experienced these hallucinations since you've been back on board?"

"Not like that. But the images randomly flash before me, especially when I'm looking at the water."

"Hopefully the visions become weaker and less frequent as time goes on. My own nightmare always occurs more when I'm stressed. What is it with these bloody horrors visiting us. . . . Fingers crossed whatever poisons they fed you in there will be out of your system in no time. I'm here if you want to talk about any of it, all right?" I hesitantly squeeze his arm.

His face relaxes and the firelight plays on his features, deepening the velvet glow of his eyes. "Thank you," he says, his voice hushed. "You risked so much for me."

I'm unable to tear myself away. I remember what it feels like to trace his face, to run my fingers through his hair. The touch of his hands. The feeling of leaning into him and inhaling his scent. Showing him I care deeply for him. Ari holds my gaze from beneath thick, dark lashes. He wears that tender expression I'd recalled countless times and dreamed every night of seeing again. He thinks I risked too much. . . . I'd risk everything for him.

Movement outside interrupts us and we swing our gazes back to the water. I suck in a breath. *Yesss.* Ari's face shines and Jojo races over, her tail wagging away.

It's an entire pod of humpback whales pausing to play before the sub.

We stand and take in the sight. I've always wanted to see them with my own eyes. They're huge, so incredibly long. The dark-gray creatures slowly spin around as we watch. Wavy lines mark their bodies and scars dot their lighter undersides. I can't believe how lengthy their noses are—and how knobbly! And they have the longest fins ever. The friendly animals twist and turn in the water, not at all phased by our presence.

Ari smiles as he watches, one hand pressed against the acrylic of the windows. "They'll always stop to help anyone they see in danger," he says. "Any person or animal. Humpbacks have saved us so many times."

Jojo barks happily at the sight, jumping around the viewport with joy and joining in with the creatures in her own way.

The whales dive and I sigh. It's a good thing Lewis borrowed my submersible because my every instinct is to check out Svalbard up close. The sights here are breathtaking. But it's time to head back to Eysturoy. Ari's family is waiting for him.

The doors open and Papa steps into the saloon. His gaze sweeps over the cushions, fire, and breakfast tray, to rest on Ari and me. His expression is thoughtful as he breaks into a warm smile.

"Salaam, Pickle. Ari, welcome, son." Papa holds Ari's gaze and a tiny line appears between his eyebrows.

"Salaam, Papa! I'll get your breakfast."

I grab the tray and look back at them as I cross the saloon. Ari moves to shake Papa's hand but is met with an embrace instead. As Papa steps back, the thoughtful expression deepens. He gives a small shake of his head, clears his brow, and gestures to the sofa. I watch as they make their way to the seating area and begin chatting away. My insides flip-flop at the sight of them together.

I dwell on Papa's preoccupied expression as I work away in the galley. What was he expecting? Is Ari not how he'd imagined? My mind races, as usual forming something out of nothing.

When I return with his breakfast, Papa gestures to the seat beside him.

"Sit, Pickle, we must talk while I eat. Bismillah," he says, lifting the cup of tea to his mouth.

Ari is sitting opposite to us, paying attention to Papa whilst also tending to Jojo as she plays with a favorite stuffed cat.

"They've had a look at the information Max downloaded," Papa says. "Only a fraction of it is of any use to us, but it's...enough." He presses his lips flat. "There are other labs."

Ari pauses, oblivious to Jojo who's waiting on his next move, and instead stares at Papa. Jojo whines.

A weight settles in my chest. More places holding creatures and possibly people, too. And in such horrific conditions. "Do they know where?"

Papa shakes his head. "There's nothing about the locations, but there's plenty of evidence to show they exist. Some of the animals are for private sale, but the rest…They're building some kind of army. They're transforming the creatures into a group who'll carry out large-scale coordinated attacks on…on your communities, son," he says, looking at Ari. "They're captured, 'trained,' and altered until eventually they comply. We saw what those eels did on our way to the lab. They're planning on unleashing other such creatures into every settlement." He sounds so helpless I move closer and place my hand on his arm.

Ari sits, muscles strained against his skin and blinking away as he absorbs Papa's words. "And us?" he finally asks quietly, his face dark now. "If they want us all dead, why do they hold some of us at these places?"

Papa swallows before answering. "The drugs they're meddling with, the techniques mentioned in the files, and the limited data recorded in them all point to the field of neuroscience. We haven't yet had ample time to investigate all the info retrieved, but from what we can gather so far, it seems the labs are working on finding ways to impact your volition. There are streams of data on the neuroscience of free will and trying to interrupt neural signals in the hopes of impacting your agency. I'm so sorry, son." He sighs and pushes the tray of food away.

My stomach heaves. "They're controlling them?"

"No, Pickle—from the records, it's clear they're far off from that. But yes, it's the area they're working on. How they determine who's sent to the labs isn't clear, but that seems to be the reason they're holding so many captive. The animals, too. They'd planned on some sort of test that day, for one or more of their most powerful creatures," continues Papa. "Their 'most rewarding specimens.' And that's why the place was so light on security when we got there—most of them had accompanied the transfer of the animals."

"Something went wrong during the test," I say, trying to remember Sebastian's words inside the lab. "I think one of the creatures they were transporting got away. Sebastian was furious with his men and ordered them to find it immediately. He said it was the best thing they'd ever discovered and that it would destroy everyone, but that first they needed to tame it. I think this secret weapon they plan on unleashing in communities is a *creature*, not firepower.... Papa, do we know what hit the lab? Something definitely attacked it—that's how we were able to escape. Did you or Oscar see anything weird?"

"'Weird'?"

"I don't know.... I feel like I saw something in the water after the lab came down. Like a giant eye..." It sounds bonkers now, even to me.

An army. We have to stop them.

Ari stares into the space, his face flushed. "A coordinated attack... Was there any indication of a date?"

"No," says Papa. "They're referring to it only as 'D-Day.'"

"Wow, they really have no shame," I say. I could vomit.

"Sebastian must be stopped," says Ari, the muscle along his jaw ticking away. "We have to find a way."

Papa takes a deep breath and lets it out in a huff. "Your father's called a meeting. And he wants us there, too. We need to start making our way back."

Ari nods. "I can help on board. Do you need me for anything?"

"We have everything under control, son. You must take things easy."

I twist my hair around my fingers. "Who else knows about this 'D-Day' plan, Papa?"

"Those Ben trusts, and Bia. But *everyone* knows of the lab's existence now." He turns to Ari. "Your father said tensions are high across the communities."

When he was strong enough to talk after his rescue, Papa told me how amphis and their allies have been covertly resisting the authorities for decades now. Blocking attacks, obstructing the transfer of innocent people to and from prisons and other places, infiltrating institutions to help break them out, and attacking security bases specifically set up to locate and destroy their communities. Again and again they've protested their treatment and pleaded to be left alone in peace. Begged for their lives. And not a single instance of trying to make those in charge see that what they're doing is unjust and cruel has ever got them anywhere. And still the leaders of each community, year in and year out, plead for patience.

"But from what I can gather," Papa continues, "this isn't like any other time. What happened at Tórshavn, and the discovery of the lab, it's caused a huge stir. Communities everywhere are demanding action. They've been onto settlement leaders nonstop since news of the lab spread. They're angry and frightened, grief-stricken. They want answers."

Papa also told me how so many are done with all the talks and quiet hope. Especially the youth, who want the horrors to end immediately. A tiny number seek revenge in whatever ways they can. Like those who boarded the *Kabul* and attacked Ari and me when we first set off from London.

Something has to change. Or before long there won't be any of them left.

Ari's Bracelet flashes; Ruby wants to chat with him. He excuses himself and leaves the saloon.

"Leyla," Papa says, scratching his chin. "Why did you enter the lab? I asked you to return to the sub, and did you? Do you have any idea how worried I was? It could have gone so wrong."

"Yes, we were really lucky nobody was harmed."

"You don't listen to me anymore."

"I couldn't return just then, Papa. What was the point of coming all that way if we weren't going to properly search the place?"

"Ya Allah, what is the point of *anything* if you don't survive it?" He stands and walks over to the viewport.

"Papa, I'm really sorry I worried you, but we found the others, didn't we? If I hadn't gone in, or if I'd come back when you said, then they might still be trapped there or worse—killed in the explosion. I don't understand—"

"I know I was absent for a few months, but I'm still your father, Leyla. You don't always need to understand; you could sometimes simply *listen*." He throws his hands up. "Yes, you found the others. Alhamdulillah you did. But you could have been injured in the process!" He runs his palm over his hair. "Do you have any idea what it's like for me? You're my child.

My *life*. Anytime you're out there I may as well hold my breath until you're safely back on board." His voice fades and he paces the viewport.

My heart goes out to him. I never want to worry him. But my throat also squeezes around words desperate to escape it now. Sometimes I'm going to have to do things he's uncomfortable with. I have to be allowed to make mistakes, and I hope to learn from them. And I've already spent enough years being afraid. But as I watch him now, the words refuse to leave my lips. It must be so hard for him, raising me on his own all these years and now living every day with the fact that we're fugitives.

I don't regret my actions at the lab at all. But I also hate this....I wish he'd stop worrying so much.

"Papa, please," I say, walking toward him. "You have to trust me. I know I can be rash, but I promise I'm trying not to be anymore. I can't risk losing you or...or anyone else dear to me. But we mustn't be afraid to do the right thing, remember? I did what felt right, like you always taught me to. Why's that changed?"

"Because doing the right thing can kill you!" He draws his breath and tilts his head back, looking up at the ceiling of the saloon. "You're too much like your mama!"

"I wouldn't know," I say quietly. "You never talk about her."

Silence fills the room. Papa rubs the back of his neck and stares out into the water. His posture changes, the stoop he'd inherited in prison returning. "'The right thing,'" he mutters so quietly to himself I have to strain to hear. "Where did doing the right thing get your mama..."

I still at his words. What did Mama do? And what happened to her because of it? "Papa, what do you—"

The doors slide open and Ari enters the saloon. He takes one look at us and holds up an apologetic hand. "Sorry."

"No, son," says Papa, facing him. He takes a deep breath and motions for Ari to come in. "Stay. Our home is your home."

Ari meets my gaze and I swiftly look away.

How can the *Kabul* be homelike for him when he's even more vulnerable anytime he's near her? As if his identity doesn't attract enough hostility and injustice as it is, we have a hefty bounty on our heads. Sebastian's probably dying to get his hands on him. He seemed really eager to continue running tests on him at the lab. If Ari hadn't stayed on board after we got Papa back, he wouldn't have been captured. No, this can't be home to him.

He watches me intently now as I beckon the Navigator.

"Please rise, Oscar. And take her full speed to the Faroe Islands, back to Eysturoy. They're waiting for us."

CHAPTER THIRTEEN

I t's midmorning; we arrived back in Eysturoy a few hours ago. Ben set off the moment the storm cleared and got here just before us. Ari's home is packed with family and friends as discussions take place. I move to a quieter corner and take a seat with my cup of tea.

I chew on my lip as I look around the large room. I've never witnessed so much raw sentiment. Along with relief for the rescued people, there's shock and pain. Among the teens there's an air of helplessness, too. And from so many there's resentment and anger—a live, palpable sense of loathing for Captain Sebastian and those in power. Ari's friends and family keep getting teary every time they spot him, and it's emotional watching them.

We haven't had any proper alone time since the morning we sighted the whales. I took care of getting us back here, while he and Papa worked to keep abreast of everything going on, constantly messaging back and forth with Grandpa in London and Bia's lot at Cambridge. The journey back was mercifully event-free. Despite traveling both nights, it took us two days to reach the Faroe Islands from Svalbard. Papa didn't mention Mama again.

Where did doing the right thing get your mama...? His words won't leave me alone. Why would he say that, if something hadn't happened to her because of her actions? Is it possible this something led to her death? I'd always been told she passed away peacefully in her sleep, but now I can't help wondering.... Waiting for Papa to speak more on it is torture. And judging from how busy the discussions taking place before me are, it'll be a while before I can ask him.

The lab's existence really has created a wave of unrest in every amphi community around the country. And it's gathering momentum.

They've had enough.

A settlement in Cardiff discovered a plan to protest openly. A small group was so fed up they'd actually intended on swimming through the city carrying placards. As if they wouldn't come under fire in seconds. Youths in Belfast snuck out of hiding to break into the council offices there and paint all over the walls. They left messages and even artwork highlighting their plight. And in Bradford a gang attacked a protein plant in objection to everything going on. Such incidents are increasing in severity, and it's all playing right into Captain Sebastian's hands.

Those in charge fear it's only a matter of time before the government exploits the actions of protesters to escalate the vile treatment used against the communities. The media is working tirelessly to remind everyone of the unimaginable danger posed by amphis. Footage and reports have been manipulated and doctored. And it's all doing its job.

I've never witnessed the national sense of fear this heightened.

I notice Papa excuse himself to Ben and make his way toward the quieter corner I've settled in. I drain my cup and lean in as he draws near.

"Leyla?" His expression is serious. "I must speak with you, child. Could we—"

"About Mama?" I hold my breath.

He nods. My Bracelet flashes but I ignore it until it stops. "It's really loud in here, Papa, we can go sit in a quieter room if you—" My Bracelet flashes again, and this time it's a message. I frown as I read the text moving across the wristband. "It's Theo. He says it's urgent."

Papa wrinkles his brow. "Take it," he urges. "I'll be with Ben if you need me, Pickle. Theo's been working with Gideon as he helps those down south. I hope things haven't escalated further.... You'll let me know what's going on? We can chat later."

After promising to speak with him as soon as I'm free, I make my way out of the noisy space and find a small, empty room.

"Didn't mean to worry you," Theo says, sweeping his hand over his platinum-blond hair and trying his best not to look worried. He's never been able to hide his emotions, though, and his pale-blue eyes remain cloudy. "But word on the back streams is Westminster is out for blood. They've been on Ari's case in a big way. I got wind of it from several sources. They've put every resource into finding him again. They obviously realized he's been helping you all along. Add the fact you've now broken him out of that place, and yeah, he'll want to watch his back out there. He needs to be real careful, Leyla."

A chill sweeps over me. Westminster is especially after Ari because of his association with me. I mean I suspected it, but still I feel sick. "I'll let him know."

We chat some more. Theo can't wrap his head around the discovery of the lab. "Charlie and I were just discussing it; it's wild. They're sick and twisted, the whole lot of them. Mum's in shock; we can't talk about it in front of her. Can't believe you guys went right in like that. Need me or Tabs to do anything?"

I shake my head. "You're already doing enough by helping Gramps and Charlie when they need it." I look over my shoulder as faint voices rise from somewhere, but it falls silent and I carry on. "Everyone's working out what they can do with the info they've collected all these years, the evidence of their treatment. Papa said they've tried for so long to release it to the public, but even with Bia's help and the might of the Den, it's always discovered and blocked."

"Wonder if I can help there?"

"No harm in asking Charlie if you can help with the tech side?" I sigh. "All this time we were oblivious to what's been happening right under our noses. Now that we finally know the truth we have to *do* something. If we speak up, people will listen. It's not us in the firing line—" Voices rise once more, and promising Theo I'll be in touch again soon, I wrap things up.

When I open the door and step back into the corridor, the voices are much clearer. They're coming from a room at the end of the passage. The door's open and I recognize Ari's low tones. I move toward the sounds. Ari needs to know the authorities have taken a keen interest in him. He must be more careful than ever out there.

A woman's voice drifts out of the room, terse and agitated. "Ben's a fool, walking on eggshells around their kind. At last the time comes for us to stand up and take action, and what's he doing? Holding more meetings!"

"I know you're upset. We all are." Ari's voice dips lower, as if he's holding himself in check. "But there's no need to undermine my father's efforts—he's doing the best he can."

"No, he's an embarrassment to us all." Her tone rises, biting now. "Mind, if he were really Faroese, he'd not be such a coward, but what can you expect from an outsider?"

There's a pause, and when Ari answers, it's with an unmistakable edge to his voice. "He belongs here as much as anyone else. He's dedicated himself to helping this community. And you've said enough."

I should probably turn around…but I keep going until I'm standing in the doorway. I spot Ari and Lewis together, and the woman pacing opposite them. She looks to be in her sixties, arms crossed and an exasperated twist to her mouth.

Ari whips his head around, his jaw clenched but his eyes softening slightly when they meet mine. "Everything okay?"

I press my lips together, suddenly wishing I'd waited until later to speak to him, but he gestures for me to enter. I step inside and join him. The woman stills and lowers her head to study me before giving it a small shake.

"You can't stay away from them, can you?" she asks Ari without taking her narrowed gaze off me.

"Yer stepping out of line now, and if I were you, I'd leave," says Lewis.

She blinks, her eyes widening as she turns to Lewis. "You might drop in on us whenever you like, spending all your time with this family, but don't you for a second assume you can order me around. Or that you're one of us."

Her lips press tight when Ari lays a hand on Lewis's arm. What on earth is her problem?

Ari's shoulders rise and fall and his face is thunderous now. "You're being rude to our friends. Leave," he tells her through gritted teeth.

"I beg your par—"

"*Now*," he insists.

Her eyes flash. "Foolish lad," she spits out the words, nostrils flared. Throwing Lewis and me a last icy look each, she moves near the doorway where she pauses and fixes her gaze on Ari. A hint of pity surfaces in her expression. She points absently to Lewis and me and purses her mouth.

"You choose them over your own people now. When it was *their* kind that ensured you were found stranded alone and lost out there—your birth family probably killed."

CHAPTER FOURTEEN

Ari had been all alone in the water when Ben first met him.

After the relative's outburst, Ari asked Ben and Ruby to tell him it wasn't true, that they hadn't found him in such confusing circumstances. But they couldn't deny it. In a daze, Ari asked them for any clue they might have as to the identity of his birth family. But nobody has any idea. Ben and the entire community up here had exhausted all efforts at the time, and came up with nothing.

Ari left us at that point, and Lewis went after him. The next couple of hours were a blur of emotion from all sides.

Many in the community accused Ben of derailing the urgent discussions. There were bigger, more important matters than his personal woes, they insisted. Some even said the fact he wasn't native to the Faroe Islands but originally from London shouldn't be overlooked. That visibly upset Ben, as they've been in Eysturoy for over a decade. And so Ben had to let Ari go for now, and return to the discussions with Ruby. Papa did what he could to help calm the situation.

I needed some space so I'm back on the *Kabul*. There wasn't any point hanging out at Ari's if he wasn't home and Papa was busy. Freya's with me. She was left confused and anxious by what unfolded and wanted to come with me. Ruby and Ben agreed a break from all the tension at home would do her good and she'll be spending the night on board the *Kabul*. We jumped in the submersible and got here without hassle.

It's late afternoon now, several hours since Ari left. Oscar warned of a small quake a few leagues away. Even a small one can trigger sandstorms and tsunamis, and I really hope Ari's all right wherever he is.

I message Papa to say I'll come pick him up tonight. He wants to remain overnight, though. He's tired, plus he doesn't want to leave Ari's parents alone. Ruby and Ben are anxious about Ari, and Papa will be staying over so he can be there for them.

The thought that Ben found Ari lost and all alone in the water is alarming. I wonder where Ari is right now. Maybe he's out there, swimming around as he tries to make sense of it all. I shudder imagining him drifting in those depths. I truly don't know how they do it. Hopefully he's inside somewhere, safe and warm.

The submarine has taken Freya's mind off things, thank goodness, and she can't get enough of walking the length of the vessel, staring out of the viewport, and chatting with Oscar. When I bring up the simulated sea chart for her, her eyes almost burst out of her head in wonder.

We wash and change into our pajamas after dinner. Freya wants to sleep with me, so I put her in my bed. Jojo curls up in her Bliss-Pod on the floor beside her.

Freya sighs as she looks around, her eyes shining. "I can't believe you have your own submarine. A whole submarine!"

"I can't believe you can breathe underwater!"

She grins and begins playing with the mood lighting. When she speaks again, her voice is lower, subdued. "Leyla?"

"Hmm?"

"Today's been awful. And everyone keeps talking about what's happening, you know, because of that lab."

"Yes. That place should never have existed. But they're going to try and fix things."

"Will Ari be okay?" she asks. "I hate them—whoever captured him and all the others and took them there. And if anyone hurt him before Dad found him, then I hate them, too," she says firmly.

I take a moment to answer. "It must be alarming to learn that about yourself. We have to just be there for Ari. It must be so confusing for him, but we have to hope that in the end he'll be all right."

She pauses, deep in thought, before speaking again. "Leyla...do you think non-amphis will ever love and care for us as much as they love and care for one another?"

There's a physical tugging in my chest at her words.

All the history we access through Jeeves tells me we'll always point to someone else, always need an "other" to reassure ourselves we're somehow superior, to feel better about our own lives and ways of living. We've done it forever, way before amphis existed, and we'll most likely do it until the end of the world.

I realize Freya's still waiting on an answer. Could non-amphis ever love and care for amphis as much as we do one another?

Could we really accept humans who can breathe underwater as "one of us"? Humans who lack in nothing, and whose only "crime" is an extra ability.

How did we ever manage to convince ourselves the difference was a negative thing?

"Yes. We're capable of real, unconditional love for one another, Freya. No matter who we are. So whatever happens, we should never stop hoping for and demanding better."

Her curls bounce as she nods, processing my words. "I saw you before you even came to Eysturoy, you know. I watched you on-screen in the London Marathon. You were great. We all wanted you to win because Mum and Dad know your family is good and kind." Freya plays with the lighting, settling on a golden hue to the room, and brings up her bed-time reading. She swishes open the book, beaming as text and pictures glimmer before her. "'Night, Leyla. I'm going to listen to the next chapter of my book before I sleep."

"That's fab. Good night, you queen." I leave the room to the sounds of her giggling uncontrollably as the narrator describes how a little boy called Charles McGuffin has turned into a snake and found himself in the girls' toilets at school.

The idea of schools always fascinates me. All our education is provided by Jeeves. The thought of attending a whole separate place for learning, along with so many others around your age, sounds like such fun. I think I'd have loved it.

I return to the saloon. I feel too restless to even read tonight and so I walk right past the cozy armchair by the bookcase. The Lumi-Orb suffuses a rose-pink blush over the viewport, and I throw the cushions down and sit by the windows. Papa was finally ready to talk to me about Mama earlier. I check my Bracelet. It's too late now; he'll be exhausted. I'll ensure he tells me tomorrow.

I stiffen when there's movement outside. Someone's swimming toward the sub. I peer into the gloom and feel an unexpected release of tension. It's Ari. The vessel's dimmed exterior lights barely capture his form, but I know it's him and my shoulders relax. He draws closer before pausing to hover in the depths before me, blinking away as he stares. Another shape comes into sight and it's Skye, his pet dolphin. She's so attached to Ari she followed him all the way to London when Grandpa asked him to watch over me. I wave at the dolphin and she flaps a fin in response. I'm so glad she's with him now.

Come on board I want to say to him, but I don't know if he's ready. He propels himself forward to cover the distance between us. I stand and move closer to the window. We instinctively reach out and place our hands on the acrylic at the same time, our palms pressed together as if touching. And once more I get the weirdest feeling.

I can't pinpoint it, but it's there every time we do this. As if it triggers a memory I've no recollection of now. As before, Ari looks slightly bewildered as his gaze rests on our hands. This exact moment always feels strangely familiar. I shake the weird feeling away and smile at him before leaving to make my way to the galley.

When I return to the saloon with food and hot chocolates, Ari's on board, as I'd hoped. He's sitting by the window, washed and changed, and I feel infinitely lighter. Skye is gone and the water is clear.

We sit in the soft rosy glow of the viewport with me drinking my chocolate as Ari eats.

It's difficult to stick to my resolve to stay away when I know he's hurting. "Freya's in my room so yours is free if you want it," I say.

He looks uncertain at first, but then nods. When he's eaten, he sits still, his expression pensive as he stares away at nothing in particular.

"Ari, do you want to talk about it?"

He takes a moment before speaking. "I went home," he says quietly, his gaze fixed on the floor. "Mum had gone to bed with a headache, but Dad was still awake and we talked a bit." He lifts his shoulders a fraction in a slight shrug. "Dad found me alone in the water." He rakes his fingers through his hair. "Whenever I used to ask about my past, they always said the same thing, that they didn't know who I was before I became a part of the family. Now I realize how true that was." He takes a deep breath before continuing. "I was around five, Dad said. I was alone and in shock, and I wouldn't speak. He knew I'd experienced something serious, but he could never find out what. It was months before I started talking again, and by then I'd either forgotten or blocked out whatever had happened to me. Nobody had a clue who my biological family were—they still don't. Dad said his cousin added the 'probably killed' bit to it herself. Thankfully he never saw anything like that."

I feel like my heartbeat has slowed down, and I want nothing more than to wrap my arms around him. I can't bear to see him like this. "I'm so sorry, Ari."

He nods and rubs his face. "I can understand why they didn't share all the details with me, especially when they had no answers. It was a difficult decision, but they were worried telling me might trigger the trauma. They promised each other they wouldn't lie to me if I asked, but it never crossed my mind. I sometimes asked about my past, but never really wondered about exactly how they first met me, you know?"

"Yes."

He takes off his necklace and twists the beads in his fingers. "I was wearing this when Dad found me." He holds it up, rubbing his thumb across an inscription on the beads. "It's a proverb, written in Mauritian Creole. One day I asked so many questions and Dad, desperate to provide some answers, took a wild guess and told me I'd had a Mauritian ancestor. When I started asking more questions as I grew older, he had me take a DNA test so I would know who I was, where I came from. That's when we discovered I have mostly South Asian ancestry. After that, Dad urged me to learn Mauritian Creole in the off chance it was my birth family's language."

Wow...I truly don't know what to think. "What does the necklace say?" I ask him.

Ari tilts his head at me. "*Ca ou pédi nen fè ou va trouvé nen sann.* What you lose in the fire, you will find in the ashes."

We fall silent, each lost in thought.

Ari puts the necklace back on, and his eyes soften as he watches me now. The seconds stretch as we stare at each other and then, dammit, color creeps into my cheeks. His own face also turns a warmer shade and we avert our gazes at the same time. Tabby would be utterly ashamed of me.

I clear my throat. "Oscar?"

The Navigator appears in an emerald-green velvet jacket. "My lady. Good sir."

"Oscar, secure the *Kabul* until morning, please. Like always, put her in stealth mode. And is everything else all right?"

"All is rather satisfactory, my dear. The odd unexpected quake does still insist on making its presence felt, however, and so I fear visibility will be at a disadvantage in the morning. And understood on the instructions, my lady. I implore you not to worry."

I picture Captain Sebastian's face and a tremor slides across my back. "There are people who'd hurt us when we haven't done anything wrong, Oscar. We need to make sure they never find us."

"Ah, my lady. I do find that one should always forgive their enemies; nothing annoys them so much."

Whaaat. "They can go choke, Oscar."

He blinks. "A most intriguing sentiment, my dear."

Ari grins.

I dismiss the Navigator and push my hair out of my face as I turn to Ari. "You must be exhausted. Try to get some rest? God knows what tomorrow might bring."

He stares into the space, looking deep in thought.

"You're all right?" I ask.

He nods. "It's what you just said. I never thought on the day you showed up at the lab that it might go any differently to all the other days.... And I never thought today would be so... you know." He shrugs slowly. "It feels strange to recall anything of my life with the same perspective as before, even though none of that has changed."

"Gramps has a quote hanging in his home, a statement mentioned in the Talmud: *Gam zu l'tovah*. This, too, is for the best. It's one of my very faves. But... it's not always easy to try and make the best of what we're given, is it?" I take a deep breath and blow out my cheeks. "Ari, I'm here if you want to talk, all right?"

He nods slowly, his eyes shimmering in the soft light, two amber pools reflecting everything good and beautiful. Oh how I'd missed him.... How at once he's so comfortingly familiar in a way I can't even explain and yet the most exciting person I've ever known. I can't believe he's back and safe. It was the longest month without him. He holds my gaze and my heart races, my insides fluttering away. How many times I'd imagined once more being alone with him like this. He tentatively reaches across, his hand finding mine. I grasp his fingers, unable to look away from him. His face, his blazing eyes, his soft mouth. He leans in toward me.

And Theo's words earlier come crashing into my head.

My stomach quivers and I pause, dropping my gaze. Reluctantly I let Ari's fingers slip out of mine. I swallow to ease my dry throat.

How quickly I let my guard down.... I have to be more careful.

"Leyla?" he asks gently, rubbing his jaw. "What is it? What's wrong?"

Tell him. I could just let him know they're hell-bent on capturing him again. That for his own sake, he mustn't get close to me again. That's what my heart wants to do. But my head says once Ari knows I'm staying away from him out of concern for him, and not because I don't feel the same way about him anymore, he'll ignore his own safety.

"It's late, Ari," I whisper, unable to resist a quick sidelong glance his way as I stand.

Questions swirl in his eyes and linger at the corners of his mouth. Muttering good night before he can voice them, I stumble away.

I slip into bed, plant a kiss on Freya's curls, and turn on my side. I try to block out the look on Ari's face but it's no good. My heart aches and I don't know what to do. All I know is he's in enough danger as it is, and even more vulnerable when with us. Just knowing he's on the *Kabul* tonight has my heart in my mouth. Papa's words come back to me about how he can't breathe properly whenever I go off alone. Is this what it feels like?

A heavy sigh escapes my lips as I turn on my back and stare at the ceiling.

This, too, is for the best. The Talmudic quote seems exactly opposite of how we think when we suffer from the seasickness, when everything seems hopeless and unbearable.

There are so many painful and difficult discussions being had around the country right now as amphis process the existence of the lab. They want and need to be accepted as equals. But are Britons ready for that? Because to do what's right and just would require change.

And we are not terribly good with change.

CHAPTER FIFTEEN

I awake to a note from Freya: She's out for a quick swim and will stay close by. It's unnerving to read, but this is their home and I have to trust she knows what she's doing.

After a quick wash and change, I head for the saloon with Jojo. As soon as Freya's back, we can breakfast together. It looks like Ari's still asleep. There's a sinking feeling inside whenever I recall pulling back from him last night. I peer out into the water to take my mind off it. The sub's no longer in stealth mode and Eysturoy's murky early morning current laps the vessel's nose. The turquoise depths back in Svalbard now seem translucent by comparison.

"Oscar? Everything all right?"

The Navigator materializes. "Good morning, my lady. Everything is most satisfactory, though as predicted the environment is currently rather capricious. Alas, not a day for rousing adventures!"

"I see. Thanks, Oscar. And ooh, you're dressed pretty stellar. And so bright and early?"

He looks as if he's off to attend a ball or something. A silk quilted jacket covers an embroidered shirt, and a fabulous red flower is tucked in his hair.

He fiddles with a large, dainty ring on his finger. "My dear, one should either *be* a work of art, or wear a work of art." There's a flush to his cheeks as he raises his eyebrow a fraction. "I don't suppose the gentleman Lewis will be gracing us with an appearance?"

"I've no idea, Oscar." I gaze out at the dense and shifting waves, and pause. "Wait, what did you say?"

The Navigator offers a secret smile. "I was merely wondering if the dashing—"

"No, about the water today."

"I beg your pardon." He straightens and clears his throat. "Visibility is reduced out there, my dear, due to what appears to have been another quake last night. It caused quite some damage to a part of the seabed."

I rub the back of my neck. Freya's out there.... I know she does this regularly, most likely in all kinds of weather, and she did say she'd stay nearby, but still it makes me feel uneasy. Best to be safe.

I head downstairs for my sub. There's no need to worry Ari. He has enough on his mind right now, and I'll be back in a tick with his sister.

The waves are definitely a little choppier this morning, and I switch on all lights as I navigate the shrouded water. I can't spot Freya near the sub, or even by the surrounding ridges. Maybe she wanted to go home on a whim. I head in that direction, peering out for any sign of her. I realize I've no idea how far she's comfortable straying from the community when in the water. I doubt she'd be allowed outside of their security boundaries, though. When I can't spot her at these depths, I dive even lower. And when there's no sign of her by the seabed, I rise as high as I dare in the more turbulent current. Nothing. Surely she wouldn't go too far when visibility's reduced. Except she did mention how she loved to go out by the rift to collect rocks. *Especially after a sandstorm.* Ari didn't like her going alone, she'd said. And there'll be good reason for that. I need to locate the rift.

The only rift I know about is the main one, created when Greenland nearly snapped in half during the disaster. The tectonic plates there shifted it to an almost ninety-degree upward angle. But obviously there are smaller ones around here, too, and at least one is close enough for Freya to regularly swim out to.

Oscar sends me coordinates for the only possible rift it could be, and I follow the craft's instructions.

It really is impossible to see much. How on earth can Freya even swim in this, never mind spot beautiful rocks? At last, though it's still not visible to me, Oscar tells me I'm by the rift. I circle the area. *Come on, Freya.* There's no sign of her. I should've woken Ari up. He might've known exactly where she was and reached her right away. But he's going through enough already, and I don't want to add to his troubles if it turns out to be nothing. I set my lights to flash; hopefully the continual blinking away will catch her attention. Finally I spot her, thank goodness.

Freya's hovering away in the distance. I continue flashing my lights until she slowly turns around, eyes wide in a frozen expression. Something's wrong.

"Come on!" I gesture to her.

She shakes her head. Again I beckon her toward the sub, but she raises her hand and points behind her. I draw closer.

As I pass her, she gestures wildly for me not to go any farther. A foreboding settles in my stomach as I keep going. I pause the vessel and peer around. I can't see a thing. And then there's movement right on the edge of my vision, in the depths below. As I stare at the spot, the water shifts. Something stirs on the seabed. Just like last time.

No, no, no.

I'm turning around to tell Freya to get out of there, when waves hit my vessel. There's the flash of something but it's gone before I can pinpoint it. The water fills with endless churning. Again, something whips through the current ahead. And then.

Oh God...This has to be a nightmare.

Gigantic limbs wriggle as they stretch through the water, and the biggest living thing I've ever seen rises out of the depths. A monster. It's a monster.

I forget to breathe. I forget everything.

It's no creature I can name. It's a terrifying, hulking mass before me. Where's Freya?

It pauses in the distance. I think my heart has stopped. *Please protect us, God.*

It's green-black and oily looking. It's all endless swaying arms and tentacles and mammoth suckers. There's something nebulous about it, as if a colossal blot of ink has come to life. Wisps of color seep from its body into the water around it. And then a ghostly tentacle, tipped with countless toothed suckers and a spear-like end, reaches out of the gloom to feel its way toward me. My chest and throat grow hard, crushing me from the inside. *Please, God, let Freya have left the area.* I see black spots.

Kill the lights. I force my frozen mind to work, but before I manage to actually do anything, the beast wraps the pointed tentacle around the sub.

And pulls me toward itself.

I grab hold of the sides of my seat. "Oscar! We're in trouble! Can you hear me? There's something in the water! Freya's with me!"

My arms thrash through the air, slamming everything as the vessel rocks and jerks to and fro at the mercy of the monster. Alarms blare through the craft. I squint through the tossing waves, desperately trying to spot Freya. My thoughts scatter as I try to hold on. This has to be their secret weapon, the thing that wiped out so many lives in Tórshavn. It's the creature Captain Sebastian and the officer mentioned: *We tame that thing, and we win the war against the savages*, he'd said. Control *this*?

It's all I can do to try and hold on with quivering hands. My head hurts and my neck aches as the vessel heaves and lurches.

"Freya!" I call out when I spot her cowering on the seabed. She's covering her face. The grotesque beast swings its limb low with me in its grip, and when I sight her again I flash all my lights. The creature becomes frenzied, but at least Freya looks up.

"*Go!*" I scream and gesture for her to get the hell out of here. I nearly sob with relief when she turns around and bolts away through the water.

I kill the lights and almost immediately the monster seems less agitated, though it's still trying to crush the vessel. The sub creaks and my whole body trembles. I'm not sure how much longer the craft can hold out. And then the creature suddenly releases me. The sub hurls away and I grab the throttle and joystick, working the wings like mad to try and counter the spinning. A swift glance over my shoulder and there's so much churning it's almost impossible to spot anything. But then I do and I cry out, half focusing on my vessel and half staring at the sight ahead. It let me go because it was distracted.

Ari distracted it.

He's in the water. Suspended there, a tiny figure in front of a shadowy devil.

At last, the sub stops spinning and I turn in Ari's direction. If only my submersible had firepower! I move in, closer and closer, until I can see exactly what's happening. When something falls through the water, I realize Ari has a knife in each hand and is slashing away at the tentacles as they try to squeeze him to death. He breaks free and ducks and dives, darting under and over the endless, slimy limbs, never letting up with his knives. I can't stop shivering as my vessel jerks in all the chaos, and it's only a matter of seconds before the monster notices me again. Its eye is massive—a ball of inky blackness surrounded by boils. It blinks and the dread is surely going to swallow me whole.

Even though Ari moves faster than a sailfish, dodging expertly as he hacks away, nothing slows the beast down. I need to stop shaking or I'll never be able to help.

Forcing myself to focus, I move back, away from it. I need distance. Its limbs are endless...slithery tentacles rippling out across the waves. It's no good—without real help, we'll never survive.

I have an idea...and thank goodness Papa's at Ben's because it would've killed him with worry.

"Oscar! Track me and bring the *Kabul* here. It's an emergency! But rise, and stay high, all right? Let me know when you're two hundred feet above me! Has Freya returned to the sub?" *Please, please, please.*

The Navigator assures me the submarine's on its way. "And Miss Sterling's presence is detected on board as we speak, my lady."

Tears prickle my eyes with relief. My breathing's so hard and fast it feels as if my lungs might puncture any second. I move back toward the heinous thing.

Ari spots me and gestures frantically, urging me to get out of there. I flash my lights and the creature turns its attention to me again. Between us, Ari and I keep distracting it from each other, dodging its hideous resolve to end us. At last, Oscar informs me they're here, right above us. I catch Ari's attention and, signing away frantically, tell him to distance himself from the beast. He looks exhausted.

"We can't win this, Ari! It destroyed so many in Tórshavn! Only the *Kabul* has the power to take it out. I want Oscar to fire on it—but we need to get out of the way first!"

I get back to the Navigator. "Oscar, do you have a fix on the creature attacking us?"

"Indeed, my lady, our sensors are off the chart!"

"When I give the word, I want you to target it with everything we have for a Grade 1A attack. *Everything*, got it? But you *must* wait until I tell you it's safe! Don't descend. And if our firepower somehow misses the target and the beast finds its way up to you before we're back, blast it out of the water with everything else!"

"With pleasure, my lady!"

I turn back to Ari, who's kicking and slashing away at a gnarled limb twisted around his leg now. His face strains as he hacks at it nonstop until at last he shakes free of it.

"Come on! Oscar's ready to fire!"

"It will follow us!"

He's right. "Let's try and get on top of it and hurt it somehow. Look at its head, it looks soft and slimy—we could strike there!"

But it's not that simple. Every time Ari moves to swim up, the creature manages to grab him in yet another tentacle. Very soon he's not going to have any energy left to fight it. I bring the sub right in front of its horrifying face and distract it with my lights. Ari manages to slip past it. When he gestures he's ready, the vessel charges through tentacles to rocket up beside him, and the animal lashes out to locate us. We look down at its head, viscous and stumpy.

Ari bolts close and rams his knife into the gloopy spot right at the top.

The blade digs deep and the creature writhes and lashes out, limbs slicing the waves in every direction.

"Now, Ari!" I shout, signing away like mad. "Grab my wing!" The second he nods to let me know he's ready, I bolt away, counting to twenty. We're going to feel the impact, but there's no way around it—any longer and it'll either get away, or catch up with us.

"*Now*, Oscar!" I shout. "Hit it! And track it if it moves away!"

Within seconds, the sub rocks violently. The craft spins out of control and is carried along. My heart hammers away as I work to counter the balance. When I finally get it back under control, I've no idea where we are. And I can no longer see Ari. I can't see *anything* for all the churning. The choppier current rolls over the submersible again and again.

"Oscar, is the *Kabul* all right? Update, please!"

"My lady, everything is satisfactory on board. And all our efforts hit their target. I am no longer able to detect any movement."

Oh wow, we got it! Relief washes over me, though it's a little tempered by Ari's absence. "Oscar? If Ari returns to the submarine, I need you to let me know instantly. And tell Freya I'll be back any minute!"

Images crash into my head of Ari caught in the *Kabul*'s firepower. It's not even logical—we weren't in the firing line. I take deep breaths. I have to trust he's safe and pray for the best. He's somewhere around here—he was knocked away in the turbulence, that's all. Keeping my eyes peeled for any sign of him, I get my bearings and slowly trace my way back to where we were attacked. The craft sways in the increased waves. I switch every light on and dive when I realize I drifted too high with the impact. My pulse races as I imagine the creature suddenly looming before me. But instead I'm met with floating debris.

I gulp as fleshy chunks drift past the vessel. Arms, tentacles, suckers, and pieces of torso, with dark and wispy tendrils leaking bile into the water. It's all over the depths, in a thousand pieces, and very definitely dead. *Yesss.*

It was far too dangerous to leave alive. I wouldn't put it past Sebastian to have tried to save its life so it could continue ripping communities apart. I can't bear the thought of what it did to the people of Tórshavn, but it won't be harming any others ever again. We did it! I turn my head, and pause.

It could be the adrenaline playing tricks on my mind, but the water looks different to my left. I'm not sure. There's a flickering, a shadow to the current in the far distance. . . . I swerve the sub in its direction.

The shadow stretches as I draw closer. The flickering becomes specks. Glimmering specks. *Lights*. And the slinking shadow . . .

The shadow is a hulking Blackwatch vessel.

I swallow and open my mouth to speak. "Oscar." I can barely get my voice out. "Listen very carefully to me now," I say when he responds. "This is an emergency order. Get out of here. Hide. Lock the pool door right now, don't let Freya leave the sub, put the *Kabul* in stealth mode, and contact Papa. Tell him to let everyone know Blackwatch themselves are in the area, and that you missed them. . . . They somehow evaded our systems, which means the community could be vulnerable, too. Look out for Ari— he'll be trying to find the *Kabul*. . . ." My voice trails as my throat dries up.

Oscar gets to work.

Wiping my hands on my thighs, I grab hold of the throttle and joystick. The sneaky vessel starts moving toward me. I'm left with no choice but to slowly reverse as I keep my eyes on the growing shadow.

I jolt when something hurtles toward my sub from above and drops right in front of me. Ari. He's waving his hands frantically, telling me to get out of there. I nod, gesturing for him to hold on to the sub so we can speed away. I'll look for a range to hide in; we can do this. Ari swims around to the side. I turn to face him, my hands ready on the controls the second he gives the go-ahead.

A force hits my sub.

I don't know what it is. I only feel it. It strikes at my very core. And a terror unlike any I've felt before fills the moment immediately after.

Only Ari registers when alarms burn my ears.

Only Ari makes sense when the craft lurches.

Only Ari is clear. His face, how it contorts with shock, how his eyes bulge as he watches, and how he thrashes around, shouting. Screaming.

The vessel shudders.

And when I plummet, when I hurtle down, down, down, I think of everyone I love.

And as the sub groans and its sides press in on me and something cracks so loud I imagine the seabed has splintered, I think, *Forgive me, God.*

And then I surrender to the unknown as it chokes every ounce of life from me.

Nothing is so painful to the human mind as a great and sudden change.

Mary Wollstonecraft Shelley

CHAPTER SIXTEEN

I am lost in the dark.

I have no idea where I am. I forget where I was.

I forget *who* I was.

I have no idea who I am.

There is a memory. The answer. It's there—right there, on the edge of this...whatever this is. So pressingly near. And yet so utterly, gallingly, out of my grasp. I wonder what it is. If only the pain would stop. But it burns. Not a flaming, hot scorching, no. A bitter, mind-numbing cold. A chill frosting my thoughts and freezing my insides, causing them to blaze, blaze, blaze.

I can't breathe.

I can't breathe. I keep screaming this, but it changes nothing.

Please. I can't breathe.

Nothing changes.

There is nothing. Only an emptiness. An absence. A vacuum I can't explain, can't determine.

I am lost in the dark.

CHAPTER SEVENTEEN

There is a memory.
I am not alone in this world.
There is something more. An all-encompassing truth.
A light at the heart of this abyss. I just need to let it in. Except.
I'm falling. I've been falling for so long and it never ends. And.
I can't breathe.
I keep screaming this but nobody listens.
I can't breathe.
I beg you, come and help me.
Because I can't breathe.
But nobody comes.
I reject it. The void. This unknown. Sucking me in. I reject it all.
Because there's a memory. And if there's a memory, then there is a me.

Me.

I remember who I am.
And I open my mouth. To scream.
I scream soundlessly, so hard and for so long, the void sucks me under again.

CHAPTER EIGHTEEN

I'm vomiting.

I can't stop vomiting.

And every time I hurl, I think there's nothing more to bring up. My insides are being ripped out of me I think.

I'm Leyla Fairoza McQueen.

My mama was Soraya Bibi. My papa is Hashem McQueen.

This isn't one of my nightmares. It's really happening.

I'm not falling.

I am adrift.

Where I am exactly, I've no idea. It hurts to think too much. I've tried. But there's an incessant *thud, thud, thud* hammering away inside me. Something bears down on my skull and it's going to crush my head, mash my brains away. A force presses on my body, squeezing my rib cage tighter and tighter. And there's a grinding pain, a relentless, sharp scraping against my throat and insides.

The vomiting stops. It's replaced with coughing and spluttering. Something keeps tensing inside of my chest, tightening and relaxing.

I cover my ears. Noise. So much noise. My eardrums ring with it. It pounds away at my temples and my head feels as if it might rupture absorbing it all. Sounds. Vibrations that reach deep, slipping into my veins until my entire body throbs with their rhythm. The thunderous roll of waves, the unending dull roar that reaches me as if from across entire oceans, the evasive *whoosh* of something passing by, the frenzied gurgle and hissing of boiling geysers, and the ceaseless bubbling and trickling of water, of streams within streams. Heartbeats. And whistles and clicks and calls—languages I don't speak, don't understand. Echoes within echoes.

And the darkness . . . the darkness is everywhere, stretching across and pouring into every corner, every pocket of this watery vault. A palpable, inky void.

I can't taste or smell anything, and everything's so eerily blurry. Everything's slower. Even lifting my hand to my face is exhausting. The pressure . . . the sheer force pressing down on me is unbearably tangible and I sense it in every cell. My body wants to give in, to just bow down to the weight of all the water.

I'm shivering. I've no idea if I feel cold, though. Still, at last I know something.

I am all alone somewhere in the deepest, darkest depths. Alone in the abyss.

I know this because now I know.

I am Leyla Fairoza McQueen, and I'm breathing and existing underwater.

Despair washes over me. I open my mouth to cry out, and several hundred million cubic miles of water rush to fill it. Cold, dark liquid gushing in.

And out.

Mama was an amphi.

It's the only explanation. And it feels true. Maybe it was also the reason she was killed. All this time I carried the dormant gene Lewis mentioned: *It's rare, but some have the relevant gene only kick in after a trigger—usually a massive trauma.*

And that's what Papa must've been trying to tell me.

The intense pain in my head and chest has subsided, and now there's only the intolerable sense of pressure, the weight of the world pressing in on me. The edge has also worn off the uncontrollable shivering; it must've been shock. Or maybe I've become accustomed to the temperature now, I don't know. Even submerged, though, I know my body's trembling. I very vaguely recall kicking frantically against the sub's damaged body and swimming out at some point.

A wriggly, pale thing drops down in the cloaked green-black depths before me and I thrash at the water until it darts away. I haven't mastered my movements yet, and it's all I can do to not open my mouth and scream. I wrap my arms around myself. The abyss bulges around me.

The noise is still there, reaching deep into the heart of me, but now there's something else, too. Silence. An unwelcome, deep hush. How is it possible the two exist simultaneously? But they do. All the noise of this world could never fill the absence of human sound.

How long have I been like this? How long have I been adrift in this darkness? Hours? Days? *Too long.* I kept slipping in and out of consciousness, I think. Back in London, thanks to my ability to become easily distracted when out in my submersible, Tabby was always jokingly accusing me of being lost at sea. Her words couldn't be truer right now.

Please help me, God.

If God made me and God made this entire universe and is Lord of all the worlds, as I believe, then this, too, is His will, and He wouldn't abandon me now. I keep praying as I move, trying not to die of fright every time I spot distant shadows and formless shapes. This deep in the heart of the abyss it would be so easy to forget light even exists.

I kick as something soft brushes against me. When I turn to look, my gaze rests on the strangest creature. Small and dark, yet with a totally transparent dome for a head. I can see right inside it. I stare at it as it passes by, opening and closing its tiny mouth.

Every time I open my own mouth, every time I breathe in and out to try and see how it works, it's so frustrating because I've no idea. I can't see myself, and I can't feel any gills on my neck. I'm just me, but swimming, breathing, existing deep underwater.

The sense of clawing for air has gone, thank goodness. For the longest time I felt I was suffocating. But that, at least, has ceased. I will never forget that feeling.

We are human, *Leyla. We are you. We lack nothing—we only possess more.* Ari's words to me, after I went into shock on discovering his identity.

But nobody prepared me for it, for this.

I wave something away. And then another. And then, oh God, I'm surrounded by giant insect-like creatures drained of all color. Endless legs wriggle away and their tentacles twitch as I thrash the water. I move my limbs as fast as I can, and oh, the effort it takes as I swim through the ghostly swarm. I want to vomit except I know, painfully so, that my insides are empty now. Finally I lose sight of the creatures.

I've felt a certain level of fear all my life, mostly a dread of anything I don't know. But I have never known terror on this scale. It's relentless. I forget for a few seconds, become momentarily distracted, and then I remember my situation, where I am, and once more it bears down on me from all sides. A shrouded, menacing unknown. And a sense that everything's too primitive, that *anything* could suddenly happen.

I don't know how to survive down here. Nobody told me anything. I've no idea how to navigate the current, which creatures to avoid—nothing. And there's no sign of anyone. My Bracelet's only a shriveled-up band on my wrist now. Am I an easy target for predators by wearing white? I think of Ari in his perennial black.

Ari. Over and over again I replay his reaction after I was hit. The look on his face...Did they capture him? I have to believe he got away. I won't even imagine the alternative.

Thank goodness I told Oscar to get out of there. The "quakes" the Navigator mentioned were obviously chaos caused by that beast. I shudder as I recall it and quickly look around; it might not have been the only creature of its kind. I block the thought out and try to stay focused on thrusting my body forward as I slice the dense water with my hands. Though I've no idea where I'm headed, it feels wrong to stay still. Maybe they're looking for me? Papa will know what to do, and Freya will be safe at least. Thank God nobody else had been in the sub with me....Will Papa know I've survived and changed? What if he thinks I died...? He's too weak for that shock. I need to get back to him.

An amphi community. It's my only hope.

They're always designed to remain concealed to security forces, to submersibles. To non-amphis. But I can breathe and exist underwater—even in the deepest depths. They were never built to remain secret from me.

I move silently, keeping my eyes peeled as I thrust my body through the liquid with erratic strokes. I'm far too slow, but at least I'm moving. I suddenly find myself above the seabed. It's not what I was hoping for, but I continue to swim along it.

Bicycles, shopping trolleys, and a couple of oxidized and lifeless labor machines—the old-fashioned robots from several decades back—lie terminated on the ocean floor, everything now just one huge pile of rust and sponge and coral. Farther on, I shudder when I think the ground is moving. *No.* I couldn't bear it if another of those beasts rose up. But it's spiders. The seabed crawls with giant spiders at least three feet wide, and they're feasting on something. They thrash the food around, their long, spindly legs fighting over it. It's a human corpse, almost a skeleton now. My stomach rolls. I tear my gaze away from the ghastly sight.

Oh God, this is just so hard.

But I must stay focused on my own survival and keep going.

It's only after several alarming tugs I realize I've drifted into the edges of a strong current. I quickly move away, not wishing to be carried along to who knows where. When I come across what look like fish walking on the seabed, I dive for a closer look. I'm not imagining it.... They resemble anglerfish and they really are walking, using their fins to drag themselves along.

Papa taught me how to swim at Blackpool Pleasure Beach, the small resort in Shoreditch, but I rarely practiced and my limbs ache now. I'm growing tired. That's not good.

I swim over endless fissures and shudder when a wide trench approaches. A great gulf of darkness that stretches from the bottom of the world, to reach deep into its heart. Gurgling sounds bubble away in my eardrums, and there's the hiss of the earth spitting out gases, but I can't see far enough to spot any thermal vents. When will my eyes adjust to everything?

The chasm is crammed with ancient debris. Furniture and traffic lights and even several train carriages lie wedged inside, all crawling with abyssal creatures. How much of the Old World lies stuck in total darkness? How many of them did the earth swallow up? It's too painful to think about, and I shake myself to focus. I'm starting to feel empty, hungry. And it's making the exhaustion worse. How long can I last before I fall asleep right here, in the middle of so many predators who'd happily gnaw on me while I'm still alive? An army of tiny silver-gray lanternsharks dart past and I swiftly propel myself on before they spot me.

Ridges appear to my right. After a while, more rocky structures join them. A thought occurs to me: Maybe if the rocks reach high enough, and I don't veer off course, I might hit lighter water. I turn to ascend the baleful cliff faces.

I'm soon passing countless jagged peaks and trying not to dwell on the presence of the unnerving entryways to deep chambers. The mouth of a pitch-black cavern gapes at me, and a flicker of silver flashes from inside. I shudder and tear my gaze away. God knows where those subterranean passages lead, or what lingers in them. I move with haste. I really need to get the hell out of the water. The smooth, stony flanks seem to go on forever as I kick hard and continue to climb. Soon long trails of weed cling to the surface and it becomes slippery to the touch. As I force my limbs to keep moving through the creeping fatigue and I swim upward, the rock face abruptly flattens out before me.

Several homes loom on the current ahead.

I pause. Where are the lights? But of course, amphis wouldn't advertise where they live! I kick frantically now and make my way over to them. As I draw closer and realize what they are, I stop short and hover, staring. I could cry with despair.

They're Old World homes. Derelict. Empty.

I rise so I'm above them, and cast my gaze around. There are more buildings. It's an entire village. I blink several times; my vision's beginning to clear. A bulky form below catches my eye. It must've been a small whale, or maybe a dolphin; it's difficult to tell now. The carcass lies stuck across a chimney, as if impaled. Its decaying flesh flaps and flutters, and there's movement all over its body as tiny sea creatures feast on its remains.

I propel myself away to take a closer look around the village. It feels utterly surreal being out here in the water and surrounded by the Old World. It's strange and terrifying and so unexpectedly stirring. My gaze flits all around. Decayed homes and drowned community spaces. An entire way of life swept away. Grief suddenly, inexplicably, floods every part of me.

I swim through the small village, my mind all over the place. Everything timeworn is something a human touched, used, created. It feels so wrong that dead things should survive when the living beings once linked to them have long since perished. I spot a huge, tiled mural, and though it's pretty faded, you can still see a row of children holding hands, a sun shining down on them. Various mollusks and sea urchins have made the artwork their home now. I can see the limited remains of a church. Its cross, though slightly bent, is still visible on top of a spire at the center of huge interlocking archways that loom in the current. Each arch is so abundant with reefs they appear as if decorated with flowers. The skeletal but unmistakable dome of a mosque sits close to the church, and I gaze on both.

And the sense of grief softens.

As I look on the mural and the ruins of the church and mosque, my heart expands. I'm filled with an extraordinary love for the people in this village. And this unexpected warm feeling is so welcome right now.

Pushing through the murky current, I come upon a small row of almost identical cottages. Something stirs deep inside me.

When I look on the homes, on their battered roofs and dark spaces and smashed-up fences, I see a whole world, another reality. And yet it's only us in the past. I see adults and children living and working and playing, and I don't see any water. *No water!* They breathed air, they brushed against plants and trees, stepped among flowers, petted fellow life as it sat curled up on fences and on pathways, felt all kinds of weather on their faces, bodies. How can it be exactly the same place and yet such a different world? They were us; we're them. Looking on these houses now, that world seems too much like a fairy tale to have ever been true. And yet it was. It happened. And they had all that.

Imagine if they were still inside this house directly in front of me now . . . if they looked out and suddenly saw the water. Saw *me*. Goodness, what on earth might they think of me? I'm me, and yet they would only see an amphi. But I could so easily have been them, and they me. I'm about to move away, when I fix my gaze on the house again.

I have never been inside an Old World home.

Back in London, despite all the warnings and penalties, beachcombers still enter them in search of precious treasures—which is anything Old World, really. And those suffering from the seasickness are especially guilty of it. They no longer care much about the perils as the desire to hold on to something Old World becomes paramount to them. Oftentimes looters become stuck once inside, trapped in the liquid tombs. My chest tightens; Papa made me promise I'd never enter one.

Except . . . I'm no longer in a submersible.

And now certainly isn't the time. I know it isn't. But I have to see.

I move toward the house, taking in all its otherworldly details. A gate and picket fence are still discernible, clinging devotedly on. Oh, the Old World Heritage Society would love the place! I swim over the gate that has succumbed to deep-water coral, and up the path. Despite the fact I'm swimming, not walking, and that there's water instead of air, I suddenly feel as if I'm treading in Old Worlders' footsteps.

The door is shut. The window, too, remains barred. The place was locked up. A shimmery green fish swims out of a small window space upstairs. Kicking my legs, I rise toward it. My breathing quickens as I peer ahead into the hidden space of the room. It appears soulless, empty. And though I can now see more than the few meters I could earlier, it's still unnerving. Throwing a cautious glance over my shoulder first, I ignore the tremor in my legs and kick, thrusting my body forward through the window and into the ancient home. It takes a moment, but my eyes adjust.

It's a cottage full of ocean.

I frown at first, confused by the glowing light around the space, and then as my gaze draws lower I see the floor crawls with bioluminescent creatures. Thousands of worm-like beings emit a vivid electric-blue color. They're like a brilliant moonlit carpet and cast their luminosity at least halfway up the room. I look around; no unexpected creatures or horrors appear to be lurking. Still, my pulse pounds.

The room must have been a nursery. A cot bobs around the space, too clunky to drift out of the opening. It's all spindles and seaweed and debris. I grab its edge, peer inside, and flinch. But it's only a doll, the head wedged between the cot's bars. Its face has lost all paint and the remaining plain molded features give me the creeps.

Dolls are one of the worst things Old Worlders insisted on. They simply refuse to decay, and far too many sick and dead creatures are found with the limbs and heads—or even whole dolls—stuck inside them. I gaze down into the cot. A sea cucumber grazes on patchy deep-water coral where once a baby lay.

What happened to the infant? Did it survive? If it were alive, it would be at least sixty-five years old now, and in a whole different world than the one it was born into.

In my mind, I zoom out of my setting until I'm a speck in a sea of blue; then I see only a rotating ball of water. Finally the globe is just another dot among trillions and trillions of dots existing in a once infinite nothing, a breathless void. My heart flutters. Oh how I used to love listening to Papa talk about stars being born, supernova explosions so bright they briefly outshine whole galaxies—outrageous brilliance that simmers and explodes into being all around us. How he'd glow talking to me about it all. He really hasn't been the same since Broadmoor. I need to hurry, find my way back to him. But first, just one more room.

I swim out of the nursery and spot a wide staircase flanked by banisters glistening with slimy seaweed and kelp. Again, the bright blue of luminous sea life lights up the darkness. A group of tiny, oily-black fish dart out of my way as I head downstairs. My stomach is rock hard from sheer terror, but I keep going.

Downstairs, a child's bulky pram floats through the space. A variety of swaying sponge has made a home on its hood. Something stirs inside the carriage. I gulp as a cusk eel swims out. It's chunky with frilly edges and a ghostly, ominous gray color. Its fringes ripple as it effortlessly swerves and sways its way through the room. I press back against the wall to avoid it, and my gaze is drawn to all the endless plastic drifting around. Containers and bottles and jars and toys and just about a million different things all made from the omnipresent, devastating material. The eel thankfully isn't interested in me and glides straight past to head upstairs.

Moving through the home suddenly feels intrusive and eerie, and unexpectedly saddening. But it's also fascinating and I'm compelled to take it all in.

Curtains and rails dangle lopsided from barred windows. Furniture floats adrift, covered in sludgy plant life and home to a variety of abyssal organisms. In the kitchen, I startle when a sea snake slithers out of a cupboard. I freeze, hovering there.

It spirals and stretches through the water to pause right in front of me. It's rough and stone-colored, and has a thousand tiny, eerily transparent, razor-sharp teeth. The electric blue of its eyes is piercing. My pulse thuds away in my ears, faster and faster as I hold its gaze. The snake coils slowly as its head moves to and fro as if judging me. It twists its body and then, with startling speed, bolts out of sight behind me somewhere. I begin to shiver.

A longing sweeps over me as I stare around the space, an intense aching. What I wouldn't give to be out of these waters. To rest awhile, to eat and see others. To feel safe. The longer I'm in the water, the worse things will get for me. I must keep going.

Mustering all my energy, I push myself through the weighty space and back upstairs, keeping an eye out for the snake as I float out of the nursery window. I swim down the garden path.

And jolt at the sight of the security sub ahead.

CHAPTER NINETEEN

I freeze, but only for a second. And then I dive.

I can't stop trembling because I know what they do to people like me. A chill grips me and my heart goes out to those who've had to live like this forever.

My pulse hammers away as I crouch behind a section of the picket fence in the garden. Did they see me? Should I make a run for it? It's not like I've fully mastered movement, though. I'm still swimming like I normally would—not like the others when they dart through the water so effortlessly.

I don't think they saw me. They're hovering off the ledge, facing in the other direction. Also, their distress light's blinking away; they're in trouble. I'm glad. They're the absolute worst.

Except... it's the first sign of humanity in what feels like forever. And to my absolute shame, a very tiny part of me actually feels relief at the sight of them.

My mind races. I'm exhausted. I don't know that I'll ever see anyone else in time. At this rate I'll still be drifting around when fatigue takes over, and then what?

I raise my head and peek at the vessel again. Relief sweeps through me as I realize my eyesight's improved even further in the short time since I entered the house. The blur has finally worn off. The ledge is around ten meters away, but I can now see everything clearly enough through the water.

I watch the craft. Minutes pass by, though I've no idea how many. Ten seconds can feel like an hour down here. Sure enough, a breakdown vessel soon appears. They set to work, extending all manner of robotic equipment, until at last the security sub works its regular lights and switches the emergency red one off. I very slowly move.

Staying as low as I possibly can, I edge closer and closer, all the while racking my brains for which vessel to choose.

If I go with the breakdown craft, they're less likely to have any firepower if I'm discovered and so I'll have a shot at getting away. But if I go with the security sub, it might lead back in the general direction of Eysturoy, assuming that's not where we already are.

It's such a huge risk. What if it's headed somewhere else entirely? Like London.

Both vessels start moving.

At the very last minute, using every bit of my scant remaining energy, I thrust my body through the water and lunge forward.

To grab the tail end of the security sub as it leaves.

Time blurs again. Unless I count to myself, I've no idea how to gauge it down here. The breakdown sub sped away in the opposite direction, thank goodness. I don't know what I'd have done if they'd decided to travel together.

I hold on to the tail for dear life. Luckily the sub is huge and heavy, and I crouch, wrapping my arms and legs around the piece. It isn't really the tail; it's a decorative fin above the actual tail, but it's sturdy enough and shorter than the tail itself. I couldn't risk upsetting the balance of the craft, not least because it'd rouse their attention. Besides, twin propellers flank the tail and I can't risk getting too close to those.

The vessel passes through endless water and I can't tear my gaze away. More water than I ever imagined. I've crossed so many leagues in the *Kabul*, but it never once felt like this. It's startling to move through the world without the security of a vessel.

The sub slows and I tense; maybe they've discovered me. I peer around to see if there's anywhere to hide. And then I see why they've paused the vessel.

The officers want to watch a group of sharks as they feed just below us.

The creatures are so different from any sharks I've seen. A tremor runs through my body. It worsens when I remember I'm in the water with them. I can't hide from them if they spot me. Or smell me. I hold my breath, afraid they might hear my heartbeat.

The animals must be about six meters long, their flabby bodies a pink-gray color. They wear a grim expression and are unforgiving as they battle one another for the right to the corpse of something. I startle as I realize what they're fighting over—the carcass belongs to one of their own. If my tummy had anything left inside, I'd have hurled out of sheer terror. I crouch into a ball. As soon as they're done ripping into their dead one, the craft moves again.

I hold on with everything I have; this isn't an area I can get lost in. Instead of going forward, though, the vessel ascends. Higher and higher it climbs until finally the enormous shadow of a submarine hovers far above us. I look around frantically for any idea of what to do. Security forces or cannibalistic sharks—which is worse?

I'm exhausted and hungry and I don't have any energy left to stay in the water. The craft enters the very subtle glow of a moon pool, and pauses. The vessel hovers there, probably waiting on a submersible exiting the submarine. I twist my neck in every direction—I'll need to hide if another craft enters the water. Hide where, though? Apart from a dolphin circling in the distance, it's an empty and endless dark blue all around me.

I'm waving away a small fish from right in front of my face, when I see it. Something drops from above, down through the shaft of light. I squint at it. Our sub moves forward into the glow, and the form drifts past us. And it isn't another craft.

I must be close to losing my mind out here because it takes several seconds for me to understand that I'm looking at Ari.

His eyes are closed and he's not responding. My pulse pounds away in my ears. I can't take my gaze off him. It's only when he grows smaller, and then I can barely see him, I realize the submersible is rising. I spring into action. *Bismillah.*

I let go of the fin and fall back into the deep.

Farther and farther I plunge into the darkest blue, my hands slicing through the waves and my eyes peeled for Ari. *Come on, come on . . .* At this rate I'll find the damn sharks before I do him. My hair isn't helping matters, and I have to keep flicking the long strands out of my vision as I continue on. He's got to be here somewhere.

There. In the middle of the ocean, wearing only his black bottoms and with his dark hair floating around his face, Ari drifts aimlessly. The dolphin is beside him, swimming back and forth. Is it Skye?

I plunge through the water toward Ari just as the dolphin turns and races away. The first thing I do is check his pulse, and I could cry with relief when I feel it. I grab ahold of him, but no matter what I do, he doesn't respond. The water turns murky here and there and I stare at it: blood. I peer closer at Ari and flinch when I see tiny cuts in his skin— several small slashes around his shoulders and back.

They cut him and threw him bleeding and unconscious into the depths, where ravenous sharks await. I hope whoever did this to him chokes.

His own knife isn't in its usual place around his waistband. I lift his black bottoms and his small dagger's still there, tucked into its strap half-way up his leg. The water discolors as blood seeps into the current. Any second now those creatures will smell it.

I try shaking him alert, but nothing. I struggle to move forward without letting go of him. No matter what I attempt, we either sink together or hover there not going anywhere. *Please help him, God.* Somewhere far above is the blasted Blackwatch and somewhere below us circle the horrifying sharks. We really need to get the hell out of here.

I try circling Ari's arm around me before lunging forward and kicking like mad. It doesn't work; his arms hang out to his sides as we fall. I thrash away in the hopes of halting the drop, but only lose my grip on him. *No.* I swivel frantically and feel his head brushing against my foot. Once more

I try and hold on to him. Any moment now the terrifying creatures will surround us. I shake him with energy I no longer have. Nothing.

I open my mouth and scream.

I'm stunned when I hear the sound. My voice carried in the water.

Wrapping my arms around him, I attempt to speak. At first only a stream of bubbles flows out. On my third try, I hear my voice clearly. "Wake up. I beg you, Ari, you have to wake up!"

I think I feel his body jerk against mine, but I can no longer concentrate. My mind's abandoned me. Because a dismal shape stealthily appears in the distance behind Ari.

The shark grows bigger the closer it gets.

I turn my head; there's another one, lower down. And yet another shadowy form heads for us on our left.

I twist to glance behind me, and somewhere in the movement Ari slips from my grasp again. Before I've fully turned, a shark barrels toward me, ramming my waist with its elongated nose. The force... Black spots dot my vision and I double up, breathing hard and fast against the pain. The water spins around me. I straighten and hold up my arms for protection when another one appears beside it, its tiny, glassy eyes rolling around. It bolts toward me. The entire gray-pink, flabby jaw that's tucked below its gigantic snout expands, the flesh almost reaching the end of its flattened nose. It opens wide to reveal teeth like nails. Time stands still. I stop breathing as I stare at the stained, razor-edged peaks. The shark moves in to bite.

And out of the gloom above the creature, Ari emerges and strikes.

He plunges his dagger into the top of its head, burying it up to the hilt. Again and again. The animal spins aside, lashing out at the water, its fleshy jaws snapping away.

Ari stops and hovers there, his chest and shoulders rising and falling as he stares at me. Startled. Dazed. He blinks several times and shakes his head. His eyes suddenly widen and he swings his arm, hurling his dagger in my direction. I flinch as it slices through the water, right into the snout of another shark on my left, the creature's jaw wide and close enough to have taken a bite out of me. My entire body trembles. Ari thrusts forward, his face fierce and eyes blazing as he removes the dagger. The animal spins away. I look around; there are more of them now. It's all too much.

Ari swims toward me, wraps a strong arm around my waist, and holds tight. We hover there, twisting our necks in an attempt to keep the merciless creatures within our sights. The injured two have finally disappeared. The remaining sharks circle us, enjoying the hunt.

My heart beats so loudly now I'm certain they can hear it. Every few minutes, one tries to inch closer but backs away as soon as Ari lashes at the water with his knife. They're not going anywhere, though, and every muscle in my body strains. My mind scrambles for an escape but comes up with nothing. Ari tightens his grip around my waist. He turns to look down at me, his hair floating around his face. Again, his eyes are questioning, stunned. He shakes his head and draws me closer to him.

He opens his mouth. "Are you hurt?"

I startle at the sound of his voice and stare at his lips. I shake my head in reply.

We stiffen and turn when several of the gruesome creatures advance at once. The current grows thick with fear. Ari waves his dagger and I kick and thrash away in panic, but they continue toward us, bold in their numbers. The water churns in all the movement and I try to peer through it, desperate not to lose sight of the sharks. And suddenly they're close enough for me to see right into the yawning gap of a mouth, and I pray nonstop. Just as Ari tucks me into himself and kicks wildly at them, the animals abruptly scatter.

We stare as a submersible comes into view behind the creatures, hitting them repeatedly.

It's Lewis. I cry out with relief. His eyes widen and his mouth falls open as he spies me. Someone moves forward from behind his vessel. Jack Taylor. He swims toward us, calling out to Ari and throwing him a spear. The sharks circle us again, and then lunge at us.

Ari and Jack are a blur of thrusts and spears and muscle as they take on the predatory creatures. It's all blood, snapping jaws, and endless churning.

Lewis continues ramming them with the sub. One of the animals crashes into the small of my back and pain zigzags across my spine. I turn to see Jack pull his spear out of the shark's head before it sinks away. Everything's happening at an unnerving speed. Visibility is reduced. The deep surges against us in all the action, wave after wave, as if protesting the disruption. Ari remains at no more than arm's length from me, constantly twisting his head to check if I'm safe.

At last the dreadful creatures have either fallen or fled and he closes the distance between us, his face dark as he runs his gaze over me. "Are you okay?"

I nod to assure him I'm fine, even though I'm not. I'm not all right with any of this. I'm just holding on. And I can't tear my eyes away from his body. New wounds have joined the earlier cuts and the water immediately around him is thick with blood. My head won't stop shaking at the horror of it all. Maybe it's my whole body trembling—I can't even tell anymore. Exhaustion suddenly washes over me and it's an effort not to just give in and drift away.

"Hurry!" Jack shouts. He grabs the tail of the craft and warns me of the propellers. Ari thanks him.

"Thank Skye," says Jack with a quick smile. "It's her who led us to you."

Ari's expression softens. I can't believe it. It *was* Skye; she actually left to fetch help. What might've happened if she hadn't? I shudder at the thought.

Ari circles an arm around my waist and pulls me to him. He holds me so close I hear the *thud-thudding* of his racing heart as I tremble against him. I look up just as he tilts his head to gaze down on me. His hair swirls around his face and his intense gaze searches mine, mystified. We cling together, desperate and relieved, our free hands grasping a jutting fin beneath the tail.

Lewis checks we're all ready, turns the sub around, and bolts away from it all.

CHAPTER TWENTY

P apa moves his lips, silently reciting prayers over me.

It's midmorning and we're on board the *Kabul*, on the sofas in the saloon. I have my hands wrapped around a cup of tea. Jojo's curled up beside me, refusing to let me out of her sight. It's the longest I've been apart from her and she kept placing a paw on my face for at least an hour after my return. Papa's eyes fill with tears whenever I speak about any of it so I'm trying not to, but it's difficult to avoid when he also keeps asking me questions. I'm familiar with that feeling —he needs to know.

He places a blanket around my shoulders now. I've assured him I'm not cold, but it comforts him. He asks God to protect me from harm, from the authorities. It's been a few hours since I returned, but he still can't believe I'm here, that I survived. I can't believe it myself.

I keep curling my toes against the floor and the sofa, reveling in their solidity, and I can't stop marveling at how easy it is to move my limbs. Every few moments I gulp at the air, greedily sucking it deep inside as if it might run out.

It turns out it was yesterday morning when I left the sub to look for Freya, which means I spent twenty-four hours alone in the deep. I'm trying not to think about that time in the water but it's impossible; it remains so vivid. I can still see, hear, and feel it. The horror of those endless first hours—the pain and sense of suffocation, the relentless darkness, the all-consuming panic when drifting in and out of consciousness, of repeatedly coming around to realize it wasn't a nightmare, that it was really happening and I was still stuck in that void. The not knowing. The constant wondering if I'd ever see anyone again.

I shudder now as the memories claw at me, wrapping their hands around my throat and squeezing tight, and I swiftly take another sip of the warm, sweet tea.

"Are you sure you don't want anything else to eat, Pickle?" Papa asks, his face strained as he rearranges the pillows behind me. The small of my back aches from when the shark rammed into it, and I lean into the cushioning support.

I nod to reassure him. I'm too full to even move.

Freya's fine and safely back home. When she spotted a single, endless tentacle reaching out from beneath the sand where the creature lay in wait, she was frozen to the spot. I dread to think of the outcome had that thing sensed her. Oscar did as I'd instructed, securing and concealing the submarine and contacting Papa. Ari's back home. After the Blackwatch fired on me, they captured him and took him on board their sub where they knocked him out. He lost quite a bit of blood but will be fine. He started losing consciousness on our return, and Lewis dropped me off by the *Kabul* before speeding away with Jack holding on to Ari. Ben and Ruby insisted on him getting home immediately so they could tend to him.

Papa sits beside me and stares into the space. "I was too late in letting you know, and you had to face all that without any idea." He rubs his face. "I will never forgive myself." He sounds numb.

I place my cup down and slip my hand in his. Jojo immediately spots her chance and jumps to settle in my lap. "Tell me about Mama," I say, stroking the puppy's soft curly fur.

He pats my hand, nodding. "You remind me so much of her, Leyla. And this is what she wanted for you. She spoke about it often, hoping you carried the dormant gene and that it would be somehow safely triggered. There was no way of knowing whether you had it. It scared your mother that you might not develop the ability to exist in the water. She worried one day you'd encounter trouble and wouldn't have the means to survive."

Something tugs at me inside. "Was she always an amphi or did she change, too?"

"Soraya was born with the ability to exist underwater." The corners of his mouth curl up a little as he becomes lost in a memory, and the skin around his hazel eyes crinkles. His time inside Broadmoor left him with several premature silver hairs, wrinkles, and even the tiniest hint of a stoop that worsens when he's really worried. "The first time I saw your mama out there, my heart twisted inside my chest. All I felt was fear for her, despite Soraya telling me the world wouldn't flood and crush her." He shakes his head, his face softening further and his smile widening. "She was laughing. She was quite mischievous, your mama, Pickle."

I can't help grinning. A yearning takes ahold, and oh how I wish my mama were alive. I've never felt closer to her. What I wouldn't give to see her face, hear her voice, feel her presence. So many things I don't know about my own mother. "Tell me more, Papa."

"She never let go of something, always pursued it until she had an answer."

I beam at the new insight. "Oh, I love that....A true Virgo, then."

"Oh yes. Eva and I used to tease her constantly about all her attention to detail, the endless lists. You're so very alike."

"Yes." I chuckle. "And Eva?"

"Your mama's friend, Pickle. Eva Gladstone, Edmund Gladstone's sister. They were very close."

All these years, how little I knew about my own mother.

Papa takes my hand and his voice grows serious again. "I had no idea what happened to you. Oscar contacted us and passed on your message. And then silence. Everyone searched high and low, both in the water themselves and via subs, but couldn't find a trace of either Ari or you. And then finally, while Jack was out searching, Ari's pet dolphin found him and was clearly distressed. Jack alerted Lewis and they let the creature guide them to you. That's when we finally knew you were both alive, Pickle." He takes a ragged breath. "Thank God neither of you had drifted too far. If the dolphin hadn't gone looking for help..."

I huddle closer to him, resting my head against his arm and taking in his zesty, herby smell that always instantly calms me. "We're safe now, Papa, and that's all that matters."

"You saved her life—Ben's daughter. And you put an end to the lab's vile weapon. I can't bear to be reminded of what you did; it fills me with terror. But I'm also prouder than I can express, Pickle. You have your mother's resolve."

I squeeze his arm and chew on my lip, pondering the question on my tongue now. Papa's never been in such an open mood, and I desperately need to know.

"What happened to her?" I ask. He tenses immediately. "*Please*, Papa, tell me. What did you mean when you said about Mama doing the right thing? You have to tell me. Did I die when you were taken and imprisoned? No. Did I die when I found myself in the abyss? No. I coped as best I could, and I'll handle this, too. Tell me what I still don't know."

It takes a moment, but at last I feel him nod. "It's your mama's death, Leyla," he says, and I notice the tremble in his hands. "I've always believed there was more to it."

I go rigid. A part of me doesn't want him to go on but an even bigger part hopes he'll finally share everything before he changes his mind. I force my voice out. "How do you mean?"

"They told me the cause remained unknown, and refused to say another word on the matter. Your mama...She didn't pass away in her sleep like I always said. She rushed out after receiving a message. And..." He clears his throat. "She was found dead within hours. The death certificate stated cause of death as 'undisclosed.' But I knew the officers were keeping something from me."

A chill grips me. I shudder against him and he holds me tight. I gulp at the air. It feels like I'm going to run out of it.

"You were so young; the truth would have burdened you then. So I told you she went to heaven as she slept. I was warned from questioning the certificate's accuracy and accused of obstructing the law. They said I would lose custody of you if I pursued the matter. I'd just lost your mother

and I wasn't prepared to lose you, too. I had no choice but to back off."
He pauses to take a breath. "A postmortem report exists somewhere, I'm
certain of it. I looked into it shortly after your sixteenth birthday, knowing
they could no longer threaten to take you away. Unfortunately I must have
triggered a trace, because the very next day Blackwatch stormed our laboratories at Bloomsbury and arrested me..."

I sit back and the room spins around me. I can't even contemplate what
might've really happened to Mama; my mind won't go there. All those
months I felt so desperate and helpless wondering why they'd taken Papa,
worried sick about what the real reason for his arrest could be. Everyone
was told he'd been found helping seasickness sufferers to take their lives.
When in fact all he'd been guilty of was trying to uncover the truth about
his wife's death.

He presses his lips flat, his face growing heavy. "You were barely sixteen when I finally gave in and turned your world upside down because of
it. They took my beloved Soraya, and now I'm afraid for you, little one. If
they find out..."

I rub his arm. "Do you think she was killed because of her identity?"

He nods, his mouth pinched. "I've never had any doubt. But I didn't
know how or what to tell you. I didn't want to scare you. It was a lot for
you to take in. But there was always the possibility, the dormant gene. You
had to know. But once I finally decided to share the truth with you, it was
never the right moment. And then I was too late." He grimaces.

A thousand other questions suddenly burn my throat, but I can see this
is enough for now. His shoulders have stooped and shadows linger in his
expression. I'll ask him more later today, if he feels up to it. We sit together
in silence for a good while, before chatting lightly about other things. When
the screen flashes and I see it's the twins, I'm so grateful for the distraction.

Papa insists on making me some soup and leaves for the galley.

Keeping the worst details to myself, because I hate going over it, I tell
Tabby and Theo what happened to me, and answer a zillion questions.

They keep staring, stunned, and then more intently, as if trying to spot
any visible signs of what I can do now.

"I can't get my head around it," Theo says, his eyes clouded. "You out there, in all that...I can't even picture it."

"Same," says Tabby. "It's just...who'd have thought."

"I'm shocked all over again whenever I think about it," I say. "I guess it's going to take a while to sink in."

Theo looks pensive. "You're even more vulnerable now. They're dead set on locating you for bringing down the lab. They have everyone working on it. And if they catch you again, and discover your identity..." He doesn't finish, and Tabby chews on her lip.

She meets my gaze. "You can't let them find you, Leyla. That slimy git Sebastian and his messed-up cronies are on the rampage."

Theo nods. "They're so obviously lying, and hardly anyone's batting an eyelid. The bloody media are lapping it all up. Oh, and they're still looking into Ari, trying to get ahold of everything they can on him. My mate located a trace right back to Number 10. I reckon they're aware he got away. He really needs to watch his back, Leyla."

I feel like my head's going to burst. "How would they have known he escaped the sharks? Well, we'll just have to make sure they never find us. We're moving in a bit anyway—I'll update you when it's done. We'll be safe where we're headed. We could do with a couple of days' peace, and we need to come up with a solid plan. Papa and I have to work out what we're doing next."

We chat further, mostly about the growing unrest and what might come of it.

Theo rubs his jaw. "What will you do for a submersible now?"

"It's already been sorted. Ben's lent us one. It's like yours, Tabby, a Griffith05 but the twin-seater. So while we're up here at least, I don't need to worry about that."

Tabby nods, approving. She narrows her gaze and the sparkling glint returns. "I know it was dead scary, but you have to admit, it's also flipping awesome. Do you feel powerful?"

Tabby's called away as Theo and I grin. He yawns and I take in his puffy eyes.

"You look tired, Theo."

"You haven't heard?" He runs his fingers through his hair, his expression tightening. "There was another attack yesterday evening, a tiny community in Hastings. Blackwatch had them surrounded and hit them hard." He swallows before carrying on. "Several casualties, and so many injured."

"Oh no . . ." I clasp my hands, squeezing tight as a sour taste settles in my mouth. "And what happens to the survivors now?"

"Bia's taking care of them. The Den have secure locations and Charlie and I were up all night helping sort it. The community's defense measures were inadequate. We discovered them only yesterday morning, and I spent the day planning with Charlie how best to approach and discuss security precautions with them—your granddad's been teaching me the drill. Only last week Bia's lot reached a group of families in Slough mere hours before Blackwatch blasted the area. They saved twelve people in a single morning. But this time . . ." He shakes his head. "After spending all day working on how we might help protect those in Hastings, Charlie told the others at the Den of our plan. But in the end we were just too late. The community came under attack a few hours later."

No wonder Papa seems so preoccupied; I thought it was only because of me. We discuss it some more. It's heartbreaking but I need to hear it.

Theo takes a breath when he's ran through everything in detail, and wrinkles his brow. "And that Jas fella's not exactly helping. Every time Charlie and I put our heads together to work on something, he's there on-screen, hovering in the background. I reckon he's suspicious of me. He needs to lighten up. I'm only trying to help, and your granddad asked me to."

"Sorry, Theo. I think Jas is just like that with everyone and I wouldn't take it personally. They witness a lot of stuff. . . . Must be hell on them."

A thought occurs to me and I wring my hands. I didn't want to tell them until I'd had more time to process it, but I can't unthink the idea now. I repeat what Papa shared about suspecting the official cause of Mama's death.

Theo stares, blinking. "Neptune, I'm so sorry. So *that's* why he was arrested . . ."

I nod. "Theo, do you think you could maybe...I don't know, take a look into it, please? See if you can find the postmortem report? No rush, though, take all the time you need. And only if you know for certain it wouldn't attract any attention. There can't be *any* risk of it linking back to you, I mean it."

His eyes flicker and he straightens. "Absolutely," he says, nodding confidently. "And I'll be careful, promise. I'll message you a list of the details I'll need."

The Navigator materializes and I wrap things up with Theo.

Oscar looks down at me on the sofa, and smiles that small, subdued smile of his. I really wish he were somebody I could hug. Sometimes, like now, I just want to throw my arms around him. He's the absolute best and I wish I'd known the real him.

"Everything all right, Oscar?"

"Indeed it is, my lady. At your command, we are set to go."

Cradling Jojo, I make my way into the viewport. The vessel is stationary, still in Eysturoy. The Navigator joins me and we gaze out into the murky depths.

"Oscar, head straight for the coordinates at Bergen."

The *Kabul* hums into action.

Ari's aunt lives in Bergen, in Norway. She weds in two days' time and has invited us to the ceremony. After the last couple of days, everyone coming together to celebrate something good is exactly what we all need.

We already have permission to travel into Norwegian territory, so that's one less thing to worry about. I stare into the water. An amphi wedding. I'd never even imagined they get married. They— My thoughts scatter as I focus on my use of "they."

You're one of them.

I swallow and wrap my arms around myself. It's difficult to process it. I was outside in that, for all that time. I wasn't crushed and I didn't drown. I breathed and swam through it.

The submarine starts turning. Most of Ari's community will travel to Bergen tomorrow. I'd rather set off now and know we've safely reached the location in plenty of time for the wedding. Besides, I could really do with a break from these waters. Blackwatch don't operate that far and I desperately need a diversion from everything that's happened, if even a brief one.

Papa said I should think about getting back out there as soon as possible, otherwise I could develop a fear of the water after my experience. And that fear is dangerous for us because diving directly into the water might prove our only means for an escape. But I'm not ready to go back out there just yet.

I tilt my head in the Navigator's direction. "I can swim, Oscar—out there. I can breathe underwater. My mama could do it and now so can I. I was out there for hours."

A slight crease forms in his brow. "How did that feel, my dear?"

I peer at the water, rubbing the back of my neck. "It was dreadful. It felt like it was never going to end and I'd be trapped down there forever. But once I realized what had happened to me, and the pain died down, and when there weren't any scary creatures around, it was also miraculous. I mean, I was still petrified the whole time, but I also felt a part of something bigger than me. And there was such a strong connection to others—to Old Worlders." I shrug. "I can't really explain it, but I definitely felt something. It was really sad that they are no longer here. But being so close to the traces of their lives, and the ways they tried to understand and make sense of stuff, I also felt so comforted and heartened."

Oscar fiddles with a silk rose tucked into his waistcoat. "Ah yes, my lady. Terrifying and miraculous are an apt way of putting it. You know"—he cocks his head, fixing his soft gaze on me—"it takes a great deal of courage to see the world in all its tainted glory, and still love it."

"But, Oscar, how did I not know? All these years, how come I didn't realize I might be carrying the dormant gene?"

The Navigator shakes his head and gently waves away my words. "Oh, my dear, only the shallow know themselves."

The *Kabul* speeds up and heads for Norway.

Ari will be at the wedding. I haven't spoken to him since my return.

Warmth radiates through me at the thought, despite my resolve to remain distant from him. I hope he's all right. I can't shake off the image of him drifting unconscious through shark-infested waters.

More calls come in, keeping me busy. Charlie gets in touch from Cambridge. As soon as I'd returned, Papa alerted Gramps to what happened, and Grandpa updated Bia. Charlie heard what happened and is as stunned as the twins were.

"I can't even take it in," he says, concern clouding his eyes. "Sounds like hell." He tilts his head to the side. "And whoa, you really never knew yer mum was one?" He shakes his head. "Can't imagine how scary it must've been for you. Chuffed to see you looking right as rain now. You had me dead worried when I heard!" He leans in. "You want anything, you know where I am, right? Don't mean to scare you, but you wanna watch out for yerself more than ever now. Keep me posted?"

We discuss the attack last night, before Jas beckons him away for something.

Grandpa's next. He wants to know everything that happened. There's fear in the green pools of his eyes, despite him doing his best to hide it from me. He's deathly afraid for me. I say what I can to reassure him, before he's interrupted with a call from Bia and we vow to chat more later.

I was already Britain's number one enemy, along with Papa, but now I'm also different. Now the authorities wouldn't even have to justify their treatment of me.

I take deep breaths and rub my temples.

Getting away from here for a bit, and attending a wedding with Ari, couldn't have come at a better time.

CHAPTER TWENTY-ONE

I t's almost midmorning, on the day of the wedding. The ceremony will be held in the evening.

I pause from reading the Qur'an and throw a glance toward the porthole in my bedroom, tilting my head as I realize something. I never shut the blind last night. And it doesn't bother me. It used to be the first thing I did every evening.

The vessel is stationary high above Bergen, and it's our second day here.

As soon as I've finished reading my surah, I move beside the porthole, gazing into the water lapping the side of the *Kabul*. Papa's in the saloon chatting with Ben. Ari's family arrived last night and are staying somewhere in Bergen. Ben and Papa have a lot to discuss in light of the growing tensions around the country. Ari's much better, his dad assured me. I can't wait to see him today.

Yesterday we had showers fitted in the pool room. Papa hired someone Ben recommended here in Bergen, insisting it's far too inconvenient for me to have to traipse dripping wet to the bathroom after any trip in the water.

Oscar materializes beside me sporting an olive-colored velvet jacket and intricately embroidered shirt. "My lady, I have conducted a survey of the vicinity. There is nothing untoward to report."

"Thanks, Oscar. Wow, you look very dapper."

He nods, his face shining as he places a hand on his chest. "Of course, my dear—looking good and dressing well is a necessity, whereas having a purpose in life is not. And I feel especially compelled to enter into the right spirits for the upcoming nuptials." He smooths down his hair and a gleam enters his eyes. "I take it the gentleman Lewis will be gracing the ceremony with his fine company?"

"What? Oh, I've no idea, sorry, Oscar."

I return my gaze to the water outside. The current seems much calmer here than it is around the Faroe Islands, and there's a green tinge to this part of the Norwegian Sea. I peer into the waves gently lapping away at the circular window. How vastly different things are in Norway.

Non-amphis are entirely aware of their amphi community here.

I was totally stunned when Papa told me, and have been looking into it.

The Old Worlders who lived in this part of Norway relocated farther inland before the disaster. Despite global scientists at the time insisting that moving away from the coast would make *no* difference to anyone's chances of survival—because once the asteroid hit, water levels would rise enough to cover every habitat around the globe—people still fled the sight of the seas. The bulk of Norwegians all settled in the east of the country. When some of the second generation of amphis secretly left Britain in the '50s, a group headed for Norway and settled in the uninhabited west of the country. Nobody knew they were there.

Edmund Gladstone's press conference in the '80s, when he told us about the existence of amphis, sent shock waves throughout the world. Suddenly all nations were on high alert for the terrifying British killers, and sent out their respective armies to search for them. It had been decades since the "Anthropoids" first started living among us, they said, and who knew how wide they had spread. Norway went for a different approach.

Not totally convinced by the "evidence" the British government provided to back up the PM's claims about the violent nature of amphis, Norwegian authorities reacted more prudently. Unlike Britain, and soon after most of the world, they would never preemptively attack them, they insisted. If any were already hiding out in their waters, then as long as they posed no threat to Norwegians—and none had been discovered—they would be left alone. To date there have never been any problems here. Heartened by the country's determination to give them a fair chance, amphi community leaders here contacted the authorities and an agreement was reached. As long as they stayed west and never ventured anywhere near non-amphi communities, Norwegian authorities would leave them alone.

It's so far from what we've been led to believe back in London. We've always been told amphis are enemy number one, everywhere they exist. And it's nowhere near to being free and respected and having equal rights, but I can't deny the relief at knowing we're not actively hunted and murdered *everywhere*. Oh, how low the bar is.... I return my focus to the view outside.

I wish I still had my submersible. I could go out in Ben's, but it doesn't feel the same. I think it would've been pretty cool to race over Bergen. The waters are so calm, so clear here. There really is something magical about the place. I pace my room, arms still wrapped around myself.

I've broken the law countless times, traveled illegally, escaped attacks, hacked into files, and been chased. I've free-fallen into the deep and broken into prison and outraced the Blackwatch. And I should've died when my sub plummeted, when it crushed under the weight of this world. Instead I spent twenty-four hours alone in the abyss.

Back when I first left London, when the *Kabul* crossing the capital's borders sent me into a panic, Ari said I was braver than I think. He's right. I definitely am. I survived all that and more.

And I promised myself I'd never again let fear control my decisions.

I walk into my closet and slip on a long black dress that flares out at the waist.

I head for the saloon and have to suppress a smile when I enter. Poor Oscar. Papa's got him sitting drinking tea with him and Ben, and the Navigator looks more than a little bored. He nods absently at whatever they're saying as he daintily lifts his cup and takes a sip.

I wave to catch Papa's attention. "Sorry, Papa, but I think I might need Oscar for something."

"What for, Pickle? He's happy here with the men!" He turns to the Navigator, gesturing. "Drink, eat, Oscar. Or I will be offended." He pushes the plate toward him.

The Navigator looks on his own tart he already has in his hands and seems perplexed by Papa's words. Poor thing, he has no idea how Pashtun hospitality works.

I turn to Papa. "I'm dipping my toes into the water. You mustn't worry, Papa. I don't need anyone with me. I'll be fine and will remain close to the submarine, promise."

His face relaxes and he nods away approvingly as he and Ben exchange a quick look. "Yes, good idea, Pickle. This is the best place to do that; it's very safe. But still, stay alert."

Jojo's sitting curled up in the viewport, the lazy mutt, totally ignoring her exercise bone. Hopefully she'll be good for Papa while I'm out there. I'm about to turn, when I'm pretty certain the Navigator just threw me a pleading look. Oh dear!

"Papa, I might need Oscar's help."

"Yes, yes. Ensure you have everything you need," he says, turning from something Ben's explaining to him, and nodding at the Navigator to confirm.

Oscar bows respectfully, then hastily places his cup down and joins me.

"Before you go, Leyla," Ben says, and I turn to Ari's dad. "I wanted to thank you in person, too. You saved Freya's life. It doesn't bear thinking what might have happened if you hadn't found her. And it's the second time you saved our son. As for the heinous creature you killed...Neptune alone knows how many lives you've saved, not to mention you were lucky to get away with your own intact. If only they'd had a submarine in Tórshavn, they might've stood a chance against that monstrosity. Everybody's deeply grateful to you."

"Thank you, but I'd truly never have survived the monster if Ari hadn't been there. And I think if Lewis and Jack hadn't shown up when they did, the sharks would've had us...." I shudder as they flash before me. We chat a little more and then I leave the room.

"And how might I aid my lady?" Oscars asks on the way to the pool, looking instantly chirpier.

"Oh, it was nothing, Oscar. You looked really bored in there, that's all. You're actually free to go." I stop and smile at him.

He pauses, before straightening. "My dear, you are as a light in my world."

Oh, he's too much! I love Theo anyway, but I love him even more for giving me Oscar. I know the Navigator isn't real, but he's real enough to me. "Oscar, I'm hugging you in my mind. Right, I must get in the water."

"Of course, my dear. Experience everything! Let nothing be lost upon you."

There are three showers and they look fab. Papa was right; we definitely need them. I rush back out and fetch some towels, toiletries, and a change of clothes, and hang them up, ready.

When the pool door slides open, I stare down at the dark-green water. I look back at my hands, arms, legs. I peer at my skin but there's no sign of my body's changes. None whatsoever. It's astonishing. Taking in deep breaths, I gulp greedily at the air. *Bismillah.*

I dive headfirst into the ocean. *Whoa!* I shudder at the impact—the water's bloody freezing! At any moment my body will adjust to the temperature, but right now it's unbearable. And oh great, I realize I'm holding my breath.

I picture my mama out here. Beautiful, kind Mama. And how she wanted this for me. How she prayed I'd develop this ability so I'd have more of a chance at surviving this world. I release my breath and then, trying not to dwell on it too much, draw a long one in, and out again. I watch as the water flows with such ease you'd think I'd always been able to do this. It's astounding. I shake my head and peer around.

A world of water. An endless expanse of liquid and I'm suspended right at the heart of it. The noise is overwhelming; it's a constant, riotous murmur all around me. I look down at my hands and legs. Nothing feels different when I rub the skin on my neck. The skirt of my dress keeps rising to swirl around my knees, and I really didn't think this through. Next time I'm covering up.

Kicking my legs, I move out from under the *Kabul*'s shadow. The speed with which my body's adapting to the environment is alarming. My eyesight has adjusted remarkably swiftly. I can see clearly for at least twenty meters in every direction. It might not be the upper lighter waters, but thankfully it's also nowhere near as dense and gloomy as the depths I found myself in back at the Faroe Islands. The abyss is a whole world unto itself and I never again want to find myself drifting through it. I no longer feel cold either. The noise is still there, though, the ever pervasive, ceaseless *thrum*. If the water had a heart, I swear it'd be this thrumming sound.

The current is almost a deep jade color, and remains calm. I squint; there's nothing to see at this height. I forgot to do something about my hair, dammit. It floats all around my face, and I have to keep pushing it out of my vision. I accidently flick a tiny red fish and the poor thing swiftly darts away.

I dive until a lengthy pipe comes into view below, stretching through the depths and passing out of sight both ways. I swim closer. It's a rusted brown and I descend a little farther to investigate. The "pipe" is actually the top of a suspension bridge.

Shadowy vertical cables loom into focus. There's a quiver in my stomach as I take in the bridge, the way it reaches across through the current and out of sight. There's something sad about it. Who used it? Where did they go? I peer at a dense part of the cables in the distance; there's a wreck tangled up in them. When I look up, the *Kabul*'s hazy form is barely visible now. I mustn't dip any lower. The wreck catches my eye again and I swim toward it.

It's a small plane, its wings all smashed up. Seaweed fills the cockpit and hangs from the craft. I move closer, around its broken wing, and brush aside some of the slimy plant life blocking the cockpit. Immediately the blur of a sea creature darts out past my face and into the water behind me. I look back after it, but it's already gone. I turn around to the cockpit again, and freeze. The pilot's still inside.

My stomach drops and I can't move. I can't stop staring at the Old Worlder whose plane fell out of the skies a long time ago, and who's now ended up tangled in a bridge that lies at the bottom of the world. The remnants of their clothing are barely discernible, and the body is almost a skeleton. Vividly patterned sea anemones cling to the empty sockets of their eyes.

I move away and, taking care to keep the plane in sight as a point of reference, drift along over the bridge's deck. How many people must've traveled this bridge…It stretches defiantly through the current before me. Sea life darts between the rustic metal of its sides. A small school of silver fish swims alongside the structure before turning to cross it just ahead of me. As it flickers by, the floor of the bridge moves, the grit that's settled there shifting. I pause and narrow my eyes. It's a stonefish, I think; they're always camouflaged as they lie in wait. Sure enough, the enormous lumpy animal materializes from the sand to pounce on the small creatures and swallow a mouthful.

I scan the waves for any Eyeballs, but they look clear. One thing I've noticed since leaving British waters is there aren't nearly as many Eyeballs around anymore. I'm so used to them constantly watching your every move back home in London.

"Leyla…"

I startle when I hear Ari's voice from somewhere behind me, but the shock is instantly replaced with joy. I close my eyes and listen to him as he says my name again, his tone hesitant, curious, but with an unmistakable edge of wonder. It feels miraculous to hear his voice through the water and I'll never get used to it. I turn slowly around, my eyes fluttering open, and lift my gaze. And there he is, dominating the depths before me, several meters away. We stare at each other.

Ari closes the distance between us, his powerful limbs slicing the waves as he propels himself forward until he's floating right in front of me, his eyes flitting all over the sight of me in the water. He shakes his head, his eyes wide and his mouth slack. The corners of his mouth lift and his expression takes my breath away.

His color's returned, thank goodness; there's no sign of the blood loss. He's barefoot and wearing only black bottoms. His beaded necklace hangs around his throat and a dagger around his hips. My eyes scan his body to check his wounds. The gashes he'd received are still visible, but they've been attended to and are now sealed. And apart from several further superficial cuts and small bruises he picked up during the shark attack, he seems all right.

He slowly circles me. His hair swirls around his face, and I can't tear my eyes away from his intense, molten-brown gaze as he returns to pause in front of me. He's so beautiful. He commands even this vast and boundless space.

Long strands of my hair float forward and I swish them away. We can't seem to stop staring at each other as we hover in the waves over the bridge.

I open my mouth and marvel at the sound of my own voice. "How are you feeling?" It's amazing. I'm chatting with someone in the deepest depths. It really is unbelievable.

"I'm good. You?"

"Oh wow." I stare at his mouth as it moves. His voice isn't muffled and I can hear every word as clearly as if we're indoors. "Say something else, Ari."

"I missed you, Leyla McQueen."

I could happily float away. "I missed you, too."

We lock eyes as we hover there. And I realize what that constant *thud-thudding* is since Ari turned up. I can hear his heart. My gaze rests where his heart is, and then travels higher, taking in his full lips, all the honed angles and cryptic grooves of his face, the way his hair sways around him and how the waves cradle him with such grace he appears weightless.

What are you doing? I mustn't let my guard down again.

I quickly swallow and tear my eyes away to point out the surroundings. "So much I need to learn."

He pauses, considering me a moment, before clearing his expression to give a brief nod. "Yes, but I can teach you. Just go easy on yourself, okay? Your whole life you breathed air and now you can take in lungfuls of liquid without choking. With a little time and practice, you'll master it all. I'll show you everything you need to know."

I fidget. "If you're feeling up to it, then do you think I could learn something now?"

He grins and we get to work.

First up, we tackle how to drown out the constant din. It proves much easier than I'd anticipated, and in no time I'm able to tune it out. It's still there, but already it's reduced and muffled. If only I'd known this before falling, it would've made a world of difference. That pounding slipped right inside my head, under my skin, in my veins. I look down now and rub my wrist where my Bracelet should be.

"Leyla, what happened that morning?"

I quickly fill him in, recounting what took place from the moment I found Freya's note to when he joined me in fighting that beast.

He nods slowly. "Oscar told me you'd gone after Freya and I left to find you both. That's when I saw you and the creature. When it came under fire, the force knocked me off balance, and the next time I saw you, Black-watch were there. I watched you fall after they hit you...." He clamps his jaw shut, taking a moment before carrying on. "And then all I recall is a force and I blacked out." His face falls into shadow.

"I hate them so much for what they did to us. God, I still can't believe they actually feed people to sharks..."

"Leyla," he says gently, "what happened after you fell?"

I tell him everything I experienced after the sub was hit. It was the scariest thing ever, but I came through it.

His face darkens and his posture goes rigid.

"I survived, Ari. We're here, right now, so they didn't win."

Every muscle in his face is tense. "You went through all that alone. It should never have happened to you."

I could just hide in his arms. Damn my resolve not to get close to him. I turn away from him. "It shouldn't have, but I can look after myself, Ari."

He falls silent a moment, before continuing. "Yes, you can. It's important you know we don't have an innate sense of the environment out here. And we aren't guaranteed safety from it in any way. We're humans who can breathe underwater, and that's it, Leyla. We have no built-in survival skills for the deep. We're stronger than non-amphis and we've never been known to catch hypothermia, but nothing more. We have to be very careful. Even those of us *born* with the abilities don't venture into the abyss. You're lucky to have made it out...."

He waves his hair out of his face and fixes his gaze on a point between us. I suddenly don't know what to do or say. I only know there's nothing I want more than to close the gap between us. It takes every ounce of will to resist the urge and look away. Bergen better be as safe as everyone says because even now he might be vulnerable around us.

"Hey," I say, desperate to break the sudden awkwardness. "How come you hardly move your arms? Mine are starting to grow tired already."

He watches me closely a second longer, before clearing his expression with a little shrug. "It's okay, we just need to work on your buoyancy control. And not only to save your arms. You need full command of your movements so you don't hurt yourself knocking into things like sharp wreckage and cliff faces. We can practice this now, too, if you feel ready?"

We discuss it a bit more. I'll also need to know how to react when I'm faced with predatory creatures, he tells me. I note he says "when," not "if." I try not to dwell too much on it, and hungry to learn how to be faster, stronger, and safer, I focus everything I have on his instructions.

We spend the next hour working on controlling my buoyancy and basic self-defense moves.

"Okay, great," says Ari. "That's enough for today."

I've managed to perform precise maneuvers that will enable me to dodge anything traveling toward me at speed, and I just swam my fastest lap around the *Kabul*. It's amazing.

A bright-yellow seahorse drifts between us, oblivious and slow. We grin as we watch it move on.

"Do you want to explore a bit?" Ari asks. "There are several abandoned Old World neighborhoods nearby."

I take a moment to consider it, despite the sudden lightness in my chest. "And we definitely wouldn't be going anywhere near the abyss?"

He grimaces. "You shouldn't ever have drifted out that far and deep. No, we never willingly journey to those depths, Leyla—I meant the old city seabed."

A thrill goes through me at the thought of exploring an actual Old World city up close. "And we're safe here?"

"It's a small town on the outskirts of Bergen. Non-amphis are leagues from the place," Ari reassures me.

"Then yes, I'd love to. But I have to let Papa know. If he knew you were with me, he wouldn't worry. He was so keen for me to get back out here so I don't develop a fear of the water. Your dad's with him."

"Yes, I know. It was them who told me you were in the water."

"Was it now." I roll my eyes. They didn't think I could look after myself.

As my gaze catches Ari's necklace, I remember that on top of every-thing else going on he's also had his own recent shock to deal with. "How are you feeling now about . . . you know?"

His hand flies to his necklace. He shutters his gaze as he twists the beads. "I wish I knew more. My dad left no shell unturned at the time and came up with nothing, so I've been thinking I'll have to try something else. Once the wedding is over, I can give it some attention." He looks away into the current.

We hover there, staring silently into the secretive folds of the waves as they roll on around us.

"Because I can't help thinking, Leyla," he adds quietly, "what else I don't yet know about."

CHAPTER TWENTY-TWO

I can't believe I'm going to visit an Old World neighborhood with Ari—that we'll be swimming in and around it. Despite his reassurances, I think it's going to be a while before my first time in the water doesn't shadow every trip. Thankfully the nerves pale against the thrill of knowing I'll be experiencing pre-floods life up close. New places just waiting for me to explore. And how different it'll be when I'm not lost or alone!

"I wonder what we'll see, Ari?"

He waggles his eyebrows. "We're going to swim through an ancient town center, let you see it in person for the first time. And there's at least one place I think you'll really like."

"Let's go!"

We move side by side. The bridge stretches across the deep, blanketed in sea sponge. Tiny varied organisms sway on the current in every shape, color, and pattern. I once read somewhere that some of the sponge in the water is thousands of years old. Thousands! The mind boggles. All the mighty empires and nations that rose and fell above the water, and down here the same little sponge thrived and survived them all.

The brief training has worked wonders already. I no longer feel heavy; my limbs barely even register. We slice our way through the waves until at last Ari indicates we're at the right spot, and we dive. All manner of creatures drift past as we descend. The hazy silhouettes of ancient mountains loom into sight. Lower still and ghostly reminders of Old World life come into view, scattered forever along the seabed.

We pass by a high-rise, sludge and slimy plant life clinging to its many balconies. In Britain, submersibles must keep their distance from Old World buildings, to both protect us and preserve the revered sights. This is the first time I've ever been this close to an ancient high-rise. The rusted frame of a bike remains locked against the railings of a balcony, and on another one a canopy stays lodged in the cramped space. To think they had so much sun they actually sought shade from it! The canopy flaps away, and it takes me a moment to realize something's inside. My pulse quickens as I move closer. It's a stingray, and it's found itself trapped in the fraying canvas. I pull at the end of the pole until finally it dislodges. The creature darts out, its fins frantically oscillating away as it swims on.

I secure the pole and join Ari, who's busy taming a lengthy sheet of plastic. He draws it toward himself before wrapping and securing it around one of the balconies. We move on, diving down to street level. There's so much debris piled up: vehicles and dead trees and pylons and furniture, and parts of buildings that came crashing down. We turn into a narrow, cobbled alley that's mostly intact. Stony buildings loom on either side of us.

"Look, Leyla."

I follow Ari's gaze and spot the bloom of white jellyfish ahead. We slow down, watching them pass gracefully through the street. There are around a dozen of the wispy creatures, all about a foot wide and equally high. They're completely translucent apart from their glowing edges and stomach pouches. They drift silently through the stone alley, filling the space between the ancient buildings.

We turn into a wider street, and at last Ari stops by an imposing structure. Unlike the other buildings in the street, this one's ornate, its carved stonework still visible and its columns defiant.

"I thought you might like this place," he says, and gestures for us to go inside.

The doors hang bent, barely holding on. We swim through the grand archway. A huge, elaborate chandelier lies on the floor, all rusted iron arms and coral. A winding staircase ascends the space, diverging at the top. Ari and I follow the stairs up and a hefty flounder fish darts out of our way. Slithery plant life clings to the banisters, slipping into the water here and there, and the flicker of scales reveals tiny fish grazing away. We turn right and swim through the ghost of an elegant interior before finding ourselves floating over a little balcony. We're inside a theater.

We swim over the boxed space and into a cavernous and imposing hall. Seating and endless boards and other debris drift around us.

"Careful," says Ari, peering into the distance. "There are eels around."

"Ugh." I stay alert.

The grand stage catches my eye. Its curtains are barely hanging, their elaborate fringed edges swaying in the water. I swim to the very front row of seats, the only one still mostly in place, and hover above it. I gaze at the stage and imagine I've come to the theater with Mama and Papa.

We rode here on our bikes. Perhaps through a park. Maybe it was raining. I bet there were birds flying in the sky and some clouds high up above our heads. How would I feel sitting here watching a play set underwater? What would I imagine life in the oceans to be like? Would I think it magical? Or would it make me feel afraid because it's the unknown?

Ari swims toward me, smiling. "Enjoying the show?"

"Ari, how do you think you'd feel about the oceans if you'd been an Old Worlder?"

"I've never considered myself in relation to the Old World."

"Oh."

I look around, taking it all in. A place once full of endless possibilities—whatever you could imagine, in fact. I love it. It's different from Clio House, the enormous reenactment hall back in London. We're allowed to only act out historical events in Clio House, but on these stages Old Worlders explored everything imaginable. . . .

I sense Ari stiffen beside me and his hand moves for his knife. Following his gaze, I look over at the stage, and freeze.

Something glides across it.

My mouth turns sour, and my pulse races. I back away. It looks alien. And suddenly I can *hear* it, too, and oh God, my eardrums feel as if they'll rupture. The sound is like screaming. A shrill faraway screech that surges and ebbs, over and over.

"What *is* that, Ari?"

"I don't know. I've never seen it before." He's poised, ready to defend. "There are countless animals we know nothing about, and some of them prove vicious predators."

Not exactly what I was hoping to hear. I sense a tremor in my legs. It's the creepiest thing I've ever seen. The creature is a pale ghostly color. Its incredibly thin arms and tentacles are so alarmingly long you have to tilt your head up to locate its body. Except there isn't one...only a head. It looks like an insect on multiple stilts. I've never seen any animal like it. The edges of its head sway, wavering in the water. Its tentacles drag across the stage as it moves. Thank God I never came across *this* when I was alone out there! I can't bear it and yet can't look away. The thing floats slowly across the space, thankfully away from us.

"Ari, I think we're done here." I flash him a wobbly smile.

He nods and we kick away, swimming up and out of the theater. Once more we push through the current, passing street after street, schools, parks, hospitals. We swerve to avoid a drifting truck that's come unstuck, and rise to swim over rows of rooftops and chimneys. This morning's practice has truly done wonders. Despite swimming so fast, I don't feel tired at all—my movements are already so much more streamlined. And controlling my buoyancy's made such a difference. The current is calm and still here.

"Sorry about back there." Ari breaks into a rueful grin. "No idea where that thing came from." His face suddenly brightens. "Look."

He points to a dark mass below and I take in the sight as we swim over it. It's a colossal ancient ship, positioned eerily upright.

"It's an Oneraria, Leyla...a freighter of the Roman merchant fleet," says Ari, his voice full of wonder as we drift past it. "I check her out anytime we visit relatives up here. The disaster must have dislodged her from who knows where and the current carried her here. She's only holding up because she's stuck in the ground."

"What? That's from Roman times? *Wow*. I can't believe something from the Roman Empire still exists!"

Astonishingly, a large sail still hangs from a leaning mast, though it's ripped in places and almost see-through.

"Ari, I suppose we can visit any shipwreck?" I say as we leave the vessel behind. "There are so many ancient ones containing endless treasures. A couple of years ago several Americans set out to find the *Merchant Royal*. It sank off the coast of Land's End in 1641. Guess what? It was carrying gold, silver, and jewels that would be worth billions today. Their sub hit trouble and they ran out of air. But we could just explore every ancient wreck, right?"

He shakes his head. "It's too dangerous. Most of them lie in the abyss. And even if we found any, what would we do with ancient treasures? They'd take everything we discovered, right before capturing us."

Any mention of capture really tears my heart up. "I hate them. They're so busy dividing us all, while our world drowns. Maybe one day they might see sense."

"Do you really believe their hearts could be changed?" He pauses to hover before me, his gaze concentrated as he waits for my answer. I almost forget the question.

"Yes, I believe it."

We bob away in the water. Ari nods slowly to himself, before staring into the space. His eyes grow stormy.

"Ari…?"

He shutters his gaze and swallows before replying. "Do you think *they* had a change of heart?" he says quietly, twisting the beads around his neck.

It takes me a moment to realize exactly what he's referring to. I open my mouth and close it again, taken aback. He means his biological family. It's heartbreaking. I've been so wrapped up in everything going on, I'd never stopped to think he might be contemplating such a thing. My chest grows heavy at his words.

"I'm so sorry. I can't imagine how unnerving it might all be. There

could be a thousand reasons why your dad found you alone in the water. . . ."
I feel useless. It's massive news and probably on his mind twenty-four/
seven. I wish I could help him. The look on his face tears my insides. I lean
forward and rest my hand on his arm.

I wonder what he blocked out as a child. He said he couldn't speak
when Ben found him. Whatever he'd witnessed must've been horrific. . . .

His features soften as he holds my gaze. "There's one last— Move!"

He pulls me out of the way as a humongous grouper, easily over a
meter long and equally wide, floats lazily by.

I stare in alarm. The limbs of an octopus wriggle away in its mouth.
When I turn to Ari, eyes wide, he's grinning and shrugs. The creature
drifts on past us.

Ari draws closer again and tilts his head, studying me. A secret smile
plays on his lips.

"Leyla?"

"Yes?"

"Do you trust me?"

My heart races. "I do."

He wraps his arms around me and kicks. We rise.

I twist and turn against him. "Where are we going?"

"It's a surprise."

Oh gosh, why did he have to say that word! It takes all my willpower
not to break away from him with excitement. We ascend the depths and
I'm reminded just how fast Ari is. I hold on to him tightly. The waves
grow bigger and our hair swirls all around us, but still he climbs. We stop
briefly whenever there's something interesting to see. Gradually I realize
the color of the water is starting to lighten. Ari pauses again, indicating
something ahead.

"Over there, Leyla. Ever seen one of those?" I can barely hear him because
he's whispering. I turn and realize why he's speaking with such awe.

I shake my head at the sight of the strange and delicate creature. "No,
never. What is it?" I hold my hair back so nothing obstructs the sight of
the beauty drifting only several feet from us.

It's exquisite. So fluid. It looks like a liquid form slowly, gracefully moving around the water. There's no face, no limbs that I can see, yet you know it's a living thing. As it swirls around, I glimpse a tinge of orange-gold to its skin, and then it's suddenly almost transparent and I can see the slightest hint of its insides.

"They're called *Deepstaria enigmatica*," says Ari. "It's a jellyfish, though it doesn't have any tentacles. They're something special."

"It's unlike anything I've ever seen. It's mesmerizing."

We continue to ascend. The current turns stronger as we enter the higher turbulent waters. I spot ropes and pipes and other signs of energy and power installations, some of them connected all the way up to the surface. We whiz past the most amazing sea trees. They're not the kind hanging high above London. The skeletal frames that hover over the capital are from over three decades ago and the half-dead slimy produce sold down at the markets is the worst. These towering inverted pyramids are abundant with nutritional vegetation, and it's amazing.

The water turns increasingly choppy and we start to sway as we climb. And then my gaze flits across the waves that at some point turned from darkest jade to a glittering, lustrous turquoise. I twist to look in every direction and suck in my breath as I process what I'm seeing.

I wriggle against Ari. "Please stop." I can barely get my voice out.

He pauses, and we hold on to each other in the rougher waves.

My eyes widen as I look around. I suddenly feel light-headed. "Ari…"

He smiles, twisting his head to take in the surrounding sight, and looks back at me. His face shines brilliant and bright.

I shake my head. My heartbeat races, *thud-thudding* away. It's a dream. We're swimming in sunlight.

"The water. The light… Ari."

My whole life I've seen footage of the sun's rays. How they used to fall over the land, how the light reflected on varying surfaces and bodies of water, and how differently it manifested at certain times of the day. Warming, nurturing, illuminating.

Even though we're now deep under the oceans, the sun is still here for us. It literally lights up our world. Where would we be without the solar spheres illuminating the depths? And the closest I've ever been to it is when Ari once took the *Kabul* higher to show me the last of the sunlight as it trickled down through the water. It was much weaker than this because the submarine was lower down than the altitude we're at now, and I watched from inside.

Nothing has ever prepared me for this moment. It's as if I'm in a trance.

I let go of Ari and drift through the luminous waves. I turn in the light dancing on them, lift my arms above my head, and whirl around and around. And oh how I wish everyone could experience this. We need it. All of us. This subtle, arousing presence that revives and reminds us.

We aren't forsaken down here.

I catch Ari watching, and pause. We stare at each other, and I'm suddenly filled with distress at the thought of never being close to him again.

"Leyla, what is it?"

I shake my head.

"Please," he asks softly, searching my face. "You can talk to me." And something inside me crumbles.

"Westminster is really keen on finding out more about you, did you know? They're running all kinds of searches on you, so you need to be really careful. And—Well, you're in even more danger when you're with us…when you're around me. The bounty on our heads is massive, and you're—"

Realization breaks out on his face. "Leyla…Is that why you've been hesitant around me? I thought I was losing my mind." He rubs his face, his eyes wide. "I'm vulnerable all the time, everywhere. It's nothing to do with you. We've *always* been hunted. I'm in no more peril around you than I have been my whole life. You have to believe me."

The last of my resolve drowns. A weight washes away from me, and I swim to Ari.

In what world did I ever think I could stay away from him?

The filtered sunrays streak him, and his skin is all light and shadows, the warmest golden shades and richest browns. He peers out from under thick black lashes flecked with bubbles. I love how his eyes change intensity depending on whether he's in or out of the water, and right now they're two blazing suns brightening up my world. His face ripples with liquid light and my insides flutter. He stares back with the most wondrous expression.

The water laps between us as we bob away. My dress bellows up around me and our hair takes on a life of its own in the tempestuous waves. I close the distance between us and reach out to him.

When our mouths meet, nothing else exists. I forget we're hovering in a world of ocean. I forget everything. There's only here and now, and this beautiful soul that completely out of nowhere came surging into my life. And how I'd be so utterly lost without him now. He was perfect for me before my change. He's perfect for me now. And he'll remain perfect for me no matter what else happens.

Ari cups my face as we kiss, his palms gently brushing my skin. I let go of everything and get lost in him. My fingers rake through his hair as our lips stay pressed together. There's nothing else—only the sweet and fiery taste of him. His hands move from my face to twine his fingers around the length of my hair, and I melt against him. I can *feel* his heart as it beats wildly away. Around and around we twirl in the water as our lips refuse to break the connection. Finally, slowly, we pull apart to gaze into each other's eyes.

There's so much I want to say to him. About his capture, and his time in that tank. About how happy I am that he's back, safe, that he's here with me and it means everything to me. And that no matter what happens now we'll face it together.

I raise my hand and hold it up in front of his chest. Ari looks down on it and his face softens, his hair swirling around it like a cloud. He moves his own hand to match it. We press our palms together. And it's a jolt.

An uncomfortable jolt to my memory.

A blur of confusing images and ominous feelings surface. I shake my head and look at him. His smile wavers. He's squinting as he looks at our hands.

"Ari…" My stomach tenses.

A line appears between his eyebrows as his gaze fixes on our hands. He shakes his head, his eyes clouding. "Leyla…?"

I snatch my hand away and close my eyes to focus on the images crashing into my head. When I reopen them, I see my confusion mirrored in Ari's expression. "My nightmare…Us touching hands seemed to trigger it and so much of it came back to me, and with such clarity. I stood there, a little girl, and outside in the water there was…this *boy*. How did I forget all these years. I blocked it out, blocked *him* out. It was a little boy out there. He looked at me, and…"

Ari blinks repeatedly. Disbelief swirls in the depths of his gaze. He swallows before speaking. "He looked at you and—" He rubs the back of his neck and gives another shake of the head. His voice drops even lower. "And he swam up to your window and placed his hand on it." Ari takes my hand and again presses his own to it. "And you copied him, covering it with your own from the inside. And you smiled. And he smiled. And… we both laughed."

Silence.

"Ari," I finally whisper. "How do you know about *my* nightmare? And why are you saying *we*?"

"Me. I was outside in the water. Leyla, you saw *me*…." His voice is tight and his expression stunned. "I remember now. Water, feeling joy, our hands, and terror."

"You're saying my nightmare is actually a memory? And that our nightmares are of the exact same moment?" I can't stop shaking my head, and he hovers there, his face shadowed with bewilderment. "Ari, I've had the nightmare since I was a little girl, since I was four."

"I must be around five in the flashbacks. Blood. There was blood everywhere, Leyla…"

"Yes, yes. Blood clouding the water. It *did* happen. It *was* you.…We were both there. It's real. It actually happened."

"The visions I've been plagued with since my time in that lab, of something that took place in the water, it was a memory. And my sense of

189

someone watching it unfold . . . it was you. I see you clearly now, all those years ago. I turned around in the water and you were standing on the other side of the window. It was you all along, Leyla."

I can't believe it.

His expression is intense as he continues. "And it has to be linked to when Dad found me. . . . I'm around that age."

I don't know what to think. "We both placed our hands on the window, covering the other's, and maybe that's why whenever we touch hands like that now, it always triggers the memories. Clearly of something we've both repressed . . ."

He wraps his arms around me. "It's okay," he says, though he can't conceal the endless questions in his voice. "We'll find out what it means."

"We're both haunted by the very same moment in our pasts and all this time we never knew."

His eyes are two whirlpools of chaos as he nods, processing everything. His hand flies to his necklace and he twists the beads around. "A long time ago, we already met."

"Yes," I say, hugging myself. "And, Ari, exactly what happened when we did?"

CHAPTER TWENTY-THREE

Bergen is mesmerizing.

Beside me in the submersible Papa twists and turns in an effort to take it all in as we follow the wedding invitation's directions through the evening water toward the ceremony.

I've kept quiet about what I discovered with Ari earlier: that we share a memory of the same moment from years ago. It's not only that Papa would definitely worry, but I can't handle it myself either. Not right now. Ari and I agreed we'd keep it to ourselves until we have more time to make sense of it. We had to return almost as soon as we found out, or we'd be late for the wedding. I really, really want to forget everything for a few hours. It'll still be waiting for me afterward anyway. I straighten in my seat, determined to enjoy my very first amphi ceremony.

We're headed for the station as there aren't enough hatches at the venue hired for the wedding. All guests must park at the station and make the rest of their way via public transport. My pulse races as I process everything I'm seeing.

Bergen is a dense, urban city sprawled across a mountainous landscape. It's full of high-rises and domes, and so much of it is interconnected. See-through tunnels stretch through the deepest-green waves, both just above the seabed and also crisscrossing higher up to connect the looming towers. The place is so vibrant and I love it! Ledges glow with sleek, modern buildings, and ropes bearing phosphorous business signs and directions stretch between rock faces. Lights blink and beam from the homes and the water glows with color and illumination. People are busy with their lives and dart by in submersibles. It's dazzling!

"There, Pickle." Papa points to a lengthy see-through structure that has endless tunnels leading off: the station.

A school of shimmering pink salmon scatters out of my way as I approach one of the countless hatches on the side. I turn my head, and my eyes widen at the sight of someone in the water, casually working away on the hatch next to ours. She wears a bright neon vest and grins and waves over at us before continuing to replace the watertight seal. She has an ease about her I've not seen in a single other amphi. I can't believe it. An entire city of amphis, and all of them living out in the open. Wow, this sight would be unthinkable back in London.

We park the sub, and as we make our way down to the terminal, several people turn to stare at us, causing me to tense. Captain Sebastian declared us Britain's most wanted and had our pictures plastered all over the news. Papa turns to me now, a reassuring look on his face as he shakes his head softly.

"They're admiring your outfit." He smiles.

I glance down at my lehnga. I only wear traditional desi clothes on special occasions because though I adore how they look, I do spend an awful lot of time fiddling with the outfit. This particular lehnga actually belonged to my mama. Papa saved all her traditional occasion wear for me. It's dark purple, and tiny silver sequins twinkle away in the embroidery at the neck of the cropped blouse and in the folds of the skirt.

"Mashallah, look at you, Pickle," Papa says, his hazel eyes bright as we take the stairs. "Your mama would have been so proud." He holds out an arm and I move in close. As soon as I inhale his familiar zesty scent, my shoulders relax. "My two Kabuli perees," he says quietly. "Both fierce in their own soft ways."

Kabuli perees. Papa always refers to Mama and me as his fairies from Kabul.

The wall by the bottom of the stairs is mirrored, and I quickly check my hair to ensure the jewelry's still secure after the trip here. I left the lengthy black strands loose as usual but added a little wave to them today, before decorating them with a full matha patti. The hair jewelry is draped across my hairline at the front and its central piece rests on my forehead. I love desi jewelry so much, and weddings are pretty much the only time I get to wear it. Mama's silver antique kara flashes on my upper arm. I peer closer at myself in the mirror, like I have done countless times since I developed my new abilities, but astonishingly there's no hint of them.

Papa tugs at his elegant burgundy kurta. His hair's grown a little longer, and though it'll be a while before he's once again sporting a head of brown curls, there's finally some semblance of his old self.

We head into the sprawling terminal. It's a vast, open space made up of a transparent shell, and a titanium skeleton that comprises endless supporting columns, walkways, and arches. People rush around to catch their trains. Papa checks our directions again.

The building is a sight I've never witnessed before. In London there are no all-translucent structures. Where the odd roof *is* see-through, the outside environment is concealed by way of projections because people find it unnerving. The only time I ever saw the water through a transparent roof was when Brighton Pier was attacked. The technology at the indoor resort faltered and suddenly we could see the real sea all around us. It was jarring and eerie. But here, while it's still a little ominous—because you can never really know what's out there—it's also exciting. And well, it just feels more *real*.

The shimmering forms of the animals in the well-lit water outside glide over the roof and down the side as they swim obliviously all around us. The huge silhouette of something larger, possibly a whale of some kind, looms in the current above as it drifts lazily over our heads and onward past a block of flats. Wow, the difference some light makes! Not knowing, and resorting to increasingly wilder guesses, is always infinitely worse.

"It's a short train ride, and then the number 57 bus, Pickle," Papa says, swishing away the wedding invitation with its directions.

We follow the instructions hovering around the space and soon we're sitting on our train as it whizzes through the clear tunnel. We stare out when it pauses at a stop. The city is *alive*.

All manner of businesses hover in the depths. A group of restaurants drift around, floating before glowing buildings to attract customers. These larger submersibles are different from the ones back in the capital; they look like the old '40s egg-shaped designs, modified with the latest technologies. Bright beams run all around the vessels, winking away to catch attention. I love it all! Once more the scenery whooshes past us as the train moves on.

"Leyla." Papa indicates our stop.

The station here is much smaller and we head for the No. 57 bus, hopping onto the bulky, cylindrical-shaped sub just in time. I squeeze in by the window even though the sides of the vessel are see-through and I could catch the view from any seat. The bus is full; families and workers and a group of teens all sit in the aisles, engrossed in either conversation or the glimmering graphics before them. Some inspect their calendars, a few check their messages, and others play various games that materialize to hover before them. I look down at my empty wrist. I still haven't replaced my Bracelet after it was damaged in the abyss and have to ask Papa to pass on messages and check in on Oscar. I need to get ahold of another one as soon as I can.

The bus pulls away and movement in the water catches my eye. I stare as a small silver-gray fin whale swims alongside the craft. A child places their hands on the windows, tapping away in an effort to catch the animal's attention. It's heartening to see how comfortable the creatures are here, how casually they venture this close to city life with no signs of panic. The bus swerves around a mountain, and a wide and brightly lit high-rise looms in the depths before us.

I ring the bell for our stop, and the bus parks by one of the hatches on the lower floors.

The venue for Ari's aunt's wedding covers the entire upper floor of the towering block. We take the lift up to the top and exit to moody lights and music, dark lanterns, vivid coral-like plants glittering in pots and planters, and joy and laughter echoing around the place. It's all blissful and soft, and warm smiles everywhere you look. Freya, sporting a black tutu dress, rushes over when she spots us, her face brightening as she wraps me in a hug.

"Neptune, Leyla, you look like a princess! And it's so cool you can swim out there now. You can breathe underwater—you're one of us!" She laughs, bouncing from foot to foot. "Come, my aunt Linde's over there." She leans in to whisper, "I spied the best food ever."

"Excellent," I say, ready to eat for England.

Papa and I move to meet Ari's aunt and her soon-to-be wife.

The place is enormous with arches separating the vast spaces. Each section appears glittery and low lit, and with a dusky sense of magic about it. We pass beautiful bare trees that you'd never guess are man-made. They line the edges of the interior, and tiny red lights hang from their stark, twisted branches. Ravens, crows, and owls sit alert on the empty boughs, staring at the people moving around. You only realize the birds are holographic when you reach out to touch them.

Freya introduces us to the brides.

Back in London most brides wear the traditional green to symbolize nature, to evoke the purity and blessings of the Old World. Some brides feel this is actually an affront to the Old World and prefer the ancient custom of wearing white. But the brides before us now are in glorious, sparkling, inky black, and it makes my heart sing to see it. It reminds me of when Camilla Maxwell, the chief historian's daughter, submitted an original story for publication. We're encouraged to only submit retellings, but she wanted to tell her own story, and even though it was rejected for that reason, it made me so happy. The brides look stunning. Ari's aunt and her fiancée chat with us a bit before other guests arrive and they have to move on.

I look up and spot the moon and stars. The waxy silver-white projections glow away against a midnight-blue sky. In the distance, other planets can be seen.

"Look, Papa."

He tilts his head up, before shaking it and pointing to the glorious, iridescent worlds. "See that one, Pickle, it's wrong. Saturn would be over there, in between those two."

I grin; he just can't help himself. My papa, the eternal astronomer. Ever since we've been able to contact Grandpa safely, they've both gone right back to discussing our universe. The simulated maps they bring up make you wish we could travel the galaxy. Papa had one open the other day and the entire saloon was a vast space of stars.

He spots Ben now and they move aside to chat. I wave at Ruby, who's deep in conversation with others, and the music drowns out her words to me.

"Ruby wants you to know Ari should be here soon." Lewis grins as he joins me, running a hand over his head as usual. The group of girls he's torn himself away from stare after him, eyes shining. He cocks his head at me. "Yer looking dead bonny, Leyla."

"You look fab, too. I think I've only ever seen you in a white T-shirt."

He's wearing a smart black jacket and kilt, and looks totally cool.

Lewis throws back a berry-colored drink and his expression grows serious. "How are you? I still can't believe it. Nearly had a coronary when I saw you in the water. You okay, lassie?"

"I'm all right now, thanks. Any news on your mum?"

As we chat, Kiara, Ari's neighbor, and his cousin Samantha spot us and rush over, and we all catch up. It's fun and feels really great to relax for once, to let go of everything and stop worrying. If the twins were here, too, it'd be perfect. The girls are thrilled I can swim out there. Just as they want to know exactly how it happened, a bell thankfully rings to indicate it's time for the nuptials.

Edgar Allan Poe, an Old Worlder who Linde and her fiancée adore, materializes to recite a melancholic poem. There are solo musical performances; Kiara's piano glimmers in the space as she plays a stunning, dramatic piece. I lift my gaze and my breath catches when it meets Ari's.

He's standing across from me, towering and beautiful, and watching me thoughtfully. I stare back, unblinking. His eyes flicker when I smile, affection softening his expression. It's impossible to look away, impossible not to recall our closeness in the water only a couple of hours ago.

He flicks back his hair. He's had a haircut and the black waves hang down to his shoulders like they used to. Though he's dressed in his perennial black, it's nothing like he normally wears. It's a long formal robe, with silver embroidery adorning the edges and collar. We don't stop staring at each other. My face warms, and I return my focus to the ceremony.

As soon as the brides have pledged their love for each other, we all pass under an archway into another equally large space where tables are laid ready for a feast. The food matches the color scheme and it's all dark reds, purples, and black. Even if it were stark white, though, I'd still ensure I tried everything. I find myself sitting between Kiara and Samantha; Ari's at another table with his parents, closer to the brides' table. The food is delicious and I lose myself in chatter and scrumptious tastes.

When I return from the bathroom afterward, everyone's making their way to the expansive windows. I locate a quieter spot with a great view of the outside. A shoulder lightly brushes mine, and I know it's Ari. My stomach flutters as I turn to him.

"You look breathtaking," he says softly, his bright eyes taking me in.

"So do you."

His mouth twitches and, wow, he looks so beautiful I have to tear my gaze away.

Only as we turn to the view do I fully appreciate how stunning the place is. A whole world lies not just lower down, but on our level, too. Bright beams shine up from every ledge and rooftop. The waters arc lit up to reveal a comforting green instead of the cloaked depths around the Faroe Islands. Here, there's nothing to be afraid of. Nothing unknown that might be hovering, waiting.

Several towering blocks similar to the one we're in surround us, and mountains lie to our right. The water is so well lit we can see homes on the ledges all the way from here. Submersibles of all kinds, private and business, drive through the current, their beams further highlighting the endless banners and signs as they expertly duck under and around them. I can even spot people walking through the transparent tunnels. And the place is so clean. Despite the efforts of several amazing volunteer groups back in London, chiefly Keep Great Britain Tidy, we've hardly made a dent in the capital's debris. But here…wow, it's the cleanest city I've ever set eyes on. I love it all.

How I wish London were more like Bergen. That there was no *Today's Terrors of the Deep*, or Wireless Man and his monotonous tone reminding us every minute of the horrors out there, or the endless projections that hide the ocean from us. That we felt safer. There's a sense of *home* about this place, and it's so moving to witness.

Someone beckons to us, and Ari and I realize we're not in view of whatever we're here to see. We hurry to where everyone else is standing watching on the other side, and gaze out. This side of the building looks out on more mountainous landscape. The water turns abruptly dark as all exterior lights dim. Everyone hushes when music sounds around the place.

Huge three-dimensional geometrical shapes, in a deep scarlet shade and glowing in the gloom, lower from above to hover before us. They look almost like spheres except they're made up of countless pentagonal shapes all fitting together. They're opaque and so delicate looking they appear made from paper. I definitely want to make one. I usually only stick to animals and people with my origami, but I'd love to try and replicate one of the exquisite shapes before us. They're decorated with intricate swirls in a fiery-gold color. The music hums away, soft and beguiling notes that rise into a crescendo, and we all let out a hushed gasp as the shapes open up and fall away to reveal dancers.

A red glow surrounds each person. They perform a dance for us and they're mesmerizing to watch. They're all poised and graceful and nobody can take their eyes off them. Their hair floats in the water around their faces, and everyone wears the most exquisite gowns in glittering, vivid shades of red and purple and shimmering black. Lengthy trains of wispy material and endless ribbons trail from the gowns to swirl around the dancers, adding to the motion as they move their limbs so effortlessly. They look like fairies! I can't tear my eyes away. It reminds me a little of Persian dancing, the mystic styles, but with more ballet. I wish Theo and Tabby were here to see it. At last they take a bow before us, and dive out of sight.

There's movement in front of the windows and only now do I see that the brides watched it all from out there, arms wrapped around each other. Wearing huge smiles, they swim up before us, waving and blowing kisses at us, and we all cheer and clap. They drift away toward a cliff edge cloaked in shadow. The spot lights up, brilliant and bright, revealing a bridge made from wooden planks and with ropes for sides. It links to another rocky ledge some distance away. Lamps hang all along the ropes, effusing a soft, honey-orange glow in the darkness.

I slip my hand in Ari's. If Papa spots me, I think I might die from embarrassment. We haven't talked about boys yet, but I have a feeling anything like dating will be supervised. I don't actually know because it's simply never come up! But I really, really like Ari, and holding his hand just doesn't seem wrong. He immediately squeezes it.

The brides, too, are holding hands while grabbing onto the sides of the bridge. They begin making their way across it. There's a collective intake of breaths as confetti drifts down on the couple from submersibles well out of sight. The multicolored bubbles shower them and it's so beautiful, specks of every color drifting down over the newlyweds. A small school of tiny fish is attracted to the sight and moves closer to investigate, swimming behind the couple as they cross the glowing bridge. The brides reach the other side and wave once more before the area is plunged into darkness again.

Fireworks light up the depths. The beams whiz and flash and form every shape and pattern, the vivid colors illuminating the entire city below in time to music playing inside. I'm almost bouncing on my toes now—I love it all. The display dies down and the room erupts into cheers as we move away from the windows. I'm buzzing with joy. Back in London, the closest we've come to including the environment in our celebrations is the acts they put on during the opening ceremony of the London Marathon. Nobody ever does anything outside during private celebrations, though. While we can't get into the waters, we could definitely use vessels and technology more when commemorating important moments!

Dance music sounds and the expansive room is transformed as lights and lasers stretch and pulse through it, and projections add to the magic. There are dark birds and glittery butterflies, silver stars and sparkling snowflakes. I feel light-headed; it's all so enchanting. Samantha and Kiara and Lewis rush to the dance floor and let go. Almost immediately everyone flocks to do the same. The music thumps its way around the space, in the walls, through the floor. It's vibrant and freeing and it's alive!

Papa finds me to let me know he's returning to the *Kabul*. He covers his ears and shouts, shaking his head repeatedly much to everyone's amusement. Ari offers to take him back, but Ben's already sorted out a lift and insists on dropping Papa off before returning to their hotel with Freya, who looks ready to nod off.

It's a relief watching Ari and his dad interact like they used to before Ari discovered more about how Ben found him. I think Ari's slowly getting over the shock. I wonder what he might dig up once he begins looking into things after the wedding. . . . Why was he all alone when Ben found him? And how is he connected to me? What on earth is our shared memory all about?

I promise Papa I'll be extra careful getting back to the sub after it's all over, and they leave.

I turn to find Ari staring at those dancing. I grab his hand before he can protest and hasten toward the others. He breaks into the widest grin and we dance and dance and dance. And it feels like heaven to lose myself in it all. To not even *think* about anything else but this moment right here and now.

When we grow tired, Ari and I wander away from the dance floor and search for a quieter spot in the adjacent space, drinks in hand. There are all kinds of interesting themed places to sit, and my eyes are drawn to a little Old World setting in the corner. It's a Victorian street complete with a row of homes all lit up in the evening, and an iron bench beneath a glowing lamppost. It's surrounded by more of the bare trees I saw earlier, and a light shower patters over the scene, causing the cobbled ground to glisten. The projected homes and rain are so realistic we stare at first. It reminds me of *Ripper's Revels*, the Victorian-era game I always played with Theo and Tabby in their Holozone.

We sit on the bench looking out at the street, the soft radiance of the lamppost falling around us as we sip our drinks in silence. When we've quenched our thirst, I edge along the bench until we're close enough to be touching.

"I'm glad it didn't ruin the wedding for you," Ari says softly, referring to what we discovered earlier. "You've been through so much, and watching you smile, laugh, and dance tonight…" His cheeks turn russet-brown and his eyes sparkle.

"I've loved it. Catching up with everyone, the ceremony itself, all the dancing. You…" We gaze at each other and the "rain" falls silently around Ari and, oh, technology is amazing. Even though I hate it because it hates me. "It feels great to take a break from all the worrying for once, even if only for an evening. And you? How are you feeling?"

He falls silent, his eyes flitting across the cobbled street. I lean in and squeeze his arm.

Ari scratches his jaw and fixes his gaze on the rooftops in the distance. "It's constantly on my mind…the fact that Dad found me like that. I want to know everything about myself, my past."

"I saw you with your mum when we were eating. Have you been discussing it with them?"

He's lost in thought a moment, before speaking. "All these questions play on my mind now and won't leave me alone." He blinks and suddenly breaks into a smile, turning to me as he remembers something. "Here." He reaches into his robes and holds out a Bracelet. "It's like your other one. I asked Theo to send over the same specs as soon as I'd recovered."

"Oh wow, I've been feeling lost without one. Thank you." I take the silver band, snap it into place on my wrist, and switch it on. "How do amphi communities send one another things? Do you have your own Royal Mail equivalent?" I'm half kidding, but he smiles secretly.

"Who has freedom to roam anywhere as soon as they graduate a certain program?"

"No way?" I grin. "Some amphis train for Explorer status just so they can run their own postal service?" He nods and we laugh. "How do you get past the tests?"

"There are ways." His gaze rests on my lehnga and when our eyes lock, we exchange quiet smiles.

"It used to be my ma—" I jump and our gazes dart to the Victorian street in front of us.

I peer ahead, frowning. "Oscar?"

The Navigator flickers in and out of vision in the middle of the cobbled street. I turn to Ari, confused, and he's staring at him equally bewildered. I look down at my new Bracelet and tap it several times. At last Oscar materializes closer to us, though he's still not stable.

I turn to Ari. "Just teething problems. I hate technology!" I try again. "Oscar, everything all right with the *Kabul*? Did Papa get back safely?"

The Navigator flickers several times until he's a lot clearer, and speaks. "Oh, bloody hell, please let this work. Leyla, are you there? Are you getting this? I can't contact Tabs because they've got a tracer on our place."

Panic rises up inside to settle sour in my mouth. The voice is Oscar's but the words definitely aren't. "*Theo?*"

We stare at the Navigator's glimmering projection.

"Are you getting this message, Leyla? If you can hear me, you need to tell your granddad to contact Mum and Tabs right away and tell them they're being watched!"

"Oh my God, Ari, it *is* Theo! He's trying to reach us through the Navigator! Why? Where is he? Theo, can you hear me?"

"Leyla, I've been detained. I just hope Oscar's getting this message. It's my only option. They took my Bracelet, but I've managed to hack into the *Kabul*'s system through a guard's Bracelet and the interface here. Hope you're wearing your new Bracelet already and hearing this. Neptune, I'm running out of time! I *really* didn't want to tell you like this but your dad was right, Leyla—there's more to your mum's death. I found the report. Your mum had cuts and burns. The cause was laser weapon—"

Oscar freezes. His hologram becomes static still.

My pulse races and my face goes all hot. The thought of Mama being attacked, of her being injured and in pain...I can't focus. Except I have to. *Theo.* He needs help. I start shaking.

"Lewis might be able to help with Oscar," Ari says, his expression heavy as he rushes to fetch him.

I pace the cobbled street, tapping away at my Bracelet, but Oscar remains frozen. They have Theo. I clutch my stomach; it's like Papa's arrest all over again. Searching for the report must've triggered a trace, just like it did when Papa tried. And Tabs and his mum aren't safe either. They need to be warned immediately.

I can't even process what he said about Mama.

Ari returns with Lewis, who takes my Bracelet, inspects it, and frowns. "Try rebooting it. Need me to contact anyone? If they have yer mate, then he's right about them watching his home."

I initiate a reboot instantly. "Oh God," I say, as we wait for the Bracelet to start up again. "We've been here for hours. Who knows how long Theo's been trying to contact me?"

Ari rubs his jaw. "We can send someone to pick up his family and get them out of there." He exchanges looks with Lewis, who nods in agreement, before returning his attention to me. "I can vouch for the sub we send, and will ensure it sets off right away. Let me know."

I squeeze Ari's arm. The Bracelet starts up without a hitch.

"Oscar?" *Please work.*

"My lady?" The Navigator appears and there's no hint of a glimmer, thank goodness.

He has no message for me from Theo, and no recollection of the hacking. He assures me the submarine is safe. All right, I must try and focus now.

First, we need to do something about Theo. I call Grandpa and he answers instantly. He sets to work while we're still telling him what's happened, jabbing away at files in his study and exchanging messages even as we speak.

"We'll get to the bottom of this, Queenie," he says, though his voice can't conceal his concern. "We'll have Terence's boy out of that place." When he hears what Theo discovered about Mama, he flinches. He stares at me, his expression pained and distant. His Bracelet buzzes and he shakes himself alert. Grandpa's voice is flat as he reads the message. "They just set a bail hearing for tomorrow. I doubt very much they intend on letting Vivian know."

They'd actually try to keep this from the twins' mother? "How dare they, Gramps. Have you passed Theo's message on to Tabs and his mum?"

He shakes his head. "If Theo says there's a tracer at work, then there's no way to message them safely. But you mustn't worry, someone's already on their way over to inform them in person. I suspect his family isn't even aware of Theo's arrest."

"Gramps, do you think bail will be granted?"

Theo promised he'd only ever look into the report as long as it wouldn't lead back to him, but still I wish I could rewind things. I wish I'd never asked him.

After exchanging several more messages with others, Grandpa turns to us. "Listen to me. You mustn't contact the Campbells; the tracer will pick it up and all hope of helping them will be dashed. We have subs at the ready should Theo be released on bail. I've alerted Bia, and Charlie is sorting things out on that end. If the Campbells need it, Bia's willing to send protection from Cambridge. Queenie, sit tight and wait to hear back from me, and try not to worry. Right, I must speak to Hashem now."

I nod. "And, Grandpa? Please wait a few minutes before you contact Papa. I need to first tell him what Theo found out about Mama. He needs to hear it from me."

Grandpa grimaces; he rubs his eyes and lets out a long sigh. "Let me know when you're done, Queenie."

I move by the huge window and call Papa. He stares, blinking and dazed, when I repeat Theo's words.

"You were right, Papa. Something did happen, and they covered it up."

He shakes his head, a stunned pain shadowing his face. "All these years...All these years I'd hoped, I'd prayed it wouldn't be something like this. That she hadn't suffered as much as I feared. They never let me see my Soraya's body."

Tears glisten in his eyes, and my own prickle with them, too. A shudder runs through me. Mama's last moments in this world were most likely painful and terrifying. God knows what she went through as her life was snatched from her.

"I'll be there soon, Papa," I say. "We're setting off any minute."

He nods absently. I end the call and let Grandpa know he's free to talk to Papa before hurrying back to Ari and Lewis, who stand speaking in hushed tones under the streetlamp.

"Nobody must find out," I say. "Even innocently, they could ruin whatever Gramps comes up with for tomorrow. I just hope they don't cancel Theo's bail hearing. Oh no, if they find out he contacted us by hacking into their systems, who knows how they might punish him." The thought of them hurting sweet and gentle Theo is just too much now.

Ari shakes his head. "Nobody will hear anything from us."

Lewis receives a message of his own and leaves.

"I need to get back to Papa," I say to Ari. "I want to be with him."

He narrows his eyes as he watches me and gestures to the bench. "You're trembling, Leyla," he says. "Take a moment before you head out?"

When we sit, he takes my hands in his. "If whatever your grandfather plans doesn't work, I'll go down there myself and find Theo. We won't let them hurt your friend." His eyes simmer under the glow of the lamppost. "They won't get away with this."

I shake my head. "You're not going down to London, Ari. They're not getting their hands on you again." I sigh and it comes out as a shudder.

Please, God, let Theo be safe.

In the short time since Papa shared his suspicions about Mama's death, I'd hoped and prayed so hard her passing away had still been as easy as possible on her. Except there's nothing peaceful or natural about lasers blasting your body.

"How much longer is this going to go on?" I whisper. "How many people have to go missing, rot away in prisons without trial, take their own lives in despair? They can't do this to us. They're meant to lead and protect us, do right by us. It's their *job*. How many more will meet a violent end at their hands?" My voice breaks and I swallow past the ache in my throat.

Ari moves closer to wrap his arms around me.

"Something *has* to change," I say, my words muffled in his shoulder. "And we need answers. They will not continue to get away with what they've done."

CHAPTER TWENTY-FOUR

I t's late afternoon and I'm in the galley making tea.

We're still stationary above Bergen. It's been two days since the wedding and so much has happened since. We can't move away just yet, not until we know what's going on.

The Campbells are missing. Theo, Tabby, and Vivian, their mother.

When Gramps turned up to Theo's bail hearing with Vivian, Theo was begrudgingly let go under several conditions—one of them being he mustn't leave London. Except, after having witnessed the shoddy but very serious evidence and charges against Theo, Gramps knew he had to get him out of the capital immediately before he likely ended up missing like Papa and so many others. Grandpa and Bia had anticipated the bail conditions and taken steps to ensure they could still help the Campbells. Shortly after Theo got home yesterday, he, Tabby, and Vivian secretly left in one of Bia's largest, high-speed submersibles. They'd been informed of our location here in Bergen and were on their way to us. In the evening, Grandpa received an emergency message from Theo: Their sub had been ambushed. Someone had lain in wait for them. Theo said he was going off grid for their own safety, and nobody's heard from them since.

I have to believe they're all right, that they made it past whoever attacked them and that Theo's simply off radar as he said he'd be. Bia has subs scouring the water for them, but there's no sign of them out there. It's an effort not to jump into the submersible and go searching for them myself, which doesn't make sense at all because nobody's more skilled and experienced at that than Bia and her people.

Who ambushed the Campbells? How did they discover Grandpa's plans to get the family out of the country? He kept it very quiet. Someone might be tapping into our systems, Lewis said, despite whatever Theo's put in place here. Or maybe they're listening in on Grandpa. So many questions. The main ones being: Where are the Campbells right now, and are they safe? I should never have asked Theo to look into Mama's death. I was wrong, and he's already paid so heavily for trying to help me. All I can do now is hope and pray things don't get worse for them.

There's some good news among all the unease. Lewis's mother is out of Broadmoor. Maud McGregor's shift ended yesterday and Lewis brought her straight to the *Kabul* so she could update Papa, Ben, and everyone in Cambridge, all at once. While she was inside that hellhole for a prison, she helped me big time with rescuing Papa; thank God she's got out herself before she was rumbled.

I return to the saloon and place a tea tray beside Papa.

He has one eye on the files glimmering before him, and another on the screen where the news is on. It's been relentless lately. Every channel is reporting only amphi-related news now, and not one of the stories is from our perspective.

There was an attack on a family spotted in the water in Cardiff yesterday, and it was horrific. It's led to some uncontrollable situations in the communities. Several individuals who've had enough have started randomly striking places. Last night in Oxford, one of them got into a large sub and launched an attack on the regional Anthropoid Watch Council offices. And from glancing at the government spokesperson on-screen now, it's clear the authorities are incensed by the assault. Security's been tightened at all AWC offices around the country. Hopefully the twins will manage to dodge the increased patrols out there.

There's currently only Papa and me on board the *Kabul*. He's constantly in touch with others around the country, trying to make sense of the growing unrest and advocating for calm and rational action ahead.

He's also liaising with Charlie to ensure the communities Papa used to aid down south are kept up to date with what's going on and remain safe.

I haven't been back in the water since exploring the area with Ari on the day of the wedding. All I can think about right now is whether Theo and Tabby and their mother are all right.

Papa and I have chatted more about Mama in the last two days than in all the previous years combined, I think. He always found it too painful and struggled with talking about her, not knowing if his suspicions around her death were correct or not. And though there's so much we still don't know, having his doubts confirmed, and the fact that I also now know, has unleashed a tsunami of memories. And I've loved hearing every one of them.

"Tea, Papa."

He nods absently as he goes through files displaying the latest updates from the engine room. I haven't been in there since he recovered. He insists on sharing some of the running of the sub and I'm more than happy with that. I much prefer keeping an eye on things in the control room instead. He glances again at the screen as the news reports another amphi attack in the last hour. This time they hit the security base at Saddle Bow.

Jojo follows me out of the saloon and into my bedroom where she plays by the porthole.

I say my prayers and am rolling up the prayer mat when Oscar appears.

"My lady, there appears to be a hostile vessel in the vicinity. A security sub, around a league away. Might I propose a firing shot? Nothing too dramatic, of course—though I do find it's important to remain earnest in such matters. Merely a—"

"We'll do no such thing, Oscar."

I groan at the news of a security sub. As if we don't have enough going on already. What are the British authorities doing in Norwegian waters? And in such close proximity to the *Kabul*? It can't be a coincidence.

My Bracelet flashes. "Leyla! We're so bloody close, but we came under attack earlier from border patrol and the sub's acting up!"

"Theo? You're all right! Oh, thank God!" Tears prickle my eyes. "Wait, what? Where are you?"

"We've not long been back online after leaving British waters. They realized we're using a security sub to get away and hit us when we couldn't produce papers. We were lucky to get this far after that. I'm having trouble stabilizing her now! Anyone around to help?"

"Give me your coordinates!"

"Oscar," I say, as soon as we know the Campbells' exact whereabouts. "That security sub you mentioned is friendly! Get the *Kabul* to this spot at once. Theo and Tabby are in trouble and need our help!"

The Navigator nods and the submarine turns around and speeds south.

I rush into the saloon just as Papa's about to exit it.

"Pickle, why are we racing in—"

"Papa, Theo's here! They're somewhere nearby, but I need to get out there because they're in trouble." We hasten down the winding staircase.

"Alhamdulillah," he says, thanking God as he lets out a huge breath. He jabs away at his Bracelet as we rush toward the pool room. "What kind of trouble? Will you need help?"

"No idea until I check their sub," I say, taking off my socks and Bracelet and straightening. "I'll hopefully be able to sort it, but if not, then I'll return and we can ask for help."

He looks sheepish. "Yes, let me know, Pickle, but still I've just alerted Ben—"

"Papa!"

I turn to the Navigator and raise my eyebrows, waiting.

"Any moment now, my dear," he says. "And…this is the spot. Some hundred feet below."

The *Kabul* slows down and I rush through the pool room.

"Drop fifty feet, Oscar."

The Navigator nods and we descend.

I barely feel the temperature of the water this time, and as I plunge through the depths my body adjusts within seconds. I dive, propelling myself on as fast as I can. Thank God the waters are so much clearer around here. There's no sign of them, and I'm pretty certain I've covered more than fifty feet. I keep diving until finally the seabed comes into view.

It's an abandoned area. I circle the spot, keeping my eyes peeled. At last I locate a hazy shape and the faint glow of lights. It's quite daunting swimming toward a security sub as opposed to racing away from one!

When I draw near, I see it's a hefty model, one of the larger sizes, and they're grounded. Finally I'm close enough to see the problem: The vessel's tail has become trapped in an old industrial-sized fishing net that's stuck to the seabed. I swim around the robust craft to the front. My heart lifts at the sight that greets me and it's all I can do not to thrash at the water with joy.

Tabby's peering through the sub's window, looking the other way. It really is them!

"Tabby!" I plunge toward her. Vivian, their mother, is beside her and I wave at them, grinning like mad. Oh my gosh, wait until they spot me!

Vivian starts screaming. Tabby's eyes widen when she sees me, and she stares, stunned.

Oh! "Hey, it's only me, you daft cow," I sign.

Theo comes up behind his mother and sister, panic in his expression and a tool in his hand. His mouth falls open when our eyes meet. And I remember.

I recall the shock of seeing Ari in the water for the first time. Seeing Ari as what we've always been led to believe is the most evil creation ever—a human that can breathe underwater.

Theo turns to his sister and mother, saying something as he gestures to me. Tabby frowns and comes closer, peering hard at me. And then her expression clears, her mouth an O shape. Vivian stops screaming but remains looking very unsure.

"I'm sorry," says Theo, signing back. "They didn't recognize you. You're actually the very first amphi we've ever seen with our own eyes. Wow, Leyla, look at you!" He shakes his head, his smile wide and warm. I could hug him to bits. His expression turns somber. "The sub started spinning and we lost altitude. I managed to bring her down intact, but I think the tail's caught something."

I nod. "The rear fin's stuck in a massive net, but I'm going to try and clear it."

"Thanks, Leyla. No rush but we're running a tad low on oxygen."

"We're one hundred percent about to die!" says Tabby.

Oh how I'd missed them!

I race back to the tail end and try my hardest to clear the fin of the net. If only I had a knife. I fumble away with the tough ropes, pulling them until my hands turn sore. When that fails, I push against the tail as hard as I can in the hopes of dislodging the fin. It barely moves. Where are my powers, dammit—I thought I was supposed to have increased body strength now!

"It's okay, Leyla, I've got it."

I turn to see Ari swimming toward me and instantly relax; he's the most welcome sight.

"Are you hurt?" he asks as he plunges through the remaining distance to hover beside me. He takes out his knife and hacks away at the rope.

I shake my head. "I'm glad to see you. They're running a bit low on oxygen, and I was just thinking I'll have to race back to the sub and grab a knife for the net. Did your dad tell you?"

He nods, leaning in to inspect the tail, and then continues to slash away at the net until the fin comes free. He disappears to the front of the vessel.

"Ari, wait, they—"

He immediately heads back. "I think I've upset their mother."

Oh dear. I take Ari's hand and we move to the front of the sub. Vivian is beside herself, refusing to calm down. I tell the twins the vessel's good to go.

Tabby's piercing blue eyes glitter as she watches us, smiling. "Nice." She winks at me. "Gravity defying. Oh, the stuff you could get up to in—"

My eyes widen. "Tabs, Ari speaks sign."

"Oops," she says, looking not at all remorseful.

Ari gestures to the Campbells to follow us and we all head back to the *Kabul*. He swims incredibly fast, taking me along with him, and I love it.

We swim up through the pool and quickly head for the showers.

When I'm done, they're all hovering outside the room, still greeting one another. Jojo's gone wild and is leaping around everyone with joy. Tabby and Theo rush to embrace me when I exit the room and all three of us become teary.

So much has happened since we last hugged like this. Back then, we were saying our goodbyes before I left the city for the first time in my life in some wild hope of finding Papa. If it hadn't been for the twins, I'd never have been ready to leave in time. Blackwatch were shadowing me, and my flat had been turned upside down. There was so much uncertainty and fear. And so much to do. But they helped me with everything. And back then, amphis were the worst thing we could think of.

A lot has happened since. So much has already changed. *We've* changed.

As soon as we've all greeted one another, the Campbells go to freshen up. I can't find Ari. I scatter all the cushions in the viewport to make a comfy seating area. Oscar brings up the little fire again, and I'm wondering what to do about food—it's early evening now—when Vivian enters the saloon. The twins' mother makes her way over to the viewport, looking around and marveling at everything.

"Remarkable. You turned it into a warm and inviting home and I'm delighted for you, dear. Bless you, you've suffered far more than anyone your age should." Vivian's a copy of her children—the same blue eyes, whitest skin, and platinum-blond hair.

I pull a face. "It's definitely been a lot at times."

She nods, pressing her lips together. "I can't apologize enough for my reaction earlier, love," she says, her cheeks turning pink as she twists her pearls. "It—it was just alarming seeing you like that, you know? But I'm so sorry for screaming, sweetheart." She clears her throat. "Terence, he was much better at this than I am. Apparently he was even helping your—you—I mean your kind. I had no idea. I think he knew I wouldn't have coped very well. I mean, we've always been taught to be *afraid* of the Anthro—"

"Amphis. And it's all right, Viv. You've been through a lot."

"Amphis, of course. Sorry, love. Theo keeps correcting me but it's going to take some getting used to. I don't know.... First Hashem's disappearance, then you left, and then, heavens—you were 'public enemy number one!' We were all so worried about you. The twins couldn't sleep! And then they took my Theo...." Her chin quivers. "But you did it, you clever girl. You found your wonderful father."

"Thank God you all got away after the attack. I still can't believe you're here."

"All thanks to Theo. He hid. Then he shut down every system that could be used to trace us. Though of course that did leave us feeling terribly alone. He worked his magic and even managed to override the Traffic Ordinance Council's systems. And then we headed here full speed." She shudders as she recalls something. "The skirmish at the border played havoc with my remaining nerves." Vivian tilts her head, twisting her pearls as she studies me. She lowers her voice. "Do you really think you're cut out for life on the run, love? I don't know.... Maybe if you just contact the authorities and explain everything, they'll understand? Edmund Gladstone's so nice; he'd never hurt anyone. I just...I really think you should speak with them."

"*Never*, Viv. They—"

The others enter the saloon and Vivian walks away to inspect the cushions by the side of the viewport. Tabby and Theo are wide-eyed and can't stop smiling as they take in everything, and once more my heart soars at the sight of them.

"We had a quick peek about the place, Leyla. Hope that's okay!" Theo says. His hair stands upright as always, swept back into a perfect quiff.

"I know we saw it before you set off, but seeing it out here and lived-in is something else," Tabby says. "It's flipping amazing!"

"I know," I say, unable to wipe the smile off my face. "She's just perfect. Come on!" I gesture to the viewport.

Vivian prefers to sit on the sofa, where she has lots to discuss with Papa. She wants to know everything that happened to him since his arrest, and Grandpa gave her several files to pass on that were too sensitive to risk sending digitally.

Theo and Tabby rush to the viewport, mouths open. They take in the view, then glance down at the plush space, and we all smile when our eyes meet. I feel breathless.

I know the country's currently burning. But at this exact moment right here and now, I'm living a dream. We've been through so much. Papa's alive and well, Ari's back, and the Campbells are safely here with us, too. It feels unreal and incredibly precious.

I turn to Theo. "Your mum filled me in briefly on what happened on your way over."

He pulls the corners of his mouth down. "Let's not even talk about that now, or the arrest. Can't *believe* I never got around the tracer they put on the report." A flush creeps across his cheeks. "I really thought I could do it on the low, but the security was bonkers."

I squeeze his arm. "I should never have asked and I'm really sorry."

He waves away my apology. "While I was in there, I tried to dig around for any hint of where the other labs were, but nothing." He removes the ornate binoculars from their hook and tests them out.

"They're not going to let what happened at a single lab upset their plans for mass attacks," I say. "We *have* to find a way to stop them before it's too late."

"You heard protesters took out some of the signal shields around Westminster, right?" He replaces the binoculars and traces the arches framing the windows. "Broadcasting live has never looked more possible. It's top priority for Bia's lot, too."

I nod. "Same up north. A ton of people are working on it nonstop. Hopefully between them they'll come up with something soon because people are getting angrier by the day, and it's leaving them vulnerable. The lab really set things off, and whatever we're doing needs to be decided fast." It's hard to remain worried for too long right now, though. Things seem a little better already just from having the twins on board, and I can't help breaking into a smile. "Thank God you're safe, and here."

"Yeah." Theo shakes his head. "Thank Neptune we got out of there. And now I just want to catch up with *you*. So, you're okay? And you really don't feel the cold out there?!"

We sit on the soft cushions and the little fire burns away between us as we take it in turns to answer a million questions. A Lumi-Orb casts a golden glow over the area.

Theo updates me on Malik's progress after his seasickness diagnosis. He's secretly following the recommendations of international scientists instead of our own government guidelines, and is already feeling more positive, thank goodness.

"Whoa, what's going on outside?" Tabby leans forward for a better look.

We follow her gaze and there are not one but three brightly lit restaurants floating in the water before us. Ari drifts into sight.

"You have a lot to catch up on," he says. "I thought you might like some hot food."

"Does he always strip in the water?" Tabby asks, waggling her perfect eyebrows. Each time she turns her head, her short and perfectly sharp bob swings beside her face.

"Thank you!" I say to Ari before turning to the twins. "Hope you're all hungry?"

"I'm famished." Tabby rolls her eyes. "Trust me, that sub wasn't exactly a palace."

"Hey, it got us out of there." Theo frowns.

"There's plenty of choice," explains Ari.

I grin and jump up. "We're coming!" When put in charge of food, Ari will always insist on a variety.

We leave the saloon. The twins watch as I command the Navigator to activate the bridge.

Tabby's eyes shine. "So flipping cool. Like, you really are the boss of your own ship."

One restaurant at a time, the submarine's bridge extends and attaches to the hefty submersibles' own seals. Each time connection is secure, the hatches of both vessels release and we're able to cross the bridge and interact.

"Awesome," says Theo, his eyes wide as we pass through the short tunnel-like attachment. "Engineering!"

I've missed grabbing a take-away so much. The vendor in the last sub gestures to the menu hovering in the steamy air behind her, as exquisite aromas waft into the bridge. As we stand there deciding, she launches into her pitch.

"We have it all! Old World and new! All ingredients fresh from the farms! None of that reconstituted starch from the food dispenser. You want chicken chow mein, Peking duck, dumplings, sweet and sour everything, ribs every flavor, cookies, mango pudding, banana fritters, coconut buns, jellies, ice creams—"

"A little of everything!" I shout across. "All of it, please!"

The vendor looks delighted.

"I missed you." Theo grins.

All too soon we're back in the saloon with bags full of food.

Papa and Vivian eat by the sofas, and we return to the viewport with Ari joining us. I realized he felt he was intruding, so I had to insist. It's so easy between us all, as if we've known one another forever. They've jumped straight into discussing gaming. Tabby pauses between mouthfuls of ramen to keep glancing at Ari and me, her eyes mischievous and narrowed. To my shame, my response is to blush. I could strangle her. Ari thankfully can't see her and is oblivious as he tucks into his food.

"These taste bloody brilliant," Theo says, with a hint of surprise as he takes another dumpling. "So fresh."

"Mm," I manage, after chewing a mouthful of delicious keema samosa. "Other places definitely do something differently at their protein plants. The meat alone is so much tastier than what we have down in London."

After we're done eating, we sip tea and continue to chat. Jojo refuses to leave Tabby's lap and Tabs couldn't look happier as the puppy nuzzles against her. We listen, mouths open and eyes wide, as Ari—after some pleading from Theo—recounts the time he found himself momentarily stuck inside a sprawling Old World shopping center with what he thought was a horde of ghosts drifting toward him.

"I lashed out at them," he says, grinning. "It was too dark and for a moment I didn't know what, or who, they were. It took several punches and for my hand to start hurting before I realized they were only mannequins."

"I would just die!" says Tabby, eyes wide.

I shudder. "Same!"

Vivian stands, her voice carrying over to us as she asks for a suitable hotel in Bergen. Papa's mortified by the question, and I join in.

"What? No, please," I say. "You're all staying on board with us. There are three bedrooms so Tabs could crash with me, and if Theo doesn't mind the sofa in here, then you could take the guest bedroom and we're sorted, Viv. Besides, you really don't want to risk checking into a hotel when Theo's wanted back home? You never know."

"Of *course* we're staying here!" Tabby says to her mother, her eyes pleading.

After a little more assurance from Papa that they wouldn't be any trouble, Vivian accedes and retires to the guest bedroom for the night. Papa leaves, too. The last prayer of the day is all he can manage now, he says, stifling a yawn.

I take a sleepy Jojo off Tabby and put her to bed in her Bliss-Pod in my room before rejoining the others.

Ari squints as he peers out into the water. "It's Lewis," he says, and jumps up to leave the saloon.

"Lewis is the Scottish guy whose mum helped you at the prison, right?" Tabby says.

I nod. "Yes, and he's Ari's best friend."

"You love your new friends more than us." She pulls down the corners of her mouth and Theo throws a cushion at her.

She yawns. "You know what, I might turn in, too. I need the longest sleep."

"I'll show you where everything is," I say. "And you'll get a good night's rest in my room, promise."

"Rest?" Tabby asks, suddenly straightening. She fixes her gaze over my shoulder with renewed vigor, and that familiar glittering stare is back. "What's rest?"

I turn around to see Lewis and Ari have entered the saloon. Lewis walks over and slips me a little bag of several chips and other tech I don't recognize. "For yer dad, Leyla. He was expecting these today but I was held up. Make sure he gets them first thing tomorrow? They hold info he's been waiting on."

I pocket the tech immediately. Lewis notices the others.

"Theo?" He breaks into a grin when Theo nods. "Och, good to see you got here okay." His gaze rests on Tabby and his face lights up, his green eyes visibly sparkling. "And this would be..."

Theo groans. "This is Tabby, my sister. And the current national under eighteen's champ of more than one martial arts discipline. Anyone who gets on her wrong side gets a free demonstration."

"Aye? I'll hold you to that, Tabby," he says to her with a wink.

"Anytime," she replies, standing up and flicking back her bob. Her eyes scan him and they dazzle. "Call me Tabs."

"So..." Lewis waves his hand as if to indicate everyone but doesn't take his eyes off Tabby. "What are you all up to?"

Tabby bites her lip. "We were just after a nice, quiet catch-up," she says, with a glint in her eyes.

Lewis raises an eyebrow. "Aye? Allow me to complicate things for you."

Tabby glows as he joins us. It's impossible not to like Lewis, and before long we're all laughing our heads off. We chat and snack until well into the night. Ari and Lewis will leave soon and have promised to return tomorrow.

The Navigator materializes wearing a flamboyant shirt and a little lily tucked behind his ear. He's usually in his dressing gown at this time. His gaze sweeps the room and he takes a little bow before turning to me. "My lady, should I secure the pool? Am I to understand those remaining on board will be gracing us with their presence overnight?"

Struggling sounds reach our ears and we turn to see Tabby knock Lewis to the ground with one clean sweep. He lands with a *thump* and lies there on his back.

Oscar clutches his chest. "Might I inquire as to what is going on, my lady?"

"Tabs!" Theo's mouth falls open.

Tabby rolls her eyes and comes over. "Shh, I'm teaching him how to defend himself."

Theo throws his hands up in the air. "What, by killing him?"

Except, Lewis sits up with a squeak and looks at Tabby as if he's just discovered dry land. He calls out to us. "As you were." Tabby pulls him up, a satisfied smile on her face. Lewis holds up his wrist and winks at us. "Remember, Bracelet says do not resuscitate."

I've never had a sister, but I've never felt like I've missed out because I've always had Tabby. And oh, she is absolutely perfect. I feel so much lighter just from being around the twins again.

The Navigator clears his throat and I remember I haven't answered him. I double-check with Ari and Lewis and inform Oscar they'll both be leaving. Another crash and this time Tabby's fallen right on top of Lewis. An accident, I'm sure! I suppress a giggle.

"Hey, Oscar!" Tabby says as she notices the Navigator's glower. She rises gracefully to her feet and walks over with a mischievous look in her eye. "Leyla, I get the impression Oscar here can be a bit of a bad boy."

The Navigator smiles, though it doesn't quite reach his eyes. "My dear, it is absurd to divide people into good and bad. People are either charming"— he looks away and waves his hand to indicate the rest of us in the room, before settling his gaze back on Tabby—"or tedious." He flickers out of sight.

Tabby's mouth falls open and I burst out laughing.

We continue our chatter and laughter as the fireside keeps us company. I look on the faces around me and my heart expands. Two amphis and three non-amphis. How much easier life could be if some didn't consider it beneficial to divide us.

My hand brushes against the bag of info in my pocket, and I roll the technology between my fingers.

I fear for the amphi communities around the country. How many more will lose their lives as they protest their treatment? Will things ever change for us?

Are enough non-amphis willing to acknowledge how deeply unjust things currently are and inconvenience themselves as necessary to help bring about real change?

I have a feeling we're perilously close to finding out.

CHAPTER TWENTY-FIVE

The main Anthropoid Watch Council headquarters in Westminster are destroyed.

The attack took place at three a.m. As of this morning, the area around it is chaos.

Despite being told to stay away, Londoners are flocking to the spot in protest. They cite the attacks up and down the country, and demand answers and increased protection from amphis. The news is dominated by the incident. There have been retaliatory attacks on anyone suspected of being an amphi. And there's also been the odd person braving a different view, insisting they're not being told the whole truth. Their voices are drowned out the moment they express such sentiments.

I can't bear to watch it. All it does is leave me with an overwhelming sense of despair. It makes you want to shout, beg everyone to see what's really going on.

We message Gramps and he's all right, thank goodness. I wish he'd set off with the twins. It's becoming increasingly unstable in the capital, and God knows where it's going to end.

I take the winding staircase down to the lower level and give the control room my early morning once-over. All looks fine and I head back upstairs for the galley. We're expecting Ari, his parents, and Lewis to arrive any moment, so I rustle up extra breakfast and take the trays to the saloon.

Tabby already ate and is busy giving Jojo a bath. The little scallywag's lapping up all the attention Tabs is lavishing on her.

"Breakfast, Papa," I call out to him. He's pacing the viewport as he messages someone.

I place the tray carefully on the coffee table, away from where he's set out all the countless bits of tech he's been receiving. Theo's already busy going through it, decoding the encrypted files and watching the classified footage.

"Thanks," he says, pulling off his earphones and sighing.

"That all the evidence?" I ask, pointing to the tech as we tuck into scrambled eggs and toast.

"Yeah, your dad and Ben's copies. It's maddening. If we could only find a way around the shields and broadcast it. Can't believe they let me jump in on it with them—a whole online army working toward the same goal, love it." He gestures to the bits and pieces. "There's everything: footage, files, names, all the original Explorer reports, files on Broadmoor, every order given to trigger the earthquakes, the experiments they carried out at the lab, all the people gone missing these last few years, which by the way is anyone who ever questioned the status quo. There's even actual footage of attacks. It's…" His eyes widen and he shakes his head.

"What? Tell me."

But he's deep in thought, staring absently at the equipment again. "I reckon this sub is our best chance of bypassing their blocking signals and getting the info out there in time. Few places can transmit digitally via sound the way she can, while not compromising her own shields. Too risky to try it from a building…nowhere to run if it goes belly up. With the *Kabul* we at least have the option of moving fast if the tech fails and they have a lock on us." He waves a hand. "So many have risked their lives collecting this proof. We have to put it to use—and before they carry out any of the planned attacks."

"If the submarine can help in *any* way, you must use her. Do you think enough people will consider the info, though, even if we did find a path around the shields? I mean, all of the statements Sebastian's made about the protests over these past few weeks have been complete rot. They haven't even made sense. And still it's not made any difference."

Theo butters a slice of toast. "The truth's too scary; easier to pretend it isn't happening. But if we present people with enough evidence—and this would be as solid as it gets—then we make it impossible for anyone to ignore. There are plenty of witnesses from different fields who are just waiting for the chance to speak up and be heard. Even some ex-Blackwatch and security forces personnel who've promised they'll speak up once it airs."

I glance back at Papa again, who's still looking busy in the viewport.

"I'll make sure he grabs a bite," Theo says. "He's worried about the sub's defense systems and is waiting on one last delivery. You were running low after taking out the patrol subs at the lab, and that monster." His eyes widen and he shakes his head.

The others arrive and pretty soon the saloon's buzzing with breakfast and discussion about what's going on. It's interrupted constantly as news breaks out of more and more incidents. Some amphis are carrying out protest attacks, while others try to reason with non-amphis. It doesn't work, though, and they only end up captured by the authorities.

With so much information now before us, we get busy.

Tabby and I go through files, checking against the missing people's list to see if any of the names match those Lewis's mum provided on inmates in Broadmoor. Ruby checks in on the precautionary measures taken by communities in the north. She's a security expert and runs through defense plans with their leaders. Vivian's tending to Jojo. Ben and Papa try and keep an eye on what Number 10 is up to, because they're becoming more active by the hour, mobilizing every security force we have in Britain. Lewis and Theo work with the covert nationwide network of tech experts as they examine ways to hack into the national broadcasting system. Oscar sits with them, looking comfortable as he imparts his knowledge on the matter. And Ari left to check in with the officials here in Bergen who've been monitoring what's happening in Britain. Their plan of action has taken forever to decide.

Some want to gather as many people as possible and go straight down to London and request the British government put a stop to all the slaughter. Others are afraid any real action might draw unwanted attention to themselves, causing the Norwegian government to rethink their somewhat lenient stance on the amphi community here. But after putting it to a vote, the overwhelming majority has spoken, and those in charge have promised to help in any way they can if matters escalate.

The hours tick by. Ari returns around late lunchtime with another one of Bergen's restaurants in tow. The saloon is soon filled with the aromas of biryani, several delicious curries, and hot buttery naan. Everyone's ravenous. After lunch I bring in a tray of kahwah, coffee, and English breakfast tea, and we sip our warm drinks as we update one another on our progress. And then it's back to work.

It's midafternoon when Theo's cry sounds around the saloon. "Result!" He punches the air and high-fives Lewis.

"What?" Hope surfaces in Papa's gaze. "Is this true? Well done!" he says to Lewis and Theo.

"Nothing to do with me," says Lewis, and he points to Theo with a look of awe. "It was him and everybody else working their socks off."

"Alas, the gentleman Lewis is far too modest," says Oscar, offering Lewis a small, admiring nod. "And therefore it is incumbent on me to proclaim his input as of utmost importance."

Everyone looks at him slightly puzzled, before returning their focus to Theo.

"You found a concrete way around it, son?" Papa asks him.

"We did. It only took us this long because I had to be sure it couldn't be traced back to the *Kabul*." Theo goes on to explain the mechanics, all of which go right over my head.

Basically, though, he and many others have worked out how to bypass the government's blocking signals and live broadcast all the info we have.

My heart races. It's what everyone wanted. But it's also the scariest thing ever.

If we do this, there is no going back.

There's a mad scramble as Papa checks in with a bunch of people. He messages Cambridge and discusses with Bia. The Den looks as busy as ever behind her, with files hovering around as everyone rushes about the place. Despite nodding away at Papa, Bia seems distracted, her deep brown eyes not as focused as they usually are.

Papa seems to have noticed, too. "Everything okay, Bia?"

She throws a swift glance behind her before leaning in and dropping her voice. "It's nothing we can't handle. But as a precaution you shouldn't give the *Kabul*'s location to anybody, Hashem. And I mean *anybody*. No one outside your circle should be allowed on board."

Papa's eyebrows meet. "Bia?"

"There's been one too many instances of classified information making its way out of here. And to be clear, when I say making its way out, I mean intentionally leaked to Westminster." She sticks her chin out. "But I'm on top of it and things are now on a need-to-know basis at the Den. I suggest the same precaution on your end. Right, that done, we need to stay focused on present matters. So you're all set to go, Hashem?" She launches into action, bringing up files even as Papa speaks.

He nods. "I'll need a quick word with Charlie, too, and I've received the—"

"Charlie's not here," she says. "He's headed north on sensitive business. I—I needed someone I can trust without question." She pauses, pinching the bridge of her nose as she lets out a long sigh. "Besides, the tension between him and Jas has reached new levels and I'm done with it."

I watch the screen as they chat, and Jas emerges from the room behind Bia. He throws the briefest look her way before swiftly veiling his expression and moving on. Bia turns around just in time to see him exit the Den.

"I think— We need to be more cautious about who we're letting in on this," she says, facing us once more. "I just feel we should be more prudent with the most sensitive matters." She presses her lips together as she thinks, then shakes herself. "Right, let's do this." She claps her hands and clicks her fingers, urging the others into action.

Papa shifts on his feet. "You will let me know if you need my help?"

She assures him she can take care of things and disappears.

Papa swiftly gets through the rest of the people he needs to check in with. We also catch up with Grandpa, who's doing all right thankfully. If anything, he's more worried about us. Ben contacts those in charge back in Eysturoy, notifying them of the development.

Most of the people Theo's working with on this have been anticipating this very moment for years. We hold our breath.

Everything is uploaded and transmitted for live broadcast.

All of it. Every lie and truth exposed.

Theo and the grid of hackers and technicians haven't missed a trick, and it takes only minutes for Britons to be hit with the info in some way. They've covered news stations and broadcasts in public places, sent the files directly to certain individuals they know have the resources and desire to spread them further, and they've even taken over Wireless Man. My heart is in my throat. We've no idea how it will be received, or what the immediate repercussions for our actions might be.

I hold Jojo close, breathing in her new flower-scented coat thanks to Tabby, and offer a silent prayer that we remain untraceable and that all amphi communities are safe. There's no knowing how Sebastian is going to react to all this.

Before our very eyes, the official broadcast playing on-screen switches to one of the illegally uploaded files.

I stop what I'm doing. "Theo, what's that?"

"Leyla…" He gives a small shake of the head. "I don't think anyone should watch."

"Why not?"

He swallows and stays silent. My heart races, but I turn and focus on the footage playing on-screen now.

It's shot in the water.

The images seem like some kind the military record. Numbers and a counter run along the top and bottom of the screen. In the center is a target symbol. And it's fixed on a family.

I try to push down the sense of nausea insisting on rising now.

The family swims together. A man, woman, young girl, and toddler boy. They hide behind one ledge after another each time they sight their pursuer. But the target always finds them.

I hold on to Jojo and can't look away from the family.

They're now trapped. The young girl cowers and the mother shields the little boy with her body. The father moves forward, and begs for their lives. He *pleads* as he points to his family behind him. There's sheer terror in his gaze. A chill sweeps through me as I watch. Pain engulfs the little girl's face. She tries to reach her father, arms outstretched and crying uncontrollably. A fluorescent light dots her father's chest.

The laser rips into him until finally he drifts lifelessly away.

His wife and children scream endlessly. They're next. A grenade. A huge explosion. Nothing but drifting body parts afterward.

I clutch my stomach, trembling. Something brushes my shoulder and I know it's Ari. He takes my hand and squeezes it. I'm vaguely aware of Tabby comforting a crying Vivian. I turn to see Papa watching me, a faraway look in his eyes. Ruby and Ben appear frozen and exhausted. I realize they must have lived with experiences such as this family's their whole lives. I can't breathe for the weight in my chest. The family... And I'm trying desperately to block out the image of Mama experiencing something similar.

In under two minutes of the footage playing, there's a government expert on another channel pointing out all the ways in which it's "clearly false." And then there's a phone-in and the presenter consoles those who are panicking and afraid an "Anthropoid" attack is imminent.

"The footage isn't false," says a third caller. The presenter looks around the studio in alarm but the call continues. "I'm Lieutenant Violet Eastwood and I recorded that video." It goes quiet for a second. "Truth is, that family never posed any threat to us. I took their lives, but you've got to understand I was only carrying out orders. And I'm now in hiding, in danger from all sides. I just want my life back!" The line goes dead.

Ari wraps an arm around me and I cover it with my hands. All those people lost. All those needless deaths. And Mama, too, should still be here. It's unthinkable that they're no longer with us because of someone else's ignorance and ill intent. Their cruelty.

I still don't know exactly what happened to Mama.

Chaos breaks out. Every place we're monitoring is all accusations of falsehoods, denial, panic, rage, grief. And a rising sense of suspicion of the government. It's relentless and overwhelming, and people don't know how to process it. My Bracelet flashes and then it's one message after another as confused family and friends from outside Britain want to know what's happening. Someone checks the other channels and suddenly there's a familiar, slimy voice dominating the airwaves.

I freeze when Captain Sebastian's face registers on-screen. I've never seen him look more threatening. He's in his office, his cold gaze fixed into the camera. Text runs along the bottom: *Captain Sebastian. Principal private secretary to the prime minister. Emergency bulletin.*

"I cannot stress enough the treacherous nature of this act," he says. "The prime minister is disgusted. The cowardly perpetrators of these illegal broadcasts have put the lives of all citizens—of every good, law-abiding, and civilized Briton—at risk with the evil actions they've taken today. I repeat, all the footage you see is fabricated. It's false news." He clenches his jaw, straining so hard you can see the vein by his temple actually wriggle. Like the sea snake he is. "Make no mistake, if you're involved in the spread of these falsehoods in any way, you'll be considered a traitor." He straightens and stares down the camera. "In the interest of national security, we offer the citizens of Great Britain this: ten million pounds to the person who delivers the accurate source of the transmission of these seditious lies. It must be terminated before it causes irrevocable harm. And to those who say—"

The screen goes blank; Papa commanded it off.

The broadcast leaves an uneasy atmosphere in its wake, and everyone falls quiet in the saloon as we busy ourselves once more. Papa takes several further messages via his Bracelet as family and friends abroad become increasingly worried about what's going on in Britain. They're watching everything that was uploaded, along with footage of the protests in London, and are growing concerned for loved ones in the country.

It's late afternoon now. Tabby continues to inspect files with Vivian helping her. Theo and Lewis keep an eye on the transmissions. Ari's throwing knives at his target board. Every now and then Vivian steals a glance his way, her expression unsettled as she twists her pearls. She catches me watching and quickly averts her gaze. I wonder if the twins' mum would feel as afraid if it were a non-amphi practicing their knife-throwing.

Ari leaves to head into the water, insisting on scanning the area himself to ensure the sub remains safe. No amount of reassurance from Oscar can persuade him the Navigator's got security covered. I take the opportunity to head downstairs and run a more in-depth scan of the control room. Everything's so unpredictable right now and we can't afford for the *Kabul* to be in anything less than her best state. All looks good, thankfully. I return upstairs and pop my head back into the saloon.

"Just going to put the kettle on. Anyone want a warm drink?"

Papa beckons me over to the seating area where Ruby and Ben sit straight, their expressions somber.

"Sit, Pickle." He pats the seat beside him and I join him, chewing on my lip. "I've spoken again with Bia. The situation is turning grave in London. Your grandpa's alone. People are being attacked for protesting the current situation. There's no knowing where it might end. . . . The prime minister hasn't been reachable for days. Something's not right. Bia's wise to suspect foul play. She and many others will head for the capital this evening."

"What are you saying, Papa? Do you think the PM isn't in charge of what's going on?"

He shrugs. "We have no idea and that's the problem. Everything taking place, all the unrest, the orders seem to come from Sebastian. Maybe if someone were to reach the PM directly, it might make a difference. Who knows. Edmund Gladstone is no friend of amphis. It was he who revealed their existence to the world and declared them enemies. But the increase in the abhorrent treatment of them these past few years, and the creation of the labs...he doesn't appear capable of such cold cruelty. He comes across a more reasonable fellow. And as long as we're hovering here in the Norwegian Sea, we aren't going to get any answers."

My pulse hammers away in my ears.

Papa takes my hand. "I must go, Pickle. It's time for me to return to London."

CHAPTER TWENTY-SIX

"Wait, what?" Tabby stands and stares over at us all on the sofa. Everybody heard Papa's words.

I turn to him. "Papa, did you forget we're Britain's most wanted?"

Lewis straightens. "Count me in."

"You misunderstand," says Papa, beckoning everyone. "I mean only the adults. I will not have children heading into that mad—"

"Neptune, I turn *nineteen* in a few months," Lewis says. "Whatever, I'll be right behind anyway with me mam."

The others come over and take a seat. I glare at Tabby because although her expression is one of disbelief, there's also an eager look in her eyes now. We mustn't encourage Papa.

Vivian flinches, her blue eyes wide and her expression clouding. "I'm not sure I quite understand, Hashem."

Papa sticks out his chin, his gaze alert. "Ben, Ruby, and myself will head down in Bia's sub, the one that brought you here, Vivian. It's been repaired and is fit again for long-haul travel. If you wish to remain here, you're most welcome to do so. In fact, it'd put my mind at ease if an adult were to stay behind."

Vivian's shoulders sag with relief.

"*Please* don't go to London." I can't stop shaking my head. "You mustn't. Sebastian hates us. He'll—"

"Pickle." He leans over and wraps me in an embrace. "We don't have much choice. People need us. They're risking everything to protest in the capital. I've never seen anything like it. They've had enough, and so many others who didn't have a clue what was taking place all this time have their hearts and minds set now on helping to put things right. We must make a stand before momentum is lost and the current state of things continues. Everyone's efforts all these years will have been for nothing, and more will disappear and die. I have to go."

I notice Tabby and Theo exchange looks. I can't believe it; they agree with him.

"Try not to worry," he continues. "We'll stay safe. I can do a lot even in hiding. I can be there for others. We won't take part in anything reckless. Have faith, Leyla."

"That's unfair. I have faith, and I'm also rightly worried because you're heading into chaos."

"I'll be in touch throughout. Bia's taking everything with her, so we'll have ample protection once we get there. And one of her subs will split for your grandpa's; they'll watch over him until we're free to pick him up. So you see, there's nothing for you to worry about, Pickle."

They've made up their minds and begin discussing details among themselves.

Tabby wraps her arms around me.

"I don't want him to go," I whisper.

"Same, after what he's been through. I'm so sorry. But...I understand why he feels he must," she says, her voice almost wistful. "That's our city, our home. How *dare* they have us fleeing it?"

"Yes, but it's too dangerous for him to show up in London."

I know I should be proud; my papa's doing the right thing, the honorable thing. He's stepping up when it's needed. But all I can feel is this rock-hard weight in my chest now. The same feeling I had back in London when he went missing. When they drugged him and dragged him out of the capital. It's a burden that only lifted once I had him back. And now he's leaving to return to the very same place. To where that snake Sebastian is waiting for him. And there's nothing I can do to stop him.

There's a scurry of message exchanges, and Papa packs a bag. Ruby's sister turns up with essentials for her and Ben. Ari returns and is annoyingly as calm about it as the twins.

Ben turns to him. "Freya's with your aunt, son, and it's the safest place for her until we're back. You must stay here in Bergen. I don't want you heading home just yet. They're always sniffing around the islands and I don't want you anywhere near the place in my absence." He pats Ari's shoulder and his voice deepens. "We'll talk more as soon as things settle, lad, I promise."

Ari nods firmly and they embrace.

It's evening when, after further checks and arrangements, Papa enters the saloon, his hands slightly shaking as he clasps them in front of him. He goes through his plans with us and then makes us all promise a ton of things linked to our safety. He hugs us one by one. "Look after one another. All will be well, inshallah. We have to believe it will be." He recites a prayer for protection over us. I try to hold on to him for as long as I can when we hug.

They leave. I stand in the viewport with Ari, watching their vessel go.

Vivian looks like she might pass out. Theo checks on the broadcasts, and Tabby and Lewis chat quietly on the sofas.

I realize Ari's watching me, his towel-dried hair framing his face and his thick black eyebrows slightly pressed together. At least he's still here, thank God. I can no longer recall a time when I wasn't aware of his existence. Even in memories pre-Ari, I imagine him in the background living his own life, always present in this world. In *my* world.

He squeezes my hand. "Your father will be okay. They've been doing this for years, remember. We have to trust they know how to look after themselves."

It's true of course. Papa's been secretly aiding amphis longer than I've been alive, and he wouldn't have evaded capture for as long as he did if he didn't know what he was doing. He promised he'd be careful. Not to mention, he's way more sensible than I am. All I can do now is hope and pray he stays safe.

"Come on," says Ari. "Let's do something about dinner. It'll take everyone's minds off things."

But even as we get to work in the galley, my thoughts race as I entertain all kinds of reckless ideas. Like going after Papa, doing something myself to get the PM's attention, and other outrageous notions. I block each one out. Papa's a grown man and he knows what he's doing. And just as I'm always begging him to trust me, I must now trust in him.

Delicious aromas fill the saloon as we bring in trays of food. Ari was right; I feel a little better. Lumi-Orbs glimmer away as they light up the space in a warm hue, and Oscar conjures up one of his fires. Waves lap at the windows and the viewport reflects their subtle ripples.

Jojo's already had her meal and is now happily eating out of Ari's hand as he feeds her bits of ours. An array of South Asian dishes are spread before us.

Lewis rubs his wrist before helping himself to the chicken curry. "Anyone tried the AK01 dermal tats?"

To my surprise Ari waves his own wrist. "Music, all the BattleDeep games, and every major Old World forest."

I never realized he had any dermal tattoos, but then they're invisible until you're using them, at which point your wrist slightly glows.

"Whoa, when did you guys get tech-tats?" Theo asks, his face lighting up. "I've been considering an engineering encyclopedia and one of the latest Hologame collections. Mum just needs a bit of persuading."

"During a recent trip to Budapest," says Lewis. "I went for an art gallery. It's given me direct access to loads of international artwork. You definitely wanna try it out, lad."

"Er, no you don't, Theo," Tabby says when he nods in agreement. She scowls at Lewis. "You'll never catch me installing any tech under my skin other than the health ones. I don't trust tats at all." She scoops biryani onto her plate, topping it with cooling raita.

Theo shrugs. "You swallow Prognosis Pills. What's the difference between nanobots and the dermal tats? I think they're bloody amazing. You can have access to entire libraries if you want." He beams as he bites into his pakora.

233

"Oh, a creep running a stall back at the Trading Post in Cambridge pestered me about having one of those tats," I say, spooning chutney onto my plate. "I had to tase him with the brolly to get away."

They stare at me.

I pause. "What?"

Ari narrows his eyes. "I knew something was wrong when you went missing in that place! You should have told me."

"No need, I took care of it."

The twins grin, eyes wide, and shake their heads as we continue to enjoy the food.

I point out the desserts, kheer and sweet rice. "Guys, there's also kulfi in the freezer if you fancy that."

After dinner, Vivian insists on cleaning the galley, refusing our offers of help. I think she's really uncertain about the whole situation and prefers being on her own right now. Theo moves to the lavender armchair by the bookcases, with a selected pile of books in his lap and Jojo curled up at his feet. In the warm glow of the floor lamp, he inspects each volume in turn, smelling the pages and running his fingers across the words. Ari, Lewis, and Tabby chat away on the sofas, laughing heartily after Tabby asked Ari for embarrassing stories about Lewis. Lewis wrestles with Ari, trying to stop him from sharing something Lewis once did as a young boy who was desperate to "acquire Ari's powers." My chest warms at seeing this new side to Ari, how he is around others. And I'm so glad he's finally relaxing after all he's been through recently.

When I've checked everything's all right with the sub, I move into the viewport and look out into the evening waves.

Tabby soon joins me in gazing into the current.

I take a deep breath and blow out my cheeks. "It's definitely been a day."

She whirls around to face me, folding her arms and waggling her perfectly arched eyebrows. "Do you know what I really missed after you left?"

"I'm scared...."

She grins. "Let's play dressing up."

I groan, pretending I'm not secretly pleased for the distraction.

"Hey, I always love you in this one," says Tabby, holding up one of my long black dresses against her body. She towers over my petite frame and the dress is only knee-length against her.

The wide screen doors to my wardrobe stay open as we take over the expansive walk-in space inside, continuing to go through my clothes and trying on different outfits. Anything to put the day's events behind us. I already feel lighter for it.

Tabby moves to the blank wall at the back, which is made up of the same glossy material used in the twins' Holozone back in their home, and dangles the dress in front of the small scanner on the side. The system, identical to the one Tabby has at home, lights up, and a projection of Tabs appears before us in my dress. Her hologram gives off the faintest glimmer as she walks across the space and twirls around to show off the dress.

"It suits you, *obviously*," I say, grinning.

"Pick your next one!" she says, narrowing her eyes as she watches herself now sashaying around in one of my purple skirts. "Hmm, party mode," she instructs the scanner and the background switches to low lights and a busy indoor party scene. It looks so incredibly real, as if my wardrobe leads to another room where a party's taking place. Tabby's hair and makeup change, too. "That's better, but something's still off." She places her hand on her hips as we look on her smiling away mingling with everyone at the party. "Of course—try cherry-red lips," she says, facing the scanner once more, and then takes in the result and smiles. "Perfect."

"All right, I've got one!"

Tabby moves out of the way as I scan my midnight-blue dress. My hologram twirls around before me.

"Gorgeous," says Tabby.

"I love this dress."

"It was your mum's, right?"

"Yes."

"It always looks great on you, but something's missing, Leyla. I know!" She turns to the scanner. "The Dynamite Dazzle for hair and makeup, eight-inch heels, and Purple Floyd tattoos across the neck."

"What is *that*?!"

We giggle at the strange result before us.

The Navigator flickers into sight between the open screen doors.

"Everything all right, Oscar?"

He looks so elegant sporting a turquoise frock coat and pink silk cravat. His gaze runs appraisingly over the racks of clothes. "Indeed, my lady. I merely felt to ask about security arrangements for the night. The usual, I gather?"

"Yes, ensure she's fully secure and well hidden, please, Oscar."

He nods. "At once."

The Navigator adjusts his cravat and his eye catches the screen at the back. Thanks to Tabby, my projection now struts down a lengthy table in the middle of a party in some huge, packed hall. Oscar narrows his gaze and the screen changes. I gasp and break into a smile.

Bluebells. An entire meadow of them.

"Oscar, you remembered!"

His face softens at my reaction and he tilts his head. "Of course, my dear. Your most cherished flora." He gives me one of his beguiling smiles that I love so much.

I'd told him during a chat a few weeks ago and I can't believe he remembered. I watch as my hologram runs among the purple-blue flowers swaying in sun-dappled woodlands. Of all the flowers of the Old World, bluebells will always be my favorite. I can't believe people got to actually witness fields full of them. Oh how I wish I could have seen one with my own eyes. I've heard about the gardens in Abu Dhabi, Marrakesh, and Kuala Lumpur, where they have real ones growing. One day I'll see the flower for myself, inshallah.

The Navigator knits his eyebrows when the screen changes as Tabby tries a different outfit. She looks amazing dressed head to toe in black leather—jacket mine, trousers borrowed from the system—the sunlight catching her short platinum-blond bob as she strides down a busy Tokyo street. The background changes abruptly.

"What the hell?" Tabby turns scowling. "I never selected that?"

She's standing in a field surrounded by cows and mountains of dung.

I throw my hands up in the air and stifle a giggle that's trying to break free. "I swear it wasn't me!"

Tabby narrows her gaze as she stares at Oscar, whose face is now slightly flushed even as he shrugs innocently.

"Hmm, I thought you knew *everything*, Oscar?" Tabby arches an eyebrow.

"Oh, but my dear," he says, inspecting his nails, "I'm not *young* enough to know everything."

He turns to me. "Well, my lady, if that is all?"

"Erm, yes, thank you, Oscar."

He disappears and Tabby presses her lips flat. "The snarky git? I swear he changed my background. He's got something against me, that Oscar."

We look at each other and break into laughter as we leave the space to sit on my bed.

"Let me give you an *actual* makeover," Tabby says, running her fingers through my hair.

"We've already tried that a trillion times back in London and no thank you."

She grins wickedly, most likely recalling all the strange and hilarious looks I've had to wear at her hands.

"Ari really likes you," she says. "I have this urge to shock him."

"I know you do, and you'll suppress that urge."

"Have you guys done anything more than kiss?"

My cheeks warm. "No, and I'd never," I say firmly.

"I grabbed Lewis and made sure to press my—"

"I don't want to know!"

We giggle.

"Seen him naked?'

"No!"

"In his underwear?"

I fall quiet.

"Leyla Fairoza McQueen! You'll tell me everything right this minute!" She stops playing with my hair and turns to me. "Every delicious detail."

"Just once," I say, mumbling the words.

"Oh, but in my experience once can be quite enough," Tabby responds, her face shining. "Tell me."

"There's really nothing to tell! A noise woke me up—turns out it was a pod of whales nearby—and I left my room to investigate. I caught Ari just as he also decided to check on the sounds."

"And?"

"Well, he was wearing only boxers."

"Yes *and*?"

"Well...Don't hate me now, but..."

"Oh, dear Neptune."

"It's only because I bloody panicked!"

"Tell me then kill me."

"I wished him salaam."

Her mouth falls open. I don't blame her in the slightest.

"You saw a colossal hunk like Ari—and someone who flipping adores you and who you clearly worship right back—in his friggin' *underwear* and...you wished him *peace*?!"

"Well when you say it like *that*. I'm not you!"

We laugh until we roll right off my bed.

CHAPTER TWENTY-SEVEN

We're all back in the saloon. The sub's secure for the night, and a subdued Vivian brings in a tray of refreshments.

We chat quietly on the sofas as we sip our warm drinks. Afterward, Lewis sets up his easel and starts painting us.

"Hope yer all right with this ending up in one of those galleries when someone spots me talent," he says, his movements erratic as he selects and flings the hovering colors at the easel.

"*So* skillful," says Tabby, smiling coyly as she watches him. When he's done with the group, she jumps up and poses solo for him.

My Bracelet flashes. It's Charlie.

"Hiya!" he says.

Jojo gives a happy bark when she hears his voice, despite feeling sleepy. She paws at his projection hovering above my wrist.

I peer closer at him. "Are you in the water? Bia said you were traveling up north on some emergency. Everything all right, Charlie?"

"Yeah, I'm in me sub!" He bites his lip. "You alone, Leyla?"

I move over into the viewport, and nod to confirm.

"Bia sent me on an urgent errand." He lowers his voice. "Strictly between you and me, I had to go see someone in Trondheim. They had info on some of Sebastian's dealings. Got what I came for, and I'm on me way back now but"—he grimaces—"I've come stuck, about halfway between Utsira and Bergen."

"Oh no, what do you need?"

"It's the wing; looks like it's caught up in a trench's worth of freakin' plastic. I don't know, whatever I try, the sheet's not letting me go." He rubs his face. "Bia's waiting on what I have. I can't risk asking Norwegian authorities for help, and there isn't enough time to request backup from Cambridge. Blackwatch could carry out the planned strikes at any moment. But yeah, if yer not too far off, then I don't suppose you could give me a hand if yer still in the area? A nudge should probably do it."

"Sure! Give me your location and I'll hop in my sub. And don't worry, these waters are really safe so you'll be all right."

"For real?" His shoulders sag with relief. "Thanks a bunch. Passing on the coordinates right now."

The Navigator pinpoints Charlie's location.

"Oh, you're not too far away," I say. "I won't be long."

"Yer a lifesaver!"

When I end the message, I bring up the simulated sea chart just to be on the safe side, checking out the exact spot and making a note of any possible obstacles in the area. Confident of what to expect, I'm just waving away the interactive map when movement outside catches my eye. It's Ari. He hovers in the water, waving to get my attention.

His hair swirls around his face. "I'm headed for Utsira. I heard Oscar give you the location, and I can help Charlie."

"But I can do it!"

"I know, but I'm more experienced out here, Leyla. And you're needed on board. I have to go. I'll be back in no time!"

"Are you sure you don't want a sub to tag along as well?"

He shakes his head. "He's close by, don't worry." Then he bolts out of sight.

He's right about being the wiser choice to help Charlie; he's physically stronger than me and we don't know exactly how the sub is stuck. And I'm definitely the best person to watch over the submarine.

Lewis is standing behind me when I turn around. He's in his usual white T-shirt and waves a heavily tattooed arm in the direction of the water. "Ari's left to check out the area again? That lad worries too much."

"No he—"

"Lewis!" Tabby calls out to him.

His eyes light up. "I've been summoned." He walks away beaming.

Hopefully it doesn't take Ari too long with helping Charlie—sounds like he needs to be on his way back to Cambridge as soon as possible. I wonder what the info he came all the way out here to gather reveals. It must be something really damning. I rejoin the others.

Jojo's showing off nonexistent acrobatic skills to Lewis and Tabby. Theo's as busy as ever with the broadcasts. They're still playing on a loop around the country. God only knows how angry Sebastian is right now.

Back in my bedroom, I peer out of the porthole and into the evening water, and calculate Papa's journey. If all goes well, they'll be in the capital this time tomorrow at the latest. I wash and pray, forcing myself to focus because I'm so exhausted I can barely think straight. Afterward, I lie on my bed and everything that's happened goes around and around in my head.

My eyes flutter open as raised voices sound from somewhere. Ugh, I nodded off. I groan when I check the time: I've been in here several hours! Jojo's in the room, fast asleep in her Bliss-Pod. Tabby must've put her to bed. The pod's still playing its soothing music and gently rocking away. The noise that woke me was much louder, though. I quickly freshen up and make my way to the saloon. In the passageway, traces of water on the floor catch my eye just as the raised voices sound again. I hasten into the room. It's Ari.

He's hurt.

Lewis is rushing to support him.

Tabby spots me. "Leyla! The Medi-bot!"

My pulse racing, I grab the Medi-bot and make my way to Ari. He's wet and leaning on Lewis. We try to get him to lie down but he insists on sitting up in the viewport, his breathing heavy. There's a deep gash in his arm, and swelling to his shoulders and back. The skin around his ribs is darker. The Medi-bot gets to work diagnosing him.

Theo's checking on Charlie, who looks as if he's about to pass out any moment. He's impossibly pale and quivering uncontrollably.

I sit on the floor beside Ari. "What happened?"

His expression darkens as he shakes his head. "We were attacked." His voice is hoarse and he catches his breath.

"Fractured ribs," says Tabby, reading the diagnosis hovering in the air above him. "And stitches required on the open wound."

I take in Charlie's trembling state and turn back to Ari. "Another creature?"

His gaze simmers as he gives a small shake of his head, but it takes another five minutes to stabilize him enough for him to speak without pain. "Three submersibles, looked private to me."

My stomach hardens. "I don't understand. Who'd attack you here? I thought amphis were safe here?"

Lewis immediately messages Bergen officials to alert them.

Ari takes a breath before speaking. "I found Charlie no problem and set to work removing the debris. It took a while, but the wing came free. Then—" He winces, and Charlie takes over.

He clasps his trembling hands. "Ari released the wing. I was just gonna get going when we came under fire." His eyes widen. "One of the subs focused on me and the other two went straight for him. Next thing I know I'm spinning out of control and going down." He starts shaking and Theo passes him a glass of water. After a pause and several sips, Charlie continues. "They thought they'd done me in and followed the others after Ari. I managed to stabilize the craft but they'd messed up her systems and I was stuck again." He grimaces. "I had no way of getting help. Whatever they did froze me Bracelet, too. So I just hoped to Neptune he'd be okay and get away and that someone would know what was going on and turn up." He jabs frantically at his Bracelet. Theo moves in to check it out. "I've let them all down," Charlie continues. "Bia and the lot of them. This place was meant to be safe." Relief floods his face and he thanks Theo when his Bracelet finally boots up.

"Thank God they didn't puncture the vessel's body," I say. His eyes bulge at the thought.

I grab a towel and dry Ari's face and neck, careful not to brush against anyplace sore.

He clenches his jaw. "They pursued me, hitting me each time they got close." The muscles in his face strain against his skin. "But one by one I saw to their subs."

"Good," says Lewis firmly, his posture tense.

Charlie nods slowly, mouth open and expression dazed.

I touch Ari's arm and he wraps a hand over mine. Everyone falls silent. Tabby and Theo listen, eyes wide, while comforting Vivian, who's clearly struggling with everything.

"I'm dead sorry," Charlie says, looking at Ari with a pained expression. "It's all my fault. And thanks a bunch. If you hadn't gone looking for me afterward, I'd still be stuck down there. And no way would I have gotten back without you propping up me sub every time it needed it."

I can't believe it. That's how they got back here—with an injured Ari having to not only push himself through the depths, but also doing whatever he had to in order to get Charlie to safety, too.

How much longer is he meant to live like this?

"There could be more of them," I say. "We need to make sure we're safe." I beckon the Navigator.

"My lady?" He takes in Ari's state and offers his sympathies.

"Oscar, secure the sub."

I turn to Ari. "You've got to do exactly as the Medi-bot says because we need you to recover. And nobody else leaves this sub. At least not tonight."

I lean down and check his arm myself as the Medi-bot prepares to stitch it. It's a mess, and I shudder.

Ari's gaze intensifies as he catches me looking. "I took care of them," he says quietly.

I nod and sweep back his hair. I'm glad he did.

"They got what they deserved," says Lewis, applying ointment to the backs of Ari's sore hands. "Yer lucky to have made it back."

Vivian can't take any more. She sits and sobs, and the twins do their best to comfort her.

Charlie stares into the space ahead, his forehead creased. "I'm gonna need a scan on me sub if that's possible. Not sure if she can make the journey back to Cambridge."

"I can run a full diagnostics," I say. "And if she's not seaworthy, we'll fix you up with another. You need to rest first anyway. We'll deal with that in the morning."

"Yeah, just focus on feeling better." Theo squeezes his shoulder.

Charlie nods. "Sound. Thanks, mate."

He looks in shock, and completely lost. I exchange looks with Theo and he's clearly thinking the same thing. He grabs the Medi-bot to ensure Charlie's all right.

The twins' mother brings in a tray of warm drinks. I notice Vivian fusses over Charlie, but Ari...not so much. I wonder if on some level she thinks less of me now since my own abilities kicked in.

It's another hour before Ari's color improves and he feels up to talking. He swallowed a Prognosis Pill and the fractures don't look too bad, thank goodness. We go over what happened again, and then I check the time. It's very late and I want to give the vessel a quick glance-over before sorting out the sleeping arrangements. When I turn to Ari, he looks far away.

"Ari?" I call out softly. He doesn't hear me and I squeeze his arm to let him know I'm off to tend to a few things.

Though his gaze meets mine, he's still leagues away. His voice drops low. "I think— When they were chasing me, I—"

"You all right, lad?" Lewis wanders over to check on him and Ari shakes himself into focusing.

I hover a moment in case he wants to finish what he was saying, but he falls silent. He nods when I say we can catch up later, and I exit the saloon.

The passageway's comforting deeper hum greets me as I step into it. "Leyla?"

I turn to see Charlie on my heels. Recalling something I made just earlier as I was sitting with Ari, I dig into my pocket and bring out a paper model. "Here," I say, handing him the origami shape.

His face relaxes. "For me? Whoa, this is awesome. Look at Jojo. It's spot on." He turns the paper puppy over in his hands, inspecting it before his expression grows serious and he carefully pockets the shape. "Can I have a quick word?"

"Of course."

"First off, I really don't wanna impose. Are you sure it's no bother having me on board for the night?"

I assure him he's welcome anytime and he nods absently in response.

"Charlie, what is it?"

His brow wrinkles and the worried expression deepens. "Leyla, do you think it's possible someone talked? Told the authorities where we were?"

"You and Ari?"

"Yeah." His face grows heavier. "What if those who attacked us were on orders from Westminster?"

"British security forces? But what would they be doing in foreign waters?"

He shakes his head, blowing out his cheeks. "I don't know.... But I keep thinking about what happened and it just doesn't sit right. The more I think on it, the less it feels like a random attack. Except I never mentioned where I was to anyone but yerself. What if someone else knew where Ari and me were, and they told?"

I twist my hair around my fingers. "I didn't tell a soul. Ari overheard and then he was in the water insisting on taking my place."

"Sorry, don't mean to worry you. I reckon I'm just on edge from everything going on back at Bia's." He lowers his voice. "This is strictly between us, but you were right to smell a rat. We have a problem back at the Den and it's even worse than you thought. Westminster isn't listening in on us.

Someone's working *with* them, on the inside, passing on info. But Bia's on it, and fingers crossed we'll have it sorted pronto."

"We kind of got the impression from Bia that something was up. I still can't believe it. I'm so sorry."

"That lot at Number 10 wanna wipe every amphi out and there's nothing they won't try to make that happen. We wanna be more careful, especially when it comes to any mention of locations. Can't have them discovering any more." He swallows, his expression suddenly haunted, and I wonder just how much horror he's already seen in his life.

I reassure Charlie as best I can. He leaves to take a shower, and I give the sub a quick once-over before rejoining the others.

Lewis glances up as I move toward him and Ari. "Everything all right?" he asks.

I suddenly recall him standing right behind me when I saw Ari off in the viewport. Ari had mentioned Utsira. Lewis knew of the location. I could kick myself for even thinking it. No way would Lewis do such a thing.

Who attacked Charlie and Ari? And did someone alert the attackers to their location?

It can't be true. It doesn't *feel* true. It's very possible it was just a random, vile incident. I press my hands to my temples.

Sometimes I struggle with knowing when to go with either my heart or head about certain things. Just sometimes, it's really difficult to know which of the two to trust most in a situation.

I push all doubt away now as I concentrate on sorting out the sleeping arrangements. Tabby's with me. Ari will have his own room back—Vivian insists on vacating it and taking Papa's instead—and share it with Lewis. Theo and Charlie will crash in the saloon. Lewis suggests we keep watch and volunteers for the first shift.

As I lie in bed next to Tabby, who's finally fallen asleep after letting me know exactly what she's going to do with Lewis as soon as she spies the opportunity, I can't help thinking about the attack on Charlie and Ari. And hoping it really was random.

I never got a moment alone again with Ari, and he clearly needs to share what he went through today. We'll find some time tomorrow.

A restless hour later I turn on my side in the hopes of easing the weight in my chest. Instead I drift into nightmares.

The same old elusive memory of years ago.

CHAPTER TWENTY-EIGHT

I look out of the porthole in my room and into the early morning water. Tabby's lightly snoring away in my bed and Jojo's still asleep in her Bliss-Pod.

I just heard from Papa. He and Ari's parents are halfway to London now. Apart from a tense moment as they passed a security base that resulted in a brief chase, the journey down to the capital has been manageable so far. Papa looked and sounded upbeat and more like his old self. His sense of purpose seems to have finally returned. I can't deny how heartening it was to see him speaking as he used to, with his quiet determination and zeal. He promised again he'd be as careful as possible once he enters the city.

Charlie's clutching a cup of black coffee when I enter the galley. I'll never understand how anyone drinks coffee anyway, but to drink it without milk is quite disturbing. He looks like he hasn't slept at all, and stares into the space.

He grimaces apologetically when he spots me. "Morning. Sorry, didn't know what time everyone's up so I helped meself." He gestures to his cup.

"Morning, Charlie. Why've you only got coffee? Papa would be seriously insulted if he were here. You mock Pashtun hospitality! There's all sorts for breakfast."

He grins and waves his hand. "I don't do breakfast, only the coffee, but cheers." His expression turns somber again and he chews on his lip.

I pause by the Tea-lady. "Still worried about who caused the attack?"

He presses his lips flat now and stares down into his drink. "That too...Don't suppose you had a call from the Den last night?"

"The Den?" I shake my head. "Last contact I had with you lot was when Papa called Bia to discuss the broadcasts. Now that Bia's on her way to London, and you're here, there's no reason for me to contact Cambridge. Why?"

"You wanna be careful, Leyla. Bia messaged a short while earlier. Whoever the mole is at the Den, they tried to get in touch with someone on the *Kabul* in the early hours of the morning. Bia tracked several unauthorized attempts."

I line up the cups and turn to him. "What? They tried to contact the submarine?"

He nods. "You didn't hear it from me, mind. But I must admit, I don't like it one bit."

"We need to find out who they were trying to reach....Theo might know a way. Let's get onto it straight after breakfast? Try not to worry; it might just be something innocent."

He helps me rustle up food for everyone.

As we make our way to the saloon with the trays, we spot Lewis hovering by the door of the engine room and fiddling with his Bracelet. He glances up, eyes bloodshot.

I indicate the food. "Breakfast. Looks like you didn't get much sleep either." I pause. "Wait, you never messaged me for my shift! Did you wake the others up? Don't tell me you pulled another all-nighter, Lewis?"

"Och, I'll live. I'll be there in a tick," he says. "Just catching up with me mam."

Theo startles when we enter the saloon. He's standing by the screens and was engrossed in a file.

"Whoa, steady on." Charlie grins. "Only us."

"Morning, Theo. How did you sleep?"

We place the trays down on the table by the seating.

Theo stares at me, pinching his bottom lip. "I slept all right, thanks."

He flicks his hair out of his eyes; he hasn't styled it up yet so strands are falling across his forehead. Usually it's a platinum-blond wall.

I move closer to him. "What's wrong?"

He rubs his jaw. "It doesn't make sense, I know. But…security's throwing up traces of communication between the sub and Westminster."

Charlie stills, his mouth falling open.

"What?" I clasp my hands tight. "The submarine and *Westminster*? There must be a mistake, Theo."

He shakes his head. "That's just it. Maybe a one-off alert could be taken for an error, but there are several. All incoming official government communication—so anything from border patrol, security, Westminster et cetera, logs a notification. I ensured it would, before you left London. Sometime between midnight and now, there was interaction between the authorities and someone on board the *Kabul*. It's no technical error."

We stare at him.

Charlie wrings his hands as he turns to me. "Look, I don't wanna worry you, but this is one too many coincidences. You really wanna watch yer back, Leyla."

Theo looks at him, eyebrows squished. Charlie repeats what he told me—that he suspects it was British security forces that attacked them yesterday.

"I must admit," says Theo, "I was thinking the same thing last night. What happened yesterday sounds more and more suspect. But how would they know where you'd be?"

"Charlie didn't tell anyone except me," I say. "So few of us knew. I mean literally only Oscar, Ari, myself, and maybe Lewis might've heard the location mentioned, but that's it."

Theo folds his arms. "We could always be wrong. It's not impossible it was some random locals."

Charlie nods. "It could've been, yeah. But I've been doing this forever and I know undercover British forces when I see them. It really feels like this was them. But yeah, this isn't solid. Contact with Westminster is, though."

Theo narrows his eyes. "*We* were ambushed, too, on our way over here from London.... I wonder how they got our location?"

"That's another one that's had me stumped," says Charlie. "Bia and me never let anyone else in on that one. We've been real careful back at the Den, knowing we have a leak."

"We kept it strictly among ourselves this end, too." I shrug, confused.

Theo faces me, brow wrinkled. "So the only people to know we were traveling were your granddad, your dad, Bia, Charlie, Ari, and those Bia sent after us?"

I nod. "That's right. Oh, and Lewis, but that's it."

Theo's gaze flickers.

"No, Lewis would never," I say.

"He's McGregor's son, yeah?" Charlie asks, deep in thought.

I nod. "He's Ari's best friend. Ben and their entire community trust him. His mum, Maud McGregor, works for the Den."

Charlie nods. "Maud's the best, worked with Bia for years."

"But you aren't familiar with her son?" Theo asks.

"Can't say we are," says Charlie. "But I'm with Leyla—why would Maud's son work against us?"

Theo sighs and throws his hands in the air. "Okay, then who?"

I nudge Charlie. "Tell him what Bia's told you."

Charlie bites his lip. "There's more," he says to Theo, his voice strained now. "Bia traced someone at the Den trying to get in touch with the sub, without authorization. And it happened this very morning. Looks like whoever's double-crossing us at the Den tried to get ahold of one of you guys. Very likely the same person on board who tried to contact Westminster."

Theo stills. "No way?" He rubs his face. "Neptune, of course! Once they establish contact with us, they can use that connection to trace the submarine's bearings." His face suddenly hardens. "And I know exactly who it is." He turns to Charlie, opens his mouth but closes it again without saying anything. He paces the floor, his expression heavy.

"It's okay, Theo. Tell us," I say.

He pauses. "It's Jas. He's the leak at the Den."

I squint at him. "That's—What makes you so sure?"

Charlie's shoulders sag and he rubs the back of his neck. He's not at all surprised by Theo's guess.... He already knew—or at least had his suspicions.

"Because he's always there," says Theo, waving his hands in the air. "Watching, listening in. It's almost always him who answer my calls to the Den, always gets there before Charlie, as if he's watching out for them. And I've lost count of how many times he's 'forgotten' to deliver my messages for Charlie." He turns to Charlie. "I'm telling you, he's your leak at the Den."

I wrap my arms around myself. I've no idea what's going on.

Theo looks at me, his eyes clouding. "Leyla, we can't ignore all this. We were ambushed on our way up here, the mole at the Den—almost definitely Jas—is trying to contact someone on board and possibly get a fix on the sub, Charlie and Ari were attacked, and now we know there's been contact between Westminster and the submarine. We have a problem on board."

My mind's racing and a sense of nausea rises inside.

"Leyla," Theo says quietly now, head tilted and gaze still fixed on me. "Was Lewis aware we were headed north after I skipped bail?"

I picture Lewis and shake my head. "Look, I really don't think—"

The doors slide open and the others enter the saloon, chatting.

"Mum's still asleep," says Tabby. She has Jojo with her and the puppy darts to the viewport where her breakfast bowl waits for her. "I'm guessing she was awake most of the night worrying about what's going on with all the protests. I'll take her some breakfast after she's had her rest."

Soon we're all on the sofas, tucking in. Lewis yawns as he digs into the French toast.

I want to say what's going on—that there seems to be someone on board colluding with Sebastian. But voicing it aloud to everyone would make it very real, and it's too ugly a thing to establish. As I look on the faces around me I really, really don't want for it to be true. It's only a matter of time before we can't contain it anymore, though.

"Did you get any sleep?" Ari asks me.

"Yes. How are you feeling this morning?" I lean into him. "Do you want to talk about what happened yesterday?"

His movements are much slower than usual, but his wounds are healing well and the swelling's mostly died down. I'm guessing his ribs still feel sore, though he'd never mention it.

He chews on his lip. "Much better," he says absently. "It's not the attack, it's something else. . . ." He swallows. "Later," he says with a small nod.

I think about the state of him when he returned last night. He and Charlie could've died. As I eat I recall all the times I've seen Ari hurt and in pain. He had to endure yet more of it yesterday, and was forced to fight back. He has to go through all that, and I'm afraid to simply voice the truth?

"Somebody on board the *Kabul* is communicating with the authorities."

Silence.

Tabby's jaw drops.

Lewis tenses, then his gaze flits from one face to another.

Theo turns a crimson color while stealing glances at Lewis.

Ari slowly puts down his cup, his expression veiled and eyes fixed on me.

Charlie looks uncomfortable with being present. I give him a small, reassuring nod and he returns it.

At last, Ari speaks. "You're sure about this, Leyla?"

I swallow before continuing. "Theo's discovered Westminster had contact with someone on board the sub. It happened sometime between midnight and early this morning."

Lewis's nostrils flare now. Tabby stays silent, mouth still open.

"Who?" Ari's voice drops really low.

"I don't know, Ari. We just don't know."

Jojo finishes her breakfast and comes bounding over to me. I scoop her up and hold her close, thankful for the distraction.

Tabby finally finds her voice. "It doesn't make sense, though. Nobody here would do that. I mean, why would they? Think about it, Leyla, they'd have to have a *really* good motive to collude with that scum."

"I would sooner set fire to all of Westminster than work with them," Ari says, his tone unflinching.

"I'd walk out on the Den before I had anything to do with the murdering low-life running this country. And the Den's my only home." Charlie stares away into space.

"They caused our father's death," Theo says quietly.

It's heartbreaking. *Nobody* here has a motive for conspiring with those in charge. We already knew that. This doesn't make sense. If anything, everyone has a solid reason for working *against* the rot at Number 10.

"It's bollocks," Tabby says, flicking her hair back. "Everyone went to bed and nobody got up to contact the authorities."

I press my lips together and Theo shifts in his seat. He shoots another quick glance in Lewis's direction and his skin flushes further.

Lewis stayed up all night.

There's an angry glint in Lewis's eyes as he rubs his palm back and forward over his buzz cut. "It ain't me."

Ari tenses. "I know."

"I'm not saying it is, though." I have to force my voice out because the atmosphere's thick with tension now and I wish I were anywhere but here. "It's just that everyone needs to know what's going on. Also, whoever's working against Bia at the Den is trying to contact one of us on board. Bia traced multiple attempts at communication in the early hours of the morning. And if they get through, they could pinpoint our exact location."

It falls quiet. The silence is killing me.

Theo's Bracelet bleeps and he brings up several files. He whizzes through them quickly before swishing them out of sight.

He clears his throat. "I ran another scan. The communication with Westminster took place sometime this morning, and there was interference—heat-generated. Currently the only areas showing up as matching that kind of temperature are around the reactor and the engine room. The reactor compartment's off-limits. So basically whoever contacted Westminster did so from inside the engine room."

"Yer info could be wrong, lad," Lewis says bitingly.

Theo chews on his lip. "Actually, the tech on those scans is near perfect."

The look Lewis sends him could freeze the oceans.

"I haven't even *seen* yer engine room," Charlie says.

"Me neither," Lewis offers immediately. "Never been anywhere near it. And I'm done here now. I'm gonna get a lift down with me mam instead." He stands.

Ari shakes his head. "Stay."

Tabby twists in her seat, her eyes frantic. Charlie's gaze darts to Lewis and I know what he's thinking. Lewis was hovering outside the engine room as we left the galley with the breakfast trays. He said he was contacting his mum.

The situation is starting to get out of hand. I rack my brains for what to do but can't come up with anything that sheds any light on it. And though Oscar can trace heartbeats on board to their exact location, it's only possible in real time so he's no help right now either. It's very hard to believe anybody in the room could be guilty of something so malicious.

I shake my head. "Lewis, please don't leave. It's very possible there's another explanation for everything. But we all need to know exactly what's going on." I stand. "I'm off to do my rounds," I mutter to nobody in particular.

Thankfully it seems to stir everyone a little. Theo gets back to scrutinizing the files with Charlie helping him. Tabby and Lewis move to the viewport and speak in hushed voices.

What a mess. I leave the saloon and take the winding staircase down to the engine room. It's immediately hotter and noisier inside, and tanks and pipes fill the space. Jojo jumps out of my arms and races around.

"Oi, you muppet, get back here at once," I say, making a start on the inspections.

Everything looks satisfactory as I give it the once-over. I check the atmosphere control equipment and there's nothing to worry about. I'm almost done. "Oscar?"

The Navigator flickers into existence and the sight of him immediately lifts my spirits a little as I check a row of thermostats. "Morning, Oscar. You're such a welcome sight right now, you know. And how do you always know what to pair with what?" I tap one of the dials.

Oscar's decked out in breeches and a beige frilly shirt, with a velvet turquoise waistcoat finishing off the look. He offers one of his subtle smiles and nods in gratitude. "Well, my lady, my secret is that I have the simplest of tastes. I am always satisfied with the best."

I manage a small smile of my own. "Never change, Oscar. Is everything running smoothly?"

He nods to confirm.

Jojo scampers back playing with a tiny ball of rubbish.

"Ugh, Jojo, let it go!"

"Oh, how felicitous!" Oscar says. "I myself have always lived by the old *finders keepers* adage. Why, on a particularly wet evening nearby Trinity College, I once…"

I chase after the puppy, finally grabbing her, but she refuses to give up the rubbish. "Fine. You're lucky I've so much on my mind right now."

We exit and I make my way to the control room.

All looks satisfactory. Still, I double-check with Oscar and he confirms everything's working perfectly.

As I pass the pool room on my way back to the saloon, Charlie's sub catches my eye. I remember promising him a full diagnostics on the vessel.

"Charlie," I say into my Bracelet. "Can you switch on your sub so I can have her checked out?"

"Done! She's open and should be up and running. Give us a shout if there's any problem, though."

"Be good!" I say to Jojo as I leave her outside the pool room. She's no longer chewing on the rubbish; hopefully she spat it out. I enter the chamber.

While I'm waiting on the sub's test to yield its findings, I check the vessel's external HUD myself. The compass and depth gauge are off and I make a mental note to have them looked at properly. As soon as the results trickle in for the rest of the craft, I begin scanning them. The rear fin and wing took hits but they're repairable. I look on the dent in the tail and shudder; a little closer to the sub's body and Charlie would've been done for. The vessel will definitely need repairing before he sets off again.

I open the door and peer in at the cockpit. All looks good, though the dashboard's flickering here and there. Even the slightest glitch can prove fatal out there, and Theo will have to double-check that for him. The route planner's frozen on the last journey the sub took yesterday, a straight line from Cambridge stopping just shy of Bergen. I shake my head as I take in the state of the faulty dashboard. What if either of them had been fatally hit yesterday?

Who attacked them? And did someone tip them off?

Once more a weight settles in my stomach as I think of the spy at the Den trying to contact someone on the sub. And who among us contacted Westminster from the *Kabul*? I can't stand it, the not knowing. But no matter how hard I think on it, it's impossible to picture anyone on board doing such a thing. I rub my temples as my imagination conjures up all kinds of scenarios, none of them comforting. The chamber suddenly feels as if it's closing in on me.

I catch sight of the pool door and it's like a light amid all the uncertainty. An escape. I chew on my lip: just five minutes. A quick swim around the sub. I confirm with the Navigator that there's nobody in the area and he assures me it's completely clear.

I check the test on Charlie's vessel is complete. Soon as I've had my swim, I'll get on to repairs. I hasten through the hatch, removing my Bracelet and slippers as the pool door slides open, and dive right in.

The water feels tepid and the current is calm. It has the usual green tinge familiar to this part of the Norwegian Sea. Hovering below the shadow of the *Kabul*, I take in my surroundings as I breathe the waves in and out. I just really need a few minutes to myself. My dress clings to me. Swishing my hair out of my vision, I scan the waves in every direction. Tiny fish dart past, and as I hover there I can *feel* the sub. The *Kabul* effuses a gentle vibration, and when I hold out my hands I can see its effect on the water. I swim out from under its shadow, and then up the side of its body.

It's actually quite scary just how big the vessel is. She suddenly seems so vulnerable suspended in the deepest depths, as if she's too heavy and might sink at any moment. She stretches out of sight at both ends. It's a miracle we ever manage to stay hidden. Thank God for mountain ranges, and especially for Theo's extraordinary tech know-how. I run my hands over her matte body, defiant and powerful. Back when she was at the Mayfair Hangars it was clear she was a gunmetal-gray color, but in the water she only ever appears black. A dark, expansive metal tube, with a single row of glowing portholes.

Climbing higher through the waves, I reach the top of the sub and make my way over to the little acrylic dome. It covers a tiny viewing space leading off the first floor of the craft and offers a 360-degree aspect of the surroundings. I've barely had the opportunity to sit in it and watch the world go by as I'd planned.

I move around over the vessel, taking everything in. The only part of her that fills me with so much dread I can barely look at it is the huge propeller. There's something so eerie about the colossal blades rotating away on submarines. I quickly move on, toward the other end of the sub.

Hovering outside the viewport is unlike anything I thought it would be. The saloon looks so homely with its cozy glow radiating out through the windows and around its bow. It's surreal being on the outside looking in. I can't believe the vessel is mine. A safe space where I'm free to be myself. Where I can do whatever I want, whenever I wish to. *Home.*

There's not much movement in the saloon, and from everyone's body language, things are still tense inside. An ache grows as I watch them. Oh how I wish we knew exactly what was going on. I don't know where to even begin with this latest problem. One of us could be colluding with the enemy, and we're all stuck together in here. I can't see a way out.

I wave the hair away from my face and move, gliding up and over the vessel. Making my way back to the center, I hover there, staring up into the endless dark green of the liquid environment. The world floats by, highlighted by the sub's glow. Tiny creatures drift obliviously, and bubbles speckle the watery folds. As I stare into the rippled current, I go over everything on my mind. I think about everyone who knew the more sen-sitive stuff these past few days, and I try to picture them passing it on to Sebastian. My brain won't form the images.

A turtle swims into sight above, lazily flapping its flippers. It looks so carefree and I ache to feel like that again. Lately, the gaps between not being sick with worry about something have become ever shorter. The creature suddenly tucks its head and limbs away as it floats on. And then my heart stutters when I realize why it's hid like that.

I gulp at the shadowy wall of shapes as it stealthily advances in this direction from my right. It can't be more than five meters above me. An Orca pod. I daren't move, even though I know they pose no danger to me.

The pod draws ever closer, the creatures growing bigger as it does, and now I spot the calves swimming alongside their mothers. The smallest of them float along against the adults' sides. There are around a dozen of the animals, all of them black on top with white patches and underbellies. Low clicks and whistles and various nasal sounds reach my ears as the group moves through the depths. I hold my breath as the pod starts pass-ing directly over me. The adults are all rubbery flesh marred with scars and lines. The colossal creatures glide over the submarine. Goodness, some of them must be at least six meters long. It's the most staggering sight and my heart feels like it's soared to the surface. The creatures swim over, tiny eyes barely moving as the lengthy bodies glide through the current.

I sigh as I watch the pod pass. *Wow.* It commands the entire water as it goes. Soon, they're out of sight and I can't believe what I just witnessed.

How smart was that turtle to quickly hide in its shell? And how do they still know where they're headed when they tuck their heads in like that? I shake my head; if I spent my entire life out here, I'd still not know all the secrets of the deep. I'd be completely lost without my maps.

I pause as a thought suddenly occurs to me. Unease grips me.

The more I ponder the matter, the tenser I become. Soon a weight heavier than all the surrounding pressure bears down on me. So many moments and conversations that have taken place all swirl around until I feel my head might burst. But I can't unthink the thought now. It's absurd and doesn't make any sense. Except…my heart is telling me I'm right.

I move, swimming over the side of the submarine and underneath its belly until I'm back at the pool, and rise to reenter the *Kabul*. I grab my Bracelet and snap it on as soon as I exit the shower.

Jojo's right where I left her outside the chamber and I scoop her up. "For goodness sake, Jojo, spit it out." She's still chewing on whatever she found in the engine room and I try easing it out of her mouth. "Do you want to choke?"

She whines and tries to bury her face in my top but I persevere until she's forced to give it up. I fling the ball of rubbish into the nearest bin.

And pause to stare at it. I freeze as I take it in.

My suspicions are correct. They *have* to be.

"Oh, Jojo."

I try swallowing the nerves but my insides are all over the place now. I scan the length of the passageway; it's empty, thank goodness. I need somewhere to think. The engine room. I indicate for Jojo to go on upstairs in the direction of the saloon, and thankfully she does as she's told for once. I can't be distracted. As soon as I slip into the hot whirring of the engine room, I secure the door, move to the far side, and summon the Navigator.

"Oscar?" I motion for him to be discreet when he materializes. "Please stay here, in the room? I just need you to be here, that's all." He's not a real person, yet still I feel stronger for his presence right now. For not being alone.

He nods and, folding his arms, comes to stand by my side.

I sort out my thoughts. There's something I must do. Taking several deep breaths, and praying I'm making the right decision, I bring up my Bracelet and lower my voice.

At last, when I'm done, I end the call. Then I make another. I'm quivering by the time the calls are over. From anger.

I unlock the door and edge my head out slowly. All is clear. I run upstairs to my room and find what I need. The passageway feels as if it's closing in on me as I make my way to the saloon. The doors open and I step inside the space. My heart races.

Theo's standing by the screens, his brow furrowed as he peers closely at a stream of data on a nearby hovering file. Tabby's on the sofas, thanking Charlie as he moves toward her with a warm drink for her. Vivian's joined everyone and sits taking her breakfast opposite Tabby, her mouth pressed in a thin line and her gaze far away. I move through the room. Jojo's by her water bowl in the viewport, sipping away. Ari and Lewis take turns throwing knives at Ari's target board. Ari's about to throw, when he spots me and pauses.

Lewis plays with the knife he's holding. "Everything all right, lassie?"

"Did you go out into the water?" asks Tabby from the sofa. "Why's your hair damp?"

Vivian throws a glance at my hair and shifts in her seat.

"Found another alert that looks well dodgy," Theo says as he makes his way to us. "Nothing concrete yet, but someone was really keen on getting through. Charlie's going to have another quick look through the files in case I've missed anything."

"Happy to," says Charlie. "My main job back at the Den." He turns to me, hope in his gaze. "All done with the diagnostics, Leyla? Any chance me sub will make it?"

Lewis spins the knife around in his hand.

"Yes," I say to Charlie. "Your vessel will be all right. You've no idea how much I wish the same could be said for you."

I bring up my hand, point the brolly at Charlie, and zap him until he drops.

CHAPTER TWENTY-NINE

"**B**loody hell!" Theo looks at Charlie lying unconscious on the floor, checks his pulse, and stares back at me. "Leyla?"

"What the hell is going *on* around here!" Tabby shouts, rushing over.

I only now realize Ari's standing close beside me, knife at the ready, and he holds his other hand out in front to shield me. His brow is slightly creased as we lock eyes, but he nods, and I'm heartened to realize he trusts me without question.

Vivian stands, deathly pale, her hand flying to her throat. "I don't understand...."

"Mum, don't worry," says Theo. He turns to me, his eyes wide and swirling with questions.

"Maybe take your breakfast in your room until we sort it?" says Tabby. The twins' mother doesn't need to be told twice and hastens out of the saloon.

Lewis stands there, hands on hips as he glances back and forth between Charlie and me. "Yer pulling me fucking leg?"

"He had us *all* fooled," I say. "Oscar? Bring up the Den."

"The Den?" Theo says, frowning. "But they'll get a fix on the sub!" He searches my face. "What do you know?"

I turn to the screen and Jas is already waiting. Theo crosses and uncrosses his arms. We gather in the seating area where we can all see Jas.

"What about *him*?" Tabby points to Charlie.

"He'll be out of it for at least fifteen minutes," says Theo, lowering his voice as he turns to me. "What's going on, Leyla? And are you *sure* we can trust Jas?"

"Absolutely," I say, and we all acknowledge Jas before I continue. "Charlie had us believe the mole at the Den was contacting someone on board, and that if they got through they could trace the sub. He even had Bia and Papa convinced. It made one of us look suspect, and ensured the Den couldn't warn us about Charlie. Because Jas had worked it out. He was onto Charlie, and tried to tell us what he'd discovered."

Theo doesn't stop shaking his head.

"Such as?" Tabby folds her arms.

"You know all those times security forces carried out an attack shortly after Bia's lot got in touch with the communities? It was always Charlie. He's been working for Sebastian all along. When Ari—"

"But we worked together to *stop* them!" Theo wears a pained stare as he runs his hand through his hair. "I don't understand!"

"Let Leyla finish," Tabby says gently, rubbing his back.

"When Ari and I stopped at Cambridge," I continue, "Blackwatch turned up at the Trading Post the next morning. It wasn't a coincidence. *He* alerted them. He was hoping they'd capture us away from the Den. I always thought it so strange how someone with the might and know-how of Blackwatch missed the Den every time they raided the place above it. Except, they never missed it. They've always known where Bia and her group were. They left them alone because thanks to that little snake there, the communities they hunted were sometimes delivered right into their hands. Charlie simply passed on the location to Sebastian every time."

Theo blinks away as he processes my words. Ari is very still as he listens. Lewis tries to make his way to Charlie, and Tabby takes up the job of stopping him.

"How do you know all this?" Ari asks.

"I spoke with Jas after I became suspicious."

Tabby throws her hands up. "But *how* did you come to suspect him?"

"His sub. I ran a diagnostics on it and the dashboard's playing up. The route planner's frozen on his last journey. A journey registered to start from the Den in Cambridge, and end in Bergen. Don't you see? The little dick lied to us about being out here to visit someone in Trondheim for some top-secret info on Sebastian. There *was* no guy in Trondheim—he made that whole story up to Bia. He never went farther than Utsira, and that's because he wasn't aware of our exact location. All he knew was we were somewhere around Bergen. He clearly came all the way out here for *us*."

Ari's face darkens. He tightens his grip on his knife and flips it between his fingers.

"The sneaky shit…" Tabby's face is flushed.

Theo remains silent, his mouth slack.

Lewis starts pacing again. "The attack on him and Ari. Who? Why?"

I shake my head. "The damage to his sub isn't critical. He was never in any real danger. All that firepower with only a single sub in its sights and they still missed? No way. They were obviously in on it with him, but I've no idea to what end. And now I know why he was so puzzled by the beast's assault on the community in Tórshavn. He was genuinely confused because just for once he wasn't in on an attack." I turn to the screen. "Jas?"

He nods. "So Bia contacted me right after Leyla updated her, and we're getting a clearer picture of what's been going on here at the Den. Charlie became paranoid he was close to being discovered. He was especially on edge after Leyla spoke to him from Ben's."

"I mentioned how odd it was the communities were always attacked shortly after the Den discovered their location," I explain to the others. "Wow, he'd pretended to be so hurt about the attacks, the little snake."

Jas nods. "You'd rattled him. To cover his back, he started casting doubt on my loyalties, nothing major, but quietly sowing seeds of doubt in Bia, abusing her good nature. I noticed the difference in her. She grew cautious around me, started keeping me out of the loop. I couldn't work out why and…turned to Charlie. It was right after the incident at the lab, and of course now I know why he was so bloody touchy when I brought it up. The anger worked in my favor, though, because he let his guard slip.

Instead of his usual 'poor old Charlie' persona, I met a totally different person. He was off his head, accused me of being paranoid and suffering from shrub addiction. It was something else.... None of us had ever seen that side to him and I knew nobody would believe me. I stayed quiet, let him think I'd forgotten it. But I started looking into things."

Jas pauses and leans aside to pass on instructions off-screen, and the Den can be seen in the background. Everyone's busy rushing through the space. When he's done, he notices our expressions. "Once they don't hear back from Charlie, they'll suspect we've worked things out. And then they'll come for us," he says, mouth pinched. "We're well equipped, but if the full might of Blackwatch rolls in, we stand no chance. Especially because some of us already left for London. The good news is Bia said she started clearing the Den out as soon as Charlie first cast suspicion on me. She was right to anticipate an attack once Westminster realized they no longer had to hide knowledge of our existence. Except Bia thought it was because of me, not Charlie. We need to get out of here before they hit us."

I swing around to Ari. "Remove Charlie's Bracelet and check him thoroughly for any other tech."

Jas's words fill me with dread as I return my gaze to him. "Jas, go if you need to."

He casts a look behind him. "I'm okay for another minute. I became uneasy with Charlie's conduct after I started looking into things, so I took every opportunity to limit the flow of info in his direction. I tried to answer certain calls, 'forgot' to deliver messages, and so on."

Theo's face flushes with color and he rubs the back of his neck.

"Took me a while to build up the courage to share my worries, though," Jas continues. "I thought nobody would believe me—he'd already started discrediting me." His face hardens. "Then he left for the north and it was all hush-hush. Bia was on her way to London by the time I was ready to talk. No matter what I tried, though, I couldn't get through to her. When Gideon and your dad also didn't accept my calls, I realized something was up. Of course now I know he'd told them I was trying to get a fix on their locations. All I could think to do was to contact you directly. I feared something was going on, that you needed to know he was traveling up north. Except I couldn't get through to anyone. And then you called today out of no—" He breaks off to speak to someone behind him and waves at us. "Gotta go, take care. Switch to Bracelets only." The screen goes blank.

"Bloody hell," says Theo. "I was so wrong." He twists his mouth. "That lying, scheming little—"

Jojo yelps loudly and we jerk our heads toward the sound. I scream.

Charlie has Jojo.

We all rush toward him. I freeze at the sight of Jojo looking so helpless, her mouth open with her tongue hanging out, as he stands holding her in front of him. Lewis and Ari stand poised, ready to lunge at him.

"I'll hurt her. I swear I'll bleedin' hurt her if any of you so much as lay a finger on me."

My grip tightens around the brolly's handle and I don't take my gaze off Jojo. She fixes her round brown eyes on me. I'll zap him until his heart stops if I have to, before he can hurt her.

"What the actual hell?" Tabby says, her hands curling into fists beside her.

Theo rummages in the cabinet and grabs some rope.

Charlie suddenly cries out, swearing. Jojo's bitten his hand. She struggles a little before leaping down away from him and straight into my arms. Tabby launches herself at Charlie, spinning in the air toward him. Her foot hits him full force on the chest, sending him staggering back. She lands gracefully on her feet. Charlie wheezes as the wind is knocked out of him.

Ari, Theo, and Lewis are instantly on him, tying his hands behind his back. Lewis's face shines as he glances up at Tabby and she flashes him a smug smile.

Ari and Lewis drag Charlie over to the bookcases and force him into the lavender chair. Theo finds more rope and they secure him in place. Everyone's breathing hard and fast as we gather around him.

My face is hot and I take several breaths before I speak. "You need to talk," I tell him. "Tell us everything right now."

He screws his face up. "I've no idea what yer talk—"

I reach into my pocket and fling the remaining pieces of the origami model of Jojo at him. "That's the model I made for you. Jojo found it at the back of the engine room. You know—"

"The room you've never stepped foot in!" says Lewis, his voice rising as he looks on the shredded paper. He shakes his head. "And you dared to act all innocent?"

Charlie goes red as he stares on the pieces, before collecting himself. "Proves *nothing*." He blows his wispy hair out of his face, and stares dead ahead.

I point the brolly at him and he flinches. "If you don't start talking, I'll zap you again—except twice as long this time. You've done more than enough damage already. I saw your damn dashboard and your last logged journey. You never went anywhere *near* Trondheim, you liar. You stopped at Utsira because *we* were your destination!"

Realization sweeps across his face and he swallows nervously as Ari moves closer to him.

Theo folds his arms, his nose wrinkled. "You gained my trust, acted like we were mates," he says bitterly. "And all along you were just using everything I told you, for your own rotten purposes. You make me sick."

I jab Charlie with the brolly. "Why did you ask me to meet you?"

Ari leans in, his voice a whisper. "Answer her." When Charlie remains silent, he grabs him and puts him in a neck hold, the tip of his knife denting his skin. "You're in no position to stay silent. Now answer our questions."

Charlie's eyes bulge. "All right!" he says, looking dead ahead and refusing to meet anyone's gaze. "But I'm not saying shit until *he* gets this knife off me neck."

Ari lets go but stays put.

"Now talk," I say. "Start with why you asked me to meet you at the location."

He looks at Ari, who's poised ready with the knife, and my brolly pointed at his chest, and shifts in his seat. "I was gonna deliver you to the captain," he says. "What with that whole reward thing going on. More money than I'd make all year. I knew Bia had warned yer dad against letting anyone on board, so I reckoned I'd get you to leave instead—knew you'd volunteer." He finishes with a hint of scorn in his expression.

I stare at him, stunned. "And then what?"

"Well *he* went and showed up instead, didn't he?" His face grows red as he glances briefly in Ari's direction before returning his focus to me. "Everything would've been perfect if you'd only done as I'd asked, but no, you always have to—"

We gasp as Ari's knife embeds itself in the chair inches from Charlie's face. He moves toward him and Charlie goes very still as Ari pulls his knife out and leans in. "Watch your mouth."

I shoot Ari a pleading look. Charlie needs to keep talking, dammit. I turn back to him. "And what did you plan to do once I met you there?"

His whole posture is rigid. "They'd capture you. And I knew if this lot heard you were in trouble, they'd head there. Sebastian would have *everything*: Britain's most wanted *and* the source of the broadcasts. Plus a whole bunch of your kind. And I'd pick up every reward going—*millions*. And the submarine of course."

Tabby swears, then punches him, her eyes blazing. He flinches. Theo pulls her away before she can hit him again. Lewis looks thunderous; his nostrils flare as he gazes down on Charlie.

I shake my head. "You'll *never* take the *Kabul* from me. Ever. What happened when Ari turned up instead? The truth, now."

He falls quiet but as soon as Ari gets ready to aim, he opens his mouth again. "What do you *think* happened? It all went belly up, didn't it? Orders were clear enough for him after he escaped the lab, so it should've been simple. But he went friggin' wild and attacked my friends. . . . We're not allowed to operate up here, so I'd asked mates to help me out. He killed innocent people. Yer a bunch of animals!"

"Can't have been that innocent if they were willing to take Ari's life." Lewis gets ready to throw a punch. "Yer a little—"

"Please!" I say, holding up my hand to Lewis and not taking my eyes off Charlie. "What were the specific orders for Ari?"

He shrugs. "He has a terminate on sight out on him, doesn't he?"

My stomach heaves. "You're saying the rest of us don't?"

He curls his lip. "What do you take us for? We're civilized people. You'd end up in Broadmoor, obviously. But him... Orders are very clear for him. Anyone who ends him and delivers proof?" He whistles. "Massive bonus."

We all turn to Ari, who keeps his gaze fixed on Charlie, his expression unreadable.

I don't understand. Why does Sebastian feel such an intense loathing toward Ari that he wouldn't even bother with the pretense of a trial and imprisonment? I'm public enemy number one, and also an amphi, and apparently even I don't have a terminate on sight on my head. What *is* Sebastian's problem with Ari?

Charlie twists his face as he scowls. "Except if three subs didn't manage to end him, how the bleedin' hell was I gonna? And it weren't only that—without him I wasn't gonna get anywhere near yer sub. So I had to ignore orders, like. The captain would understand why, once I delivered the lot of you. Yeah, I reckoned the best thing to do was to make Ari think I couldn't go on, that I'd need to be brought to the sub. Had to think on me feet, like."

I take a deep breath. I want so badly to hit him with the brolly. "Why did you try and make out as if one of us was working for Sebastian?"

"This morning I saw Jas was trying to contact the sub. Bia had warned him against doing that. For him to go over her head it had to be big. I figured he was onto me. So I told you he was trying to trace yer sub." He shrugs. "And once I sent in me report to Westminster, I realized the sub had notifications for all government contact." His face hardens as he glares at Theo now. "And I couldn't override them. So I reckoned having you suspicious of one another would help keep the heat off me all round. I only had to stay in the clear until Blackwatch got here."

"You scheming little fucker." Lewis advances again, but Tabby holds him back. "Have you already called them?" he asks.

Charlie ignores him.

Ari moves closer again. "You'll tell us what we want to know, or I drag you into the pool," he stresses quietly. "So, have you alerted anyone to our whereabouts?"

Charlie twists his mouth, regret lingering at its corners. "No," he spits out bitterly. "I was just thinking on how I was gonna do that without setting off any more freakin' notifications."

Tabby leans in. "Wait, did you tell on Theo, too? Is that why he was arrested?"

"It weren't anything to do with me! He were poking around classified stuff, breaking the law, got what he deserved."

"How did the authorities know they'd left London?" I ask him. "So few of us knew and yet they were ambushed. You definitely had a part in *that*, didn't you?"

He looks away, and Tabby leaps on him. "You could've killed us all!"

Jojo whines and I quickly soothe her. "We're frightening Jojo!" I shake my head and Lewis pulls Tabby away.

The Navigator materializes beside us. He takes in the sight of Charlie bound to the chair and his eyes glaze over. A small smile plays on his lips. "Oh I say. I should confess to a rather tantalizing incident of my own during an initiation at Oxford. The society demanded it! Two exceedingly charming boys tied me up and—"

"Oscar?" I raise my eyebrows.

"Oh." He clears his expression. "We have company, my dear. From Bergen."

"It's all right," I say to everyone. "They've come for him."

There are five of them, with two hefty submersibles between them. The Bergen authorities will question Charlie and then detain him until he goes on trial.

He pales now, squirming around in the chair. "No! Yer not leaving me with so many—" He catches himself and purses his mouth.

Tabby balls her fists. "What's the matter? Can't face the people you've been helping kill? Don't you even realize what you've done? You've caused *so* many deaths. Whole entire communities full of innocent people! You set *us* up. We would've died if Theo hadn't quickly done something. You tried to hand Leyla over to the Blackwatch yesterday. You're a freakin' monster. You've allowed the murder and torture of people to take place. Why are you in denial about what you've done?"

"It weren't me! I was only carrying out orders!" he shouts. "It weren't me in charge of sending anyone to the lab! I just—"

"You actively took part in all the horror," says Theo. "And you knew and stayed silent about other things so you let them happen, too. You're complicit in countless murders."

Charlie's face darkens and he turns to me, his expression pleading. "Leyla, please. Yer me only hope. Yer, you know—yer not like the others. You got to see it from my point of view. We're under threat! What do you think will happen if they're allowed to live freely? They'll take *everything* from us, can't you see? And anyway, I was only doing me job, weren't I? It's them that issue the orders who want punishing, not me. Just let me get in me sub and I'll be on me way. But don't leave me up north with these—"

"Oh, shut *up*," I say. "And I'm *exactly* like everyone else, you manipulative dick. You always had to know *everything* because you were just that cut up about it all. Always getting my papa to share what he knew, making a complete mockery of him. And you could've refused to carry out the orders! If there's nobody willing to do the dirty work, then it can't take place. It isn't rocket science! Think of all the people whose deaths you've caused by handing their locations over to Sebastian. It was you who sent Blackwatch to the lab when we hit it, wasn't it?" He shrinks back. "We could have all died!" I straighten as I realize something else. "After the prison breakout, when Ari was taken, you told me not to contact anyone. You said it was too dangerous. That was another lie, wasn't it? I was practically on my own for an entire bloody month when I could have been in touch with friends and family. You've been playing us—all of us—for far too long. *Ugh*, get the hell off my sub!"

Lewis unties the ropes binding Charlie to the chair and hauls him up. "You've outstayed yer welcome, lad," he says, his expression tight.

Charlie suddenly screws his face up at me. "Yer a meddling little bitch,

271

you know that? Yer gonna pay for it, destroying the lab like that and freeing all those freaks. Don't think you've got away with it. But Sebastian will take care of you, don't you be worrying about that!"

Tabby lunges at him. "Who are you calling a freak?"

Ari gestures for Lewis to take Charlie away at once. He stands astride, hands on hips and eyes burning.

Lewis pulls Charlie across the saloon. As the doors slide open, Charlie twists his body to meet my gaze, his face and neck flushed. "Yer dad's got a nice little reception waiting for him when he gets to London. And there's nothing you can do to stop it." He swears when Lewis drags him down the passageway.

A cold zigzags its way through me.

Theo shakes his head. "He's just trying to get to you."

"He's nothing but a lying little shit," says Tabby.

I feel numb.

Ari meets my gaze. "I'll contact them," he says. "But I wouldn't trust a word from that devil's mouth."

I nod absently. Charlie was terrified and furious. He was bound to lash out in anger.

As the Bergen authorities pull away, I realize my legs haven't stopped trembling for hours.

"Communication is messy right now, but I'll keep trying," says Ari. "Nothing for you to worry about."

I nod on autopilot and turn to everyone. "Please think of anything that might need sorting now that we know he was actually working for them all this time."

They get to work at once, alerting everyone who needs to know Charlie's real identity. Vivian is back in the saloon, taking comfort in looking after Jojo.

I turn to the Navigator. "Oscar, please secure the *Kabul*. Lock the pool, and I want her in defense mode."

Although Charlie said he didn't get the chance to give away our location, we can't risk it. He's a pathological liar. And yet...I can't shake off his words about Papa.

Why aren't Ari's parents answering his messages? I leave the saloon. Back in my bedroom, I move beside the porthole and try Papa. He doesn't answer. I message Bia and she has no idea why they aren't responding. She sounds like she's still in shock from discovering Charlie's betrayal.

"Hopefully what he said about your father was more lies, but regardless, I'm going to put word out for everyone to be on the lookout for their sub," she assures me. "And once they cross into London, we'll know about it and I'll send word right away. Sit tight, girl."

Just as I'm done, there's a soft knock on the door and I tell Ari to enter. He meets my gaze and shakes his head.

"Me neither. I've tried everything but Papa's not responding. If it was only a problem with their onboard systems, they could've still used their Bracelets."

Ari nods. "Unless they've gone off grid because they sensed company."

"Of course, that's what Theo did after they were ambushed on their way up here." Some of the weight lifts off me. "I just spoke with Bia. She said they'll be keeping an eye out for them, thank goodness. Everyone's right, most likely Charlie only blurted it out to spite me. Papa and your parents will be safe, inshallah." I nod away, trying to convince myself more than I am Ari, I think. But we do know Charlie's a proven liar and I shouldn't let him get to me like this.

Ari relaxes a little. "Yes." He holds out a hand. "Come, Leyla."

"I was just thinking about this place this morning," I say in hushed tones, "when I was out in the water. I realized I've barely sat here as much as I'd intended."

"It's a great spot," he says equally quietly.

We're sitting, shoulders touching, in the tiny observatory-styled area at the very top of the vessel. There are no walls or ceiling, only a translucent dome offering a 360-degree view of the world outside. It's perfectly small and cozy with just enough room for two or three people to sit. The Lumi-Orb casts a golden glow over us. It's the quietest space on the whole sub.

As we continue looking out into the current in silence, movement catches my eye.

"Ari, look."

We tilt our heads back as the shape drifts above us.

"It's a Greenland shark," he says, smiling.

The bulky creature glides above us, keeping up with the submarine. It's a stony-gray color with a rounded snout and small fins.

"They can live for hundreds of years, Leyla. We tested a sick one back home and the animal was six hundred years old."

Six hundred years. A wave of warmth sweeps through me. Some creatures have quietly continued about their lives for centuries down here. What a strange, magical thing time is.

"Ari, have you ever swum alongside sharks?"

"Never willingly. If we meet them on our path, we keep ourselves to ourselves and they mostly leave us alone. But make no mistake; any predatory creatures *will* attack us if they're hungry, or if we insist on catching their attention. We're human beings who can exist out there, but they are animals."

"Six hundred *years*, though. Wow."

"Have you heard of the immortal jellyfish?" he asks, looking down at my face. The reflection of the water ripples across his features and the warm glow of the light casts him in all kinds of beautiful shadows. "It got its nickname because the jellyfish can switch from a mature adult stage back to its early state, just like that."

"So it can basically live forever...."

He nods. "Biological immortality." His eyes suddenly cloud. "They were testing on them, too, back at the lab."

I slip my hand in his and we both squeeze at the same time. He looks away, out into the waters for a moment, before returning his gaze to me.

"I'll never forget how I felt when I saw you standing in front of the tank. I—I was losing myself," he says in hushed tones. He draws closer and I breathe him in. The muscle beside his jaw flexes as I stare back into shimmering eyes. He leans forward and, gently cupping my face, brings his mouth to my forehead and presses his lips against it. I can feel my pulse in my throat.

"Ari?" I whisper. "What happened yesterday? You were about to tell me before Lewis joined us."

His hands slowly drop from my face and he slips them in mine as a small line appears between his eyebrows. He swallows before speaking. "When they were chasing me around the water, I had these flashes.... I remembered more about that night, Leyla."

An empty feeling settles in my stomach and I fix my gaze on his.

Ari narrows his eyes. "I was swimming in the water. I saw you, swam up to you and placed my hand on the window. You covered it with your own and smiled at me." His mouth briefly slackens. "I can still recall how I felt. I was so happy to see you smile. But then..." He shakes his head and his voice drops. "I turned away from you. There was a woman in the water. And there was blood...I started screaming." He falls silent, his brow furrowed. "And now I remember, Leyla—there was a security sub."

Questions crash into my head but I stay silent and instead reach out to wrap my arms around him. Several seconds pass before he continues.

"I had blocked it out, but it suddenly came to me yesterday during the chase. The sub hovered in the distance, firing away nonstop. And it was *him*," he says, his voice hoarse. "Sebastian. He was inside it." I stiffen against him. "There's more, Leyla.... I can recall her voice now.... She— she told me to go. And then they fired on her. She died in the water. I looked at her and she was dead. And then—then my father found me...."

Silence. I tighten my embrace and he holds on, frozen. His words swirl around in my mind. It feels like an iceberg has drifted to plant itself right inside my chest and I shiver. Ari watched his mother killed by the authorities. And it *was* Sebastian—I knew it.

We sit in a quiet embrace for what feels like an eternity, before I voice my thoughts. "Ari, the woman in the water, the one Sebastian fired on, she was your mother, wasn't she?"

He stills for a moment before replying. "Yes. They killed my mother." He pulls back so we can see each other. "Why were we out in the open in London when it's the most dangerous place in the country for us?"

"I'm so sorry. And I just don't know. . . . It's all so strange and confusing. But whatever happened that night, we do now know for certain the authorities were involved."

I could never rest until I know what happened to Mama, exactly how and why they took her from Papa and me, so I know how Ari feels.

We return our gazes to the world outside and sit in silence.

As soon as things are more stable, and we have our parents back, I'm going to focus on uncovering what happened that night all those years ago. I take a deep breath to combat the heaviness in my chest. The truth is clearly something horrific and painful. But I *will* find it out.

First though, we should assume Charlie has compromised our safety. If Westminster knows of our exact location, we're in serious trouble.

I must make sure there's no way we'll be discovered tonight, and then first thing tomorrow, we're going to have to come up with a plan.

CHAPTER THIRTY

We're back in the viewport, sitting around the fire with the others. Waves lap the *Kabul*'s bow as we munch on sweets and quietly chat.

Tabby's telling Lewis all about the martial arts competitions she enters. Theo sips on hot chocolate as he and Ari discuss one of the latest games. Every now and then Theo glances at Oscar to ask him a tricky question, keen to test how sophisticated his programming is. The Navigator reclines on the plush cushions, a few feet from Lewis. He says something to Lewis and they both chuckle. I've never seen Oscar look happier.

My Bracelet flashes. Ari snaps his attention to me, his expression expectant.

I mouth "Bia" at him and we jump up.

I take the call in the passageway where it's quieter, Ari beside me.

"We just got word they entered the capital about an hour ago," says Bia. "Don't—"

"Yesss." I smile at Ari and he nods, relief flooding his face.

"Leyla, brace yourself for what I'm about to say, girl. Charlie had alerted Westminster to what your dad and the others were up to. They were ambushed on entry and towed somewhere. We're working on where they've taken them. I'm sorry."

I think my heart has stopped. Bia's words don't make sense. I turn to

Ari for clarification, but the relaxed expression of seconds ago has darkened. Bia still talks but none of it registers.

It can't be. *No.*

They have Papa.... Sebastian has his hands on him again. And this time Papa does actually have a list of illegal activities under his belt—starting with breaking out of prison. This time Sebastian *loathes* him.

"Must go," I mutter to Bia, and I end the call.

Ari and I stand there staring at each other.

"I have to go help him," I finally say, at the exact same time he says:

"I must leave at once for London."

"Ari, no—you're to be killed on sight, have you forgotten?"

We each try to talk the other out of the decision, until finally we accept we feel the same need to go.

We reenter the saloon and I turn to the others, forcing my voice out.

"I'm so sorry, but you have to leave the *Kabul.* I can drop you off wherever you need to go, before I move on."

They stop what they're doing and turn to stare at us.

Tabby squints at me. "Er, don't be daft, why would we want to leave the sub? Why are you trying to get rid of us? And where are you headed?"

"Oscar?" I beckon the Navigator. "Ensure the *Kabul* is ready for travel in the morning."

"Hoorah, my dear!" He clasps his hands. "I must confess all this tarrying of late does not quite agree with me. But at last we shall once more rule the waves. And what might the trajectory be?"

"I'm going home, Oscar. We're returning to London."

In the sudden silence of the saloon, the *Kabul*'s usually quiet hum is a roar.

Tabby interrupts it. "You'd be arrested on sight, you know that." She folds her arms. "Have you forgotten what you said to your dad? Your Britain's *most wanted.*"

Vivian clutches her pearls.

Theo stares at me. "What's happened, Leyla?"

"I'm in," says Lewis, eyes shining. "Will let me mam know. She's preparing to head down herself with several mates. There's quite a bit of folk already making their way to the capital from all over. They saw the broadcasts and they're not happy. They want answers."

I swallow before speaking. "They have Papa and Ari's parents."

It goes silent again, and then they all speak at once and I fill them in on what's happened.

"So I *have* to go," I explain. "We have the sub, and we're going to get them back."

Tabby's eyes cloud. "I understand that, and we really need for them to be safe. But isn't there another way? They bloody *hate* you. You've caused that scum Sebastian no end of bother. You absolutely can't risk being caught."

Theo shakes his head. "No, you can't..." He straightens and folds his arms. "But if you insist on going down, then I'm coming, too."

Vivian's eyes widen.

"*You're* wanted, too," Tabby says to him. "Or have you forgotten?"

"Yes." I frown at Theo. "You are."

"This is more important," he says.

Tabby sighs. "If you're serious about going back, then I'm coming, too."

I wring my hands and try to think. "But I don't want you two to return with me. *Please*. Stay here."

"*None* of you should be thinking about going to London," Vivian says in a high-pitched voice.

"Mum, Tabs and me were thinking about it anyway," says Theo. "We can't complain about what's going on if we don't make a stand when the time comes. But it was a case of London or stay here with Leyla." He turns to me. "So if you're heading that way, we're coming with you."

I plead with them to change their minds and let me leave them at Bergen, but they refuse. We sit and chat about it. And then it's decided. Ari will drop Vivian off at his aunt's place. Everyone else will stay on board the *Kabul* and travel to London with me.

"Your mother's simply not cut out for this sort of thing, my loves," Vivian says, her face drained of all color. "You must be careful, for me. Theo, you shan't be going unless you promise not to leave the submarine."

"But, Mum—"

"No." Vivian purses her mouth. "You skipped bail, and I won't have you risking being seen. If you insist on traveling down, you don't leave the vessel. You can help Leyla locate Hashem from right here on board the submarine."

Theo pauses, furrowing his brow, but eventually offers a reluctant nod.

The twins promise to be careful and their mother then turns her attention to me, her hands trembling. "Poor Hashem. And you must be careful, dear." She shakes her head. "These protests seem to be gathering momentum....It's all rather unsettling, isn't it? I do wish we could all just get along! Who knows what might happen now....You must prioritize your safety, sweetheart. Be ever so careful as you search for your father."

"I understand, Viv. We just want to try and get Papa, Ruby, and Ben back. I don't exactly plan on circling 10 Downing Street. She's going to stay hidden, in stealth mode. And if anything, the protests are the perfect cover."

Tabby nods. "Once we're in submersibles, we'll be lost among everyone—we couldn't be safer."

"And I can help make sure the *Kabul* remains concealed," says Theo. "You mustn't worry about us, Mum. I'll look after them, promise."

Apologizing again for not coming along, Vivian asks to be taken off the sub. Her nerves can't take any more, she explains.

Ari wants to see Freya before we set off, and he needs to pack a bag. "I have to tell her what's happened," he says reluctantly. "She needs to know what's going on before we leave."

Thank goodness Freya has her aunt; she's going to need support when she hears about her parents.

Lewis will drop off Vivian and Ari, head home to gather what he'll need, and then pick Ari up again on his return to the sub. Vivian's beside herself as she says her goodbyes, tearfully hugging the twins close. And then they leave.

Theo suspends all uploads and broadcasts at my request. They've been playing for long enough now and surely everybody's seen it all. He's had to constantly keep reconfiguring things to ensure tracking remains impossible. It's time for him to have a rest.

I pace the viewport, waiting for Ari and Lewis to return. When they do, it's well past midnight.

"How did Freya take it?" I ask Ari.

He shakes his head. "I couldn't do it. My aunt is dealing with it." He looks away as he rakes his fingers through his hair.

"She's in good hands." I squeeze his arm. "I've been thinking, Ari.... What if we don't wait until the morning to leave?"

"Lewis and I were pondering the same thing on our way back. The sooner we're in London, the better."

We discuss it further with the twins until we're sure of the route down and have a brief plan for what we hope to do once we get there. We'll hide the *Kabul*, and under the guise of ordinary protesters in submersibles, we'll try to locate our parents. And we leave immediately, taking shifts to keep watch.

We gather in the viewport and I beckon the Navigator.

"My lady?"

"Oscar, if the sub is ready, then I'd like for us to set off for London now instead of in the morning. I'm sending you my preferred route and you must take note of the several deviations where security bases are concerned."

The Navigator can barely contain his joy. "I say, what a grand scheme. Nothing quite like seizing the moment! And I assure you the *Kabul* is more than ready for immediate departure, my dear."

The submarine is secured. We gaze out into the water as she rises.

The more I think on it, the surer I am of my decision—and the more twisted the knot inside becomes.

Ever since Bia told us the authorities have Papa, I've been blocking him out. If I focus on what his capture means, I won't be able to act. Anytime his face flashes before me, I feel like hurling. He was so willing and determined to go and help. I recall the state I found him in back in prison and take deep breaths. I keep telling myself I'll never again give in to fear, but it's ruled so many decisions for so long, it slips right back in without my even realizing. But enough, dammit. There's no way on earth I'm hovering around in safety up here when Papa's among monsters. Besides, we have an advantage—they don't know of our plans. And I'm going to make sure it stays that way.

"Remember, not a word to *anyone*," I say to the others.

"Yikes," says Tabby suddenly, pointing to our left. "They're *massive*."

We stare as a number of razor-sharp-teethed barracuda bolt past the viewport. They're easily five feet long, their silver bodies gliding through the current until they're out of sight.

I'm staying away from the mainland and sticking to wilder waters for as long as possible. No need to tussle with border patrol any earlier than necessary. And I'll need an escape route planned for after we find our parents. We must get out of the capital as quickly as possible at that point. Only the wilder waters can give me the kind of protection we'll need if we have to flee the Blackwatch. I must ensure my chosen course proves challenging for them.

The submarine hums, and turns direction in the surging waves. My heart races. *Bismillah*.

There's a moment's pause, and then with her familiar rhythmic *thrum* the *Kabul* speeds up, her bow piercing the dark-green currents of the Norwegian Sea as she leaves Norway and heads straight back for London.

CHAPTER THIRTY-ONE

It's early evening on the next day when we finally come to a stop in the North Sea. The sub has traveled as far south as it needs to. We're staying leagues away from the border, though, until we're sure we can slip back into Britain as discreetly as possible.

As confident of my chosen route as I can be, I wave away the simulated map and make my way to the viewport. I go over my decisions as I stare into the waves so close to home.

I've chosen to enter via Southend-on-Sea and take the Dartford Tunnel border crossing into the capital, as it's the least patrolled of London's borders. It means we're taking on mainland border patrol and the capital's own border security all at once, but that has its benefits, and I have an idea. If I can work a way around all of them, then it would save us a ton of bother.

Ari is double-checking on things in the engine room after our journey down, and Theo's doing the same by the screens. Tabby and Lewis are hard at work ensuring those we can trust without question now know of our presence. We're going to need all the help we can get in locating our parents. Beside me, Jojo gazes out happily, wagging her tail and blissfully unaware of the growing unrest somewhere out there, and the hard knot in my stomach. I message Bia.

Her expression darkens when I tell her where we are. She's in her sub, and from the shaky images and the lights around her, it's clear the waters are busy. "You need to turn around right now and head straight back for the north, girl!" She presses her mouth into a thin line. "I told you I'd put people on it!"

"Any news? Please," I say, "we're going out of our minds."

"You need to leave, Leyla, or mark my words, you *will* be discovered."

Bia and her group have more than enough to contend with. I don't expect them to drop everything they've worked so hard toward all these years and prioritize our parents instead. And I'm neither helpless nor clueless.

"But we stand a chance, if you help us, Bia. You know more than we do about what's going on right now. Share it with us. *Please.* If we at least know what we can expect when we head down in our subs, then we have more of a chance of staying safe and finding our parents."

Bia pinches the bridge of her nose. "Head down in your subs? So you plan on crossing the border in the submarine?" She shakes her head. "You'll never make it past the bases."

"There are ways we can hide, though, even out in the open. And if anyone's life is threatened, I have plans for escape for everyone on board. Where's the heart of the protests right now?"

"Around St. James's."

"Then that's where we drop into London from."

Bia's forced to make several erratic turns in her sub to avoid the growing chaos around her. When she's in the clear again, she opens her mouth as if she's about to speak, but then closes it again, her face tense as she contemplates my words. Finally, she lifts her shoulders, her mouth downturned. "We have a couple of locations they could be keeping your parents at," she shouts as she steers on. "There are rumors the old docking station in Kensington is being used as a holding center during all this. And there's the warehouse in Regent's Park—lots of covert activity reported close by. It's anyone's guess! Harrow is a no-go area, do you understand? Protests have turned violent over there." She throws a glance over her shoulders to gauge what's behind her. "The mood out here is worsening by the minute. People are struggling with the extent of what the broadcasts revealed and are starting to panic. And you've got security forces trying to cause as much damage to protesters' vessels as possible. St. James's *is* your best bet if you insist on being here, but wipe your vessels clean and— Stay in touch!"

Bia cuts off, and from the sudden flashing of lights, I know security subs have turned up in the area. I hope to God she stays safe. What *is* going on in London?

At least we have something to work on. We need to investigate the holding centers Bia mentioned.

Equipment drifts past the viewport and I peer closer. It's one of those old motorized Keep Great Britain Tidy filter contraptions of a decade ago that were meant to trap debris as they moved along. They proved largely ineffective and only added to the rubbish in the water. A familiar monotonous voice drones around the saloon and I groan as I turn around.

"Sorry." Theo grins. "Must keep on top of everything, though."

"I'd forgotten just how awfully dull he sounds."

Wireless Man is busy warning of a "hostile-looking" pod of dolphins sighted above Twickenham, and advising everyone to avoid the Ealing area where another earthquake has struck. He announces a new batch of Eyeballs, sharper and more flexible than ever before, able to reach even the most awkward of spaces. The increased surveillance will help with predicting the earthquakes, he reassures everyone.

Welcome home, Leyla.

"Brilliant," says Theo, his expression hardening. "Just what the country needed."

"An army of cameras to help predict something they secretly willfully cause? They've truly lost it. They make me want to vomit. I can't believe they're still carrying out the earthquakes. Do you think the PM knows exactly how vile Sebastian is? The quakes have *killed* people. Don't they think we're afraid enough, without adding this horror to our lives?"

Theo draws his eyebrows together. "We exposed the quakes in the broadcasts, but looks like it didn't deter them."

I fold my arms. "They're going to clamp down. On all of it. That's why the increased surveillance and another earthquake so soon after the broadcasts. And God only knows what else they have planned." I take in a deep breath and blow out my cheeks. "Are we ready, Theo? I think just before she had to go, Bia was advising we wipe our subs of all ID?"

"Good call, and I'm guessing we won't be the only ones driving clean vessels today." He glances back at the screen and the array of files hovering by the seating area, and nods. "We're still invisible to the Traffic Ordinance Council's systems, and we're off everyone else's radar, too. And if you're *sure* security bases won't spot us directly, then that's sorted. Okay, the subs."

In the pool room we cover up all identifying info on the submersibles. It takes several minutes to ensure they're no longer traceable, and then we're done.

"Right." Theo straightens. "I guess we're as ready as we'll ever be."

"We're going to go where they can't follow us—where *nobody* will spot us directly," I say when we're back in the saloon. "That's a far stronger plan than any of the alternatives." I beckon the others and they join me in the viewport.

"Engine room is clear," says Ari. He cocks his head and scowls. "Him again," he says, wagging a finger in the air to indicate Wireless Man's voice in the background. "I hated this guy when I was in London last year."

We all break into grins. Everyone hates Wireless Man.

"Okay." Lewis claps his hands. "Recap: The largest protest gatherings are around Harrow—where they've now turned violent—and St. James's Park, where we're headed, and there's another huge crowd along the Thames behind the Houses of Parliament. We have friends in the areas mentioned, so report back to Theo instantly if yer in trouble."

"Yes," says Theo. "Let me know and I'll pass it on."

"Lewis, Tabby, are you guys all right going for the old docking station in Kensington?" I ask them. "Bia mentioned it might be operating as a holding center. The warehouse in Regent's Park is also under suspicion so Ari and I will head there."

We discuss it further and everyone's on board.

Tabby fixes her gaze on me. "What if we split? Right now? Lewis and I could distract border security and take some of the heat off you as you cross."

"Never," I say. "A single submersible could never survive the might of multiple border patrol vessels. The safest place for us all, until we're above the capital, is on board the *Kabul*."

"I agree," Theo says, and rolls his eyes when Tabby scowls at him.

"Okay, that's it then," I say. "We make our way to St. James's, staying high, and once we're in the clear, we'll descend in submersibles and use the cover of the crowds to snoop around." I summon the Navigator.

Oscar clasps his hands before him. "My lady?"

"Everything all right, Oscar?"

He gives a nod. "It would appear all is agreeable, my dear."

"Good. I want us to rise as high as the vessel will safely allow it, Oscar. As long as—" Tabby's mouth falls open, but I press on. "As long as our systems aren't affected by the weather up on the surface, we'll manage if things become uncomfortable inside. It's more important we avoid a chase and possible attack. I can't risk that. If they capture anyone on board…" I shake my head. "But if we stick to waters that are only just bearable for *us*, then it guarantees the smaller security subs won't dare join us up there. At most, we might encounter the odd Explorer but they'd likely assume we were with defense. Once we're past border patrol, we cross over the Dartford Tunnel. Keep an eye on the security base at Canterbury. And the map's showing up some sort of noticeable defense installment at Gravesend, so please watch out for that, too, as we pass through."

"Understood, my dear."

The vessel hums away as she rises. The waves turn gradually choppier.

"My lady?"

"Keep going, Oscar."

Tabby frowns as the sub sways a little. "I think I'd rather we faced Blackwatch," she says. "Are you sure about this?"

"Yes. Getting involved in anything like a chase so close to the capital is a very bad idea for us. I want to try everything else first." I raise my voice. "Keep going, Oscar."

"Theo?" I call out to him.

He's back by the screens, checking the systems on the files hovering before him, and nods to say we're okay.

"Keep rising, Oscar." I turn to Ari. "Please stay on top of engine room status. Let me know if a single alarm goes off."

He nods and joins Theo by the screens.

The *Kabul* lurches slightly in the increasingly rougher current. "Oscar, slow down a little but keep going, please." Soon we become unsteady on our feet. "All right, that's enough," I say, stumbling back a few steps. "We stick to this altitude until I say otherwise."

Everyone rushes back to the viewport to take in the lighter waters. Back in Bergen I climbed to a similar altitude with Ari, but this is the highest the rest of them have ever been. The waves churn in the natural light, folding over the sub's nose to roll all around us.

"We need to keep an eye on every one of our systems now," I say. "Even the mildest magnetic storm could affect them." I turn to the Navigator. "All right, Oscar, you know what to do. Cross the borders into Britain. And you must do it all at full speed. That way if anyone spots us, we'll just continue racing away until we're safe. If it comes to that, turn toward the English Channel. That reminds me"—I nudge Theo—"if anything goes wrong while we're away, I've uploaded details of the safest route out. In that instance you have to move at once and stick to the course I've outlined. Promise you'll get out of here to safety?"

Theo offers a hesitant nod. Hopefully he'll never be put in that position.

The vessel turns until she's facing Britain, and then there's a hum as she hurtles full speed to our destination. She rocks away as we draw ever closer to the borders. No way would a submersible have been able to keep up with us in these tempestuous waves, no matter *how* sturdy the craft was! Theo updates us from beside the screens, confirming the sub's systems haven't been affected so far. I'd much rather feel uncomfortable for a bit than risk the alternative.

"Lewis, your submersible is ready?"

He confirms it is. Tabby will ride with him, while I'll use the one Ari's dad lent me. Ari will be taking Charlie's, which has now been sorted.

"Our subs are ready," Ari shouts, knowing what I'm about to ask.

The *Kabul* presses on, swaying in the choppy current as she makes her way back to the capital. Oscar's beside me as the vessel pushes through wave after wave of Britain's green-blue waters. I crane my neck in the direction of the screens.

"Theo?"

"Okay so far!"

Tabby grimaces as the sub gives another lurch. "I still think we should've risked border patrol and all the country's security forces at once over this friggin' altitude. And what if they *do* patrol at this height anyway?"

Except, apart from the passing blur of a single Explorer sub battling to remain steady in the volatile waves before giving up and diving, we come across nothing and nobody. The submarine keeps going until minutes turn into an hour, and then two.

At last, Oscar tilts his head. "My lady, we are inside Britain and nobody is in our vicinity."

I nod and my stomach rolls. I feel both relief and also a little sick, and the rocking vessel isn't helping. "Stick to the plan, Oscar. Tell me when we're over the capital. Watch out for the bases I mentioned."

"Er, speaking of bases?" Theo calls over from the screens. "They were just abandoned....In fact almost all security personnel stationed around the capital have been called in to help control the protests. I just saw the alert."

Yesss. This is exactly what we needed. Though...what on earth is going on in London to warrant such an increase in security presence there? It already has a massive police force. I message Bia again.

"In the past few minutes a crowd hit a security sub after it wouldn't stop ramming into them. They brought it down. Word spread and now everywhere you look protesters are clashing with the authorities. It's a total breakdown of order. It would be foolish to come anywhere near now!"

"We don't have any choice, Bia."

I tell Oscar to keep going and I pace the floor, trying not to lose my balance. I repeatedly glance over at Theo and the Navigator, praying I'll hear the words I'm so desperate for. The minutes feel like hours. Until finally:

"My lady, we have entered London and are approaching our destination above St. James's Park."

I can't believe it. It worked. We did it. I didn't dare imagine. But we managed to get inside the capital without incident, and no unwanted vessels are on our tail. No doubt the abandoned security bases helped enormously.

The submarine comes to a stop, still swaying as we hover high above London.

"We are at St. James's, my lady. There are no hostiles in the vicinity at this altitude. Instructions?"

"First of all, drop around fifty feet, Oscar, so we're a little more steady. But no more. As soon as we've left the sub, you must secure her and put her in stealth mode. Theo has primary status."

"I want some power, too," says Tabby, hands on hips.

"Och, you don't need any more, lassie," Lewis says, eyes shining.

"Ready?" I ask them both.

Lewis and Tabby insist on heading down first to test the waters. Neither of them is wanted by the authorities, so it feels like a good move.

"Remember everything we went over," I say. "Any sign of folk being held at the docking station, let Theo know and he'll pass it on to Bia who has people working on that. Any news of our parents and Theo will pass that on to Ari and me. Tabby, you have to keep an eye on Lewis. He mustn't go after Blackwatch or anything! Otherwise you'll have his mother to face, and believe me, you don't want to deliver bad news to Maud McGregor."

I turn away, pause, and then face them again. "Actually, Lewis, you should also keep an eye on Tabby."

Tabby beams as if I've complimented her.

"Aye." Lewis winks.

We hug and the two head off. As planned, we wait five minutes so we can be sure they're all right, and so we have a firsthand account of what's lying in wait for us before we do the same.

"Good job our vessels have been swiped," Tabby says from somewhere below. "There are Eyeballs everywhere! Other than that, it's so busy you actually feel invisible. Okay, we're headed for Kensington!"

Ari leaves next in Charlie's sub. He takes my hands as the craft starts up, his eyebrows drawn together and his gaze intense. "Listen, Leyla, you have to promise me you'll be really careful out there."

"Promise."

I make him swear the same, and then we embrace. Before long he's through the pool and I'm trying so hard not to think of the terminate-on-sight order against him.

I'm next. I drop through the opening, and as soon as the sub's out of the *Kabul*'s shadow, I hover briefly, overcome. *London.* My only home for sixteen years. The city that now holds Papa captive.

London, where everyone knows our faces and names.

CHAPTER THIRTY-TWO

The very first things I notice the moment my craft drops low enough are the Eyeballs. Tabby was right; there are so many more of them now. The canny spherical cameras can get real up close so we're all wearing hats and scarves as an extra precaution. Theo confirms the submarine is secure and in stealth mode. Ari lets me know he's waiting for me down among the protesters, and I keep descending until the city comes into view. I'm unprepared for the tsunami of emotions when it does, and my breath hitches at the sight below. I really missed London.

Lights blink away from the hazy grid beneath. I'm above Buckingham Palace. All around is a maze of Old World ruins, watertight buildings, and sprawling domes. The familiar glow of the streetlamps and solar spheres, and the endless flashing of lights from all the vessels, illuminates the city. I straighten and make my way toward the glimmering blur of subs above St. James's Park.

The city's green-blue waters are choppy with all the traffic. The crafts hover away in the depths and the waves churn and lash at our submersibles. Sandstorm beams from all manner of vehicles flash away to express the protesters' frustration and anger at what's been going on. Moving around becomes challenging.

I check in with Theo and Tabby. Everyone's okay and there's nothing to report. I'm about to message Ari to ask him exactly where he is among the throng, when the vessels around me jerk, their movements erratic. I twist my neck and can't see anything.

I startle when someone knocks into my sub. They point frantically behind them and I realize what's going on. Large security vessels are ramming the crowd.

It takes a lot of stops and starts but at last, heart racing, I manage to move slightly aside of the main throng.

"Ari, are you all right?"

"I'm okay, Leyla. I was knocked away, though, and then swept up in the crowd moving east. Theo said the closest quiet spot is Trafalgar Square. Maybe if you head in that direction it'll be safer to wait there for me? I'll try maneuvering around this lot."

"All right, yes. See you in a bit."

A small white craft catches my eye when a security vessel advances toward it. I try to warn them but they aren't looking this way. In seconds security forces move in above them and deploy the dreaded winch tucked away on the underside of their own vessel. A hook latches onto the hilt on the back of the white car, and hauls it away.

"Theo?" I message him. "Did you say protesters had made arrangements for those who are clamped and taken? There's a security sub headed west from the park toward the palace, and they're carrying a white MK27."

"Got it, passing it on right now. Everything else okay?"

"Yes, just on my way to meet Ari."

I head toward Trafalgar Square, weaving my way through the throng of protesters. As I get clear of the main hub of crafts, I spy another security sub trying to hit a civil vessel. I can't believe it. A government sub is actually attempting to damage a peaceful protester's craft, repeatedly ramming into it. They could impair the craft and kill the driver.

I sneak around to the side of the security sub. As it reverses in preparation for another charge, I make my move. Pushing forward on the throttle, I hurtle into the hostile craft. It reminds me of when I did the same to Camilla Maxwell's car during the London Marathon, when she froze from the ever-present dread.

The sub in front lurches on impact. My own spins a little but nothing I can't handle, and I swiftly stabilize it. The compact car does the same, hitting the security sub from the other side. The protester flashes their light to warn me of yet another hostile vessel approaching us from the rear, before they speed away. I take their cue, and pulling back on the joystick, I ram the throttle forward and rocket out of there. I climb as high as I can without losing sight of the city below, and then hurtle toward Trafalgar Square.

Lights blur as everything whizzes past beneath me, and I don't let up until I spot the familiar shape of Trafalgar Square. It's definitely much quieter.

I message Ari as I descend.

"Leyla, I'm still stuck over here. Protesters are fighting back so it's impossible to get through. I might be a while. I'm going to try charging through. Wait for me."

"Will do!" I hover there, hoping he isn't too long. We really need to start making our way to the warehouse in Regent's Park.

A tour bus passes by and I'm not at all surprised it's completely unbothered by the increasing violence unfolding so close to it. Old World tours are so popular you have to book a seat on the buses months in advance, and good luck trying to get a ticket during the week of the disaster's anniversary. Many of London's statues and monuments perished during the floods, and reproductions had to be commissioned. Some, like the Monument to the Great Fire of London before me now, mostly survived but had to be re-rooted. Standing beside it, a giant observing lion watches over the city—London's tribute to those who perished by water. The hefty vessel before me continues moving zealously from statue to statue.

I crane my neck but Ari's sub is nowhere in sight. Instead, I spot a familiar ornate vessel.

I stare at the sub that's all decked out like some Old World Victorian mode of transport. I think it's meant to be a carriage; I've never quite worked it out. I spot the owner through the side: Britain's chief historian, flanked by his security.

What's Lord Maxwell doing in the water? You'd think he'd be safely tucked away inside somewhere. There are mass protests going on, violent clashes all over the country, and he's one of the prime minister's two chief advisers—the other being that creep Sebastian.

I keep an eye on the sub. It rises above Clio House, Britain's largest historical reenactment hall, and keeps moving forward.

"Ari, I've spotted Lord Maxwell. I know it's a long shot, but he might lead us to somewhere useful. Why is he out here in all this? If he leaves the area, I won't pursue him any farther, promise, but I'd rather tail him than just wait here. There isn't much else I can do right now."

Urging me to be careful, Ari agrees it's odd the country's chief historian is right in the middle of all the unrest.

Keeping my distance, I follow the decorative sub. It heads in the direction of the Mall. A little farther on and the craft slows down as the giant dome-shaped building on the corner of Charing Cross Road and Shaftesbury Avenue looms before us.

Kensington Gardens? What could he be up to here? Is it possible they might be holding people here, too?

The sub pauses by the largest hatch on the side of the building, waiting for it to become vacant. The glowing white beam around the door indicates someone is busy exiting. I ram the throttle forward and steer past them, turning the corner and keeping my eyes peeled. There, a small hatch is free.

My heart races as I take the parking spot while updating Theo with what's going on. And then I switch my Bracelet to silent. I'll see it flash anyway so I won't miss anything important.

As I step into the gardens' parking bay, I pull the hat lower until it's almost covering my eyes. There's no sign of them yet, thank goodness. There's only a couple waiting to exit and they barely notice me. They're discussing the unrest outside with alarm and wondering if they'll make it safely home. I don't think this place is holding prisoners. But Lord Maxwell is definitely up to something. I hurry toward the old wooden door to the gardens. It creaks as I push it open and step in. There doesn't seem to be anyone else around. I feel instantly lighter as I scan the place.

The indoor gardens are a vast, open space, full of hills, individual little parks, and random old walls, all creating the feeling of a natural and limitless expanse. Above me the sky is a clear blue and there's no hint of the building's domed shell. The seasons rotate monthly in the gardens, and currently a bright autumn reigns. Papa told me it was Mama's favorite place in all of London.

I slowly open the door again, and freeze when I see them.

In the far corner of the bay stands Britain's chief historian, flanked by two security officers. The rest of the space is empty now. Thankfully they're busy chatting and don't see me. As swiftly and quietly as I can, I close the door and turn around to the gardens to locate a place to hide. If he's going to have any kind of a meeting or conversation in here, then I want to overhear. But I've most likely got only seconds before they enter!

Just as voices reach me from behind the door, I dart past the red postbox toward the black wrought-iron fencing and follow it as it winds around a large, lush hill. Thank God the hills aren't projections! It's always a job to distinguish between projections, props, and what's actually real in this place. I duck behind the synthetic mound just as the door creaks open.

I don't hear footsteps but I can't take any chances. I edge slowly around the hill and see him. Lord Maxwell, Camilla Maxwell's father. He's on his own; security will be waiting for him in the bay. I jump when tweeting sounds from a nearby tree and look up to spy the glimmer of several wrens and a robin redbreast flittering between its golden branches. Hopefully they won't have enticed him to wander here. To my relief, the chief historian makes his way gingerly across the gardens in the other direction. He's dressed as formal as ever, as if he's stepped right out of ancient Victorian Britain. *Where's my papa?* I want to scream at him.

I follow him, all the time looking around to ensure nobody else is here. The place is clearly empty, though, and security would never allow any new visitors until Lord Maxwell was done.

He walks past the maze, past the kennel with its huge, glimmering dog lazily snoring away inside, and around a small hill until he comes to a wrought-iron bench beneath a sprawling, autumnal tree. In the distance, London's virtual rooftops catch the light as if the gardens really are a part of the city. The chief historian sits on the bench and stares into the space ahead of him. A breeze can be seen and felt as leaves on the ground rustle and flutter around him.

"Happy Birthday, my darling princess," he mutters quietly.

I still when his words reach my ears and realization settles in. He's paying a *personal* visit. It's Camilla's birthday. And I remember how she loved this place more than any other.

Camilla Maxwell was the chief historian's only child. She loved to write. The twins and I regularly hung out with her, but her dad thought us a bad influence, and he especially didn't want her mixing with me after Papa's arrest. She continued to do so whenever he wasn't around.

Camilla took her own life on New Year's Eve. She suffered from the seasickness and it had gone unnoticed. There's a tug inside me now when her gentle face flashes before me.

The light in the gardens flickers and brings me out of my thoughts. And then I look up and my heart almost stops as I stare ahead.

Lord Maxwell stands watching me, his eyes narrowed and alarmed, and his lip curled.

"I'm so sorry about Camilla," I say, forcing myself to speak. "She really was a beautiful person and I wish she were still alive. I...Do you— Do you know where my papa is?"

He brings up his Bracelet, his expression hard.

I swallow and push the words out. "She loved to tell her own stories, did you know?"

He's poised to speak into the Bracelet but doesn't move a muscle.

My throat's dry as I press on. "She wrote and submitted one just prior to the London Marathon."

His expression betrays no emotion. But still, he hasn't summoned his security.

"But as you know, sir, an original tale is against the rules. They were only interested in a retelling, they said, and rejected it."

His eyes flicker.

It's thanks in part to all his efforts to ensure the past takes precedence over the present, all his endless advice to every department to implement this wherever possible, that led to the Royal Society for the Arts and Entertainment ruling a decade ago.

His Bracelet edges closer to his mouth. My heartbeat thrashes away in my ears. If he utters even one word the officers will be here in seconds. And foolishly I'm not carrying a weapon—not even my brolly. I never expected to leave the craft, but I should've thought of it.

He presses his mouth flat. Very slowly, not taking his eyes off me, he lowers his wrist.

"You came to her rescue," he says in quiet, clipped tones. "I acknowledge that. During the marathon, you stopped and helped my Camilla when she caught a case of wet feet. Who knows what might have happened out there had you not come to her aid. Consider this my gratitude. And know that if I see you again, I won't hesitate to have you detained." He moves away from the bench.

He looks different. There's a stoop to his gait and shadows under his eyes. It's been only a couple of months since his daughter's death.

"*Please*," I plead. "I'm looking for my papa. I know he's being kept around here somewhere. You must know where they're holding him? Please help me."

He shows no sign that he's heard a single word and walks right past me. I turn to watch as he pauses by the Memorial Fountain, the prime minister's public tribute to his murdered sister and nephew, and takes off his hat in respect. I can read the inscription from here:

In memory of Eva and Winston Gladstone, beloved sister and darling nephew, sleep peacefully, Edmund Gladstone 2087.

Lord Maxwell walks away without a backward glance. I hear the creak of the door and then he's gone. I could scream the place down. There's no way he didn't know anything about Papa. Despite my frustrations, though, I feel unexpectedly saddened by the encounter. He's aged so much in only a few months. Camilla should still be here.

I'm going to give it a minute before I check the bay; I can't risk running into his security.

"Ari," I whisper into my Bracelet. "It was a dead end. I'm headed back to Trafalgar Square, won't be two ticks. We'll just have to try Regent's Park." There's no answer. "Ari?"

The lighting in the space again briefly flickers, this time for a little longer. And then movement in the air catches my eye: snowflakes. Odd, it's not the first of the month so why the sudden season change?

I glance around and spot blossoms falling from the branches of the tree beside the red postbox: springtime. The gardens are malfunctioning. And then I stiffen as the entire park races through the seasons before my very eyes. It's incredibly jarring as all around me flowers bloom and die, branches blossom and shed their leaves, lightning strikes, and snow falls only to immediately melt under a summer sun. I swiftly bring up my wrist. Except my Bracelet isn't responding.

I jump when the crack of thunder fills the space, and hasten away. It reminds me too much of what happened at Brighton Pier, the indoor resort, when it was attacked. All the technology was affected and it was incredibly eerie.

I round the hill just in time to see the sun fall from the sky and I shudder. The projection now shines from a park bench instead. All the joyful twittering of birds suddenly ceases. The gardens close in around me and my chest aches. I pick up my pace. I'll never find Papa if I become trapped. Around another hill now as fast as I can and *boom*, the ground rocks and I stumble. I press my palms on the grass, ready to haul myself up and run, when I see it.

Splash.

A drop of water right on the back of my hand. An icy chill grips me and I can't move.

Real water plays no part in the gardens' effects.

I don't want to look up. I really, really don't want to. I look up just as there's an earsplitting roar.

And I scream as the world comes crashing down on me.

CHAPTER THIRTY-THREE

The ocean pours into the gardens.

The water is dark and raging as it flows through a dreadful gap to fill the space faster than I can think. And it's so incredibly loud.

Another chunk of the building gives way and the hole widens. A submersible spins down with the flood. I try to keep the craft in sight, but it's impossible in all the chaos. My mind races in too many directions at once, leaving me unable to dwell on any single thought.

I run for the closest, highest hill, scrambling up as fast as I can as the water smashes into everything in its path. My heart is going to burst right out of my chest if it beats any faster. All around me is the deepest rumbling sound, and the sudden crack and snapping of the gardens drowning before my very eyes. Another piece of the dome gives way and hurls out of sight. I can't stop shaking my head.

Is this what it was like during the disaster? Is this how the waters took over the world?

"Theo! Can you hear me, Theo?" I scream once more into my Bracelet, and cry out when it lights up.

"Leyla!" His voice is thick and fast. "Where are you? I've been trying to get in touch. There's been an explosion! It's madness around Westminster! And fighting's broken out all over the city now. Security's attacking any civilian traffic in sight and it's bloody chaos. I..."

His voice fades as the roar takes over, and I stare stunned at the rising waters almost at my waist now. "Theo!" I shout at the top of my lungs. "I'm still at the gardens and the building's caved in! Check on Ari, he's not answering! You need to get everyone back on board right now, and get them to safety! Can you hear me? I don't have much—"

I'm underwater.

I try surfacing but the current is too choppy. All around me the gardens have transformed into a green-blue maelstrom of churning waves filled with uprooted fencing and trees and benches, all swirling in the chaos. I splutter and retch and lose my balance until finally I stop fighting it and focus, recalling all the training Ari gave me. It's still very challenging, though. My hair's loose as usual and it floats to obstruct everything around me. I sweep it aside and look up. Most of the top of the dome has broken free and the ocean surges in, more determined than ever. The water around me swells, pushing me toward the drowned hills. I need to get out of here.

I can't believe it. I'm really in the water in London, the most hostile place in the country for us. The only safe way out for me now is a moon pool. The *Kabul*—I need to get back to her. But what if Papa's at the holding center in Regent's Park...? I've no idea what's going on. Considering what Theo said has happened, who knows where and how everyone is right now. *Please, God, keep everyone safe.*

Minutes pass as I try to work out my next move. I glance up; I can no longer spot any water pouring in. The gardens are completely submerged. A passing craft pauses by the gaping hole in the dome. Before I can register what's happening, I'm bathed in light and freeze in the sharp beam.

A security vessel.

I plummet out of the way. The sub descends. It's one of their smaller crafts, but all security subs are armed.

My thoughts race. Do I stay here, keep dodging them inside this space, or should I try and go for the opening? But it's London.... They'll spot me and fire on sight. As if on cue, a laser *pings* just a couple of feet from me and I move again as the sub draws closer. I race all around the gardens, ducking and diving behind whatever props still remain fixed, kicking and thrusting my body away each time the glare of the sub's lights finds me. The family in the footage we'd broadcasted flashes before my eyes— hunted and slaughtered and gone in seconds. I block out the images and continue to keep an eye out for the hostile vessel. Several glistening cod now swim through the park, their movements erratic as if confused to find themselves here. I peer past them and spot the sub again.

It makes a beeline for me once more. And then, as I watch, it abruptly starts rocking, its nose and fin rising and dipping alarmingly. It spins away out of control. And Ari hovers there in its wake. I cry out to him as he plunges through the water toward me. Oh, thank God he's okay! As he draws close, he holds out his arms and I swim into them.

"Are you hurt?" His voice is low and urgent.

I shake my head. "You? How come you're not in your sub anymore? And how did you find me?"

"Theo," he says with relief. He pushes his hair out of his eyes. "I'm okay. I came under attack. It's lawless out there now; no more protesting— it's a battle. They'd rather harm the people than listen to them. Here, you must take this." He removes the knife from around his waist and holds it out to me. I stare at it. "You might need it, Leyla," he urges. "There's no knowing what could happen to us."

"What about you?"

He lifts his trousers and I glimpse the one strapped to his ankle as usual. I take the knife and he shows me how to secure it around my waist so it doesn't pose a danger to me.

"Everybody panicked when an explosion went off," he explains. "Now there are people trying to flee the area and security attacking anyone they can. Those who came here armed and prepared have started fighting back. I was hit in passing fire. I guided the sub out of sight beneath Westminster Bridge and eventually managed to break out of the vessel. Good thing I'd received Theo's message just before I exited the craft or I'd have never known you were here."

"Thank God you escaped, and weren't spotted. Any news of the others?

We need to get everyone on board the *Kabul* right away, including you. I want to stay. I need to search for him, Ari."

He pulls away. We duck as a tree drifts past, its paint already mingling with the ocean. Ari's hair swirls around his face and his gaze is conflicted.

"What? Please just tell me, Ari."

"Try not to worry, there's probably a good explanation, but Theo said nobody can get hold of your grandfather and—"

"Oh no..." A tremor slides across my body.

"He might've just been called elsewhere."

"No, Grandpa's extremely mindful. It's him, Captain Sebastian. I know it. Oh God, what's happening..."

He stares into the distance, concern etching his features.

My chest tenses. "If it were the other way around, Papa wouldn't rest until he'd found me." I grab Ari's hands. "I can't leave him, no matter what. I have to—"

Ari's brow creases as he raises a hand to cup my face. I can see the bubbles on his lashes as he fixes his gaze on me. "Leyla, I'm not going *anywhere* until we've found them all, I promise." Relief washes over me.

Drifting debris heads in our direction and I shove it away, my heart hammering in my ears. I turn back to Ari. "Did Tabby and Lewis find anything at the docking station?"

"Nothing."

"Then it's the warehouse in Regent's Park where they're holding people, it *has* to be. And it just might be where our parents are. And"—I swallow, trying not to picture it—"if that's hit, too, Papa, and possibly others, wouldn't survive in the water."

"We need to get out of here." He holds out his hand and I take it.

We rise through the gardens. What could've happened to Grandpa? Something brushes against me and I jerk my arm away, before gasping at the sight. I stop, stunned. Lord Maxwell stares back through the water, his eyes wide with a terrible expression and his face twisted as if startled. His body rotates as it drifts on. He didn't get away in time. Britain's chief historian is dead. I can't stop shaking my head. Ari grabs me by the waist and thrusts his body up. We ascend until we reach the unnerving gap in the dome, and cautiously peer out.

I gasp at the sight.

It looks like war out there. In London. This would've once been unthinkable.

Subs bolt around in a panic and there are skirmishes everywhere you look. It's all we can do to dodge vessels as they hurtle past above us. I startle as the distant flashes of firepower light up the depths in all directions. London is in chaos.

And we're trapped at the heart of it all.

CHAPTER THIRTY-FOUR

"Ari!" I beckon him as I slowly surface from the gap in the roof of the gardens and, keeping as low as possible, swim across the dome. Thankfully any vessels in sight are too busy to notice us. "Let's move down the side of the building and try to find a less conspicuous spot where we can work out our next move," I say.

Ari follows suit, thrusting through London's green-blue currents. Movement, sounds, and lights fill the water around us. We swim down the side of the dome. A rusted bathtub with bulky layers of seaweed hanging off its edges sits on the street; the wriggly shadow of a creature lurks inside. We're on Shaftesbury Avenue. I scan the road in both directions to ensure we're safe. Lights glimmer above us as crafts dart by, and higher up the hazy shadows and forms of bulkier subs move through the currents.

I chew on my lip as I think.

Ari glances around, hyperalert. "Thoughts?"

"We stay at street level, swimming carefully but quickly through them until we reach Regent's Park and spot the warehouse?"

He nods. "We can do this. We find them and all head together for the submarine."

We clasp hands and are about to leave when a glow materializes over the ancient rooftops of the street opposite. Ari and I move back, pressing our bodies against a dilapidated doorway as a sub comes into sight. We have to be ready to make a dash for it if it spots us. The craft passes over without incident, though. I bring my gaze back down to street level and a huge lone halibut drifts obliviously by before turning into Charing Cross Road.

I can't believe it. Even though I've been in the water several times already, I can't wrap my head around being out here in London. It's surreal and terrifying. I can't think of another place that fears and distrusts us more.

We've barely moved on when we snap our heads up again as a small craft comes spinning down through the current. The sub rests precariously on a pile of debris in the middle of the road before us, its lights illuminating the street. It's a twin-seated civilian vessel, and as the owner activates their distress beams, the waters fill with a flashing sharp blue. I thrust my body forward, thankful of even the limited practice I've had in the water. Already my movements out here are supple and streamlined.

"Careful!" Ari joins me as we circle the craft.

Something's stuck in the propeller and he gets to work on it. I move closer to the cockpit to indicate the problem when the driver and passenger scream. They open their mouths and cry out nonstop, their eyes bulging with fear. I remember, and back away. Ari, oblivious, clears the propeller and taps the vessel's body to indicate it can go. They race out of there without a backward glance.

I forgot. For just a moment I completely forgot we were feared. And despite all the recent broadcasts, all the proof clearly highlighting how this fear was created and stoked by the government, how it's ill-founded and based on lies—how we aren't remotely the people they've been led to believe we are—it's sobering to realize it won't be easy for people to let go of their long-held terror and suspicions. It's going to take time. Of course it is. And some will probably never completely let go of their previous beliefs. And though I know all this, people's reactions to us now still hurt.

We plunge through the water and swim on down the street, taking care to stay as concealed as possible. Life glistens among the endless ruin and decay as creatures forage away in the piles of debris.

As we near the end of the road, activity increases around us. More vessels, more lights. My chest tightens when firepower darts bold and bright

through the currents overhead. We clasp hands and try to stay as inconspic-
uous as possible as we edge forward. We must get to the warehouse as soon
as we can. They're hitting buildings, and Papa would never survive.

"Oh my God, Ari."

I gasp as we reach the end of the street and Piccadilly Circus comes
into sight before us. Kensington Gardens wasn't the only place to be hit.

Everywhere you look, everything from subs, ancient ruins, watertight
buildings, and even sea creatures are caught up in the chaos. Fighting has
broken out in full force, and my head spins trying to take it all in. Ari
stiffens and I follow his gaze to catch sight of a dolphin, its body slashed by
lasers, as it floats down to settle on the ground to our right. It's all terrifying and devastating.

Ari points to a set of lights a little farther on from the creature. "It's
another vessel in need of help," he says. "But we'll have to be quick."

I don't have the heart to tell him exactly how the other passengers
reacted to us aiding them. We move carefully along the pavement so as not
to be spotted by anyone. The craft lies stuck. When we're close enough, I
indicate we're there to help them. The driver's eyes bulge when she spots
me. She stares, frozen. I again do what I can, gesturing away to let her
know we mean no harm. I watch as finally she gives a small nod.

Ari swims back to me and indicates to the driver he's sorted it. She sits
blinking and nods again, before speeding away. Ari takes my hand and
moves us swiftly under the cover of a doorway as we assess our path.

We gaze on the chaos before us, and I wrap my arms around myself.
I've seen several clashes outside now, the biggest being the one above
Broadmoor when I went to rescue Papa. But being *in* the waters as one
rages around you is nothing short of petrifying. I watch as a security sub
battles with several civilian vessels that are determined to take it down.
There's a sudden glare in the corner of my eye.

"Ari, watch out!"

A torpedoing light flashes on the current ahead, brilliant and baleful, and
we propel ourselves away from the ancient shop just in time. There's a deep
boom behind us, and bricks hurl through the water. My ears ring. Everything

turns cloudy and I lose my balance in the ensuing waves. It's all debris and sand and churning. At last we find each other again through the turbulence, moving toward the other's voice. We grab hands and swim away, darting down a narrow alleyway until we're safe from the immediate danger. Ari's expression mirrors my thoughts as we stare stunned at each other; we were lucky to get away unscathed. There's no time to dawdle, though, and we move on.

We stick to the streets for now. It's very tempting to rise in the hopes we'll get to Regent's Park faster in a straight line, but it would be a costly mistake. Everyone else is above the rooftops and we need the cover of the streets. I've sprinted through this road often enough to know if we stick to it all the way, it'll lead us to the park. We make our way cautiously, swimming past ruin after ruin. Every time there's a sub, or firepower whizzes too close by, we press ourselves up against the ancient buildings, sometimes cowering inside doorways.

"Look, Ari," I say as we make our way through Regent Street. I point at a huge shoal suspended high above us. "They're behaving oddly."

He pauses and we peer up through the current at the tuna. The shoal shimmers. There's something strange about the fish, though I can't figure out what.

Ari's voice drops. "That isn't the natural movement of tuna," he says as the shoal continues to shift out of sync with one another.

Every time you think they're about to make one of those unified turns, they'll abruptly diverge without warning.

"I've seen those before," Ari continues. "Be ready to hide."

My stomach knots. "But where could we hide from them if they come for us? We're completely exposed. They can follow us anywhere. Have they been tampered with?"

Ari stays still, staring at them. "There," he says as he points at the shoal. "Did you see that red glow? Unnatural. They're armed. Those things are bots."

I wring my hands. "Let's keep going? We'll stay as close to the buildings as possible."

Ari nods. "We carry on."

We move on as cautiously as ever through the increasingly turbulent and unpredictable waters, until we can no longer see the mechanical shoal on the current. I turn to glance at the ancient commercial places as we pass them. If we hit trouble, doorways won't be enough; we'll have to venture right inside the veiled Old World businesses. I try not to dwell too much on it as I peer inside one of the ominous spaces now.

And a pair of eyes stares right back.

I flinch and still. And then another set of eyes, and another.

"Ari…"

He darts past me right into the building.

It's a family in the water, and they've been hiding here since escaping transfer to a detention center. The child, aged around seven, was injured during their getaway and his leg is swollen. It'll become infected very soon, if it hasn't already. Ari listens to them while I return to the street to ensure we're not in immediate danger.

"We've been here for hours," says the mother, her face pale and gaunt as she shakes her head. "Every time we poke our heads out to see if we can make a dash for it, look for somewhere abandoned so we can get out of the water and tend to our boy, there's always something hovering around." She narrows her eyes. "You know what they do to us? You shouldn't be out there."

I nod as I swim closer to them. "We know. And I'm so sorry. You definitely need to move immediately. It's bad out there, but the protests also provide cover. I've not spotted a single Eyeball at street level so far and I was looking out for them. I think they've been directed to where the clashes are." I look to Ari and back at the woman. "I know a safe place. My submarine. The only problem is getting you to it."

Ari agrees the best thing for them to do now is to try and get to the *Kabul.* He warns them of the shoal of bots. "Are you armed?"

They only have knives. "I'm a dab hand with them," says the father. "It's how we escaped the vessel transporting us."

"My sub hovers several hundred feet above St. James's Park. It's in stealth mode, but my friend Theo is keeping a lookout for anyone in need of aid or shelter. The Navigator will detect you once you're near, and you have to tell Theo I sent you. He can help you and get the wound seen to. Make sure you get something to eat, and rest."

"Stick to the streets," says Ari. "Don't rise until you're at the park."

"Not a problem," says the woman, relief flooding her expression as she nods away. "I'll find a way to get to it." She shakes her head. "Why are you out here when you have somewhere safe?"

"We're looking for our parents," I say. "The authorities have them."

The woman helps the child get onto his father's back, and after I've again checked the street is clear, they head furtively and swiftly in the direction we came from. I pray they make it safely to the submarine.

Ari and I bolt on down the street.

At Oxford Circus we're spotted by a small security sub that gives chase. I lunge into an alleyway. "In here, Ari!"

I grab him when he's close and pull him inside the nearest ruin. We end up hiding for far too long inside a former estate agent's offices. A school of pale-gray herring darts in, almost giving me a heart attack. At last the craft moves on. As we pass through Portland Place, a pulse spreads through the waves and a chill comes over me.

"It's another explosion," says Ari as we pause. He points to our left. "In that direction. But we must keep going if—" He stops and moves slowly but urgently toward me as I stay hovering there. His arms circle my waist.

My body tenses. "What's—"

"Don't move."

My eyes scan the water and I spot the form of the tuna shoal above in the distance. It flickers as the fish dart erratically in every direction now, searching. An ominous crimson glow frames their dark bodies.

"It's the explosion," Ari says quietly. "Blasts always put them on edge. They're in attack mode now. Follow my lead."

He leans right and very slowly, barely moving his limbs at all, drifts into the nearest alley with me on his heels. I breathe a sigh of relief when we're behind the cover of the ancient wall. We poke our heads around it to see what's happening.

The shoal separates, with smaller groups of fish heading for the rooftops and scanning the area before racing back to regroup. I shudder and Ari wraps an arm around me as we watch.

"Not long now. They were at Eysturoy when they attacked us last year," he says, hands clenched. "They should be moving along any moment toward the spot of the explosion."

Sure enough the entire shoal twists and turns as it dives several streets away, closer to the source of the blast. I shake my head; God knows who or what they've targeted.

Once more we thrust our bodies through the water and exit the alley. Back on the main road, we again turn in the direction of the park. And freeze at the sight ahead.

The shoal of tuna hovers low before us in the middle of the road, blocking our path. It's a vast and dark form with flashes of silver as fins glisten on the current. The blot-like mass is dotted with red "eyes." Eyes fixed directly on us now. A chill spreads inside me.

"Leyla," Ari says quietly. "Do you recall the training for when we encounter hostile predators?"

"Yes?" I can barely get my voice out as the mass floats there, flickering away as it watches us.

"Then *go*."

He grabs my hand, and faster than I've ever moved in my life, we propel ourselves back toward the alley we'd just emerged from.

"Don't look back," says Ari. "It will slow you down."

We torpedo through the depths, street after street, swimming over endless low rooftops and around buildings, trying everything we can think of to outsmart the bots. Nothing's working. Each time we think we've lost them, their red glow materializes on the waves and we have to keep going. Until suddenly we find ourselves lacking the protection of the streets.

We're out in the open, above Park Square, and it's absolute chaos. We look back for the rogue fish, but with so much to process here, the shoal has scattered. A *ping* far too close reaches my ears, and I fix my focus on making sense of what's going on around me. My mind's a whirlpool as I twist and turn, taking it all in.

There are security subs as far as the eye can see. Civilian crafts are attacked and rammed, and they're fighting back with everything they have, which is surprisingly a lot. Subs that you'd never guess are armed retaliate with various weapons of their own. The waters are ablaze with vehicular lights and firepower, and heavy with debris and creatures. And people.

"Ari!" I gasp. "Oh my God, there are others in the water!"

There are at least a dozen people, all fighting alongside the submersibles. Ari stares at the back of someone and races toward them. We draw closer to the individual and I see they're busy working alongside another, tampering with the rear end of a security sub to bring it down. They turn, and I could scream with relief at the sight of a familiar face.

"Kiara!" I shout. "Where are the others?"

"Have you seen our parents?" asks Ari.

Ari's neighbor from back in Eysturoy stares at us, and just as the sub is about to take advantage of the distraction, Ari lunges at the vessel. It's soon damaged and sent spinning away.

"I don't know about anyone else, sorry!" Kiara answers, her eyes flitting around as she keeps a lookout. "Not seen or heard from them. I've only been in touch with Samantha. She's helping folk around Baker Street. The entire place came under attack and there are several casualties. The same is going on all over, you know, in every city!"

I give Kiara the location of the *Kabul* and tell her to direct anyone in need of shelter or aid to it.

She nods. "Got to go. Watch out for the octopuses!"

"What?"

But she's gone already. Ari plunges away from me as a security sub spies us, and he works with others to bring it down.

The same is going on all over. This is what it looks like all around the country. There really is no going back now.

I peer at my surroundings in a daze. How am I going to find *anyone* in this?

"Leyla! Move out of the way!" Ari's voice reaches me and I dive to the side as firepower blasts from a hefty circular sub. He continues to shout. "We need to—"

"Ari!"

My eyes bulge when I see it. A long, suckered arm reaching for him from behind. He whirls around and lashes out at the creature. It's a pale-red octopus, its pupils flashing milky-white. It's not a bot, though, and its sneaky limbs are very real as it slinks around us, watching and waiting to strike again. A tentacle creeps toward us and Ari pulls out his knife from around his ankle. I grab the one he gave me. The creature lunges for us. We slash frantically away, but the animal's proving too slippery. Just as my arms begin to tire, the octopus suddenly twists and writhes around, lashing out erratically. It slumps, limbs still twitching, and sinks out of sight.

"Look, it's Jas!" I point at one of the small spherical crafts everyone at Cambridge uses, as it races on at breakneck speed after pausing to take out the hostile animal.

Dammit, he might've known something about Papa and Ari's parents' whereabouts, but he's out of sight now.

Above us activity only increases and there are clashes everywhere you look. The water spins around me and I force myself to stay focused. We *must* find a way through it, even though it looks impossible right now.

More octopuses can be seen wrapping themselves around subs, their limbs getting into everything, and even twisting around the ankles of those in the water. I blink when one materializes in the depths before me. Their ability for camouflage is astonishing! It lunges for me but I'm ready this time and fight back without pause. It's the doctored creature or me. The waters are a frenzy of churning waves. I overpower the animal and watch as it slinks away. I need to get to that warehouse.

A shadow moves across, above us. It covers *everything*. I look up to more Blackwatch vessels than I can count. God help us...A few of the subs drift along, but too many remain in place. We all watch, heads tilted back. The undersides of the huge vessels open up, and dark compact craft emerge from within: tanks. The cube-like submersibles are heavily armored and even the sight of them on the news can make you feel uneasy. My neck prickles with fear, and I want to hurl as I realize what's coming.

It's hell as they open fire in every direction.

Everyone in the water races through the depths as the subs give chase. Ari's tugging at me, telling me to move, when I spy further movement from the vessels high above us. Something else slips into the water from their underbellies, so thin they're barely discernible. I stare, trying to identify what they are, but look away when Ari darts to me, his expression urgent.

"We can't fight all this," he shouts above the chaos. "We need to get away!"

We race around a huge friendly vessel and manage to squeeze through two security subs that are distracted with fighting civilian crafts. We maneuver through the madness, peering at anyone still in the water in the hopes of spotting somebody we know. One of the tanks spies us and gives chase. And then another. My legs quiver, and my insides feel so heavy I can't believe I haven't sunk to settle on the ground.

Ari and I bolt west of the park. We'll never shake them off here, and the cover of the streets is our best bet. The crafts are heavily armed, and we duck and dive from their firepower as, hearts racing, we plunge on, finally finding ourselves in Marylebone Road. And then I look ahead and go still. We're trapped.

Before us, not more than a couple of meters away, is a wall of civilian subs, and the drivers stare back with startled expressions.

I move forward.

"Leyla, no," Ari says.

But we have no choice. We must get them to see it isn't a hard decision to make. We're not the bad guys here and they need to let us pass, dammit. I draw closer to the subs swaying on the choppy current. I swim by several and plead, trying to get them to understand we're being followed. Behind us, shadows loom as the Blackwatch tanks catch up. They slow down as they realize they have us cornered.

The drivers of the subs before us turn to look at one another; they shift around in their seats, but that's it. I shake my head at them, stunned. Would they *really* rather hand us over to the authorities, to people they're fighting against, than aid us—just because we're different? And then one of the subs edges forward and moves aside. The woman inside gestures for me to pass. I thank her and sign.

"Do you know anything about the warehouse in the park? We're looking for our parents."

She knows sign, thank goodness. "The people in the old warehouse are gone—they took them away in submersibles. There's a group targeting all suspected detention centers, setting the folk free. Soon as they started hitting them, the authorities began emptying the rest. Everyone they were holding at Regent's Park has been taken elsewhere." She hesitates, then adds, "I hope you find your parents."

I nod absently as I thank her, vaguely aware of Ari's arm around my shoulders.

"We'll find them," I say to him, ignoring the brutal weight moving into place inside my chest and throat now.

Another sub takes the lady's cue and leans aside for us, too, and then another, and in no time there's a path for us through the blockade. We take it. The tanks advance, but the subs close in behind us. The waters fill with unnerving sounds as they lock into battle. We race away, finally stopping in a side street so we can catch our breath and get our bearings.

"They can't be that far if they've only just been taken," I say, knocking away a piece of debris drifting toward me.

Ari nods as he checks out the narrow street. "We keep searching." He squints and points down the road. "Just as soon as they're free." A small sub stops and starts above an old shed, debris stuck to its underside stopping it from moving away. "I've got it; you keep watch, Leyla."

"All right, please hurry."

I tilt my head back and take in the enormous dark form of a vessel much higher up. I twist my neck and scan both sides of the street. I'm about to glance away from the top of a new block of homes when I spot a rising shadow some distance behind it. It's a Blackwatch sub—one of their larger crafts. It continues to ascend, with something following below in its trail.

This second shadow is bulky, and it sways on the current. The sub stops rising and drives on through the waves, and the hefty bundle now drifts along beneath it. I squint as it draws closer and begins to pass over us. My body turns rigid as I understand what I'm looking at. I need to tell Ari, but I can't open my mouth.

It's a net. A net just like the one they dropped around Ari before

315

dragging him away and taking him to that blasted lab. And inside this net is a whole group of people, including children. Some spot us and gesture wildly to get our attention. They must be transferring them before their holding center is hit, knowing most of them would escape free. God knows where the massive vessel is taking them now....

I plunge through the waves after them.

Kicking and thrusting my way through the current as fast as I can so I don't lose sight of them, I reach the trapped people. Some of the children grab my arm as I hold on to the net. Every one of them is scared and crying, and the adults do their best to get them to quiet down. In no time I have Ari's knife in my hand, and I tell everyone to get back. I start cutting through the ropes, with the huge bundle swinging as it continues to move along.

"They'll pay for this."

I turn to see Ari beside me, his expression twisted with rage as he joins me in hacking away at the net with our knives.

At last the hole is big enough for the smallest children to squeeze through. They stay swimming close to the net so as to remain under its cover. Soon the gap is wide enough for everyone to swim free.

"Thank you, child! Neptune bless you!" says one of the women to me as she rounds the youngsters up. The sub moves on out of sight, mercifully unaware of what's happened.

We quickly give the group directions to the *Kabul*.

"We'll find it," a small bald man assures me. "I know St. James's like the back of my hand. This is no place for children, and I'm getting them out of here. You two best worry about yourselves now. Come with us!"

We explain we can't, and as soon as everyone is gathered, we watch as they all plummet through the waves until they're no longer visible.

I turn to Ari. "I wonder where they were taking them."

His face darkens. "The only time they ever keep us alive is to run tests on us. That's why there are detention centers." He bends toward his ankle to put away the knife, and a shape in the distance behind him catches my eye.

It's only a small shoal of fish, but there's something unnerving about the coppery creatures. I peer at the flickering mass. With teeth so long they're unable to close their mouths, and huge bubbles for eyes, the animals have this startled look. And every one of them has their attention fixed on us.

"Ari…"

He straightens slowly and follows my gaze. I yelp when the shoal suddenly lunges toward us. We turn and bolt away as fast as we can.

"Higher? Lower?" I shout as we dart through the current. "Where are they less likely to follow?"

Except the shoal immediately catches up to us, and then splits.

"What the hell's going on?" I scream as my limbs and lungs work hard to keep going. "What are they up to?"

"Stay with me!" Ari shouts.

Half the fish move into place beneath us, stopping us from diving, while the other half breaks for our left. Their faces are the stuff of nightmares and it's an effort not to freeze up. The bulbous eyes are empty, the unnaturally long teeth tusklike and translucent. The shoal forces us to lean right. And then as abruptly as they'd appeared, the creatures drop back and out of sight. My heart hammers away as we pause to gauge what's going on. And that's when we notice it—the sudden darkness.

A shadow moves over us. But before we can look up to determine what's caused it, the unthinkable happens.

Ari whips his head around to meet my gaze and his eyes widen at exactly the same time as my mouth opens to shout. No words come out, though; I think my voice has died in my throat.

A net drops over us both, instantly binding us inside.

I can't breathe. The rope might as well be around my neck. For a stunned second we stare at each other. And then we both scream "Cut!" and turn to the net, frantically hacking away.

I will my hands to stop shaking, but it's no good; I'll have to work through the trembling. My mind reels: *Don't drop the knife, don't drop the knife, don't drop the knife.* Ari slashes at the rope, repeatedly glancing above us. We're rising. I cut as fast as I possibly can.

We can do this. We've come through so much and we can do this!

In the corner of my eye, a submersible slows down in the distance. *Help us!* I want to scream at them, but they're already speeding away. I look up, and it isn't a Blackwatch vessel that has us. Its hull is a different design and not one I recognize from here.

A shiver runs through me as I feel a sharp prick in my arm.

Everything seems to immediately slow down. Ari appears slightly blurry. I blink several times, but it's no good; everything's turned a little hazy. There's movement beside us and we turn our heads to see we're surrounded. Thin, stony-gray sea snakes wriggle around outside the net. Their matte bodies look like rubbery cables, and their huge perfectly round eyes are pitch-black. They don't stop twisting and turning as they hover there watching us. One of the creatures pauses and opens its mouth wide, and before we can understand what's going on, it spits at Ari. He grabs his shoulder and shakes his head.

"I saw them..." I say, my words slurred. "They dropped from the Blackwatch vessels after the water tanks."

Ari stares a little dazed into the space. "They're bots, Leyla.... Keep going." He looks far away, and when he speaks again, his voice is barely discernible. "He was standing there."

I will myself to stay focused. Everything is all of a sudden muffled, though. "Who?"

"That night." His eyebrows are squished together, his expression intense. "In the doorway, a silhouette." His words slow down. He splays his hand and fiddles with his middle finger as if twisting a nonexistent ring. "It kept flashing. Silver, shiny. And she—she told me not to speak to anyone so I stayed quiet and didn't let them see me.... 'You can swim out there,' she said to me. 'I promise you can. You won't drown if you jump in. Hurry, they mustn't spot you.' I was so afraid." His eyes grow heavy. "Leyla, we have to keep cutting the..."

I hold out a hand for Ari. But before I can feel his touch, I slump back into the net and darkness washes over me.

CHAPTER THIRTY-FIVE

My body hurts. There's something pressing against me on all sides and a foul taste in my mouth. I sense a deep *thrum* and can hear muffled voices. I try to process all this as my eyes flutter open and I peer in the dim light. I have to blink several times before the fog clears from my mind.

I'm no longer in the water. My hands are bound, and I shudder as the net I was trapped in flashes before me. *Ari.* Taking several breaths, I will myself to focus and glance up. As soon as I do, though, my stomach drops and I swiftly shut my eyes again.

Captain Sebastian.

He's standing not fifteen feet from me, the tension oozing off him as he hisses something at another officer. Terror grips me until surely it's a solid thing weighing me down, keeping me pinned here. Wherever "here" is.

I press my eyes closed and my mind scrambles to try and make sense of the situation. I'm on board a submarine, in the passage near the back. I can hear the tanks, generators, and pumps. I'm slumped against a corner on the floor. Is Ari also here? My clothes and hair are still wet so I can't have been on board that long.

I nudge my bound hands close to my body and feel around my waist; the knife is gone. I pry my eyes open just enough to peer through my lashes. My gaze darts down to my wrist. They even removed my Bracelet, despite the fact it was ruined the moment it was exposed to the water.

As guardedly as possible, I twist my head to the side and meet Ari's gaze dead-on. I startle but quickly check myself. He gives the slightest nod and I blink in response, feeling an unexpected release of tension at the sight of him here, alive. He, too, is hiding the fact he's awake. His hair's still wet and his posture's all tension and distrust. His face simmers. He's been through similar situations so many times and I can't even imagine what that does to you.

I return my focus in front of me, and just as I do, Sebastian snaps his head in my direction. My insides twist before I remember he can't see my eyes are slightly ajar, not from that distance. I take care not to move even a millimeter, not to react to his expression—the usual icy sneer as he runs a glance over me before shifting his loathsome gaze in Ari's direction. He continues speaking to the officer beside him in hushed but irate tones.

I let my eyelids drop completely, and using the same technique I do to muffle the deep roar of the waters when I'm in them, I block out all the sounds, leaving only the vibrations of the vessel. Finally I zone in on their chat.

"What's so hard to grasp? You were only asked to pick up the astronomer and the little bitch," says Sebastian through his teeth, as if trying to contain himself. "My orders for *him* were very clear. So what's he doing here? And why is he still breathing? I want him off this vessel and put down. Lose him now before Ed gets wind of this mistake, got it? It's Prime Ministerial Sub One for fuck's sake, not some compound to hold their kind. And I want to see the evidence, understood? No more mistakes. I never want to see his goddamn face ever again. Ed only asked to see the McQueens—before they finally get what's coming to them."

My heart is so loud it's a miracle it hasn't burst out of my chest, and I've gone all clammy. Ari's in deep trouble.... What are we going to do? I can't bear to look his way. A pain spreads in my lungs and pushes up to lodge itself in my throat. And oh God, do they have Papa, too?

Ed. He can only be referring to Prime Minister Edmund Gladstone— he identified the vessel as the PM's official sub. We're on board the prime minister's submarine and we've done so many illegal things....I dig my nails into the palms of my hands. How do we get out of *this*?

"Y-yes, sir. And there was an attack on Broadmoor." The officer's voice trails as if he's afraid to deliver the news. He clears his throat before continuing. "A mass breakout followed, sir. I've ordered—"

This time I flinch as the slimy snake swears the place down. God knows where all this is going to end. At least the prisoners are out of that hellhole. If only I could think of something that would help get us off here before they harm Ari, but I can barely focus. I very carefully open my eyes a little and raise my gaze in their direction.

Sebastian's Bracelet flashes.

"I'll prepare to leave, sir," mutters the officer, hurrying away. He passes through the hatch at the end and is gone.

Sebastian jabs at his Bracelet before answering, placing the call on private. He speaks in hushed tones, mostly cursing the person he's talking to. He's done and advances toward us, when his Bracelet flashes again.

"Seb," says a voice.

"Ed."

It must be the PM. Once more he swiftly places the call on private. His expression darkens as he listens, and his hand curls into a fist.

"There was no need for him to concern you with this, Ed," he says, an edge to his voice and his words rushed. "Just a small error and I'm taking care of it. Yes, I understand that, but I don't think—No, of course not, but you have enough on your plate. Ed, I really think you should let me handle this, I know what I'm—" He bites his fist as he listens. "No, sir, as you wish. I'll have them sent right over."

He ends the call and punches the locker beside him, visibly denting it. The knot in my stomach tightens a hundredfold. I sneak a glance at Ari, who meets it, wary and alert.

Sebastian pauses. "Damn your curiosity, Ed," he mutters, tracing the scar across his cheek as he thinks.

He summons an officer who joins us immediately. "Wake them up and take them to the drawing room," he says. "Ed wants to see them. And bring the astronomer, too," he adds before hastily turning around and passing through the internal hatch.

My mind races and Ari's expression mirrors the same uncertainty. What the hell is going on? But at least Ari's safer now. I think. And they do have Papa. But…maybe this is even better than escaping. It's what Papa had hoped for—to somehow contact Edmund Gladstone directly.

The officer calls for two more guards. They approach us, roughly shaking us "awake," and aim their weapons at us as we stand.

"Nobody speaks unless spoken to," the blond at the front says curtly.

I move, heart hammering away.

We follow them through the hatch and into the next section of the sub, where the very first thing I see is Papa as he exits a door next to the galley, flanked by guards. My muscles weaken at the sight of him. He's alive at least. *Thank you, God.* Ari twists his neck to look past Papa, but nobody else comes through the door, and my heart lurches at the look in his eyes. Hopefully Ben and Ruby are all right. My gaze rests on Papa and my pulse races.

It's the most terrifying, jarring experience in the world to see someone pointing a weapon at a loved one. At least he doesn't look hurt, thank goodness. His eyes widen when he spots me. I quickly nod to reassure him we're all right. Papa turns to Ari and opens his mouth, but before he can say anything, a sour-faced red-haired officer behind me shoves me forward and we all move on down the extensive passageway. Hopefully the *Kabul*'s managed to remain shielded and the others are all safe.

I try and take in as much as possible about the sub we're in. Sebastian hinted at us being punished after this meeting. Though the PM isn't anything like Sebastian, there's no knowing what might happen, and my gut tells me any government vessel I'm on I need to know my bearings. As soon as my eyes scan the place, it's very apparent Prime Ministerial Sub One isn't your average vessel.

There are no portholes at all—unheard of for a submarine this size. The PM's personal motto *No past, no future* hangs as a bronze engraved plaque in every section we move through. Banners proudly displaying the national crest fly from tiny poles on the walls by lockers, bunk beds, and even the raft mountings. Everything is top notch—the fittings, the technology, the entire design. The switchboards alone are the most minimal I've ever seen. The sub's safety precautions are unbelievable, and we pass through hatch after hatch. Even its rescue equipment is beyond excessive, looking to be enough for a thousand people. The entire place reeks of paranoia. I twist my head as I take in the design of the air ducts and purifiers. They're clearly the latest models but have been fashioned to appear like the vintage styles of the earlier 2040 vessels.

"Eyes up front!" shouts the officer behind me and I quickly face straight ahead.

It's so quiet, and everyone we pass, all the officers and crew, speaks in hushed tones. I spy glimmering files hovering over a station that has a bright red *Rule Britannia* sign above it but have barely glanced at the info when the officer behind barks once more.

"I said keep your eyes straight ahead," he says, his tone biting. And then he speaks up to the officer in front of me as if we're invisible.

"This ain't right. They shouldn't be here, shouldn't be anywhere *near* Sub One. Makes me sick to my stomach to see their kind here. I'm telling you, we should just—"

The guard leading us pauses and turns around, his gaze cutting. "The *only* thing we should do is focus on carrying out orders without questioning the prime minister's judgment." He whirls back around and we continue making our way through the vessel.

Finally we turn to face a door of polished wood. The sour taste in my mouth worsens. The door slides open and we're ushered into an unexpectedly spacious room. There are now at least five officers to our rear and a few more to the sides. We move farther into the lengthy space and see that it's empty.

"You'll wait here. Don't move or touch anything," says the blond officer.

I raise my bound hands to him. "Could you please untie us?" I gesture to the officers. "There are so many of you; we couldn't possibly do anything."

He looks down at my hands, then at Ari's and Papa's, and rubs his chin.

"Nice try," says the red-haired guy. "But we know exactly what you're like. You'd slaughter every one of us in a heartbeat if given the chance." He shakes his head at the other officer, who shrugs at me and looks away.

I could strangle them both as I let my hands drop. Beside me, Ari stands rigid, jaw set, and his lips pressed flat. Papa looks determined, ready for some answers. Except we're Britain's most wanted, two of us amphis, surrounded by Blackwatch officers. I don't think we're going to get what we want. I straighten in an effort to combat the quiver in my body, and scan the spacious room.

An abundance of ancient lamps ensure the space is brightly lit. Armchairs and coffee tables are placed together to create several seating areas, and a writing desk leans against the far wall. Everything is Old World, or at least designed to be. Framed maps and antique portraits of past British prime ministers and others cover the regency-green walls, and all the furnishings are a rich, deep wood. Several sculpted busts watch over the space. The most noticeable thing is the "window," and all three of us stare at it now. It's square-shaped and designed exactly like those of Old World homes. Velvet curtains hang open, and the view outside is that of a lush green garden surrounded by a picket fence. A butterfly flutters past and pink blossoms drift down from the branches of a tree in the distance. Despite the beauty and clarity of the projection, it feels strange to view such a scene from the inside of a submarine.

There's movement in the corner and we all turn to see a part of the paneled wall slide away. Edmund Gladstone, Britain's prime minister, walks in, his soft green gaze taking us in. He gives Ari a brief second glance as he moves toward the writing desk. Right behind him is Captain Sebastian.

Facing the PM and pointing to his right-hand man, I can't get my words out fast enough. "Please help us, sir. We aren't guilty of so much we're accused of! He's been lying nonstop. He framed my papa and—"

A guard's weapon in my face causes me to catch my breath.

"No!" Papa cries out as he takes a step toward me, but another officer does the same to him. He pleads silently with his eyes for me to stay quiet.

Edmund Gladstone gives a quick shake of his head, glowering at his officers. They lower their firearms. The PM stops to lean against the front of the desk. Sebastian moves to stand by a polished drinks cabinet, completely unbothered by my outburst. He makes me sick. I think my expression betrays my feelings because his face tightens, the vein near his temple wriggling as he locks eyes with me. The look he sends me would cut through bedrock.

"If that's true, then I sympathize, Miss McQueen; it's important you know that," the prime minister says softly and earnestly. "I don't condone lawlessness." He runs a hand through his dark-brown hair before gesturing to the portraits of past prime ministers. "But you must keep calm. Please remember where you are. For us, there are no circumstances in which we might forgo conducting ourselves in a civilized manner. It's who we are; it's the pillars we stand on. In this space, in our company, you will remain composed and polite. I have a few questions for you and your father, before you're taken away, and I'm afraid I must insist on appropriate decorum from you."

I don't know what I was expecting but I'm so confused by his words. He appears to be more bothered by *how* I said what I said, than what I actually said.

Sebastian wears a slight sneer on his expression, and I quickly look away before I'm pushed to blurting out more.

"We're more civilized than some of you will ever be," says Ari.

I turn to see his knuckles are white as he clenches his fists and fixes Sebastian with a dark look.

Edmund Gladstone shifts his gaze to Ari. "They tell me you're the firebrand determined on helping these fugitives?" He pauses to stare at him, and a tiny line forms on his brow. "Did you infiltrate Number 10? Where have I seen you before?"

Ari resumes his wary expression and stays silent. Sebastian turns around and pours himself a drink. I could scream. To hell with "decorum."

"The chief historian is dead," I say.

The prime minister's eyes widen. He swings his gaze to Sebastian, who shrugs.

"We've not heard anything, Ed. She—It's lying. It's what they do, cause mischief. Up to something, no doubt. Unless it had a hand in killing him..."

"You saw this yourself?" Edmund Gladstone asks me. "Lord Maxwell dead?"

"Yes, he was at Kensington Gardens when they were hit, sir. I saw his body in the water. He drowned." I turn to glare at Sebastian. "And I had nothing to do with it."

Grief pools the PM's eyes. He visibly shudders and hangs his head.

Papa clears his throat. "So much pain and death. So much suffering caused by your policies, sir," he says quietly. "This chaos around us is a result of that. If you would—"

"The nation is in chaos largely because of you two," the PM says quietly. He clamps his jaw as he takes in Papa and me. "We had everything under control until you stirred unrest and brought about disorder, and now my chief historian is no more. I wanted to see you for myself before they take you away. See my mistake. Did you assume damaging an entire laboratory and bringing it down would *help* your cause in any way? Why is violence always the first resort for your kind?"

My body flushes at his words and the space closes in on me. Where do I even start? And what does he mean by referring to us as his "mistake"? Why does he believe everything Sebastian says to him, dammit?

Ari leans into me, half shielding me with his body. The PM notices and once more narrows his eyes as his gaze lingers on him.

"Where do I know you from? Is it my Blackwatch you snuck into? Speak up."

"They don't belong here, Ed," Sebastian mutters. "Let me take them out of your sight."

I grind my teeth at the way they fire away their questions and how they speak about us as if we're not even here.

The PM tilts his head. "A long time ago, I took pity on the McQueens and spared your lives. I have of course come to regret it since."

What does he mean? I turn to Papa, but he's wearing a haunted look in his eyes as he stares into the space. Enough, dammit.

"Don't you care?" I ask the PM as I point at Ari. "Don't you even care that a five-year-old boy lost his mother and grew up never knowing his biological family, never knowing where he came from? All because *your* right-hand man fired on her in the water here in London, killing her right under your nose. He was lucky to escape with his life! How is any of that acceptable to you?"

Edmund Gladstone stills. He very slowly raises his gaze to Ari, his lips parting as he watches him. He turns toward Sebastian, who drains his glass and slowly places it on the cabinet's surface. They lock eyes and exchange a long, unreadable look. Finally Sebastian relents and gives a slight nod. My shoulders sag in relief—at least he's admitted it, thank God. The PM looks frozen. So Papa was right…the prime minister *isn't* aware of everything his right-hand man does.

Sebastian points at us. "All of this could have been avoided, Ed, if you'd just let me have my way. I told you—"

"That's enough, Seb," says the prime minister coolly.

Sebastian presses his mouth flat and falls silent. I daren't hope too much too fast, but could it be the PM might hear us out?

He returns his focus to Ari, staring intently at him. "What happened? What do you remember?"

"He was in a security sub," says Ari, his voice low and his shoulders rising and falling. "I was in the water with my mother, but he didn't see me. We weren't hurting anybody; we were trying to get away. He opened fire on her, hitting her repeatedly." He swallows before continuing, his whole body tense. "Until she died."

Papa flinches. "That's unforgivable."

Sebastian raises his eyebrows at Ari. "Not quite," he says.

"Seb," the PM stresses with an edge to his voice as he shoots him a sidelong glance. "Let him speak." He fixes his gaze on Ari again and nods encouragingly.

Sebastian bristles at the dismissal and presses on, not taking his eyes off Ari. "It's true I did terminate one of your kind that night, but there's a small error in your account of events." He ignores the PM's threatening glare, and abruptly shifts his gaze onto me, the hint of a sneer at the corner of his mouth.

"The freak I took out that night was Soraya McQueen."

CHAPTER THIRTY-SIX

I t feels as if someone has their hands wrapped tight around my throat, and I see black spots in front of me. It's fallen silent in the room. Finally I turn to Papa and all color has left his face.

"*Why?*" I manage to whisper at Sebastian. "Why would you kill my mama?"

"Why wouldn't I?" Sebastian's face grows red as he moves to pause beside the towering classical statue in the corner. "It's the *law*. She was the enemy." Spittle flies from his mouth. "And she was in the way."

"I said *enough*, Seb," says the prime minister. He seems slightly shaken and there's an unmistakable warning in his voice. He drags his footsteps around the desk and stops behind it.

Papa looks broken. I want to run to him, wrap my arms around him. But I'm frozen to the spot.

The woman in the water was Mama. That's how she died. Violently. She must have been terrified and in so much pain. Ari was there when it happened. How? Why? My thoughts are chaos and my throat grows ever tighter.

"Law? Legality?" Papa asks Sebastian, his voice hoarse. "Powerful people can legalize *anything*. What about what is *right*? You took my wife and then falsified her death certificate. You robbed my daughter of her mother. You hurt my Sor—"

Papa moves toward Sebastian.

"No!" I scream.

Everything happens so fast it's over before I can process it.

"Halt!" shouts the officer closest to Papa.

Sebastian raises his weapon.

Ari lunges toward Papa and shoves him out of the way, sending him stumbling back.

And a loud *crack* fills the space.

My heart stops. *Please, God, no.* My eyes flit frantically over Papa and Ari for some indication of what's just happened.

Edmund Gladstone stands pointing a small ancient gun at Sebastian, his hand trembling. And the statue beside Sebastian is splattered with blood. There's a collective gasp around the room.

Captain Sebastian stares back glassy-eyed at the PM. A growing spot of crimson on his forehead trickles down his face. He reaches up to touch the wound and snarls, his features twisting at the sight of his wet fingers. He takes a step forward but sways sideways into the statue. His attempt to grab it fails and he falls to the floor with a heavy *thud*. The bust comes crashing down on top of him, sending pieces scattering across the rug.

"Sir . . . ?" The guards stare stunned at the PM's right-hand man.

"Is anybody hurt?" Edmund Gladstone asks quietly.

We shake our heads. I sob with relief, and Papa, Ari, and I huddle close together. Papa trembles, prayers slipping quietly from his lips now, and Ari looks dazed. Any one of them could've been as Sebastian is now. My whole body quivers and I can't stop the tears from flowing.

"Thank you," says Papa to the prime minister.

The PM nods absently. He turns to the officers in the room, taking in their expressions. "I will not have lawlessness," he says, his voice shaky as he lowers his weapon. He replaces the gun in the drawer and comes out from behind the desk. His hand still trembles as he runs it through his hair. "We're Britons, not some scavengers of the deep. The moment we let go of what makes us great—the moment we act uncivilized, we're lost. We are an advanced species and nation, and must behave as such."

I've no idea what's going on anymore and I can't stop shaking.

"This isn't who we are." Edmund Gladstone stresses, his mouth pinched and his expression etched in regret as he sweeps his gaze over us. "We're better than this."

I want to run and hide somewhere until I've processed everything. It feels like the revelation about Mama's death is going to swamp me completely. At the same time there's a tiny, very distant, wave of relief, too. With Captain Sebastian out of the picture, there's the faint glimmer of hope—this whole nightmare might finally be close to ending.

Papa's face mirrors the shock and grief I feel about Sebastian taking Mama's life. And still he gives me a small reassuring nod as if to say, *We finally know the truth, Pickle.* Despite the whirlpool in my mind, I return the gesture, numb. He rubs his chest and I look on his bound hands. I should ask Edmund Gladstone to please untie us now. He actually killed his right-hand man to save us.... The PM stands quiet, shoulders slightly hunched, playing with his ring as he gazes into nothing.

We startle when the door opens and a small officer rushes in. Urgent voices sound from out in the passageway. The officer is about to speak when she spots Sebastian and her mouth falls open.

The prime minister glances briefly at his former right-hand man. A pool of red spreads around Sebastian's head. Edmund Gladstone swiftly averts his gaze. "It's under control," he says curtly. "What is it?"

The officer straightens. "Sir, it's Number 10. They're struggling. Multiple attacks in the past hour have resulted in several casualties."

The PM's face hardens. He pushes his shoulders back, twisting the ring on his middle finger as he paces before the desk. "How could they have allowed that to happen?"

The government's headquarters are under attack.... It's unimaginable, and yet all I can see is the image of Mama dying in the water all those years ago. My mind has stopped working, I think. I so desperately needed to uncover the truth and thought I was prepared for it. But I wasn't. I'm not. Something has me in its grip, and I just want to scream and scream.

My body doesn't feel like my own—it's as if my limbs aren't going to move when I want them to. And poor Papa. He was right all along to have suspected foul play. The truth is unbearable....And yet still, it's better than not knowing. At least now we finally know.

The officer is dismissed with a nod, and it falls silent. I tear my gaze away from the sight of Sebastian's twisted body on the floor and take a step toward Papa, to try to console him.

"You were there," says Ari quietly.

I turn to see he's moved a little, standing separate from us now, and I follow his gaze.

It's fixed on the prime minister.

Ari stares at the PM's hands. Edmund Gladstone's ring on his middle finger flashes silver as he turns it. At Ari's words, he stops twisting it and falls dead still, his lips parting slightly.

"You were there," repeats Ari. Every muscle in his body is rigid, his brow creasing in concentration. "'Go, Ari,' she said to me. 'Run to the pool room, and don't let him see you leaving.'" He pauses, swallowing before he continues. "'Don't let your uncle Edmund see you.'" He shuffles back a step, his jaw slackening.

Silence.

I stop breathing and try to clear the fog from my mind. The officers stand motionless. The PM opens his mouth to say something, but then closes it again. Nobody utters a word. There's only the hum of the sub as it continues to hover high above London.

"I see her now....I finally see my mother clearly." Ari shakes his head. "She wasn't the woman in the water." He spins around, his gaze frantically skimming over the portraits on the wall until he moves past all the prime ministers and pauses.

On a photograph of Eva Gladstone.

I exchange a confused look with Papa as Ari stares at the picture of the PM's sister, who was ambushed and killed by amphis.

Ari slowly raises a hand and points to it. "My mother. *She* was my mother." His eyes widen as he stares at Eva Gladstone.

I clear my throat and push out a few of the sea of words stuck in there. "The prime minister is your uncle?"

Ari blinks rapidly, staring with a dazed expression.

He nods repeatedly, as if just realizing it himself. "Yes...he's my uncle. He was there that night, in our home. He stood in a doorway, calling for my mother while she secretly urged me to leave." His eyes widen and flicker. "Yes...she told me it was a game. I had to go without anyone spotting me and hide behind the filters at the side of the house. She said—" Ari turns to me, searching my face, and the confusion in his gaze deepens. "She said *your* mother would find me there. She kept promising I wouldn't drown if I played the game and jumped in...." He focuses once more on the PM. "Except it wasn't a game, was it? She was afraid. Why was my mother afraid? Where is she? What happened?"

Papa stares at Ari. His hand flies to his mouth. "You're *Eva's* son? But he died!"

Edmund Gladstone grimaces. He pulls his eyebrows in and stares down at his feet.

I wring my hands. "Papa?"

"We all mourn his sister's death every year, Pickle, remember? Eva Gladstone. Hers and her little boy's..." Papa wrinkles his brow. "Winston, that was his name. Your mama mentioned him a few times."

An icy wave rolls over me, numbing me. Ari is Winston Gladstone, the nephew the prime minister was supposed to have lost when amphis attacked his sister's sub. The brutal ambush that shocked the nation. Except Winston never died.... He's now *Ari*.

"So that's why I wasn't afraid of him when I saw him," I whisper. "We're taught to be deadly afraid of amphis and I always was. But I wasn't scared of Ari when I saw him in the water that night—because I must've recognized him." I picture the little boy in the water and try to recall seeing him before that night, but nothing comes to mind. I was only four and it was all so long ago. But it would also finally explain why Ari's always felt comfortingly familiar to me on some level.

Tears prickle my eyes until they spill over my cheeks. My mind races as I recall what Papa said about Eva Gladstone and Mama being close friends. I can't think clearly for trying to find some clue in that as to what exactly happened to Ari, and why Mama was killed.

"She *begged* me to trust her and jump in," says Ari, his stare pained and his voice hoarse. "She kept looking over her shoulder and asking me to hurry, promising me I wouldn't drown. So I jumped...." He clutches his throat. "I couldn't breathe. Everything burned. I kept vomiting. It was so cold." He shudders. "I wanted to do as she said and wait behind the filters, but..." He shakes his head. "I tried to get back inside. But when I looked up, the pool door was shut. My mother really didn't want me returning...." He blinks and turns to me. "And that's when *your* mother found me."

I move closer to Ari, taking deep breaths. None of what anyone's saying feels real.

"Where are my parents?" Ari asks the PM. "Did my mum survive the 'attack' on us, too?"

The guards exchange furtive looks, uncertainty lingering in each one.

The prime minister's expression is intense, and he once more plays with his ring as he stares silently ahead of him.

"What did Sebastian mean?" I ask him. "He said you wouldn't let him have his way. What was he referring to? Why did you lie about your nephew's death? What really happened that night? Why did *he*"—I indicate Sebastian's corpse—"kill my mother? Tell us!"

Voices rise from the passageway and a distant alarm blares out. The door opens and it's the small officer again.

"What now?" snaps the PM, his voice dangerously low.

"Sir, we're surrounded and coming under attack. Local fire, and nothing we can't handle."

Papa and I exchange looks. *Who's out there?*

Edmund Gladstone leans back against the desk. He nods, his nostrils flaring. "Rise," he says. "They will eventually have to fall back. And then we must get to work on fixing this mess and bringing order back to this country."

The officer confirms and hurries away.

"I must know," says Ari, his voice laced with desperation. "Where's my mother? What happened to her after I left? And why did I grow up far away from here with Ben? Who could we tell now? I need to know, for myself."

The sub starts climbing.

The PM presses his lips together in a slight grimace, and blinks away at Ari's words. "It—it really is you," he finally says with a slight shake of his head. He wipes his brow and straightens. "I was a good brother. Eva never needed for anything. And I loved you, Winston. You were my every-thing." He swallows and looks away. "Everybody had to be immediately tested, starting with those in positions of power—and our families. We had to identify any infiltrators so we could protect the nation. The consul-tant who tested your mother and you was a friend. I received a call. Eva was clear, but there was an anomaly with your results...."

We listen in silence.

Ari trembles. "And?"

The PM moves to sit in the chair behind the desk. He focuses his gaze on Ari. His color blanches and a dazed look comes into his eyes. He rubs his face, but the distant expression remains.

"Your results displayed rogue genes....Anthropoid DNA," he says flatly. "I told the consultant it was a system error. I said there was no way my Winston was one of them. I had only just been elected to this nation's highest office. As if my new responsibilities weren't enough, I was alerted to the existence of enemies among us. And then what do you know—mere days into our new testing program, my own nephew is identified as one. It was a lot to deal with. Seb had newly joined the ranks of the Blackwatch. I enlisted his help and we dropped by your home. The consultant met us there." He blinks away as he continues to stare at Ari.

My heart races. Even as we need to finally hear this truth, anticipating what he might say next is agonizing.

"Your mother had been made aware of the results shortly before I was. We dropped by and I told her the specialist needed to run a quick test on you. I didn't want to worry her with anything more than that. Eva was the light of my life. She said she understood and went upstairs to fetch you. We had no idea at the time that she'd already messaged her meddling friend Soraya McQueen. Seb left to check what was taking so long, and discovered you'd left. He and Eva struggled. Your mother gave him that scar across his cheek. He told me you were gone, and that was when I realized it was true... realized what you were." His eyes are far away now.

"And what did you do?" Ari asks quietly.

"I couldn't believe it. Some days it still sends me reeling," the PM continues as if he hasn't heard Ari. "My own nephew, an Anthropoid. You broke my heart, Winston. But even then I sacrificed my principles and reassured my sister. I would let you live, I said. I would send you away to Broadmoor and nobody need find out. While I could never forgive her for allowing one of them into her life, and for bringing you into this world, I would ensure her secret was safe. For all our sakes. And she could always have another child. Do you know what my own sister said to me in response to my offer of help?" He swallows before continuing. "Your mother looked me in the eyes, and said, 'It wasn't Yusef, though. My husband wasn't the amphi, Ed. He drowned, remember? Which can only mean *I* am. And more than that, I know in my heart it's true.'"

Papa and I stare at each other, speechless. Ari draws a ragged breath, and I hear him whisper "Yusef" under it, as if trying out the name. I lean into him as the PM continues.

Edmund Gladstone narrows his eyes. "She said, 'I'm carrying the dormant gene, Ed, and I'm proud of who I am.' No shame, no understanding of what that meant. She said, 'I'm more human than you'll ever be.' She was out of control. *I* was the monster, she insisted, not the Anthropoids." His hand shakes as he wipes his brow.

The vessel gives a slight lurch and Sebastian's body moves. The room spins around me and I shake myself alert.

"That's it..." Papa says, staring at Ari. "You reminded me of someone when I first saw you, but I couldn't place you. It was Yusef. I'd seen him around a couple of times. You look so much like him, son."

"What happened to her?" Ari's voice is low and choked with emotion, his gaze piercing Edmund Gladstone's own.

The PM nods away to himself. He pinches his throat. "I am the *prime minister*. I've dedicated my life to this nation and only ever done what was *right*. Leaders must be prepared to do whatever is necessary to lead, even when—when it breaks your heart to do it. I—I took care of Eva. Of course I did. It remains the hardest thing ever demanded of me as head of this once great nation, but she left me with no choice. She was no longer my sister." He sticks out his chin and there's the slightest wobble. "I terminated your mother."

CHAPTER THIRTY-SEVEN

Ari stands dead silent, his breathing shaky. I move my bound hands close to his and grab his fingers. He squeezes mine.

"You murdered your sister?" Papa says. "You took her life because she was different than you? My God, Prime Minister, what have you done...?"

Edmund Gladstone narrows his eyes. "You don't think I've suffered? I had to end my own sister's life. She forced me to behave in a manner I'm not wholly proud of, one that haunts me to this day. And for years I have had to live with the knowledge one of those devils shared my DNA, my blood. I began questioning who *I* was." He shakes his head. "Seb took care of the consultant so there would be no witness to her treachery. And then he left to find Winston."

The sub sways and Papa grabs on to the nearby stand of a giant Old World globe standing on the floor.

Ari turns to me, staring blankly. "I remember now. I spotted your mother, like mine said I would. She took my hand and showed me another way around to your home. She—she saw something, became distracted. And that's when I spotted you in the window. I didn't know we were in danger; my mother told me it was a game. I paused in front of you and that's when it happened, Leyla. I turned and..." He shakes his head and we squeeze each other's fingers. "I'm so sorry. I see it all so clearly now, what happened to your mother. Ben found me. He grabbed me and told me to swim as fast as I could. We swam for so long...." His voice trails, exhausted.

"No wonder we couldn't find you," Edmund Gladstone says now, his mouth pinched. "We left no shell unturned, but there was no sign of you. The morgue confirmed the body as Soraya McQueen, and I ordered Blackwatch to her home. It was imperative I find you."

"Your mama left in haste without saying anything," Papa says absently as he turns to me. He rubs his chest again as if in pain. "I was busy with you when your mother received Eva's message. She dropped everything and raced to help. I waited all evening. And then they turned up, the Blackwatch. They said your mama had been found dead. They never mentioned their involvement."

"Let me assure you I didn't take pleasure in *anything* we had to do in light of that night's events, McQueen," says the PM. "The most important thing is that you understand and believe that." He stands, hands gripping the sides of the desk as the sub sways. "We couldn't link the Blackwatch to the area that evening in light of Eva's fate. And so Seb told you Soraya was already dead when she was found. You had to be questioned—we needed to be sure your wife hadn't shared Eva's message with you. And of course you had to be tested. Your wife wasn't human, and there was a good chance you and your offspring were also enemies. Luckily for you, you were both clean...." He twists his mouth. "Our greatest failure has been our inability to produce a test that would accurately determine the dormant gene."

A haunted look breaks out on Papa's expression. "You don't understand what you've done, do you? You ruined our lives. And just when my little girl needed me the most, you kept us apart for days, interrogating us. You threatened to take my child away!"

"It could have been far worse!" the PM says incredulously. "Seb wanted you dead! He insisted we were unsafe as long as you two were alive, but each time I persuaded him enough people had already died. I wouldn't hear of it. Neither of you revealed Anthropoid genes. We are not savages.

But of course in the end Seb proved right about you going on to cause trouble."

The vessel rocks and the Old World globe rattles in all the movement. I push down on my soles in an effort to maintain my balance. We need to stop climbing. The PM doesn't seem to notice any of it. He turns to Ari.

"We gave up searching for you after a few years, agreeing you had most likely died that night. Still, Seb set up an alert just in case. He would receive notification if there was ever any trace of you in the system. And then, after all these years, you turn up alive and well.... Seb must have been notified of your identity at the lab. Perhaps he was right to keep the news from me." He shrugs. "I'm not sure my nerves could have taken it. Our sensibilities are more sophisticated than yours, you must understand."

The furniture in the room clatters. All I can focus on, though, as I hold on to Ari, is the weight of the truths unfolding before us now.

All that time Sebastian was running searches on Ari after we rescued him from the lab, I thought it was because he was with Papa and me. I thought it was best for him if he stayed away from us. But it turns out it was because of who *he* was—the PM's own nephew. *That's* why Sebastian was desperate to recapture him.

The way the PM talks about Ari leaves a bitter taste in my mouth and my face burns. *Enough.* I'm so sick and tired of being afraid.

"You're unbelievable," I say to Edmund Gladstone. "You didn't kill Sebastian to 'maintain order'.... You killed him because you feared he might reveal the truth. That you murdered your own sister...and you were prepared to lock away your young nephew, have him languish in the hell that is Broadmoor. And then you turned around and blamed your own heinous crimes on an entirely innocent people. All this time...This whole time we thought maybe you didn't know everything your—"

"Hold your tongue. No need for vulgarities!" His eyes widen. "Remember where you are." He gestures to the portraits of past prime ministers on the walls.

Papa pleads silently for me to be quiet, but I look away from him.

I recoil at the PM's words. "'Vulgarities?' You're more offended and

shocked by my listing actions you've taken than by the horrors themselves....Carrying out the crimes is acceptable to you, but my mentioning them is impolite? Can't you see how utterly twisted that is?! You said
Sebastian pulling a weapon on us isn't who you are, but it's *exactly* who you
are. Just because you can't bear to acknowledge your past actions doesn't
mean they didn't take place. They don't disappear from you ignoring
them—they happened!"

We stumble as the sub's motions become erratic. Footsteps can be
heard pounding along the passageway. The door opens and several more
officers rush in to ensure the PM is all right. I glance at Papa and Ari; we
need to get off the damn vessel! But even if we rushed some of the guards,
the others would open fire. We're unarmed and stand no chance against
firepower. And out there in the passageway are more of them. He's going
to kill us all.

I grit my teeth and turn to him. "There's clearly a storm taking place
on the surface. You have to stop rising!"

Edmund Gladstone curls his lip as he steadies himself. "I can smell
the fear on you from here. How do you think our brave Explorers reach the
surface? She's merely acclimatizing, that's all. I have infinite faith in the
human spirit. There's *nothing* we can't conquer if we keep faith in who we
once were. I'm taking her all the way to the surface, where I guarantee you
we'll thrive."

The surface...We're doomed. I don't care how advanced Prime Ministerial Sub One is or what its hull is made of, nothing is a match for the
furious weather on the surface—not in the middle of a storm.

The vessel pitches and everyone loses their footing again. I can only
imagine the size and velocity of the waves lashing at the sub now. As soon
as I've regained my balance, I shake my head at his men. "Please, you have
to listen to me! I've seen the reports myself. It's scientific fact! We can't
survive on the surface—not for decades yet. We breathe filtered air, and if
the onboard systems are affected up there, then you could suffocate!"

"Spare us your ridiculous facts and figures," Edmund Gladstone
says bitterly. "If those incompetent fools hadn't given in to the disaster,

I wouldn't *need* to worry about keeping us safe down here. Where did all their data get them?"

"Except it was *scientists* who predicted the asteroid and determined exactly how we'd survive down here. You're here *because* of them. Humankind would've otherwise died out!" I shout.

"What's a man to do?" Edmund Gladstone asks his officers. "If I lull Britons into a false sense of security, they'll let their guard down and we all become vulnerable. They'll forget who we are, where we come from. That's why I made existence of the amphis public knowledge. If Britons knew about the horrors we faced down here, they'd understand why my surfacer policies are the only answer to such devilry." He turns back to me. "No more from you. You will answer for the damage you've caused this nation. You *will* follow the laws of this country."

There's a pounding in my ears as my pulse races. He actually thinks he can justify all the ways in which he's failed us. He shifts his stare onto Ari, breathing hard and fast as he takes him in. Then he motions to an officer.

"Secure them in the back. The moment we regain control of Broadmoor, I want them taken and locked away. Indefinitely. Understood?"

My heart goes out to Ari, who stands staring at his uncle with a stunned expression.

"Sir?" An officer checks his Bracelet. "The hostiles have fallen behind. Should I give the order to cease ascent?"

Edmund Gladstone shows no sign of having heard him and doesn't take his eyes off Ari.

His guards move toward us. Papa pleads with them to let Ari and me go. I'm just stepping back, when we're all sent scrambling as the sub gives a sudden, violent lurch. Cries fill the air. The space shudders.

I stagger sideways, heart pounding as I grab a chair's armrest to stop from hitting the floor. I'm vaguely aware of Ari reaching out for Papa who looks like he's fallen. Books from the shelves go sprawling across the room. Sebastian, and pieces of the statue that fell on him, roll around on the floor. A ruckus sounds from the passageway. And the "window" flickers before the garden disappears entirely as the onboard technology becomes affected. Even as all these things register, I'm not really focusing on any of them. Because a guard fell behind me.

And his weapon has landed right next to my feet.

We both dive at once for the gun. I wrap my bound hands around it and lift it away just in time.

"I'll shoot!" I raise my voice over the din as I whip my hands up above my head to point the hefty weapon at the roof of the submarine. I lock eyes with the prime minister. "Let us go or I *will* do it."

A murmur spreads around the room.

I don't take my gaze off the PM. "A weapon this size will blow a hole right through to the pressure hull and sink this thing, and you know it. Even if your men shoot, I'll still manage to press this switch. *We* might still make it if the vessel floods, but you and your officers will be gone. Don't make me do it."

Edmund Gladstone stiffens, his neck and face turning a blotchy red. Then he blinks and slowly stretches a corner of his mouth. "And kill your own father?"

I don't flinch. "You're so sure he isn't an amphi."

The PM's sneer falters.

Papa, God bless him, swiftly conceals his alarm at what I've done and said, and instead sticks his chin out.

Edmund Gladstone's officers glance at one another, for the briefest moment all of them betraying a hint of uncertainty. They clear their expressions when they turn to him for instruction, but he's busy staring at Ari now, lips pressed together.

Ari holds his gaze. "You killed my mother—your own sister—in cold blood. You faked my death, lied to the country, blamed our murders on innocent people. You," he stresses, "are *nothing* to me."

The prime minister startles. "Everything I've ever done has been for the good of the nation," he says.

I lock eyes with him. "There's *nothing* good or healthy about living in a climate of terror and uncertainty, and with a sense of displacement. *Everyone* deserves a place they can call home! You've robbed us of our peace of mind. The rise in seasickness numbers, and lack of any real treatment for those suffering, is because of you. Because of how you govern. We could learn to manage it! But instead of helping sufferers, you exploit the condition to further push your own agenda for living up on the surface. Because *you're* afraid. Fear governs your every decision and law, and now we're all drowning in it. And then you have the nerve to try to distance yourself from the outcome? That isn't how it works!" His expression darkens, but I jab the weapon in the air and press on. "You fake earthquakes to ensure we remain fearful of the environment down here. That's unconscionable. You've lied about *us* since the day you discovered we existed. You've abused every bit of your power to have people believe we're the enemy. You're a disgrace to yourself and this country!" My face burns.

He twists his features. "Your inferiority to us is irrefutable. But I'm no monster! Why do you think the labs exist? If I can just make a breakthrough with what we're working on, you can change and make yourselves useful! You could *help* us down here. I'm *saving* this country! The quakes, too, are for the people's sake. We cannot have Britons forgetting their rightful place in the world. I ensured minimum loss and—"

"What's minimum loss to you?" Papa asks breathlessly. "There's never been a quake without loss of life. Their blood is on your hands."

"Don't you see?" I continue. "We can live with hope, while also planning for returning to the surface when it's scientifically possible and safe to do so. It's not one or the other—we can do both!"

The prime minister steps forward. "We were never meant to live in this bladder of the planet," he says, bitterly. "My ancestors didn't win wars and die so we could pass away into extinction down here."

"Stop manipulating their memory. And open your eyes—we're still alive!"

I can't believe we're at the mercy of people like this. An entire nation crumbling away at the whim of someone utterly unfit to lead.

The familiar *ping* and *whoosh* of firepower reaches my ears. We all whip our heads around to the main door. Something's definitely going on out there!

Several officers rush to the PM's side. "Sir!" They flank the prime minister, protecting him. The rest split between keeping their weapons fixed on me and aiming for the main door. Just as I'm about to gesture to Ari, to indicate the guard closest to him because her gun might be within his grasp, a deep *boom* rocks the place and sends us all scattering.

I wince as I land on my side, and the room spins. The sound could only have been an explosion. I blink away until everything clears, then drag myself up. Ari managed to stay upright. Papa nods to assure me he's all right as he pulls himself up off the floor. I turn in the direction of the door when—*bang*. The polished wood blasts right into the room. I yell and dive out of the door's path as it goes crashing into the desk at the back.

Ben and a bunch of others stand panting in the gap, all heavily armed. *Oh, thank you, God!*

There's movement at the back of the room as the PM's guards swiftly escort him toward the panel in the wall he'd emerged from earlier. Just before he steps through, Edmund Gladstone pauses to throw Ari a glance. His expression is unreadable. And then it clears, replaced by an unmistakable hardness. He turns around and disappears. The panel locks shut behind him.

Ben and the others aim their weapons at the officers inside, who have their own firearms fixed on them in return. An alarm rings out.

"We're only here for them!" Ben shouts. His gaze wanders to us. "Ari? Leyla? Everyone okay? Hang in there, Hashem." He returns his focus to the officers. "We're not interested in anything else here. A single stray shot could bring everyone down, and enough have died today. Let them go and we'll walk away."

The blond officer and another hesitate, exchanging looks.

"Like hell you will," says the red-haired guy who shoved me down the passageway on our way here. And he opens fire.

I flinch as the drawing room becomes a blur of firepower and a cacophony of terrifying sounds. Shouting is drowned out amid the blaring alarm and the *whoosh* and *ping* of the weapons. Everywhere I look is a shocking sight. Ari catches my and Papa's attention and gestures frantically to the desk, his hands now untied. We all hasten toward the table and dive behind it.

I turn to Ari. "What do we do?"

"Stay here. I'm getting help."

"No, wait!" I shout.

"Wait, son, I can help!" says Papa.

But he's gone. I edge my head out from behind the desk until I can see what's going on.

"Ari!" Ben rushes inside the room, stepping over debris and ducking fire as he does. I spot Kiara, Jack, and Samantha as they engage in a shootout with the officers. Some of the prime minister's men fall, while one drops his weapon and races away. My heart misses a beat when Tabby stumbles into the room engaged in hand-to-hand combat with an officer. Thank goodness she's okay, but I really wish she wasn't here. She wouldn't survive if the vessel became flooded.

Ari shouts, asking about his mother, and Ben assures him Ruby's fine. Ari then yells something at Kiara and Jack, and they whirl around to face the desk. They rush toward us.

"Mr. McQueen," Kiara says as she produces a knife and begins cutting Papa's hands free. "I need to get you off this sub at once. Come!" She beckons him when it's done. "Lewis is waiting for you."

"Not without Leyla!" he says.

"You need to go," says Jack. "Lewis's sub only carries two, and you need to get off before the rest of us. You must hurry. We'll help get you to the pool room safely!"

Tabby, red-faced and breathing fast, races toward me. She whips out a knife and sets to work slashing away at my bonds.

"*Please*, Papa," I say, holding his gaze. "I'll be right behind. You have to trust me. Please go!"

He blinks at my words, and then nods slowly. Jack and Kiara help him up. Ben, Samantha, and a now armed Ari cover for them as they make their way through the room, dodging firepower as they go.

"I can't believe this madness!" Tabby shouts over the noise as she cuts away and we watch Papa go until he's out of sight. "Are you injured?"

"I'm all right! What about Theo and the *Kabul*? Is there news of Grandpa?"

"All's good so far! Gideon too—he's okay!"

"Oh thank God! There were people desperate for help and I directed them to the *Kabul*?"

"They made it—loads turned up and they're all safely on board!"

I could cry with relief.

"Ben and Ruby were separated from your dad and taken to the same place they were keeping Gideon. When it was hit, Ruby quickly got your granddad into a submersible and headed straight for the *Kabul*. And when one of the Cambridge lot spotted you guys trapped in the net, they alerted Ben, who gathered us to come fetch you."

Thank God *something's* going right. "Tabs, how are you getting off?"

Tabby throws her arms around me when my hands become free. "It's been taken care of." She reaches into the small pocket on her chest and pulls out a Bracelet. "It's one of theirs. It'll give me access to their subs. Swiping it was Theo's first instruction!"

"All right, we need to get to the pool room fast and get the hell off this sub!"

I glance back around the desk. They're fighting physically, too, now. Ari's a blur as he takes on the officers, delivering blow after blow while evading firepower.

Tabby grabs my hand. "Ready?"

I nod and we move forward cautiously, ducking constantly as we navigate the mayhem unfolding around us. We decide to make a run for it through all the chaos. I'm almost at the doorway when an officer grabs me from behind, and hurls me back across the room. A slither of pain races up my side as I land, and my gun rolls a few feet away. My neck aches as I crane it in the other direction and Ari comes into focus.

His face flares with rage and he grabs hold of the Old World globe, jerking it until it breaks free of its fixtures. He propels it through the room. It lands right in the chest of the officer who hurt me and sends him staggering back. Ari brawls with two of them at once, landing blows on each in turn.

From the doorway Samantha cries out as she takes a hit to the leg. Tabby is closest to her and rushes to her rescue. Ari shouts for Tabby to get out of there, assuring her he's following right behind with the rest of us. She grabs ahold of Samantha and they disappear into the passageway. My head spins from trying to stay on top of what's happening as I haul myself up.

Ari's making his way over to me when he winces and grabs his arm. I gasp as blood seeps through his fingers. The guard responsible is in the corner, preparing to take aim at him once more. I lunge for my gun and fire in his direction. Ari and I move.

"Dad!" he shouts as we pass Ben, who's still fighting.

"Everyone's out?" Ben asks.

"They've gone, it's only you guys. Come on!"

Ben nods and calls back those remaining. We all bolt out of the room and rush through the vessel. Lights flash and pulse away from every corner as switchboards and control panels warn of the altitude we're at.

My heart sinks when we sight Samantha and Tabby still on board, moving at seahorse speed because of Samantha's injured leg.

"Please, Tabs," I plead. "I'll hold on to Samantha. You go get into a sub!"

Tabby shakes her head. "I can't. There are more of them ahead. Kiara, Jack, and several others are on it!"

As soon as the others have cleared the way, we move on down the vessel. We meet further resistance when we pass through another hatch. Some officers appear afraid of us and let us pass, while others are more concerned with the state of the submarine and barely glance our way. But still several guards pull their weapons on us and Ari takes them out as we race toward the pool room. There's no sign of Papa; hopefully he and Lewis got away.

I spot movement out of the corner of my eye as guards hiding ahead take aim at us. Crying out to warn the others, I swing my weapon in front of me only just in time. An officer aiming for us misses as my weapon blasts his arm and he stumbles back. It's chaos once more. Ari and Tabby join in, and the others pivot around to take on those closing in on us from the rear. The noise suddenly feels too much, and there's a nonstop ringing in my ears. The submarine shudders ominously, and items roll off the racks above our heads. The remaining officers behind us panic and scatter.

"They're getting away! We should make Gladstone pay for what he did!" someone shouts.

"This isn't the time!" says Ben. "Go—get off this Neptune-forsaken vessel!" He pushes through and gets ahead, beckoning the rest of us to follow.

We reach the pool room. Lewis's sub is gone, thank goodness. Tabby rushes around to the chamber and accesses a single-seater. Ben holds open the maintenance hatch for the rest of us. "Jump, jump!" he shouts as we all race through and head straight for the pool. "Dive in and clear out before the submersible needs it." He secures the hatch again behind us.

"Jump, son!" he shouts at Ari.

"I'm the strongest, Dad—I go last. I'll be right behind Tabby."

The sub sways, and the lighter color and fierce churning of the waters as they lap the sides of the pool signal the hazardous altitude we're at. And then through the window I spy two officers race into the room. One of them darts to the control panel and slams his hand down on a flashing orange switch.

"No!" I shout. "They're closing the pool!" I beckon those remaining. "Quickly!"

The countdown begins immediately, echoing around the space. Ben glances up at the claw carrying Tabby's sub over now.

"Go, Dad!" Ari shouts. "They need you!"

Ben dives into the water. Seconds later Tabby's vessel is lowered into it. She drops and clears the opening in record time, just as the pool's cover begins gliding across the gap onto the ocean. *No.*

Ari and I clasp hands and jump.

CHAPTER THIRTY-EIGHT

We stare at the newsreader on-screen as we process the emergency bulletin.

Edmund Gladstone is dead.

They all are—everyone who remained on board the PM's official sub a week ago as it rose to the surface.

Papa looks shaken as the words echo around the saloon. We both utter the Qur'anic phrase usually recited when we hear of someone's death. He takes a seat beside Grandpa, who quotes a similar prayer in Hebrew. Ruby and Ben watch with their hands covering their mouths. Ari, Theo, Tabby, and I are standing as we take in the words and images streaming live now from Newsbots up on the surface. Mercifully they don't film the interior of Prime Ministerial Sub One.

Nausea rises inside to settle all sour and itchy in my mouth and throat as the newsreader continues, and we can't tear our eyes away.

This morning, Explorers were sent to investigate when all contact with the PM's sub was lost. They battled to reach the vessel only to be met with a horrific sight once they boarded her. A violent magnetic storm had messed up the systems on board, and the atmosphere control equipment became ineffective. There's evidence those on board opened the exterior hatch to breathe the air up there, without stopping to wear appropriate breathing and protective gear. The standard atmospheric oxygen levels above the surface, which were already dangerously low, had worsened due to a month-long storm. Britain's prime minister and the majority of his cabinet were found suffocated, with some also displaying fatal burns. The footage replays and finally we turn to one another.

Papa, Grandpa, Ruby, and Ben sit stunned as they quietly consider the update, each looking exhausted. Messages begin flooding in about the latest news and they discuss the developments with others. The rest of us make our way into the viewport.

Jojo wags her tail as we gaze out in silence. The familiar green-blue waves of the waters around Britain lap the submarine's bow in the late afternoon. We're hovering high above Wimbledon. The morning after we escaped the PM's vessel, we dropped off the people we'd rescued at a designated safe building way below us. Maud McGregor, Lewis's mum, and her friends took charge of it and are looking after those seeking safe passage out of the capital. We chose to stay in the area for the time being and help them.

Everywhere you look, the country's gone through hell.

It's been just over a week since we came down to London. A week since the government attacked the protesters. A week since everyone who'd had enough, along with those who were only now discovering the truth about our situation, and others who'd heard for so long but didn't believe or care at the time, all rose together and said *Enough*. All Anthropoid Watch Council offices were destroyed. And it's been three days since a steady stream of truthful accounts finally began receiving airtime on the news.

My screaming at Edmund Gladstone proved more consequential than I could ever have imagined. Every word exchanged in the drawing room was recorded, in keeping with Prime Ministerial Sub One protocol. Everyone heard the truth, including what happened in the past with Mama and Eva and Winston Gladstone, the PM setting up the "earthquakes" that took so many lives, his horrific plans for amphis, and his endless lies to the public in some misguided attempt to keep us safe—they heard it all. The recording was played everywhere, even abroad, and still runs on all the channels.

We turn to face the screen again as the newsreader announces yet another development.

"An emergency interim government has been sworn in, in the last hour. They will remain in charge until the country is stabilized enough to hold elections." She goes on to talk about the temporary new government, and who will assume which role, before adding, "What's left of the late Prime Minister Gladstone's cabinet and the Blackwatch is suspended with immediate effect. We understand that acting Prime Minister Smith will be holding a press conference in a few days' time. In the meantime, the new cabinet has declared one of its very first acts as government to be the identification and immediate suspension of any and all further experimental laboratories, detention centers, and illegal prisons."

There's a collective gasp around the saloon as her words sink in. I can't believe it. Finally. A wave of heat flushes through me. Edmund Gladstone's horrific plans for us, which the files we downloaded at the lab hinted at, were fully laid bare once his offices were overrun.

The PM wanted us to "carry out our original purpose": To serve non-amphis.

He envisioned us working away down here once everyone else returned to the surface. The best way to deal with us now, he'd recently decided, was to reduce us to the passive workforce Old World scientists had originally hoped we'd be. That's why they were experimenting on amphis at the labs. It would remove us as a threat, while ensuring they need never enter the depths again. A shiver runs through me anytime I think on it. That such a setup seemed perfectly acceptable to him. The majority of humanity up on the surface while a submissive minority lived deep below and served them. And I guess even that situation he'd have gradually made justifiable to the people. It never happens overnight. If it did, we'd object to so much of what we now consider acceptable.

The newsreader pauses, her eyes flickering as she receives yet another update, and takes a breath before continuing.

"As of this moment, all current laws concerning amphis are henceforth suspended. No amphi is to be stopped, detained, or harmed due to their identity. Further details will follow suit."

Ben and Ruby break into sobs. Ari moves over to the sofas and the family huddles, overcome. Tears run down the rest of ours faces as we look on. We cannot even imagine. How much they've had to suffer as a people. How long they've dreamed of this day.

The twins and I go to the galley and put the kettle on. Tabby is tearful and red-faced as she lines up the cups for the Tea-lady. I stare into the space, blowing out my cheeks. There are no words for what's now unfolding around us, and for the unspeakable horrors that have taken place in all the years and decades before today, and for the pain and further loss of life during the last week.

We take the tray of warm drinks inside and all gather around the sofas.

Papa rubs my arm, nodding away silently. On top of everything else, he's been mourning Mama all over again after finding out exactly how her life was taken from her. He'll sit there gazing into nothing and won't even hear me calling to him. The laboratories in Bloomsbury where he and Grandpa used to work were damaged this week, but it's barely registered with him. Buildings can be rebuilt, they both said when they heard about their beloved labs, but you can't bring back a single life lost.

Over the course of the evening, within hours of the news about the fate of everyone on board Prime Ministerial Sub One, and the new interim government and revised laws regarding amphis, protests begin to cease.

I move to light up a Lumi-Orb in the viewport, and Ari comes up behind me and wraps his arms around my shoulders. I lean back against him and we stand there in silence, looking out into the evening current. He sighs, a long and heavy exhale, and I cover his arms with my own. Edmund Gladstone was his uncle, and he murdered Ari's mother. And now his uncle is dead but his people are, at long last, hopefully going to be free. I can't even imagine what he's going through. And I guess one of the things we'll never know for sure is whether the PM killed Sebastian because in that moment he actually felt compelled to save his own nephew, or whether he shot him in the hopes of burying the truth with him.

The night we escaped the PM's sub, Ben finally told us what happened, how he came about raising Ari as his own child.

Ben lived in London and kept himself to himself. One evening while in the water, he spotted a security sub and hid as usual. When he saw the vessel open fire, he realized something was going on. He noticed Ari, who by then was distraught, having—unbeknownst to Ben—just witnessed Mama's death. Ben acted fast. He grabbed Ari and left London, going far north to the Faroe Islands in a bid to keep Ari safe. Ari went into shock and stopped speaking. The community put word out, asking anyone who might know anything about him to come forward. Nobody did, because the only amphis who knew Ari's real identity were our mothers, and they were now both dead.

They concluded Blackwatch must've killed Ari's family that night. Ben wanted to adopt him and everyone agreed it was in Ari's best interests. They couldn't decide on what to call him, until Ari was the first name they unanimously liked. It's an Old Norse nickname meaning *Eagle*, Ben had explained to us. They never discovered Ari's background. Ben fell in love with Ruby in the Faroe Islands and settled there with her. Ari started speaking after six months but never once mentioned the past or his real name—he'd blocked *everything* out. For the first time in his life, Ben took an interest in fighting for amphi rights. And that's how he met and befriended Grandpa a few years later. And why last year, when Ben feared for Ari's safety after the attack on their community, and Grandpa feared for mine after Papa's arrest, they agreed sending Ari to London to watch over me would be best for both of us.

I can't believe amphis really might stop being hunted and killed.

The atmosphere in the saloon is one of deepest relief, and also the saddest feeling ever. Tears slip from my eyes to roll down my cheeks. I take a deep breath and shudder. Ari tightens his embrace around my shoulders.

How did the treatment of amphis ever become acceptable? Why did we never question the government's line on them?

Why did we so readily choose to condemn an entire race of people based on somebody else's views instead of using our own hearts and minds?

Ari was right that first day we met on board the *Kabul*. Before Papa went missing, I was content in my own little bubble, completely apathetic to what was happening to others.

Our government first made its actions necessary. Then they made them legal. They made them normal. They even made them right.

I wipe away my tears. Still, today is a new start, inshallah.

NEW YEAR'S EVE, 9 MONTHS LATER
LONDON, GREAT BRITAIN

The waters darken as it approaches. I hold my breath. We're *all* holding our breath.

"Music low!" I shout over my shoulder, and the noise of the party dims a little. The few who were still unaware of what's happening abandon their dancing and rush over to join us by the floor-to-ceiling windows of the spacious home.

The creature's shadow comes into sight in the distance. I can't believe how close to the city it's swimming... it's only meters above the rooftops. We tilt our heads back as it draws closer until it's passing right over us, and we watch open-mouthed. Warmth spreads through me. It's never-ending.... Its considerable body glides effortlessly through the winter current like a solid wave rolling through the area. Despite looking on from inside, we can clearly see it's a gray-blue color, its skin all blotchy and noticeably scarred in places. There's a lightness in my chest and I feel breathless.

An actual blue whale is passing through London.

A half-laugh escapes my throat. It's too much! None of us have ever seen one before. We crowd even closer to the windows.

"It's a female," whispers Kiara in awe. "Lord, it must be at *least* a hundred feet."

"I heard their hearts are so big the heartbeat sounds like drums when you're in the water," says Samantha.

I can believe it, too.

"They can hear one another from even three hundred leagues away," says Theo, his eyes shining as they meet mine. "Reckon you'd swim alongside one if you saw it?"

"Absolutely!"

We stare after the magnificent creature, up at the flukes of its tail swishing powerfully through the night's current until it's out of sight, headed in the direction of Chelsea.

"Music up!" I shout. Everyone rushes back to whatever they were doing, and the first New Year's Eve party I've ever thrown is once more in full swing.

Papa, Grandpa, and Ben will have observed the whale from upstairs. They wanted to finalize a presentation they were working on, before returning downstairs for the PM's New Year's Eve speech. Ben heads a commission that focuses on amphi rights. It was set up in the weeks after the protests and national change that took place nine months ago. Papa and Grandpa take an active interest in it and help out a lot.

"I'm not going back to my friggin' game," Tabby announces, her eyes glinting as she moves closer to me. She gestures to Lewis over in the far corner, who's standing by a table with a chessboard glimmering over it. He's waving his arms to beckon her back but she ignores him. "I swear that rascal Oscar helps Lewis out whenever we're playing."

She shouts over the music in their direction. "Play with each other—I'm sure Oscar would bloody love that."

Lewis shakes his head and smiles wickedly. Oscar smooths his hair with his hand as he leans back in the chair to throw us a look of innocence I absolutely know is feigned.

I grin. "I'm sorry, Tabs. But you can't say a bad word about Oscar to me!"

I gesture to the Butler standing nearby with a colorful drinks tray. Tabby grabs a glass containing a sparkly red drink, and the robot bows his head before moving on with the tray.

"Do you think Samantha's into Theo?" Tabby asks as we watch the others dance. Samantha, Kiara, Jack, and Theo are half dancing, half chatting as lights pulse all around us. "Hope so," she continues, her eyes sparkling as colored beams play across her face. "I might one day have nieces or nephews who can breathe underwater!"

I roll my eyes and we grin.

Jojo's fast asleep; it's past her bedtime anyway, but tonight she played endlessly with the ball Tabby got her for Christmas. Chasing after the holographic toy as we "throw" it across the room seriously wears her out. She wised up to the juicy bone and refused to pursue it anymore, the muppet, but we're onto her.

Ari's upstairs working on an urgent treatment plan and promised to join us the second he's done. They found a basking shark drifting through Kingston a few days ago that was clearly agitated and unwell. As suspected, technical equipment was traced in its body. Ari's part of a team tasked with overseeing the rehabilitation of all the sea life captured and used by Edmund Gladstone's government.

I pull down on my embroidered velvet blouse and straighten the chiffon layers of my lehnga skirt.

"Seriously," says Tabby, smiling, "black is your color. And you should totally let me give you one of the new NightSpell makeovers. I promise I'll—"

"No thank you!" We laugh.

Ruby and Vivian chat as they visit the table of food. Ruby's also on the amphis' rights commission, but wisely decided to take today off. Freya's playing a game with Becca Taylor, Jack's little sister. All I can see is flashes of bright yellow light and a score glimmering away before they wave their hands again at something in the air. I can't believe the place is spacious enough to comfortably fit everyone.

All charges against us were dropped and we were awarded a significant amount in damages—for the false allegations against Papa and his wrongful arrest, his imprisonment, Mama's murder, the destructive raid on our flat, and our capture. It was enough to buy us this home near the twins. We moved Gramps in with us.

I sigh as I look around the dreamy, warm space with the cozy fire crackling away at its heart. *Home.* Our former flat was cramped and worryingly damp, so this house will never stop feeling heavenly to me. It's the first home Papa and I have ever owned, and I'll never get used to walking through it knowing it's ours. What a year. So much has happened since New Year's Eve 2099. Back then I was on board the *Kabul* with Ari and we were illegally crossing the London borders in search of Papa.

I gaze now on the faces around me. My whole life I only ever spent New Year's Eve in front of the screen with Papa, excited to watch the countdown and celebratory laser shows. Though we socialized and knew many people, it was only Grandpa and the Campbells we spent most of our time with. And now our home is filled with friends. With new family.

It took Papa several months to get past the pain of what happened to Mama. The change in him now is heartening. He's the papa I used to know, before his arrest, once more strong and full of life. As soon as the laboratories are ready again in another couple of months, he and Gramps want to resume working there. Astronomy is in their blood and they can't imagine not studying our universe. In the meantime, they've been working from home.

"Och, you can't be mad at me over a chess game," says Lewis to Tabby as he joins us. "You can't be the champ at *everything.*"

"Like hell I can't." Tabby appears shocked. "And you're both flipping cheats." She looks away.

"Oh I say," says Oscar, frowning as he comes up behind Lewis. He tugs on his fur-trimmed overcoat. "What a positively direful word to use, my dear. I dare say I was merely *guiding* young Lewis here." He inspects his nails.

"Yeah, cheating." Tabby glares at Lewis.

"Sorry." Lewis's mouth twitches and his eyes sparkle as he takes in the sight of Tabby pouting.

I look at the time. "PM's speech is any minute."

As if on cue, Papa, Grandpa, and Ben appear on the stairs. Ari's with them.

Countless heads turn as Ari makes his way down. No matter who, they always notice him. I feel suddenly wide awake. My insides flutter now as they always do when I take him in. He's dressed in his usual all black, sharp and soft at the same time. His shirt hugs his chest, and his hair hangs in waves around his shoulders. My heart soars when I meet his glittering gaze.

He moves toward me, breaking into a slow smile as he takes me in.

"You look beautiful," he whispers. "I missed you."

I smile back, loving every second of this exquisite feeling in my chest right now. "It's only been a couple of hours."

Soon we'll be spending more time together. The Sterlings just finalized their move down to London. Ben was originally from the city and he's very much looking forward to returning.

Ari takes my hands gently, brushing his thumbs over my kara and bangles, and meets my gaze. As ever, I lose myself in the intense amber of his eyes. Someone clears their throat and I turn to see Ben and Grandpa watching us. Ben grins and nods.

Gramps takes in my outfit and his face crinkles as he beams. "Beautiful, Queenie." He pats my arm, and he and Ben head toward the screen on the far wall.

"You look so much like your mother, Pickle." Papa smiles as he draws closer. He runs his hand over my head, before gesturing to Ari and me. "It's about to start."

We join him in catching up with the others for the PM's speech.

The blank surface flickers into life, and I command the music a little lower. Some continue to dance and chat away while most gravitate toward us to hear the speech. Prime Minister Achebe's face fills the screen and her soft, assured tones carry around the space despite the music.

Bia Achebe used to run the Den in Cambridge, and was wanted by Edmund Gladstone's government. She kept tabs on their activities for years and tried to highlight and share news of all their wrongdoings. At the time, many believed she was seeing problems where there weren't any, and she was even accused of being a troublemaker. In the end, almost every one of her fears and assertions proved entirely perceptive and accurate. When the truth of the old PM's administration began unfolding in public and Bia's efforts came to light, there was unanimous support for her to run for election. And here she is, the first Black woman to lead Great Britain.

A committee was set up to conduct an inquiry into everything. It's so frustrating anytime I see footage of them processing events and details. I'm truly grateful for all the positive changes. It's just that sometimes I can't help thinking *So what?* about an inquiry.

An inquiry can't undo everything. It won't bring back the dead and it can't erase the pain and trauma. People have suffered too much. And some say we need a record of everything that happened, so we can learn from our errors. Except history is full of inquiries about the actions of rogue governments, and it's never prevented the same from happening again and again. Who knows. But at least our communities are, for the first time ever, able to live openly and freely. And most people have stopped referring to us as Anthropoids.

One of the biggest problems we face now is that some think granting us our full human rights, and privileges they've always had themselves, somehow means we're taking away from them. They're genuinely unable to see we only want to be treated equally. But you can't stop progress.

Prime Minister Achebe's mention of the seasickness draws my attention back to what she's saying.

"We are already seeing significant improvement with levels of the malaise in those who have begun seeking treatment," she announces. "As you know, one of my first acts as prime minister was to offer seasickness sufferers full and intensive aid. It had previously only been 'treated' with increased exposure to anything Old World. The Department for Health didn't believe the malaise could be eased any other way, and they not only banned the successful treatments of other countries but also concealed that vital information from us. We now know there are drugs and all manner of therapies that have helped sufferers elsewhere in the world, significantly moderating the disease's effects. I will not accept further needless loss of life." She goes on to talk about plans for the crumbling transport infrastructure.

It's unbelievable how so many had to suffer and die because of one man's insecurities and ignorance. But he couldn't have sustained his rule alone. Numerous systems had a hand in upholding it. Countless media outlets were found guilty of focusing largely on what the government said, instead of conscientiously monitoring and reporting all its actions and their effects. Edmund Gladstone was polite; he was calm and smiled and seemed reasonable. No matter what he did, we made excuses for him, assumed his intentions had to be good—despite his actions clearly showing otherwise. Even Papa felt at the time the PM must be unaware of everything going on, which, looking back on it now, doesn't really make sense. The interim government sworn in after Edmund Gladstone's death found a shocking amount of further labs and secret prisons. So many people still await trial, including that double-crossing snake Charlie.

Everywhere you turn, London is being rebuilt. They even paused all Explorer projects until the city's infrastructure has been sorted. So despite facing a trenchful of obstructive laws, and further challenges from those who fear treating us as equals means them having less in some way, in a mere nine months things really are already changing for the better. Since Bia's government, and specifically the educational programs they've been running, many have gradually let go of their fear and are even getting used to sometimes seeing us in the water. One day, inshallah, they'll see all the ways in which we are exactly the same, instead of focusing obsessively on this one area in which we're different.

A small Maid-bot interrupts my thoughts as it whizzes past me to mop up someone's drink.

Theo squeezes my arm. "Fancy a sprint tomorrow morning?" he whispers. "Start the New Year off on a high? I can let the others know. And maybe you can come back to ours afterward and I'll show you the new game? It's ready!"

"I'd love to!"

For the last two months, Theo's been teaming up with amphis to design new games.

At long last, the Royal Society for the Arts and Entertainment lifted the ban on creative works set anywhere other than in the Old World, and there are endless exciting projects underway. Theo's been working alongside several like-minded tech-obsessed amphis to create Holozone games set in the water. Players will actually be in the water and go off on quests and adventures! I can't wait to see all the exciting stuff we come up with now that we're no longer limited in that way.

Oh how I wish Mama were here to experience all this change. We held a joint memorial for her and Eva Gladstone, Ari's birth mother. At long last, Papa and I got to say goodbye to my beautiful mama.

To my shame, I realize I've missed the rest of the PM's very first New Year's speech when the screen switches to live streaming the countdown against the bongs of Big Ben.

"Three, two, one. Happy New Year! Welcome, 2101!"

We all shout and break into endless hugs and expressions of hope and joy. Even Oscar joins in, ensuring he wishes each person a happy New Year—including Tabby! Grandpa embraces me before covering his ears and swiftly retiring for the night.

"Happy New Year, Pickle." Papa holds out his arms and I rush into them. He flashes one of his lopsided grins. "And hopefully this one will be a little easier, inshallah. I am so proud of you. And your mama would have been, too," he says, kissing the top of my head.

"I love you, Papa."

We chat a minute longer and then he, too, escapes to his bedroom. I sense Ari's presence beside me, and there's a rush of something so inexplicably wonderful inside, a stirring that always takes over my mind and slips into my veins. He clasps my hands, his expression sparkling. He smiles and as always, the tenderness melts away the edges of his honed angles, softening them completely.

"Happy New Year, Leyla Fairoza McQueen," he says in that gravelly voice of his that I love so much. It's becoming increasingly difficult lately to tear my eyes away from him.

"Happy New Year, Ari."

He cocks his head and considers me a moment. His gaze intensifies, velvet-brown with flashes of gold, and dark lashes I could hide behind forever. "You realize you light up my world?" he breathes.

I move closer and lift my hand to trace his face, gliding my fingers over his forehead, carved cheekbones, across his fluttering eyelids. My cheeks warm and my tummy flip-flops away. His face radiates as he cups my own. And as always, I forget everything when our lips meet.

We seem to lose ourselves in each other whenever we kiss. It doesn't matter what's going on around us, there is only the sweet, maddening taste of him and a place so deep inside him into which I just fall, fall, fall. And I never want it to stop. I can sense a connection to him that I can't fathom, can't describe. But it's always there, beautiful and precious and intoxicating. We pull away, reluctantly, breathlessly. He's such a breathtaking sight, his expression tender and dazzling. His father was beautiful, too, and we learned more about him once everything had settled.

Yusef Francois was from Mauritius, and a Muslim. He fell in love with Eva, Edmund Gladstone's sister, and they had little Winston Gladstone Francois. When Winston was two, Yusef, who had no amphi DNA, was traveling on a bus when an earthquake struck. The sub was hit and flooded, drowning all those on board. The quake was one set up by the authorities, and so it turned out Edmund Gladstone had been responsible for the deaths of *both* Ari's biological parents. Ari has since reached out to Muslim relatives he never knew he had, and also began studying Islam. Lately he's even taken to greeting Papa with a *Salaam* and it's an effort not to just throw myself at him when he does!

Cheering sounds and we turn to the screen as it cuts to the live fireworks display. We watch as beams pulse and stretch and lasers spin through the waters by the old Thames riverbank, before the feed cuts away to Edinburgh and a sweet rendition of "Auld Lang Syne." Everybody links arms and sings along.

Afterward, everyone but the teens—who continue dancing—call it a night. With Ben looking too tired to drive, Ari leaves to drop his family off back at their hotel. Tabby's performing a slow number for Lewis and it absolutely looks like she's forgiven him for cheating at chess. The illuminated green-blue waters catch my eye as they lap the expansive windows, and I make my way over.

A vividly patterned starfish sits resting against the surface, stretching out an arm and wriggling it as if in greeting. The midnight current is calm and clear, and in the far distance I can just make out the glowing lights emanating from the homes opposite. I wrap my arms around myself.

One day I'm going to swim above the city's rooftops. And then I'm going to rise, kicking and ascending all the way to the very top until I break the surface of this world. I know I am. I know in my lifetime we're going to find our way back to the open air, inshallah. I *will* one day feel the sun itself directly on my face.

I sigh as I turn my head to the right and peer into the current.

She's there—somewhere in that direction, parked inside the Mayfair Hangars. The *Kabul*. There's a tug now, as always, a deep ache inside coupled with the feeling I can fly.

The London Marathon Committee rescinded their request to have the sub returned to them. I'm not sure I was ever going to, even if they hadn't changed their minds. A part of me would rather go on the run with her than give her back. She's mine.

"It is the most peculiar thing, my dear," says Oscar quietly, fiddling with the turquoise brooch on the breast of his coat as he stops to stand beside me in the viewport. Satisfied the jeweled pin sits straight, he lifts his gentle gaze and fixes it on the waters. "But it would appear my Navigation system has been updated recently, the programs running back-to-back. And yet I hold no recollection of any proposed voyage...."

I glance back in the direction of the hangars and take a deep breath. It's time.

"I'm so grateful for everything," I say. "I still can't believe it. Everything that's happening and how things are going to be better for us all from now on. But some days...some days I can't breathe, Oscar. I'm standing still. And you know, I don't think I was ever meant to stand still for very long."

He tilts his head at me as he processes what I'm saying. His eyes flicker and a faint, familiar smile plays on his lips. I haven't seen that spark since his Navigation role was put on hold. "Then that must be redressed, of course.... You must be allowed to be yourself." He leans in. "Everyone else is taken, my lady," he says softly, his face shining. He raises an eyebrow delicately as he waits for me to go on.

A school of yellow mottled flounder fish comes into view, swimming right up to the window and pausing to take in all the lights. I look over my shoulder and everyone is busy celebrating the birth of a new year. I turn once more to Oscar, who still watches me expectantly.

"It's true. I've been visiting her recently, the *Kabul*, updating all her systems. Theo's been helping." I swallow before continuing. "Oscar...there's an entire *planet* for us to enjoy. And Grandpa and Papa have a couple of months clear before they start work at the labs again. This is our chance. There are places Gramps and Papa have always dreamed of seeing, sites in the Holy Land that hold great religious meaning for them. And from there, well, Afghanistan isn't that far off when you think about it. Which, erm, I have done, a lot. Papa hasn't been back to Kabul since I was born, and lately he's always going through images and footage of his and Mama's families. I have relatives there I've never met; my whole life I've only ever talked to them via a screen. But we now have the single, most excellent submarine to ever exist. And why stop there? The Dubai and Tokyo marathons...Oh my gosh, I'd *love* to race them. Do you know how thrilling and unique their circuits are? They're spectacularly interactive!" My face warms. "In Tokyo, contestants race through this entire holographic city that's projected onto the existing one. Imagine!" My heart races and I take a breath. "We're finally free to actually *live* our lives, Oscar."

His eyes gleam. "Yes," he says breathlessly, a slight flush entering his cheeks. "Oh yes, my dear. Voyage. Adventure. Once more we shall rule the waves!"

He glimmers briefly before stabilizing again, and my heart soars at the sight of him. Gone is the fur-trimmed overcoat, and in its place, he now sports a royal-blue velvet cape with a matching brocade waistcoat and smart breeches. He pats his hair.

I beam at my Navigator. "Welcome back, Oscar!"

"My lady." He bows his head with a swish of his cape. "And what might the trajectory be?"

"Oh, Oscar . . . Everywhere."

THE END

*There will come a time when you
believe everything is finished.
That will be the beginning.*

Louis L'Amour

ACKNOWLEDGMENTS

At long last, my dream of creating an underwater world has been fully realized. The Light the Abyss series—*The Light at the Bottom of the World* and *Journey to the Heart of the Abyss*—has been a labor of love, and a personal lesson in determination. Discovering Leyla McQueen's story, and bringing it to life, remains one of the most thrilling, satisfying, and challenging experiences. And I'm grateful to everyone who played some part in this journey.

Thank you first and foremost to my beloveds, Aswila, Mariam, and Ibrahim, for all your unwavering support, understanding, respect, and enthusiasm throughout the years it took me to write these books. You proved to be my fiercest champions. Much love to the rest of my family, and infinite gratitude for your support. Special mention to my niece, Juwairiah Khan, who zealously read every early draft (you'll always be a queen to me, Jojo!).

I've encountered some amazing souls during this journey, far too many to mention here, but if I might quickly name a few who have my heartfelt gratitude: Samantha Shannon (Samantha, you're not only a remarkable writer—truly one of the best creators of fantasy—but the best human, too; sincere thanks for everything), Sajidah K. Ali, Eric Smith, E. K. Johnston, Marieke Nijkamp, Courtney Kaericher—a brilliant critique partner and friend, all my early readers, and my steadfast Lightbearers. You've all been wonderfully supportive, and I'm deeply grateful.

Sincere thanks to: My agent, Rebecca Podos, who saw the heart and potential in this story and took a chance on me. My editors, Ruqayyah

Daud and Alvina Ling, and the entire Little, Brown team—I'm deeply grateful. To name a few: the lovely Janelle DeLuise and Hannah Koerner in sub rights; Sasha Illingworth in design; the brilliant Marisa Finkelstein and Andy Ball (thank you so much for the physical copy for copyedits!); Katharine McAnarney and Marisa Russell in publicity; Emilie Polster, Bill Grace, and Savannah Kennelly in marketing; Christie Michel and Victoria Stapleton for all matters school and library; Patricia Alvarado in production; publishers Jackie Engel and Megan Tingley; Nisha Panchal-Terhune in creative services; and the entire rest of the LB team. Thank you so much for all your help with getting the book out there and ensuring it reaches readers in its best form. Much gratitude to artist Shane Rebenschied for my gorgeous covers. And to Shiromi Arserio for doing such a great job recording the audiobooks for the series.

Huge thanks to Michael O'Donnell (aka Moose), who was a research scientist at the University of Washington's Friday Harbor Laboratories when I first began writing this series. Moose was so kind, patient, and enthusiastic with any questions I had relating to the science of my underwater world. I'm also indebted to Adam Wright, who at the time held the position of CEO at DeepFlight. Adam was wonderful and considerate in answering all submersible-related questions back when I was planning book 1. He went above and beyond when he also generously gave me a mini tutorial via Skype, covering the basics of driving a submersible!

So much admiration and respect for those Muslim SFF authors whose works I've been lucky enough to discover so far and who inspire me with how they've paved the way writing their fantastical, diverse stories. They are Sabaa Tahir, Saladin Ahmed, G. Willow Wilson, Shannon Chakraborty, Ausma Zehanat Khan, Sami Shah, Nafiza Azad, Tahereh Mafi, Samira Ahmed, Hafsah Faizal, and Karuna Riazi. I can't wait to explore the other stories already out there, and I urge all lovers of sci-fi and fantasy to check out the brilliant works by these talented authors.

To all who have helped promote the Light the Abyss series in any way and strived to put it in the hands of readers: Thank you. I'm deeply grateful for every one of you.

The book Freya is reading when on board the *Kabul*, is *Charlie Changes Into a Chicken*, written by Sam Copeland and published in 2019 from Penguin Random House Books. Sam is the country's most beloved children's author, a former Mr. United Kingdom, the number one literary agent in the nation—and the most powerful man on earth.

Unwavering love for the city of London, where a story lingers in every alleyway, on every bridge, and in every lookout. You are undeniably the best and most inspirational of them all.

Finally, thank *you*, dear reader, for giving this series a chance. For selecting a science-fiction story with a Muslim lead. For choosing to follow my beloved Leyla into her underwater world, and for sticking with her until it was a better place for everyone. I appreciate you more than you could ever know. May you always find the light in everything you do.

London Shah

OUR OCEANS

Our oceans and all they sustain are in great peril. There are many organizations and charities working diligently in an effort to halt the catastrophic damage being done. World Oceans Day, celebrated on June 8, has evolved into an entire global movement. It's doing amazing things in uniting the conservation action and rallying the world to protect and restore the planet's oceans. The following list contains just a few of the brilliant, dedicated organizations and charities doing great things to save our oceans. Almost all of them depend on donations and volunteers.

Bahamas Plastic Movement
Blue Frontier Campaign
Coral Reef Alliance
Coral Restoration Society
Environmental Defense Fund

Global Ghost Gear Initiative
Greenpeace
High Seas Alliance
Lonely Whale
Marine Conservation Society
Marine Megafauna Foundation
Mission Blue
Monterey Bay Aquarium
Natural Resources Defense Council
Ocean Conservancy
Ocean Defenders Alliance
Oceana
Oceanic Preservation Society
Pangeaseed Foundation
Plastic Oceans International
Project Aware Foundation
Ric O'Barry's Dolphin Project
Sea Shepherd Conservation Society
Surfers Against Sewage
Surfrider Foundation
Take 3 for the Sea
The 5 Gyres Institute
The Nature Conservancy
Woods Hole Oceanographic Institution
World Wildlife Fund

A DISCUSSION GUIDE FOR THE YOUNG-ADULT SERIES LIGHT THE ABYSS

The Light at the Bottom of the World (Book 1)
and *Journey to the Heart of the Abyss* (Book 2)

THE MAIN CHARACTER, LEYLA MCQUEEN

1. Consider Leyla's sheltered life at the start of the series. In what ways can her story be seen as a coming-of-age tale? Discuss her growth. Analyze who Leyla was in the beginning and how her worldview changes by the end. What factors contributed to this change?

NOSTALGIA

1. What statement is the author making about nostalgia? Explain using specific examples from the text.
2. How much of a role should a nation's past be allowed to play in its present society? Defend your view with examples both from our world and the text.
3. In what ways did the author convey that this underwater society lives largely in the past? What tools did Shah utilize to show how much of a dominant role the pre-floods world still plays in this submerged existence?

TRUTH AND TRUST

1. In book 1, just after Leyla and Ari ring in the New Year onboard the submarine, Ari tells Leyla the truth won't set her free. Leyla rejects this and passionately believes "the truth is *always* better." Do you agree with her? In instances where the truth reveals something painful and traumatic, would you still appreciate knowing the facts? Or do you see no point in being made aware of the truth in these instances?
2. After her flat is ransacked in book 1, Leyla contacts her grandfather and says, "You should have told me the truth. From the very beginning. . . . I

know you mean well.... But you could have just trusted me with it."
Her grandfather agrees. Do you think adults should trust children
and teenagers with the truth even when they know it would greatly
distress them?

OBEYING THE LAW

1. By the end of book 1, Leyla breaks her father out of prison, and they
   are both accused of terrorism and labeled Britain's number one enemy.
   Is it acceptable to break the law when we believe we are in the right?
   Do you think those who cross the line between legal and illegal actions
   are reckless, or do you feel they are courageous when morally in the
   right?
2. Toward the end of book 2, with regards to his secretly aiding the government in their relentless persecution of amphis, Charlie says, "I was
   only doing me job." Leyla responds with, "You could've refused to
   carry out the orders! If there's nobody willing to do the dirty work,
   then it can't take place." Can you justify being a good, loyal citizen
   and performing a government-sanctioned job without question while
   that role aids in the oppression and persecution of innocent people?

OTHERING (US VS. THEM)

1. Othering those different to us is a constant theme throughout the
   series. In book 2, when Freya asks Leyla whether non-amphis could
   ever love and care for amphis as much as they do for one another,
   Leyla realizes how throughout history we "always point to someone
   else, always need an 'other' to reassure ourselves we're somehow superior, to feel better about our own lives and ways of living." What are
   the consequences from such othering that arise in our own world?

LIGHT

1. The title of book 1 is *The Light at the Bottom of the World*. Analyze and
   explain the meaning of this title. Who or what do you think the identifying "light" is referencing? Can you think of multiple possibilities?